1956
UFO ANNUAL
Unidentified Flying Objects

M. K. JESSUP

SAUCERIAN PUBLISHER

ISBN:978-1-7366564-3-3

© 2021, Saucerian Publisher

MORRIS K. JESSUP
March 2, 1900 - April 20, 1959

Prologue

It is generally a good idea to return to the classics in any genre. This also goes for UFO literature. Rereading a book after ten or twenty years is a rewarding experience. You will discover new data and ideas you didn't notice before. The reason, of course, is that you are, in many ways, not the same person reading the book the second or third time. Hopefully you have advanced in knowledge, experience, intellectual and spiritual discernment. A good starting point is to reread the UFO classics in order to understand the deeper mystery involved in what happened during that era.

Morris Ketchum Jessup (March 2, 1900 – April 20, 1959) was an American ufologist. He had a Master of Science Degree in astronomy and, though employed for most of his life as an automobile-parts salesman and a photographer, is probably best remembered for his writings on UFOs.

Born near Rockville, Indiana, Jessup grew up with an interest in astronomy. He earned a bachelor of science degree in astronomy from The University of Michigan in Ann Arbor, Michigan in 1925 and, while working at the Lamont-Hussey Observatory, received a master of science degree in 1926. Though he began work on his doctorate in astrophysics, he ended his dissertation work in 1931 and never earned the higher degree. Nevertheless, he was sometimes referred to as "Dr. Jessup". He apparently dropped his career and studies in astronomy and worked for the rest of his life in a variety of jobs unrelated to science, although he is sometimes erroneously described as having been an instructor in astronomy and mathematics at the University of Michigan and Drake University

Jessup achieved some notoriety with his 1955 book The Case for the UFO, in which he argued that unidentified flying objects (UFOs) represented a mysterious subject worthy of further study. Jessup speculated that UFOs were "exploratory craft of 'solid' and 'nebulous' character." Jessup also "linked ancient monuments with prehistoric superscience"; years later similar claims were made by Erich von Däniken in Chariots of the Gods? in 1968 and other books.

Jessup wrote three further flying-saucer books,UFOs and the Bible, The UFO Annual (both 1956), and The Expanding Case for the UFO (1957). The latter suggested that transient lunar phenomena were somehow related to UFOs in the earth's skies. Jessup's main flying-saucer scenario came to resemble that of the Shaver Hoax perpetrated by the science-fiction magazine editor Raymond A. Palmer—namely, that "good" and "bad" groups of space aliens were/are meddling with terrestrial affairs. Like most of the writers on flying saucers and the so-called contactees that emerged during the 1950s, Jessup displayed familiarity with the alternative mythology of human prehistory developed by Helena P. Blavatsky's cult of Theosophy, which included the mythical lost continents of Atlantis, Mu, and Lemuria.

Jessup attempted to make a living writing on the subject of UFOs, but his follow-up books did not sell well, and his publisher rejected several other manuscripts. In 1958 his wife left him, and he traveled to New York City; his friends described him as being somewhat unstable. After returning to Florida, he was involved in a serious car accident and was slow to recover, apparently increasing his despondency. On April 19, 1959, Jessup contacted Manson Valentine and arranged to meet with him the following day, claiming to have made a breakthrough regarding an event known as the Philadelphia Experiment. However, the next day, April 20, 1959, in Dade County, Florida, Jessup was found dead in his car. A hose had been run from the exhaust pipe into a rear window of the vehicle, which had filled with toxic fumes when turned on. The death was ruled a suicide. Some believed that "the circumstances of Jessup's apparent suicide were mysterious", and conspiracy theorists contended that his death was connected to his knowledge of the Philadelphia Experiment. Although some of Jessup's friends suggested that he may have been driven to kill himself by the "Allende Case", others said that he had been extremely depressed, and had discussed suicide with friends, for several months.

Saucerian Publisher was founded with the mission of promoting books in Science Fiction. Our vision is to preserve the legacy of literary history by reprint editions of books which have already been exhausted or are difficult to obtain. Our goal is to help readers, educators and researchers by bringing back original publications that are difficult to find at reasonable price, while preserving the legacy of universal knowledge. This book is an authentic reproduction of the Jessup's 1956 Arco Publishers Ltd, London, England printed text in shades of gray. **IMPORTANT**, despite the fact that we have attempted to accurately maintain the integrity of the news, the present reproduction has missing and blurred pages, poor pictures from the original scanned copy. Because this material is culturally important, we have made available as part of our commitment to protect, preserve and promote knowledge in the world.

Some of the topics covered in this publication are: Clyde Tombaugh's UFO and artificial satellite search, angel hair, moon anomalies, the race to develop a man-made UFO, anti-gravity research, Lincoln La Paz's investigations into fireballs/guided missiles, Wilbert Smith and Project Magnet, preparations for Operation Deep Freeze and the International Geophysical Year, the Kelly-Hopkinsville incident, the reasons why pilots don't report sightings, an invisible UFO formation, plus an abundance of incidents involving planes, fireballs, UFOs, explosions, dogfights, explanations of the appearances of atmospheric phenomena and weather balloons. At the end of the book is included the Air Force

Regulation regarding UFO's (AFR 200-2 regulation).

Great, but unpretentious, this edition is a rare symbol by itself of what was going in the dawn of the modern UFO phenomena.

Editor
Saucerian Publisher, 2021

CONTENTS

❖ APRIL ❖

❖ MAY ❖

❖ JUNE ❖

❖ JULY ❖

◇ JULY-AUGUST ◇

◇ SEPTEMBER ◇

❖ OCTOBER ❖

❖ NOVEMBER ❖

❖ DECEMBER ❖

ILLUSTRATIONS

INTRODUCTION

"Where can we get up-to-date information and the latest details on UFO?" "What were the most important events in the field of UFO this year?" "Are there any pictures which have never been published?" "Do you know where I can find a list of the major sightings during recent months?" "How can I find out what is happening all over the world with UFO?"

Questions such as these have been deluging your editor for months.

Serious students of UFO have long been advocating a central Bureau of UFO Investigation—a place where *all* pertinent information can be sent for study and evaluation, then be published for the edification of all interested parties. The problem has been —where, how, by whom.

In an effort to begin such a "clearing house," I have undertaken the enormous task of assembling and evaluating as much contemporary UFO material as possible.

The UFO Annual, therefore, is a compendium of current reports, UFO sightings, and of scientific data relating to UFO either directly or indirectly. *The UFO Annual,* is and will be the nearest thing to date to a "central clearing house" for any and all UFO reports and investigations.

We must have an *Annual* for UFO because we have no other medium for effecting a general distribution of new knowledge, or interchange of intelligent analytical thought, in a field so new, so startling, so universal in concept, that both organized science and distraught governments have panicked in the face of the impact. The Press seems unable—or unwilling—to separate fact from fiction or hoax.

We must have a UFO *Annual* because we have to establish a focal point for individual sightings, observations, analyses and even hypotheses. That focal point, therefore, will be *The UFO Annual,* care of the Arco Publishers, 10, Fitzroy Street, London, W.1. M. K. Jessup, editor. Supplied with full individual reports, news clippings, magazine articles, etc., we will sift and evaluate and supply a composite, analyzed picture, as clearly and as definitively as possible.

We have to have an *Annual* for the UFO because even the news clipping services fail to give us the entire flow of data. These services serve so many clients that no one source gets more than a substantial fraction of the few reports which have been appearing in the press over the past three years. As an example, there was a tremendous UFO manifestation over Cincinnati, Ohio in August, 1955, witnessed by verified thousands of honest and objective people. Yet the clipping services sent not one press cutting! Still, the local papers *did* carry the event in some editions, and we obtained them through private channels. The wire services ignored the whole event. Why?

We have to have a UFO *Annual* because the only thoroughly

objective radio-TV reporter and commentator to give ten million listeners the current truth about UFO is no longer broadcasting. Why?

We have to have an *Annual* because information which is freely published in some foreign countries never reaches the United States through normal news channels. Why?

We have to have a UFO *Annual* because no other medium is assembling scientific data and discourse pertinent to UFO operations, and making it easily available to all of the people seriously interested in UFO.

We have to have a UFO *Annual* because we believe that the *whole* record of this strange adventure should now be assembled, catalogued, distributed and maintained for posterity. Our most poignant regret is that we did not start an *Annual* eight or ten years ago. And we earnestly solicit those who have maintained libraries of clippings and reports since 1947 to donate them to our common library, which we hope, eventually, to present to the United States Library of Congress as a specially dedicated collection.

And we have to have a UFO *Annual* because we desire to help clarify and crystallize the general trend of thought and concept anent this great phenomenon!

The UFO Annual, therefore, is a catalogue of interesting events which do not come to the attention of the general public; it is a medium of expression for those who think seriously about the problems inherent in the study of UFO; and for those who will cooperate by contributing to a pool of common knowledge and speculation. *The UFO Annual* is an attempt to chronicalize a vast field of new and qualitative knowledge.

The UFO Annual is a permanent record of the myriad major and minor events related to UFO.

There are tremendous difficulties in assembling such a mass of material in a new field of study. We have used newspaper reports wherever available, but we do not feel that we have had as complete coverage as we desire in this field. We have studied resumes in magazines and books. We have scrutinized the correspondence coming to *The Case for the UFO* and have been gratified at the great interest of readers. Some of their reports have been included in *The UFO Annual,* and we hope to have others for use in the future.

Perhaps the most gratifying feature to date, however, has been the incontestable *proof* of what cooperative observing and reporting can do. Here is an example:

In July, two readers of *The Case for the UFO* communicated their startling observations to your editor. One lives in Washington, D.C., the other in Illinois. Each saw a spot on the Moon, on the night of July 5th, 1955: a round spot! One reported it at the exact center of the Moon's disc; the other said it was near the edge of the Moon. That established two base lines: one on Earth, one on the Moon. With these two lines, and the known distance from Earth to the Moon, it was at once possible to locate the UFO in space— 95,000 miles out toward the gravitational neutral.

But—one observer gave the apparent size of the UFO in terms of comparison to the lunar crater Tycho, and from that known unit of measurement our mathematicians deduced the approximate size of the UFO: 48 miles in diameter!

How do we know it was a UFO? The answer is simple—one observer saw it hover for three minutes and then move off the moon— that's controlled motion . . . and control means intelligence!

Thus can cooperation and comparative observation be of inestimable value.

Unfortunately, we could not print every item that came to hand. A long and fascinating treatise on gravitation, for example, was sacrificed in order to bring you more current sightings. We omitted some redundant material where there were multiple reports of similar objects. We have tried to include some of the negative and biased newspaper comments and editorials in order to be fair and impartial—and to provide a true, clear, comprehensive picture of UFO and 1955.

Sometimes we had to decide between two items, of which one was sensational and other basic. Where the sensational item contained vital data, we published it; if it did not, we retained the more prosaic but meaty feature where it seemed truly worthwhile to UFOlogy as a whole.

You will meet a few new words in this volume. We speak, for example, of the *Omniverse*. A coined word, it is to be regretted that we cannot give full credit to the individual and/or organization which may have originated this all-encompassing phrase. We first saw it in some of John Pitt's writing, but later discovered it in other, earlier works. It is an all-inclusive word and supersedes *Universe*, much as *Universe* displaced *World* decades ago.

UFOlogy (You-fol-o-gy) has been coined in *The UFO Annual* to cover the field of investigation of what the Air Force has called Unidentified Flying Objects. Thus we have the science and study of the Unidentified Flying Object.

We have made this *Annual* a reporting medium: a newsbook. While we have been generous with comment, we have tried to avoid extensive analysis and dogmatic opinion. There is more than one reason for this. First of all, we feel that a reporter should merely report, and should serve the interests of all analysts and speculators, without prejudice or slant, so that each can have objective data for his own purposes. But secondly (and we believe, even more important), we are convinced that the science of UFOlogy is in too young and too chaotic a state to justify any firm hypotheses at this time. We say this deliberately and advisedly, in the face of a number of books and articles which claim to present definitive answers, whether from revelation, telepathic communication, journeys in space-ships, scientific analysis, or just plain hoaxing. We feel that much more research must be made, and more scholarly books compounded, before definitive answers can be predicated—unless and until the UFO's do make intelligible contacts with the mind of man.

The raw material of UFOlogy are facts, reports, observations and scientific data. The tools of UFOlogy are imagination and creative thought. The strength of UFOlogy lies in its courage and determination. The warp, the woof, the essence of UFOlogy is sincerity of interest and purpose.

The goal of UFOlogy—as is the goal of true religion and true science—is *Truth!* . . . the truth of basic and philosophical reality.

In order that readers may know what they are dealing with, however, your *UFO Annual* Editor desires to state without equivocation that we believe there is a serious and substantial basis for the reality of UFOlogy. We believe that much truth has been suppressed. We believe that UFO of several kinds have been a part of this Earth-Moon-Binary Planet system for thousands of years. We believe that there is intelligence, and that there are probably intelligent beings, in "outer" space, some of which may come from other planets and some which exist in what we may call open space. We believe that whole new fields of knowledge are opening up to mankind, perhaps comparable to present day zoology and botany. We believe that the human race is in the opening labor spasms of a quantum expansion of mentality and environmental concept. We believe that the field of UFOlogy is too serious and too vital for us to permit it to be sneered into oblivion or laughed out of existence.

We believe it is time to clean up the field by speaking truth and eschewing nonsense; and having done so, to demand that truth be spoken to us without nonsense!

Your editor wishes to express his sincere appreciation to the many who have toiled and researched in the preparation of this *UFO Annual,* for their wonderful cooperation in an effort to make this the most comprehensive volume possible.

To Peter Kamitchis, we owe much original thinking and comment, research in libraries and the world of news, and constant encouragement and appraisal of material.

To James Moseley, our deep gratitude for many interesting clippings and worthy items.

To Maryalice Bassett: thanks for moral support and many helpful suggestions.

To John Bessor and John Pitt: our thanks for constructive suggestions and kindly criticism.

To Kathryn Siddons Ford: our thanks for keeping the personal reports moving to your editor.

To Francis Kettaneh: our appreciation for facilities and assistance.

To Mr. Len Stringfield: for his generous and enthusiastic assistance.

To Virginia Belmont, John and Margaret Storm, Courtland Hastings, Robert Bartlett, and others: thanks! Thanks for many, many things.

And *mille grazie* to the many, many contributors of personal reports and experiences. We assure you that each and every letter, each and every sighting, is carefully filed and appraised.

Lastly, my sincere appreciation to my publishers and to my literary representatives for their unstinting efforts and wholehearted cooperation at every turn.

M. K. JESSUP

Washington, D.C.

THE **UFO** ANNUAL

JANUARY

In starting the UFO reports for the year 1955, we quote the following from the January issue of C.R.I.F.O. *News Letter,* an excellent UFO news sheet published by L. H. Stringfield, 7017 Briton Avenue, Cincinnati 27, Ohio. Later in the year this publication changed its name to ·C.R.I.F.O. *Orbit.*

THE ALTAI-HIMALAYA SIGHTING

(Case 86, 1926) While rumors were rife in January of this year that saucers were a U.S. weapon of German ancestry, the writer received a letter from Frank Edwards, which said in part: "The hokum about these things being of U.S. origin can be handled neatly if you will ask your informants how these 'U.S.' discs happened to be buzzing around the Altai-Himalayas in 1926. . . . I was sprayed with it regularly—but the Himalaya question always left them high and dry." On Frank's tip, the writer procured the book, *Altai-Himalaya,* written by Nicholas Roerich (copyrighted in 1929), from the Public Library. Referring to pages 361-2, the text reads as follows: "August 5, 1926—something remarkable! We were in our camp in the Kukunor district, not far from the Humbolt Chain. In the morning, about half past nine, some of our caravaneers noticed a remarkably big black eagle flying above us. Seven of us began to watch this unusual bird. At this same moment another of our caravaneers remarked, 'There is something far above the bird.' And he shouted in his astonishment. We all saw, in a direction from north to south, something big and shiny reflecting the sun, like a huge oval moving at great speed. Crossing our camp this thing changed its direction from south to southwest, and we saw how it disappeared in the intense blue sky. We even had time to take our field glasses and saw quite distinctly an oval form with shiny surface, one side of which was brilliant from the sun."

Those of you who think the UFO complex is something new and faddish, will find this little item a bit of an antidote to scoffing, and maybe it will help keep your feet on the ground.

Incidentally, C.R.I.F.O. stands for Civilian Research Interplanetary Flying Objects. Its publication is one of the best and most objective reporting agencies in the world.

Lima, Peru, on the West Coast of South America, started off the New Year with a report of five flying saucers in formation. They were very bright, silvery in color, hovered over Lima, and were seen for several minutes by many people.

On January 2nd, Venezuelan pilots and crews saw a bright disc, and several other reports of like nature came during the first week of January.

From the British newspaper, *Sunday Dispatch*, January 5, 1955, showing that the British, too, were sensitive to the bureaucratic concealment with which they are also plagued:

M.P.: TELL ALL ON FLYING SAUCERS

The Air Minister will be asked in the Commons on Wednesday if he will make public a report on flying saucers which an officer on the Air Staff has refused to release.

Major Patrick Wall (Conservative, Haltemprice), gave notice of his question after reading in last week's *Sunday Dispatch* that the report prepared after a five-year probe, will not be made public.

"Unless there is a security risk, which I don't think there is, the public should know the truth," he told me.

"If the Air Ministry have found the answer to whether or not they exist it is of great interest to everyone."

The following comes from the *Flying Saucer Review* (Seattle) published by the Space Observers League, Seattle, Washington. (Not to be confused with the *Flying Saucer Review* published in England.)

On January 5, 1955, at 4:45 p.m., while I was on my way home I was driving north on Eagle Rock Road in Los Angeles. When I got in front of 468 Eagle Rock Road, I had the impression something was falling in front of me. I slammed on my brakes so rapidly that my car skidded sideways and partially blocked the street. I opened the door of my car and getting out on the left and looking almost overhead was what first looked like a fairly large box kite.

It was of a material which did not reflect light and my first thought was that it was covered with some type of cloth but further observation seemed to make it appear as a dull metal. It did not appear aerodynamic in shape or structure and except for some light grey lines on the upper part of it, it did not appear to be anything I had ever seen or been aware of before. As I was parked across the street partially blocking passage, other cars stopped behind me and at least one other person (in the car directly behind) got out of his car and joined me as we watched this object. Up to this point I was only curious as to what it was.

Suddenly it moved. Not as anything I have ever seen move, that is, slowly gaining speed and then settling down to a steady speed; but its movement was more like the movement of a searchlight across the sky. It moved parallel to Eagle Rock Road and completed the distance from over my head to being out of sight in perhaps a second or two. At the time I first saw this object I was not over fifty feet and possibly as little as twenty feet from being directly under it.

Its size appeared to be about that of an automobile from my observation position. It hung absolutely motionless during my period of observation, until it made the soundless, effortless movement which carried it out of sight. During my observation, the object retained an angle of 45-degrees to the ground with the portion having the grey lines as the higher part.

While I have not had any experience with aircraft or aircraft observation, I have had some training in other types of observation, having served in an Intelligence Section where some ability in this line was required. I do not care to hazard any opinion as to what it was that I saw, but to the best of my knowledge I have never before seen anything like it."

The Oshkosh (Nebraska) *News,* January 6, 1955. Although there are some vague details, this appears to be honest reporting.

MEN WON'T SAY WHAT THEY SAW

What did some Oshkosh people see in the southwestern skies Sunday afternoon? They don't care to say because it is too near after New Year's and they don't want to be listed as among those "seeing things."

However, the fact remains they did see something. One entire family watched a bright round object in the skies southwest of Oshkosh and another man watched the same object.

Mr. and Mrs. Harold Lake and family of northeast of Oshkosh saw the bright object. They noted that it did not seem to move but was stationary for a period of over three hours. So, they presumed it was not a balloon and not an airplane.

They endeavored to contact the *News* office staff but were unable to They did talk to Samie Street though, and he too observed the object, watching it for over an hour at intervals of ten and fifteen minutes, always finding it in the same location.

No one wanted to mention "flying saucers" but someone did. None of those observing the object cared to say what they thought it might be but since they are all reliable residents of the community it appears that there was something unusual in the sky Sunday afternoon.

The Windsor (Ontario) *Standard,* Thursday, January 6, 1955, has the following bonafide sighting:

WHITE DISCS IN SKY PROBABLY REFLECTION
OF SUN ON JET PLANES

Were they flying saucers? That is the question a resident of Windsor would like to have answered as he called the *Windsor Standard* to see if others had noticed two white objects or discs cross the sky over this village, Wednesday noon.

The white objects were seen shortly after two jet planes flew over Windsor, the vapor trails making a cross in the sky. These white objects seemed to follow the vapor trails, but in the opposite direction the jet planes were taking.

One explanation given this newspaper was that the white objects might have been the sun shining on the metal fuselage of the planes and reflected on the vapor trails. Did others see the white discs?

The North Adams (Massachusetts) *Transcript,* January 7, 1955, reflects the bewilderment of a lone observer who wished he had had just one witness:

GREYLOCK RESIDENT SIGHTS 'SAUCER'
IN SKY THIS MORNING

A Greylock resident still was trying to find someone who could support his testimony that he saw what was a flying saucer or the equivalent in the southeastern sky early this morning.

Ray Merrigan of 30 Foucher Avenue said that shortly before dawn he was startled to observe a stationary saucer-shaped object low in the heavens in the southeast which bore no resemblance to any astronomical phenomena with which he was familiar. The object of an intense whiteness, he said, hung just below the overcast, and had the same general shape as that usually described in flying saucer reports.

But he was unable early this afternoon to find anyone else who
had beheld the same spectacle.

The Escondido (California) *Daily Times Advocate* records
an interesting observation by a local lady whose report has the
approval of an expert and well-practiced saucer sighter:

BRIGHT, ORANGE-COLORED OBJECTS SEEN;
HEADED WHERE?
TO PALOMAR MOUNTAIN

Call them what you may, flying saucers, mysterious lights, glowing balls or even reflections of the sun. But they seem to be back
with us again.

Latest report of a very bright round object comes from Mr. and
Mrs. Charles Griffith who live on Rose Avenue. Mrs. Griffith said
she sighted the "thing" about 9:30 p.m. Friday and watched it
intermittently for about forty-five minutes until it disappeared.

"It was north of us," Mrs. Griffith said, "and seemed to be heading in the direction of Palomar Mountain. It would move across
the sky and then seem to just hover for awhile. After stopping,
the object would then move slowly on again."

From her hillside vantage, Mrs. Griffith said the object seemed
to have color—orange in hue. The light just got fainter and fainter
until we could see it no longer," Mrs. Griffith continued. "At first
we thought it was a star but then it started moving. And I don't
think it was an airplane."

It was just somewhat more than a year ago, December 31, 1953,
to be exact—when a silvery object, torpedo-shaped, hurtled across
the Escondido skies during the morning hours, caught fire and
burst into two pieces. The object was also sighted by a trained
observer with the Civil Aeronautic Administration in San Diego,
who followed it with binoculars.

Authorities said it was "definitely not an aircraft," but came to
the conclusion that it was a day time meteor.

George Adamski, co-author of the book "Flying Saucers Have
Landed," said then that the object was a flying saucer and could
have come from Mars, Saturn or the star Wolf-359.

In August, 1954, a flying saucer forum was held at Adamski's Palomar Gardens at the foot of Palomar Mountain toward which the object sighted by Mr. and Mrs. Griffith was headed.

The January 8, 1955 edition of the Mahonoy City (Pennsylvania) *Record-American,* portrays the nervous fright of some children, too young to be hoaxers, as they see a flying saucer, or UFO:

HAZLETON CHILDREN REPORT SEEING "FLYING SAUCER"

William McGlynn, 12, and his sister Marlene, 15, of 104 S. Pine Street, Hazleton, reported that they saw a flying saucer at 8:10 o'clock last evening as they were crossing Juniper Street at Pine, in the city of Hazleton.

The boy saw the flying saucer or what the United States Air Force terms more accurately, perhaps, Unidentified Flying Object, before his sister did but immediately called her attention to the UFO.

It appeared to the boy that the round, flaming body emitted a spark as it hurried through the sky at great velocity. He said it was circular in shape and glowed like fire, and at the height that it was travelling appeared to be as large as the pupil of the human eye, "much larger than the stars that were out," he explained.

"I ran like the dickens after I saw it, all the way home," the boy added.

Frederick, Maryland, is not very far from the nation's capital where there has been a good deal of UFO activity. It is also quite close to President Eisenhower's country estate. The Frederick *News,* January 8, 1955, reported the following:

SEES "FLYING SAUCER"

The first "flying saucer" seen in these parts in some time was reported sighted about 6:25 p.m. Friday by Miss Joann Harris, near Dickerson. Miss Harris said the light orange and yellow object was shaped like a cigar and was traveling very fast between Dickerson and Washington. Others watched the progress of the object with her.

Trenton, New Jersey, was visited by a UFO, as recorded in the Trenton *Times* of January 12, 1955:

THREE REPORT "FLYING DISC"

Nicola Bilanco of 517 Tyler Street reported today that when he stopped for a red light at the corner of Liberty Street and Cedar Avenue while walking yesterday he saw a circular flying object in the sky. He said it was about 5:40 p.m.

Bilanco asserted that a friend with him and an unidentified woman also spotted the golden colored object. He estimated that the disc had a tail of fire and was traveling at the rate of about 300 m.p.h.

Lieutenant William J. Raymond, public information officer for the Ground Observer Corps Filter Center, said that his bureau has no record of any unusual or strange flying objects seen in the air around Mercer County for the past month.

The Newport Beach (California) *Newport-Balboa Press* published the following on January 13, 1955:

SAUCER? LOCAL PAIR SEE OBJECT

Report of seeing a flat, brilliant, disc-shaped object in the sky early Saturday morning over Corona del Mar was told to the *News-Press* by Mr. and Mrs. F. P. Preston of Lido Isle.

Preston said they saw the object about 6:30 a.m. and watched it for twenty or thirty minutes before it faded from the sky as morning light took over.

He said it moved from right to left for a distance about ten times its width which he estimated at a quarter of an inch from his vantage point. The object would swing back and forth for a few moments then it would hang stationary, he said.

Once when an airplane passed in front of the object, Preston said, they could estimate the relative size of the brilliant object and the plane's lights which were pin points.

This was not the only activity at that time and place, however, and the same issue carried the following indication that several objects were around, and seen by corroborative witnesses:

FLYING DISCS PAY RETURN COUNTY CALL

Flying saucers or objects were reported over the Orange area Tuesday night.

Although police received only one call, the Santa Ana switchboard was flooded with calls as residents in the northern Santa Ana area reported seeing what many described as "two fire-balls" traveling from south to north.

One observer, Jerry Hayes, Orange, said the two brilliant objects flew over at about 6 p.m. Tuesday and faded out within about five seconds of their first sighting.

Though many reported the objects as "possibly flying saucers," according to police, Herb Barr of Garden Grove, tower operator at the Orange County Airport who was on duty at the time, said he listed the objects as meteorites.

Barr, a trained aircraft observer with twelve years' experience, said he first sighted a single object at about a thousand feet elevation, proceeding from southwest to northeast coming from about the vicinity of Newport Beach.

He added that the meteorite split in two as it passed within about half a mile of the tower and immediately went out.

From the Jersey City (New Jersey) *Journal,* January 13, 1955; we wonder why there always seems to be so much confusion over UFO sightings?

OTHERS SAW "TRAIL OF FIRE"
HUDSON FLYING SAUCER REPORT
STIRS AIR FORCE FUROR

Like the fairy tale character Chicken Little, who reported that the sky was falling, Louis Penkalski, the Jersey City man who says he saw a "flying saucer" in town, has caused a furor that is spreading.

For one thing, the Air Force, in military terms, is sending the report "up through channels."

It's Serious

For another, several persons have come forward to say that they, too, saw "something" although none have been as bold as Penkalski to say it was a flying saucer.

The Air Force in Newark, which is charged with the responsibility of finding out what goes through the skies, takes all such things seriously.

A fact, according to Major Clinton McMillan, provost marshal at the base, is that Penkalski's claim will be forwarded to the Air Technical Intelligence Center at Wright Patterson Field, Dayton, Ohio.

Not Their Baby

"It's out of our hands," McMillan said today.

Meanwhile, three Jersey City residents solemnly reported that they also saw "something" in the west Monday at dusk, at the time Penkalski definitely asserted he saw a flying saucer.

"It was something big and blue and it looked round and shot straight across the sky," said William Nafey of 275 North Street. "It looked like sparks or flame was coming from it."

"Flying Ball"

"My first impression," said John Coppola of 80 Lincoln Street, "was that it was a burning airplane. As it traveled it left a trail of fire about three thousand feet up."

Robert Sullivan, a 12-year-old newsboy, of 350 Van Nostrand Avenue, said that he saw "something that looked like a flying ball about four thousand feet up, coming west over the Metro Glass Works on West Side Avenue," when his attention was attracted.

Penkalski also said he saw the thing flying over Metro as he walked towards his home, 401 Woodlawn Avenue, early Monday evening.

The Air Force, when informed by a report that other people besides Penkalski had seen the thing, said it would add their names to the report.

A boy of West Caldwell, New Jersey, saw a flying saucer.

reported as follows in the *Caldwell Progress and Verona News,*
January 14, 1955:

BOY REPORTS STRANGE OBJECT IN THE SKY

Gregg Mitchell, 14, of 24 Farrington Street, West Caldwell, reported seeing a large, red ball in the sky with streamers on it, about
4:30 Monday afternoon, while walking on Caton Terrace, Caldwell,
with Arthur Geraldson of 17 Thurmant Road, West Caldwell.

Gregg, who made his report to Hugh Long of the Ground Observer Corps, said that the object disappeared to the north in about
eight seconds. He applied for a job as an aircraft observer, but was
told that he was too young. He was, however, praised for being
alert.

From the *Jersey Journal,* Jersey City, New Jersey, January 14,
1955:

MANY CLAIM TO HAVE SEEN "WHAT'S IT?"
FLYING SAUCER REPORT BRINGS
RUSH OF STORIES ABOUT "IT"

Reports of Jersey City's sky ball snowballed into the *Jersey
Journal* today as the Air Force investigated the "what's it?" which
blazed through the heavens.

Here's what they said happened at 5:30 p.m. Tuesday.

Theodore Lewandowski, 31, of 71 Van Nostrand Avenue, a long-
shoreman, and his co-worker Michael Melnick, 30, of 41 Van
Nostrand Avenue: "It was darting through the sky at a tremendous
rate of speed . . . in a straight and horizontal direction."

Orange and Blue

Mrs. Leonard Ross, 53, a housekeeper, of 51 Audubon Avenue:
"It was just a big round ball of orange and blue fire."

Norman Owens, 49, of 268 13th Street, a checker: ". . . like a
large blue ball of fire with whitish flame spurting from it that grew
red toward its end. It lasted about five seconds. It seemed like a
meteor to me."

Mrs. John Matsko, 46, of 231 Van Horne Street, housewife: "It
was like a very white, bright light that had a tail trailing behind

it that turned duller red and then orange toward the end of it . . . it went in a straight line."

Edward Zedlath of 52 Fulton Avenue, machinist: "I thought it was a shooting star. But it was so big I don't believe it was . . . it had a tail of fire and lasted about thirty seconds."

Alfred Esposito, 12, of 22 Claremont Avenue, and Edward Patey, 14, of 375 Jackson Avenue, said they saw it. "It was crossing the belt of the constellation Orion."

And there were others, too, verifying the ball of fire.

It was a growing line of company for Louis Penkalski, who reported the sky ball to the *Jersey Journal* Tuesday evening.

Penkalski claimed it was a flying saucer.

Who knows? After all, Stanley Sajkowicz, of 15 Bayside Place, an engineering student, told this story:

"I met a man as I was leaving school who seemed greatly agitated . . . he was holding out his hand and told me he had some pieces of metal that had fallen on the roof of his home."

At about sundown on January 14, 1955, a large fiery or flaming object was seen apparently falling near Idyllwild, California, and a B-47 jet bomber had a wing damaged by "an unknown object." The plane fortunately made a safe landing, as the wing was not totally destroyed. Although a search is said to have been made, no fallen object has been reported. The Air Force, with customary discretion, has failed to enlighten the public on the real cause of this "accident."

There were several reports on the black fog of London. The following story (Associated Press) of January 17, was sent in by Bill Raub from California:

10 BLACK MINUTES
LONDON WRAPPED IN FOG

A thick belt of darkness wrapped itself around London early Sunday afternoon mystifying and frightening thousands of people and driving the birds to roost.

Freakish in every way, it lasted only ten minutes and disappeared with the swiftness and suddenness with which it came. But while it lasted one of the world's biggest cities experienced a near mass panic.

Women screamed in the streets. Others fell to their knees on the sidewalks and prayed. A man at Croydon groped through the inky blackness outside Croydon Hall shouting, "The end of the World has come!"

A spokesman for the Air Ministry's meteorological office said: "There has been nothing in my experience to equal it."

He said it was caused by an accumulation of London smoke under an extremely thick layer of cloud.

A newspaper seller in Piccadilly Circus, the heart of London, said, "It was pitch dark and then the place went silent. It was lonely, frightening and awful. Then someone began to scream he'd gone blind. I was getting my wind up when it all of a sudden came clear."

Throughout the year, the southwestern part of the USA had more than its share of fireballs, many of them of the Kelly-green class. The Plainview (Texas) *Herald* gave a rather complete report of one in its January 18 issue, as follows:

IN SKY OVER PLAINVIEW

A strange, glowing ball of fire appeared in the skies over Plainview Tuesday night, January 11, exploded twice, and then raced off to the west.

No one knows what it was. Many people saw it.

The time has been set as 11:22 by E. J. Raper, 1110 West 8th. He was up at the time and looked at his watch. Other reports from those awakened by the object ranged from 10:30 to 11, but none looked at their clocks.

"I heard an explosion, and went to the back door," Raper said. "The whole yard was lit up. I looked to the west and saw what appeared to be an extra-large, bright object in the sky.

"It zigzagged to the west and a little south, then looked like it dropped. It was as big as a bushel basket."

Raper could give no estimate of size or height, but said the object appeared to drop toward the ground, possibly fifteen to twenty miles west of Plainview.

"It was like a round ball, all light," he said. "Then the light dimmed and it looked like an object burning."

Fred Kouba, Amarillo, who was staying at the Hilton Hotel, said his room lit up and he heard an explosion. H. S. Hilburn, 707 West 13th Street, also reported hearing the explosion, which he said, "sounded like dim thunder."

Mrs. Allen Hannah, 1506 West 7th said: "Something wakened me, then I heard an explosion. It sounded like two cars running together.

"Our bedroom was flickering with light, like the house next door was burning. I ran to a west window, and right above our neighbor's house was an orange object. It wasn't exactly round, and was moving.

I thought it was coming towards me, so I ran to an east window on the other side of the house to see it pass over. It didn't, so it must have been going in the other direction. I thought for a minute the moon had gone on a binge," she added.

The object seemed to make no sound except for the two explosions. Mrs. Katie Weber, 806 Joliet, said she heard "a rumble, like thunder."

She added, "Then my room began to brighten. I looked out of my bedroom window, and saw a huge ball in the west. It was bright yellow. It disappeared to the west. Afterwards a smoke streak came across the sky going east. I thought maybe it was a jet plane."

Mrs. C. C. Keller, 1204 West 7th, said that her room lit up, and on looking out of her window she could see a big ball of fire. Bob Wayland, Southwestern Public Service employee, examined the antenna yesterday afternoon and found no damage.

The antenna was probably directly in Mrs. Keller's line of vision, and as the object dropped to the west it appeared to slide down the antenna, Wayland believes.

One local amateur "flying saucer enthusiast" said, "Something was definitely in the sky last Tuesday, and it will be interesting to track down what. However, the descriptions of the object do not classify it as one of the 'flying saucers' which have been reported all over the world in the past few years. They are rarely known to produce sound of any sort. My guess would be a meteor, or else some electrical disturbance in the atmosphere."

The *Herald* is especially interested in getting information on the object, and anyone who has a further report is invited to call Bob Hilburn at the *Herald* office.

The following was probably a bonafide meteor, but the local press thought it important enough to publish in the Redondo Beach (California) *Daily Breeze*, January 18, 1955:

METEORITE SEEN OVER MANHATTAN

If anyone thought they saw a flying saucer over the eastern part of Manhattan Beach last evening they were mistaken, according to Bob McMahon, 906 11th Street, Manhattan.

McMahon said it was a meteorite, whose light lasted for approximately ten seconds. He said the meteor was like a reddish-white ball of fire, giving off a bluish haze. He turned to his son's textbooks on astronomy and found meteors travel from seven to forty-five miles a second. McMahon said from his home the meteor was in the vicinity of Venus.

Another report of the same date appeared as follows in the San Diego (California) *Evening Tribune*, January 18, 1955. Undoubtedly the observing public has become more conscious and observant of meteors, bolides and fireballs during the last few years, but even so, we believe that there are more spectacular fireballs than in past years. The green ones are especially noteworthy as various reports will show throughout 1955:

CELESTIAL OBJECT GLOWS
ACROSS SAN DIEGO SKIES
METEORITE MAKES APPEARANCE,
LEAVES LUMINOUS TRAIL

A glowing meteorite stabbed across the Southern California sky at dusk yesterday, as hundreds watched in wonder. Scores of San Diegans called the *Evening Tribune* to report seeing it.

It shot across the heavens at 5:35 p.m., half an hour after sunset. All who saw it, from the Mexican border to Santa Barbara, said it appeared to cross the zenith directly overhead and disappear in the northwest over the Pacific.

It left a luminous trail in the sky.

Blue-white or green at first, the glowing ball of fire turned yellow and then red in color an instant before it vanished into vapor, consumed by the heat of its speed in the stratosphere.

"It went through every color of the spectrum," said H. M. Fousie, who saw it here.

There was a note of skepticism, however; some who saw it noted a pattern of vapor trails apparently above it at a high altitude. They suggested a high-flying jet bomber may have fired a flare.

The *Daily Express*, London, January19, 1955:

A Southport man reported a disc-like object over the sea at Southport, yesterday. The object was reported also by coast-guards. Mr. Peter Walsh, the observer, reported the object to the police.

The Liverpool (England) *Echo*, January 19, 1955:

A brilliant fireball flashed over Northern Ireland, going in a N.E. direction, and was seen by many people. It passed at a great height and emitted red sparks, although being of an almost pure white color. A second one, seen later, was not nearly so bright. Dr. E. M. Lindsey, director of Armagh Observatory, saw the first one, and claimed it was "only a meteor." But he admitted he has never seen one so bright.

England was pestered with fireballs during January, just as was the U.S.A. The *Eastern Daily Press*, January 19, 1955, reported the following seen at Norwich and Wrexham, at 7:10 p.m.:

REPORTS OF DISC-LIKE OBJECT
OVER NORWICH

Reports have been received that a luminous, disc-like object was seen in the sky by people in Norwich and Wrexham at 7:10 on Monday night.

"It was moving at an incredible speed," said Mr. Giles, of Hollywood Meadow Drive, Wrexham. He added that the object, blue-green in color, lit up all the ground. "At first I thought it was lightning."

At the same time the object was seen by a Norwich man who was in Robin Hood Road; "It was at least 20,000 feet up," he said, "and looked like the reflection on clouds of a search-light—but there was no beam."

The object, "circular and rounded at the bottom," went in the direction of Yarmouth. Children in the Robin Hood Road also saw it.

On January 21, 1955, the Santa Ana (California) *Register,* reported a green-blue flare seen off the California coast:

Sheriff's deputies today reported a resident of the Capistrano Beach area had seen a bright flare approximately three miles at sea last night. Investigating deputies said they were unable to see any craft in the area and theorized the flare may have been an extra-bright meteor. It was reported about 8:45 p.m. and said to be greenish-blue in color.

The *Dundee Courier,* January 22, 1955, in an article which is evidently a follow-up from an earlier report comments that a "green moon" was seen over a wide area. This, obviously, was no common, or garden variety, meteor.

EVEN MANCHESTER SAW THE "GREEN MOON"

Letters are still arriving from readers who have seen the "green moon" phenomenon reported in the "Courier" on Wednesday.

It has even been to Manchester! A reader there, Mrs. Olive Spencer, 12 St. Augustine Street, Monsall, was on her way home from work when she saw it, "a green ball of light" in the sky.

Nearer home, in Dundee, Mrs. Anne Brett and her daughter Jane, were walking down Hindmarsh Avenue, where they live, when a sudden green glow caused them to duck. "It seemed to be heading straight into Dens Park," said Mrs. Brett.

Someone was taking a personal interest in this event, besides the honest observers. The article listed over thirty names and addresses of observers who sent in letters, but you and I know that thirty thousand written reports would not sway an entrenched scientist.

An unidentified British report, January 23, 1955, has this to say about the remarks of Air Marshal Lord Dowding anent UFO's:

"BE KIND TO SAUCERS"

Air Marshal Lord Dowding wants to be kind to flying saucers.
"It's rude to fire AA guns and send fighters to shoot them down," he told the Flying Saucer Research Society in London last night.
"Besides, you never know what they could do to you."
Lord Dowding, chief of Fighter Command in the Battle of Britain, believes saucers come from planets hundreds of years ahead of us in scientific knowledge.
"There is no material we know of that could travel 9,000 miles an hour—the recorded radar speed of one saucer—without becoming white-hot," he said.

Lord Dowding is known to be one of the high British officials who is at least open-minded regarding the reality of visitors from space.

For ready reference, most of the important cases reported by C.R.I.F.O. are numbered as well as dated. The following is no exception. Note Editor Stringfield's analysis and comparison with other similar events. Maybe any one occurrence can be facetiously laughed away, but the effect of several happenings can be cumulative:

(Case 45, Darby Township, Pa., January 23, 1955.) Hard on the heels of the Lake Washington incident comes a parallel case resulting in tragedy to William C. Cunningham. Through his bedroom window, crashed a blazing missile about the size of a grapefruit on an obvious mission of menace. Attempting to throw the metallic "fireball" outside, Cunningham suffered severe burns on his right hand. Preliminary investigation of the pieces of strange metal, found embedded in the window sill and on the roof of a nearby parked car, indicated the object might have been a meteorite. Some twenty-five pieces of the object, the largest a sliver about ten inches long, were recovered. Fire Marshal Francis X. Joseph said that when he subjected the metal to 1700-degrees heat with a propane torch, it would not melt. It glowed red but kept the same shape when it cooled. A characteristic of the metal, Joseph said, is that it is a dull silver on the outside, shining brightly on the inside when broken open. Joseph also said that he tested the fragments with a magnet, but got no reaction. Dr. C. P. Oliver, astronomer, and Dr. I. M. Levitt, Director of Fels Planetarium, both expressed doubt that a heavenly body was involved. Dr. Oliver said that it may have been a home-made bomb. Dr. Levitt pointed out that most meteorites explode when they are from ten to thirty-five miles away from the earth. However, both agreed that the metal should be examined at the National Museum in Washington. (Credit: John Otto, H. G. Rovner, Dr. L.D. and J. Douglas.)

C.R.I.F.O. editor's evaluation: Note striking similarity to the two recent incidents at opposite ends of the country. Recall, too, the molten metal burning Portola Road at Woodside, California. Recall the incident of a similar small, round, red fireball that pierced a metal signboard near New Haven, Conn., in August, 1953. None has been satisfactorily explained. Regarding the Darby incident, why, if the projectile were home-made, did it enter the room (second floor), explode, and at the same time, leave other fragments outside on the ground and on top of a parked car? We agree with Oliver and Levitt that the projectile should be further examined before calling it home-made.

The Darby episode was carried by the Associated Press wire service, and clippings have come to us from various parts of the country, indicating a widespread editorial interest in the event.

Petersburg, Virginia, is about 130 miles south of Washington, D.C. The Petersburg *Progress-Index*, January 23, 1955, indicates that UFO's were active in southern Virginia in January. The description of an "unorthodox-looking" object may logically be chalked up as the understatement of the month.

MAN DESCRIBES OBJECT IN SKY HERE

Flying saucers reared their controversial heads in the sky over the Petersburg area last week for only the second recorded time since the mysterious objects reached a publicity peak in the nation about eight years ago.

An employee of the *Progress-Index*, who preferred to remain anonymous, reported sighting an unorthodox-looking object flying over Ettrick. The only other recorded "saucer sighting" incident here also can be credited or blamed upon this newspaper.

In the summer of 1953, staff members of the paper spotted an unidentified, silvery disc moving across the sky east of Petersburg. Unimaginative skeptics proclaimed it nothing more than a weather balloon, but a few of the original observers held on to their original belief: that it was a flying saucer.

People in this area may have seen flying saucers since then, but they have not recorded it publicly.

The man who saw a saucer last week wrote a description of the experience for posterity, "just in case posterity wants it." This is his story and he's sticking to it. "At last it happened. I have seen a 'flying sauc—,' well at least it was a flying something.

"Let's begin over. It was in the sky. I don't know if it was flying, being jet propelled, sucked along by the moon's gravity, or pulled by a string, but there it was. And I am fearful of having people look at me with that facial expression which is half disbelief and half pity. One can hardly afford to admit he saw one of these objects without having his sanity questioned.

"At about 5:18 p.m. Thursday, I swung onto Grove Avenue, and about three hundred feet west of Short Market Street I noticed what at first appeared to be a vapor trail in the western sky approximately a third of the way between the horizon and the zenith. It appeared to be hanging over Ettrick, close to the Appomattox River. It could have been a thousand inches or a thousand feet, but from my perspective, and the assumed distance, it was long. I had reached First Street by the time I realized it was not a vapor trail. It had sharply defined outlines, and the out-of-sight sun gave it a silvery glow.

"Apparently it pointed approximately north-south, with the northern end listing. The list was about 25-degrees, and as best I could determine it did not change the slant: but it was moving westward. I did not realize this immediately, but when I reached the Ettrick School on Chesterfield Avenue, I stopped to observe it better. Then I knew it was going away from me. I placed it in line with some utility wires for reference, and by doing this convinced myself it was moving at a good clip, but maintaining the same slanting position.

"I drove out on River Road, and kept it in sight most of the time until I again stopped in front of the J. S. Ritchie home about two miles from Ettrick. The object had gone almost out of sight, but still slanted on the north end. I watched for about a minute and drove on. It was hardly visible by then, and I turned from River Road and that's the last view of it I had.

"About eight to ten minutes had elapsed from the time I first noticed the object until I lost it. I seriously doubt that it was a conventional aircraft. If it were a dirigible it must have been enormous and I could not see any understructure. It did not appear to be cylindrical, nor circular. If it was circular, I saw it edgewise. The most accurate way I can describe it is to say it appeared to be a bright silvery stripe, with right angle corners, painted on the sky. But there it was, and it moved away.

"Now, if someone comes along and reports that a large commercial or military aircraft passed that way at that time yesterday I'll be compelled to buy a pair of spectacles."

The southwest fireballs seem to have been earliest in New Mexico, but they soon spread to other states, as witnessed by the following report in the Durango (Colorado) *Herald-News*. We suggest that you give careful attention to the green fireballs, which are not normal meteors, for they continue to puzzle science at the end of 1955.

SEEN IN DURANGO SKY

A green "fireball" or meteor which burst into brilliancy in the atmosphere, was visible in Durango shortly after midnight Wednesday. Mr. and Mrs. Walter Foster, 774 Eighth Avenue, reported the meteor to Harold Peterson at the Telluride Iron Works this morning.

Peterson, who lives at 140 West 22nd Street, keeps data on all such phenomena which occur in this area. He reports his findings to Dr. Lincoln La Paz, regional meteorologist at the University of New Mexico in Albuquerque.

Anyone who sees a fireball or anything similar in this area is asked to report to Peterson. He records the time it was seen, the direction of fall and approximate location. If he sees it himself he takes a bearing by the stars.

The Fosters saw the fireball as they looked to the southwest from their bedroom window. Dr. La Paz says such meteors are not uncommon. But when one hits a person, it is exceedingly rare. When a woman in Alabama was hit by a meteorite recently it marked the first authentic such case. Dr. La Paz had predicted it would happen in this century. As a matter of fact, Dr. La Paz is waiting for someone else to be hit by a meteorite. He predicted that two people will be hit by falling heavenly bodies in the 20th Century.

Boys playing tag after school don't usually get so excited about anything that they run to the sheriff's office about it, but these lads who saw a flying saucer felt they had a duty to perform, as note in the Burton (Ohio) *Times-Leader*, January 27, 1955:

THREE BOYS REPORT SEEING "FLYING SAUCER"
WHILE PLAYING IN CHARDON

Visibly moved by their adventure, Richard Street, 14, Charles
Bender, 14, and Edward Wettstein, 14, rushed into the sheriff's
office about 9:00 p.m. Thursday and told Sheriff F. John Phelps they
were sure they had seen a flying saucer. The boys said they had
been tobogganing in the rear of the Chardon Avenue School and
were walking up the lane there when they saw a brilliant object
stationary in the sky.

They said that, as they looked, it suddenly took off at a terrific
speed, continuing in a northwest direction until disappearing. They
described the object lit by brilliant amber light on the smaller top
and also on the longer bottom, the light divided by a space which
was not illuminated.

"We never saw anything like it before," said Bender. "It seemed
to take off at greater speed than a rocket."

The boys estimated distance of the object at about five miles
away when they discovered it. They said they had gone to the
sheriff's office to report as they had read that this was the thing
to do when any such unusual object was seen in the skies.

As January drew to a close, it was evident that UFO activity
was not limited to any single locality. The following report in the
Escondido (California) *Times-Advocate,* January 29, 1955, shows
that California was, however, holding its own very nicely:

FLYING SAUCERS REPORTED
OVER VALLEY CENTER

By Jeanne Gist

Flying saucers are frisking and frollicking about the heavens over
the Valley Center area now, it was reported Friday by Mrs. Ann
Rubalcaba.

According to Mrs. Rubalcaba, she and her son and daughter

watched the elusive little discs for several hours Thursday evening. There were seven, to be exact.

"My children first spotted them in the early part of the evening and called me. They seemed to be playing a sort of tag with each other—darting about. They glowed all over. We got them focused in my son's small telescope later and they were completely round. One of them appeared to have two distinct lights towards the front. They even seemed to be signalling each other as they would grow dim at times and then brighter," she stated.

They watched them until nearly 10:30 when they, the saucers, "just disappeared." Mrs. Rubalcaba promised to call this reporter if she sees them again. Who knows, maybe they will return some night soon so their meanderings about the heavens can be observed through my son's new telescope—that is, if I can get it away from him long enough to peek myself.

The Pacific northwest, is perhaps, the "home" of flying saucer lore, as Kenneth Arnold is, perhaps, the "father" of it. Both made the headlines in the following report and interview in the Le Grande (Oregon) *Observer*, January 29, 1955. The story was carried by the Associated Press to other parts of the country and appeared as far east as Charlotte, N.C., in the *Observer:*

EERIE BLUE LIGHT SAID LIVE "THING"

By Fred Schneiter

Kenneth Arnold, the Boise, Idaho, flying businessman, who first reported the presence of "flying saucers" almost eight years ago, said today he believes that the "bouncing blue light" of the Blue Mountains really exists.

The lights have appeared half a dozen times and have been seen by an equal number of people in the area. Three *Evening Observer* reporters investigated the reports with an all-night vigil on the cold Weston Elgin highway Thursday night but saw only a bright eerie Morning star rise over the horizon.

The snowplowmen claimed, "That isn't the light we saw before." Manuel (Swede) Erickson and Barney Thompson said they first saw the Bouncing Blue Light almost two weeks ago. First it sat in the middle of the highway; then rose in the air, bouncing and swaying back and forth.

Robert Backus, also with the Highway Department, said he observed the Blue Light a few nights later.

Descriptions of the Bouncing Blue Light tallied.

Whatever they are, Kenneth Arnold told the *Evening Observer* in a telephone interview from Boise today, that he doesn't think the snowplow operators are suffering hallucinations.

Arnold has made an extensive study of the strange reports since he first told the world of a flight he observed while flying near Mt. Rainier in June 1947. He has sighted five flights of "saucers" since that time.

"I have almost two hundred reports of this sort of phenomenon," Arnold told the *Observer*.

The description of the Blue Light sounds like a helicopter Arnold admitted, "but what is a helicopter doing in the middle of the woods in the middle of the night?" He pointed out that the men who saw the light the past few weeks said it didn't even sound like a helicopter. The light gave off a steady humming sound, whereas a helicopter has a choppy tractor-motor sound.

The Blue Light of the Blue Mountains reportedly moves slowly, apparently trying to avoid the men as they attempted to get a closer look at it.

"This tallies perfectly with all other reports I've had of saucers at night," Arnold said.

Erickson said the light gave off an occasional flash, "like somebody shooting off a flash camera."

"That is also typical of flying saucers," Arnold added.

Arnold, who is an expert on the reports, if anyone is, says he believes the things are actually living organisms, "sort of like sky jellyfish."

He cited two incidents where flyers had encountered such objects at extremely high altitudes. "My theory might sound funny, but just remember that there are a lot of things in nature we don't yet know," Arnold pointed out.

He noted the Blue Lights usually make their appearance after some sort of disturbance on earth, "like an earthquake, or something," the flyer said. "Whatever the lights are, I think they just come down to look us over . . . I believe they are harmless, or we would have had trouble with them long ago," he added.

He doesn't believe the "little men" stories. "I believe that whatever they are," the flyer explained, "they are living organisms, and not controlled by any type of Man from Mars."

The Pasadena (California) *Star-News*, January 30, 1955, has a very short item: Fireball reported seen over Pasadena area. It said: What one witness described as a "flaming fireball" and another as a "burning weather balloon" was sighted early yesterday evening over northeast Pasadena. Pasadena police said they had "one or two calls" about it, however, there were no reports from neighboring cities. Fireballs, if you hadn't noticed, are not local things. Why wasn't this "burning balloon" seen elsewhere? Does everything, even if burning, have to be a weather balloon?

It may just be that California has more UFO sightings than Florida, but we doubt if it has more per capita than Florida. The *Sun*, of Clearwater, Florida, offered the following on January 31, 1955:

ODD LIGHT SEEN IN SKY OVER DUNEDIN

Maybe those flying saucers are back again. At any rate, something funny was going on in the skies over this city last night, and there are no less than five witnesses to attest to same. But if the peculiar light spotted was seen by others, police of two cities have no reports of them.

K. M. Pearce Jr., Union Street (dividing line between Clearwater and Dunedin) told the *Sun* this morning, he, his father, and Mrs. F. Stuart Mann, 717 Wilkie Street, noticed a reddish-yellow light in the sky at 10:00 p.m.

"It looked to us about the size of a basketball," he declared. "It would burn brightly, then dim, but hung stationary in the sky for about five minutes, while we watched it. Then suddenly, it began to move rapidly to the south. The light went off. We looked ahead to about where we thought it should be, and then suddenly the light came on again. Finally it disappeared."

He described the location of the light as about over the Belle Haven, or old Mecca area, east of Dunedin on road 580.

Mrs. Adeline Yeager Wood Street, and Mrs. R. W. House, driving back to Dunedin together after a choir rehearsal at the Clearwater First Methodist Church, also spotted the strange light in the sky. "We saw it up there in the sky," Mrs. Yeager said this morning, "and at first we thought it was the reflection of a light of some kind in the windshield, but soon realized it actually was in the sky. We watched it all the way into Dunedin but lost it suddenly as we turned off Edgewater Road."

Mrs. Yeager placed the odd light in a different location from the Pearces and Mrs. Mann, however, saying it looked as though it were over the main part of Dunedin.

Inquiries to five different residents in the Belle Haven section elicited nothing. They reported they had seen nothing in the sky, but added they had been indoors at the time. When queried, both Dunedin and Clearwater police departments said officers on duty last night had reported nothing amiss in the sky, nor had they received any calls on the subject.

Here is another item from C.R.I.F.O.—this one from "down-under." In passing, we may note that the Australia-New Zealand area is very UFO conscious. Not only that, but the governments down there take the UFO very seriously, and the UFO clubs are treated with respect and as worthwhile adjuncts to UFO research. UFO were seen in Australia by astronomers as long as eighty years ago.

(Case 70, New Caledonia, January, 1955.) A caretaker of a gypsum mine reported a "luminous mass" that remained motionless for twenty minutes and then made off at a terrific speed. Two men on deck of a coastal trader reported a "large circular object" that remained motionless before speeding away, while a woman reported

a huge yellow luminous ball seaward from Noumea continually
inflating and deflating before disappearing. Still another report described a sausage-shaped object which remained stationary for at
least half an hour before disappearing. (Credit: H. Fulton and G. L.
Menefy, New Zealand.)

Some items, like the following report in C.R.I.F.O. *News-
letter* do not leave much of a mark on the evanescent memory of
the public. It's too bad, for it is the cumulative effect of many
of these "little" events, which proves the case for the UFO in
spite of bureaucratic secrecy. The significance is not lost on
your editor, however:

(Case 44, Lake Washington, near Seattle, January, 1955.) Equally
mysterious are the strange objects that pierced the aluminum dome
of an amateur astronomer's observatory, causing havoc inside, and
which, ironically, burned the owner's astronomy books. Of specula-
tive interest, the objects, described as "hot stones," were found
fused to particles of the dome's aluminum. Hence, by this token, it
seems manifest that the "hot rocks" were possibly under some magnetic influence, which takes us, in turn, to another question: How
may we explain the cohesion between aluminum and a "hot rock"
or a meteorite?
This phenomenon brings to mind the notorious Maury Island
affair of 1947 (near Tacoma, Washington), where the storied Harold
Dahl witnessed a saucer discharge twenty tons of hot rock, and/or
slag amidst other ferrous and non-ferrous materials. Recently in
Chicago, John Otto showed me a specimen of the Maury Island
"rock." Otto says it looked similar to the Lake Washington frag-
ment which was shown over John Daly's TV newscast. For details
of the Maury Island adventure, we recommend reading *The Coming of the Saucers*, by Arnold and Palmer, and Chapter IV of *Flying
Saucers on the Attack*, by Harold T. Wilkins. By the way—where
are Dahl and Fred Chrisman since their experiences of 1947?

In closing out the month of January, we are impressed with
the sparcity of press reports available for study. The military

would have us believe that this is because of a falling off in sightings, and a lack of interest by the public. It is true that UFO sightings come in periodic waves, which have been largely explained. That portion of the public who like to have a paternal government tell them what they may believe, and what they may not believe, are smugly taking up the party-line that UFO are wholly imaginary. Nevertheless the sparcity of sightings in 1955 is not real. The press is not publishing all that happens.

Obviously there has been nothing come to hand in January which is of outstanding interest, but there was a steady trickling of information which continues to add weight to the evidence in the case *for* the UFO.

UFOlogy is a lusty infant, and a growing science.

FEBRUARY

Some English friends of the *Reporter* sent a notice from the Swindon *Evening Advertiser*, February 2, 1955. It says that several people saw a strange white object in the sky over Swindon at 9:00 a.m. of the 2nd. One witness said: "It had a curved end like a boat, and something like a turret on the top." Officials at the control towers of Vickers-Armstrong Ltd., and nearby R.A.F. establishments told the *Evening Advertiser* that they did not see the object.

For the benefit of our overseas friends, I can suggest that *our* control tower operators often say the same things.

The Palm Beach (Florida) *Times,* February 2, 1955, shows that Florida was doing all right in the UFO field in February. And don't forget that Florida, together with a triangle of points east and south, is the vast area of disappearing ships and planes. In point of geographical area, this triangle is as awesomely puz-

zling as was the incredible decade (1877-1886) in point of time.
Here is the report:

REPORTER SEES WEIRD CELESTIAL OBJECT

A star-tiny piercingly brilliant UFO triangled its erratic way
across the low early morning western sky today and was observed
by an early shift reporter of the *Times* nearly due west northwest
of Delray Beach.

The UFO followed a darting eccentric pattern for approximately
six minutes, steadied hoveringly, then gradually sank below the
tree-top level, dimming from diamond brightness to almost pale
saffron.

The reporter alerted Waybe Self, meteorologist at PBIA Weather
Bureau. Later, Self, moving from his weather station across the
airport to USAF installations, said he could not sight the object,
but explained the possibility of high cloud condition blotting one
star after another in the Seven Sisters just ahead of Orion. This, he
said, can give the illusion of a UFO moving in space, often appearing as though stars eventually merge into one single light.

The reporter, neither bilious, bibulous, nor bicarbonated, characterized the brilliance, relatively, as intense as that of a naval de-
stroyer's gleaming blue-white searchlight.

Self said a Delray Beach telephone operator, too, reported "a
small ball of fire," observed, but in the eastern skies. This could
have occurred, since the reporter, enroute to the *Times* office by
car along A1A, lost sight of the UFO behind trees, only to have it
reappear quite low to the southwest as he neared Boynton Beach
Inlet.

He said the astonishingly swift movement of the UFO could be
likened to a "celestial fireball" in motion.

Not all reports of interest have to do solely with UFO sightings. The Grand Rapids (Michigan) *Press,* February 2, 1955,
carried a report of statements by a sagacious and experienced
inventor and manufacturer in the aeronautics field. It *may be* that
his opinions are no better than yours or mine, but there is a deal
of comfort in knowing that he does agree with us.

LEAR ASSERTS SAUCERS REAL

FLYING PHENOMENA EXISTS,

DECLARES INVENTOR

William P. Lear, aviation pioneer and inventor, believes flying saucers exist and are piloted through outer space by beings "of superior intelligence," the Associated Press reported Wednesday.

Lear, board chairman of Lear, Inc., which has its biggest factory in Grand Rapids, was quoted at a conference with newsmen in Bogota, Colombia, where Lear is visiting on a goodwill trip.

Lear told newsmen he believes flying saucers widely reported over this continent, but never proved to exist, "probably come from other planets beyond our range of observation." Last year he made a statement that an artificial satellite to the earth was being planned by the US government as a military observation platform. Officials later said the matter is under study.

Lear did not amplify further on his flying saucer opinions.

The professional protestors against all UFO phenomena would do well to consider the time grouping of some of the sightings. It seems no accident that there are frequently instances where completely isolated reports originate from points hundreds or even thousands of miles apart, describing similar objects seen independently by observers who never heard of each other. For example, the date of February 2, 1955, produced sightings over very distant areas. Compare those which have gone before with the observation of pilots Celis and Cortes of Venezuela, flying between Barquisimito and Valera. It was a bright day and the flight was progressing normally. Suddenly the Captain and co-pilot saw a remarkable, round, "machine" which rapidly approached their plane. It was greenish in color, rotated counter-clockwise and had a glowing red ring around its center which emitted flashes of brilliant light. Above and below the ring were portholes . . . you guessed it: the radios were cut off and reports did not get through to the airport control towers, although the first few words of the message were heard before communication was interrupted. Fortunately the plane was not otherwise molested.

A few days later the captain of the ocean liner *Vera Cruz* reported that a great luminous UFO passed over his ship at fantastic speed. The sighting was verified by crew and passengers.

If saucer sighting can gain respectability from associations with superficial dignity, then here is one that should carry some weight, The Pasadena (California) *Star-News,* February 3, 1955, carried this report of a UFO above the staid Hall of Justice:

FLYING "SOMETHING" SIGHTED IN SKY ABOVE HALL OF JUSTICE

A flying something streaked over Pasadena at 8:00 a.m. today. Two city gardeners stationed at the Hall of Justice, Ed Malvin and Ben Cluball, told police they were at Arroyo Parkway and Union when they saw a round silvery object proceeding west at a speed fast enough to overtake and flash by an airliner in the same sky sector.

Police received no other calls on the object, which the gardeners also said was flying considerably higher than the plane.

The *Lake County Examiner,* Lakeview, Oregon, February 3, 1955, tells of a very strange light in ribbon-like shape. There is an off-side possibility that this was one of those rare things called an auroral arch, but we (too) are skeptical. Anyway, here is the description:

PHENOMENON OF LIGHT SEEN

A ribbon of light was seen over Lakeview by at least three persons last week, a light not explained by the vapor trails of high-flying aircraft. George Down reported that the light was seen by him and his wife, and it was seen also by Mrs. Stewart Hanna.

Down told the *Examiner* that he and Mrs. Down saw the golden light about 9:00 p.m. on Wednesday, January 26. It appeared to climb thirty or forty feet above the houses then leaned to the northeast moving slowly. It was gold color and appeared to be a ribbon a few inches wide.

The light then moved northward and Mrs. Down went outside and watched it move across town.

High-flying aircraft passing here at sundown have left vapor trails which appear reddish gold in the sunset light, but Down and Mrs. Hanna said that the light appeared to be fairly low over the houses. It appeared to drift, rising once but never going fast.

February 3, 1955, seemed to be quite a day for lights, particularly in Oregon. Here is an account (Le Grande *Observer*) of a blue light that bounced. For a while it created somewhat of a hullaballoo in the neighborhood:

BLUE LIGHTS AND NOISES DON'T DIE . . .
THEY JUST FADE AWAY . . .

The bouncing blue light is reported back in the Blue Mountains, but veteran flying saucer watchers claim this light is just a bright star.

Russell Grisson, Cove, said he saw the blue light in the sky near Winham Tuesday night.

Gene Russell and Chuck Kennedy saw the light with Grisson that night and said it was only a star. Russell and Kennedy, both of Elgin, have made frequent night patrols into the Blue Mountains in search of the eerie blue light which was reported bouncing around the area two weeks ago.

The mystery of the strange rumbling noises has been solved. W. E. Pearce, civilian executive officer at Ordnanee, reported that light charges have been set off in the demolition area near there. Larger charges have been set off on the range at Boardman.

Pearce said that if atmospheric and humidity conditions are right the sound of the blasts would carry as far as Le Grande.

Other theories are that the rumbling noises are blasting being done by the State Highway department near Starkey.

A. I. Hoover, of the CAA *Reporter*, heard the blasts while working on the beacon in the area and speculated that the noise was blasting being done in the Ordnance area.

Note that this blue light is in one of those areas where there are mysterious atmospheric rumblings. These things are an old standby in the data of Charles Fort, but their number and intensity seem to have increased since we have had a great increase in UFO sightings—or maybe we just notice them more than before. In any case neither we nor Fort have ever been able to explain them, although it is queerly true that Fort accredited them to spatial sources, thereby showing a weird prescience for the spatial awakening we are now undergoing.

On the 4th of February the Washington *Post* announced the finding of a sunken city in the two-mile high waters of Lake Titicaca in Bolivia. Just possibly this is not connected with UFO, but I will point out that the area surrounding that mystic, sky-high lake is a region of the oldest traces of pre-flood civilization known, and if we did have a race with space flight before the flood (see *The Case for the UFO*) this was certainly one of its headquarters before the time of glaciation. The story:

DIVER FINDS SUNKEN CITY
DEEP IN LAKE TITICACA

A Chicago diver said today he has discovered the ruins of a submerged city in Lake Titicaca—the world's highest large lake.

William Mardorf, 29, explored the bottom in search of Inca gold. So far he has found none, but the stone implements he brought up excited archaeologists. Mardorf descended two hundred feet in "the sacred lake," as it was called by the Incas. Its waters are frigid, since the lake is more than 12,000 feet above sea level.

He found the stone walls of the submerged city ninety-five feet down, near the mouth of the Escoma River, near what is known as the Enchanted Island. Mardorf said he took photographs with an underwater camera.

Even traditions of the Incas of that now mountainous region relate to beings arriving "from the sun" who taught agriculture and stone work. It's the old old story of the coming of "sky people"—a story prevalent throughout the world-girdling belt of megaglyphic stone works. It's a link with prehistoric use of space flight. The great megaliths of Nasca, Peru, are not very far away and these were so obviously designed as signals to space. Churchward says that these mountain tops, intra-mountain tunnels and caverns, were built before the Andes Mountains were raised.

Whether or not we need air police to curb the molesting planes by UFO's, here is a good story about two silvery UFO's and a big plane, over Southern California, as told in the Pasadena *Independent,* February 4, 1955:

MAYBE WE NEED AIR POLICE?

Reports of an impending air disaster together with flying saucer reports yesterday had police observers on their toes. Officers from both Pasadena and South Pasadena were alerted for a possible disaster at 3:30 p.m. when patrol units spotted a four-engine Globemaster cargo plane losing altitude and apparently "in trouble" over the Arroyo sector.

Police units headed for the area when the plane dropped to as low as three hundred feet as it flew south toward South Pasadena. South Pasadena officers observed the "flying boxcar" skim housetops into Alhambra, where it gained altitude and flew out of sight into Los Angeles skies.

To add to the confusion, two city gardeners Ed Malvin and Ben Cinball, called police attention to *two silver objects* which they saw overtake a high-flying plane at 8:00 a.m.

The gardeners who made the observation at Union Street and Arroyo Parkway, said the strange objects could have been flying saucers. Police had no other reports that night.

Here (in the Buffalo (New York) *Evening News* of February 5, 1955) is something which certain reactionary astronomers would doubtless like to call a mirage, but we think they might have a tough time convincing Mrs. Dawson. This business of hovering is a UFO characteristic, and somehow it is part of the hidden key to the UFO's power and maneuverability. The event took place over Lake Erie:

WOMAN REPORTS A "SPACE SHIP" OVER LAKE ERIE

The Air Force Ground Observer Filter Center at Pittsburgh has undertaken an investigation of a report by a local woman who said she saw three times what appeared to be a space ship over Lake Erie near her home.

Mrs. Harold Dawson, 39, of Dill Park, North East, reported seeing the object Dec. 5. The craft was described by her as "about the size and shape of a fishing tug."

As she watched, however, she related, she became aware the object was not afloat on the water but hovering 6 to 8 feet about it, undisturbed by the rolling waves. Brilliant orange lights were visible. She watched it for about ten minutes, she said, beginning about 1:40 a.m., and then went to get a pair of binoculars. When she returned the lights and the object were gone.

Her report for the Filter Center said the craft had a double row of square ports or windows. Atop the strange machine, she said, was a bulb-shaped dome from which emanated the orange glow.

About ten other persons in the Ripley-North East area said they saw the same orange glow on Dec. 5 but had not attached particular significance to it.

Here is another of those succinct items from the C.R.I.F.O. *Orbit*, the UFO reporting sheet of Cincinnati. We have a comment to make after you read it:

UFO WITH LONG BLUE TAIL OVER JAPAN

(Case 89, Shimizu, Japan, Feb. 5, 1955) Early risers, at 5 a.m., saw it over Shimizu, a small port town. A newspaper delivery man,

Yukio Tanaka, on bicycle, said the object, shaped like a disc, had a long blue tail, which illuminated the road. Other witnesses agreed, and added that they saw it streak toward the Pacific. One witness said as the disc moved out toward the sea there was a sudden explosive sound and the object disappeared from view. The story was carried in the *Nippon Times,* Tokyo, and sent in by Harold Fulton, N.Z. (Ed.: Object may have been a bolide, but if so, then we must admit on basis of the frequency of such reports, that the earth is presently in the midst of the Great Bolide Age.)

Editor Stringfield may have thought he was making a flippant remark about that "Bolide Age," but it *could* be true. This solar system sweeps through a tremendous amount of space in a year's time, at a speed of eleven miles or so per second, and the earth spirals along with it at some eighteen miles per second around the sun. It could be that we *are* passing through a region where there is a concentration of the stuff of which bolides and other space trash are made, and that we are simply sweeping up a greater-than-usual amount of debris. It could also be that a swarm of them in normal cometary orbits is passing the earth. It may be . . . but your editor is a little inclined to string along with Stringfield.

The following article from the Columbus (Ohio) *Dispatch* of February 6, 1955, has quite a bit of general knowledge about astronomy which you should really absorb if you wish to understand the problems of artificial satellites and astronautical dirigible widgets. Note especially that the speed of any body, artificial or not, which travels in an orbit around the earth, will depend only on its distance and not on its size. This is a point not easily understood by laymen.

ASTRONOMER IN ARIZONA HUNTS A NEW MOON

A search for a possible second moon of the earth is now going on in Arizona, where skies are generally sparkling clear. Clyde Tombaugh, discoverer of the planet Pluto, is conducting the search.

Several other planets have more than one moon, and there is no reason at hand why the earth, too, might not have an extra moon or so. Mars has two moons, Phobos and Deimos, that are only about 5 and 10 miles in diameter. If we had another moon as large as these, it would have been sighted long ago.

Tombaugh's search is for much smaller fish. With his ingenious methods a "moonlet" only 25 feet across could be seen at a distance of 100,000 miles, and a clean, white tennis ball could be seen "up there" even if 2000 miles away.

Now just what point is there of spending time and money scanning the skies for a moon probably no larger than the State Capitol in Columbus, or even more likely, no larger than a trolley bus, thousands of miles out in space?

An astronomer would say, "just for the added chance it would give for the study of the antics of gravity." With the sun, moon and earth all pulling this way and that on the defenseless moonlet, it would be quite a nice problem in celestial mechanics to keep hour by hour track of its position. Such a problem would be good exercise for an astronomer, and especially for one of the modern "electric brains" computing machines.

But the government, footing the bill for this search, has other uses for the moonlet, if found, and for the search itself. The same techniques used in this moon search can be used to follow guided missiles, and, someday, perhaps, to track a space ship on its way from the earth to the moon.

Real fun begins, however, if a tiny companion to the earth should be found. Once its orbit is calculated, its rapid course across the sky could be easily followed. If it proved to be 10,000 miles away, it would have to make one swing completely around the earth in just 6 hours. The law of gravity says it must have this speed, or else fall down to earth. It's only the moon's speed (the regular moon, now) that keeps it from falling to earth. Its outward centrifugal force just balances the inward pull of the earth's gravitational pull on it.

The uses to which such a moon could be put would be many. Tracking it from several observatories simultaneously would lead to super accurate maps of the earth. And if we look to the future, such a moon would make a fine "space station" from which to observe the earth and from which to launch space ships. We can imagine, perhaps in the rather dim future, an expedition to this nearby moon to set up continuously operating television transmitters which would send back to us minute by minute views of various parts of the world. But towering above all practical uses, as far as the scientist is concerned, would be the knowledge that such a moon exists and a knowledge of its size, motion, and structure.

In his search, Tombaugh is making use of the fact that the unknown moon would show considerable speed across the sky. Like a news photographer who "pans" his camera, moving it to "stop" the motion of a runner, to give a clear picture of the runner while the background becomes a mere blur, so does Tombaugh sweep his telescopic camera at predetermined rates to "stop" the small moon. If he discovers a new moon, it will appear on his photograph as a small dot, while the background stars will appear as luminous lines.

This method saves light, concentrating the wanted light into a pinpoint instead of losing it by trailing, while the unwanted light of the stars is smeared into thin lines on the photograph. Examination of the photographs is much easier that way, too. All one does is to look for a spot, disregarding the many star trails.

Astronomers are wishing Tombaugh luck. It would be nice to have another moon. If there's anything up there, this search should reveal it—even, yes, even "flying saucers."

The *Daily Telegraph*, London, England, of February 7th, brings a report of a mysterious object and blast over New Zealand:

FLYING BARREL EXPLOSION—
NO WRECKAGE FOUND

A mysterious explosion of terrific force shook the west coast of New Zealand's South Island to-day after people reported seeing a strange silver shape flash overhead. Observers at widely separated points described the object as cigar-shaped and travelling at tremendous speed.

They said it threw out a dazzling light. It lost altitude as it moved inland towards the Southern Alps. At two places inland observers said it was in two parts, comparable in size to a 40-gallon drum and a large saucepan.

The "flying barrel" was first reported as it crossed the west coast. It was seen 200 feet above Inchbonnie, a farming community 30 miles inland, and then flew towards the mountains.

The explosion was heard and felt over several hundred square miles. It was heard at Greymouth and people farther south reported a pronounced earth tremor. A tall column of smoke was seen, rising from the Southern Alps. No wreckage has yet been found.

This explosion was noticeable enough to get some reporting in United States papers, and just to show you the difference in the type of reporting, we bring you also the write-up in the Fall River (Massachusetts) *Herald-News* of February 10, 1955, covering the same event:

ITEM FOR YOUR FLYING SAUCER JOURNAL

Here's one for your Flying Saucer Journal.

At about 5 p.m., on Feb. 7, dozens of New Zealanders saw an object resembling a skyrocket zooming over the mountain range in the southern part of their island, where it exploded with such force that it was heard in towns many miles away. The gigantic shock waves that ensued resembled the noise created by a great earthquake.

New Zealand's scientists explained that the mysterious explosion was probably caused by the bursting of a meteor upon contact with the earth's atmosphere, but no confirmed Saucerite is going to fall for that. The trouble with scientists is that they always have an argument designed to disparage the Saucerites' conviction that worlds in the outer spaces are trying to communicate with ours, and that if they can't accomplish it peacefully they'll do it eventually in a way to make us sorry.

If we were to become excited about the New Zealand Saucer, it wouldn't be because we thought it was launched by Martians. We would be speculating as to whether or not it were some diabolical rocket launched somewhere in Red Russia.

Your editor is, perhaps, a little inclined to go along with the meteor theory, but in that case we certainly are backing Stringfield's idea that we are in a space volume sown with meteors and bolides like a wartime minefield!

"Mysterious explosions" are not new to us. Fort reported hundreds of them. 1955, no matter what its deficiencies in other directions, produced its share, and we refer particularly to those over San Francisco, Florida and the South Central States. Throughout the history of these "booms" it has often been difficult to decide with certainty whether the detonations originated in the air or under ground in the form of earthquakes.

Here is a good sighting by a citizen of Pennsylvania, as told by the Hazleton *Standard-Sentinel* of February 7, 1955:

REPORTS SEEING "FLYING SAUCER"

Joseph Sherrock, 306 Putnam street, West Hazleton, reported seeing what the U.S. Air Force has termed an "unidentified flying object," at 1:45 o'clock Saturday morning. Sherrock and two co-workers, Edward Haburshock, West Hazleton, and John Kochie, Foster Townships, all saw the UFO at Gowen, where they are night shift coal stripping workers.

They saw what appeared to be a large star in the southeast sector of the sky. The object was a bright amber hue and as they watched, it broke into two sections which both ascended higher into the sky and then traveled in a westerly direction until they disappeared over the horizon.

Sherrock estimated their time in flight as about three or four minutes and said the fiery amber color seemed to dim considerably as the two sections traveled farther away.

The amber color is rather typical, as it is not too different from the usual orange light. The breaking into two parts is one of a growing number of instances where these UFO bodies are found to be articulated, or co-joined in some manner, as in cases of "mother ships" and "satellite ships."

Florida is back. This time it's the Melbourne (Florida) *Times* of February 8, 1955, and again it's a big meteor. Definitely there are more of these than usual, in the past year or two. Whatever may be their true nature, there are certainly definite proofs that we have encountered a time and space region containing an unusual amount of space debris and spatial activity, be it flying saucers or otherwise. It is not too far-fetched to assume that one accompanies the other to some extent.

BIG METEOR SEEN OVER LOCAL AREA

Charles Dare, local businessman, and other Melbourne area persons, reported today that they saw a big meteor flash across this section last night.

Associated Press dispatches reported that the meteor was said to have looked "like a ball of fire 10 to 15 feet in diameter," and flashed across South Florida before it burned out over the Everglades.

Hundreds of persons from Central Florida to Cuba reported seeing it. Several motorists near Miami reported they swerved to keep from being hit.

Pilots flying over Fort Pierce and Key West reported it as did two pilots flying the Atlantic between Miami and Nassau. A ship near Cuba radioed it had seen the meteor:

"I thought it was coming in the window of my plane," said Capt. Francis Black, Eastern Air Lines pilot en route to Miami. "I was over Fort Pierce at the time on a trip from Detroit. It looked like a ball of fire 10 or 15 feet in diameter.

"I took my plane up about 1,000 feet to keep from getting hit but I felt a little foolish when I got to Miami and learned that a pilot flying over Key West did the same thing."

The Miami Weather Bureau took a sober view of the occurrence:
"It was no different from hundreds that fall every night. It was a
big one but it probably burned out at about 20,000 to 30,000 feet
over the Everglades about 30 or 40 miles southwest of Miami International Airport."

The size of this thing, and the extent of its influence, can be
seen from the following report in the Miami Beach *Sun* of February 8th:

FROM OUTER SPACE
EXPLOSIVE VISITOR!

South Floridians were still talking about their "visitor from outer
space" today. The big question is "which way did it really go?"

The visitor was a big blue-green meteor that flashed across the
sky last night, then exploded as dozens of pilots and thousands of
excited witnesses on the ground watched. As in the case of certain
more controversial aerial phenomena, there were almost as many
versions as there were witnesses.

Two airplanes as far apart as Ft. Pierce and Key West—a distance of nearly 300 miles—tried to "dodge" the fiery ball. Several
motorists near Miami Beach said they swerved to avoid being hit.
Another pilot at Havana, Cuba, reported the meteor went right over
his plane.

Other spectators who swamped radio, newspaper and police switch
boards with calls described it as "big as the moon," "a crashing
plane," and "a big green saucer with a long, white tail."

Hank Tonkin, public service meteorologist, had a less imaginative
explanation. The meteor was "a big one," said Tonkin, "but no
different from hundreds that fall every night—except that this was
closer to Miami."

Newspapers all up and down the coast of Florida reported the
weird experiences of drivers and pilots when the green fireball
passed over. The Palm Beach *Post*, February 8, had a long
account, but typical is the following from the conservative Miami
Herald, of February 7th:

PILOTS AND DRIVERS "DODGE" FIERY BALL

South Florida had an unexpected visitor in the sky about 7:30 p.m. Monday when a bluish-green meteor zoomed from southeastern skies and was sighted by residents and air travelers from Fort Pierce to Cuba.

Two airplanes—one flying over Fort Pierce and another over Key West, some 300 miles from there—tried to "dodge" the fiery ball. Several motorists in Dade county said they swerved to keep from being hit.

"It was as big as the moon!"

"A plane just crashed!"

"It was a big green saucer with a long, white tail!"

Those were some of the reports from excited witnesses. But there were hundreds of other calls to The Herald and Police and Coast Guard switchboards in the area, and each caller had his own special version.

The visitor from outer space "was no different from hundreds that fall every night" according to the Miami Weather Bureau, "except that this one was closer to Miami."

"It was a big one," said Hank Tonkin, public service meteorologist," but it probably burned out at about 20,000 to 30,000 feet.

"There is no doubt but what it was seen by so many people because we had about 80 per cent humidity at that time and that helped a lot.

"It burned out somewhere over the Everglades, about 30 or 40 miles southwest of Miami International Airport."

The control tower at the airport reported receiving calls from two airplanes over the Atlantic between Miami and Nassau and from a ship in the vicinity of Cuba.

"The control tower was lighted by a green glow," one of the men on duty there said, "and we received another call from the control tower in Fort Lauderdale."

"I thought it was coming in the window of my plane," said Capt. Francis Black, a pilot for Eastern Air Lines. "I was over Fort Pierce at the time on a trip from Detroit. It looked like a ball of fire 10 or 15 feet in diameter.

C

"I took my plane up about 1,000 feet to keep from getting hit but I felt a little foolish when I got to Miami and learned that a pilot flying over Key West did the same thing."

Several Navy ships and planes and many commercial ships and aircraft reported that the meteor was one of the largest ever sighted in the area.

But C.R.I.F.O. gets reports from everywhere, and Stringfield has been puzzled by the coincidence of fireballs at the antipodes of Florida and New Zealand. In his March issue he says:

FEBRUARY, FIREBALLS & THE FACTS

(Case 66, Florida, Cuba, Salt Lake City, February 7, 1955) Fireballs, sometimes synonymous with meteors, came thick and fast in February. Checking the astronomy book, I found no meteor showers scheduled for that month, so I checked with an authority—a leading astronomer. He told me that he too could find no reference to any "showers." So, indeed, here was an anomalous situation.

And then he continues:

Let's look into some of the evidence. Hard on the heels of New Zealand's sky extravaganza February 7 (to be reported in a future issue based on details just received from Harold Fulton) came another of equal impact. Few papers carried this story of February 7. It ran something like this: A big meteor flashed across South Florida flaming so brightly that the pilot of an airliner tried to dodge it with his plane. The flashing light was spotted by hundreds of persons. Two airplanes over the Atlantic between Miami and Nassau and a ship near Cuba radioed that they had seen it. Several motorists near Miami said they swerved to keep from being hit. One pilot, Capt. Black of Eastern Airlines, reported, according to AP, "I thought it was coming in the window of my plane. I was over Ft. Pierce at the time. It looked like a ball of fire 10 to 16 feet in diameter. I took my plane up about 1000 feet to keep from getting hit, but I felt a little foolish when I got to Miami and learned that a pilot flying over Key West did the same thing." (Credit: J. J. Brenner)

From the press account, the fireball is easily explained away as a meteor, but other and less easily explained evidence was smothered. Thanks to the investigations of pilot William B. Nash, of Miami, who sends CRIFO the following report, we learn differently.

We quote from Nash's letter: "Very odd meteor—I did a little checking, and found that a PAA airplane crew with Capt. Charles Elmore in command saw three bright white lights due South of their DC6B as they crossed Biscayne Bay 1200 feet high on a west heading to the airport enroute from Nassau. The lights were 15 degrees higher than the aircraft. They were much brighter than aircraft flares and larger. They appeared to hover with the front two connected by a line of light between them. Suddenly they blinked out. The tower saw them too—couldn't identify them. The time was 8:35 p.m. The lights had fuzzy edges and were round. Clear night, no inversion—to bright for reflections. Four persons on Biscayne Key reported odd lights moving at sea about 8:05 to 8:15 p.m. Many persons and pilots saw a very bright streaking object at 7:55 p.m. (see reports UP and AP). Airplanes at Ft. Pierce, Vero Beach, Havana and over Andros Island in the Bahamas reported a bright green object as big as the moon with a long white tail. No sound reported. The times of sightings varied over a forty minute period from 7:55 to 8:35. Some meteorologist who didn't see it tagged it a meteor. The PAA pilots say that what they saw was no meteor. A Marine pilot over Andros Island said it landed gradually on Andros."

Supplementing the Florida incident, same date, is another report of a similar object passing over Salt Lake City. Personnel at the Salt Lake Municipal Airport's control tower noted that the object was sighted at 7:55 p.m. Curiously, the night before, Feb. 6, at 9:42, a similar object flashed across the sky. In both cases the objects were likened to exploding stars. They streaked across the sky from south to north at great speed and disappeared over the horizon. (Credit: H. B. Williams.)

So that's the story on the Florida-New Zealand combination.

I know Bill Nash, and know that Bill is a sober, serious and reliable pilot, and good observer.

Maybe there *is* more in this than meets the regimented eye of the meteorologist.

Maybe there was even more to the meteor story. Did we really hit a celestial nest of these green "birds?"

Here is the story of a woman 2000 miles from Miami, as told in the Walsenburg (Colorado) *World-Independent,* February 8th:

WOMAN THINKS METEOR APPEARS

A Walsenburg woman Sunday night saw a bright light as she looked through a window in her house, and the next morning found a small quantity of inorganic material which she thinks might be what is left of a meteor.

Mrs. Mary Kimbrel, 220 Elm, said she saw what appeared to be a fire coming down at 8:30 p.m. Sunday. She said the small quantity of inorganic substance was found the next morning on the top of the ground. There was no hole.

She said she felt a faint thump when she saw the bright light.

Mrs. Kimbrel said her husband, Perry Kimbrel, thought the inorganic material was clinker from a stove. The substance has been brought to the World-Independent. It has the appearance of having been heated.

At this distance in time and space we don't know what the "inorganic material" was; the description is certainly vague. But somehow it doesn't sound like any ordinary "accepted" meteoritic material. What kind of "swarm" *did* we run into on February 7th, 1955?

Even Ireland may have shared in this heavenly splash, for here is a little clip from the Belfast *News-Letter* of February

9th. We lost a part of the clipping, but this was certainly some kind of UFO:

FLYING SAUCER?

MYSTERIOUS OBJECT SEEN IN SKY OVER NEWRY

Mystery still surrounds the identity of the object seen in the skies over Newry on Saturday afternoon. Patrick M'Keown, a 35-year-old electrician, was motor cycling to his home at Maghernahely, Bess-brooke, Conty Armagh, with a pillion passenger, when he spotted the object in the sky directly over the town. He describes it as a large, clearly defined black circular object . . .

The list of crashed and disappearing planes becomes ever longer. On February 9th, two jet fighters crashed under very confused circumstances at Goose Bay. The Air Force reported that they collided in the air, but authenticated press reports said they crashed separately, five minutes and some miles apart, with no explanation as to what happened. On the 8th, a brand new B-57 jet bomber exploded over Maryland, under test conditions. It had just started a flight from the Glen. L. Martin plant at Baltimore. On the 9th, two Canadian jets crashed in New Brunswick, and again there was no explanation.

Other cases of like nature are recalled, such as an F-100 which disintegrated over California in October of 1954. The authorities stated that the F-100 met *aerodynamic conditions never before heard of by man!*

The following account from the Delray (Florida) *News*, February 10, 1955, *may* have been the same meteor seen by so many others, but the description and direction of flight would seem to indicate that it was more likely another object of the same group:

FLYING SAUCERS INVADING DELRAY?
SOME THINK SO!

It was reported that a huge, multi-colored object sped flaming across the sky at about 7:30 p.m. on Monday, February 7, and disappeared in the direction of the Gulf of Mexico.

Mrs. C. B. Perkins and Mrs. Edward Meredith were among the many others in Delray who saw the mysterious ball. "Seeing it was a once-in-a-lifetime experience, something I never expected to watch . . . a most impressive sight," said Mrs. Perkins.

On February 10th, William P. Lear again stated his confidence in space flight, and speaking as one who knows what he is talking about, he predicted that vehicles of the future would travel with equal facility on the ground and in the air. He admitted that he and his pilot had seen a flying saucer during a recent flight.

Throughout all of these fragmentary reports and discussions there is a continuous thread of hints that we are on the verge of producing "Flying Saucers" through a combination of gravity control and unlimited nuclear power.

The following is another C.R.I.F.O. case. It is undoubtedly related to the same epidemic of "fireballs" which plagued the entire earth over the previous week-end:

FIREBALL DIVE BOMBS MAN

(Case 68, Auckland, New Zealand, February 10, 1955) Mr. C. M. Callander, greenkeeper at Mt. Roskill Bowling Club, had walked on to the green with a tin and a knife. He was bending to lay down the knife when a fireball ranged in, landing inches from his feet. Callander said it was impossible to say how big it was, and admitted, "I ran for my life across the paddock, but it was gone when I turned around." He described the fireball as bright red, coming from behind and out of a clear sky. It was followed by a loud clap of thunder which came from directly overhead. The ball left no mark on the green. This report comes from Harold Fulton, and we note it with interest and speculation, comparing it with New Haven's red fireball which showed more destructive proclivity.

Now, if this was what the astronomers faithfully call "meteoritic material," why did it disappear after landing at the observer's feet? We cannot resort to the threadbare "there in the first place" explanation, for it wasn't even there in the last place!

Mississippi had some excitement, too. The February 10th edition of the Indianola *Sunflower-Tocsin* reported the following:

FLYING SAUCER CREATES INTEREST
OVER INDIANOLA

Wednesday morning many Indianola citizens saw what appeared to be a "Flying Saucer" passing over the city. It created much interest as to exactly what the thing was. A local man called the Air Force Base in Greenville and reported the object and a couple of jets were sent up to investigate.

Soon after the object was spotted by the pilots it was overtaken and identified as a "weather balloon." The point of origin was unknown. The balloon was drifting almost north by east and at a height of approximately 35,000 feet.

Those who saw the object were not too alarmed as they were suspicious of the fact that it probably was a balloon, but were unable to identify it at such a distance.

Perhaps there is an element of humor in the following second-hand item from "down-under," but please note the similarity of the "poached-egg shape" to some of the flying saucer or space-ship "photos" you may have seen.

The Kansas City (Missouri) *Times* of February 10th reported from Melbourne, Australia, via Reuters:

POACHED EGGS NOW FLYING!
AUSTRALIANS ALARMED
BY STRANGE OBJECT IN SKY

Melbourne newspapers were overwhelmed by calls tonight from people who said they had seen a "flying poached egg."

One witness said: "It had a yellow core surrounded by a white edge—like a colossal poached egg. I heard peculiar whining noises as it flew away to sea."

Although these flashes, fireballs, etc., were stretched out over a few days' time, their similarity seems to assure some relationship. Here is a report from the Metaline Falls (Washington) *News* of February 19th:

MYSTERIOUS FLASH

A. A. Shackelton and others report seeing a mysterious flash about 6:30 Tuesday evening in the sky north of town, followed by a roar three or four minutes later. George Day, while driving, and his passengers, also saw a flash south of Ione, and a report came that it was observed at Colvim.

Mrs. F. E. Appel, who lives at the boundary, comes up with a report that they had a winter electrical storm in their vicinity at that time.

One would hardly call this flurry a typical "meteor shower" . . . but what kind of an incursion from space *was* it?

And, what was the little item picked up by Mr. Nevison, as told in the St. Petersburg (Florida) *Times* of February 11th? The timing was certainly coincident with the flurry we have been recording. This little gadget had those provocative markings "almost like letters." Marked with letters and from space? Like the little stone from Tarbes?

Here is the story:

OBJECT THOUGHT TO BE METEOR
IS FOUND HERE

A visitor from outer space dropped in on the Nevison Antique Shop, 5151 Park Blvd, Pinellas Park, Wednesday night, in the form of a small meteor.

"I heard a noise on the roof about 10 p.m.," Nevison said, "and looked out the front door. There was a black object on the sidewalk which looked like a toad."

But when Nevison's cat avoided the object, he took a closer look and found it to be a lump about the size of a silver dollar and three times that thickness. He noted raised markings "almost like letters."

Several friends and neighbors have told Nevison the object is a meteor. He plans to check with an authority for positive identification. No damage was reported.

Even the shape of that little item is like the little stone of Tarbes, France, reported in detail by Charles Fort. And the size: a few millimeters thick and about an inch in diameter!

At about this time, in 1955, a pair of new books came out—both by English authors—and the following brief review appeared in the Houston (Texas) *Press* of February 11, written by Carl Victor Little:

TWO NEW BOOKS ON FLYING SAUCERS

. . . In one of two new books just published by the British Book Center, Leonard G. Cramp studies the Adamski text and photos and confirms Adamski's stories that flying saucers indeed have landed.

The Cramp book (*Space, Gravity and the Flying Saucer*, $3) carries 27 drawings and six photographs.

Author Cramp, member of the Interplanetary Society of England, concludes that photos of flying saucers (large circular space ships) taken by Adamski in California and snapshots of mystery craft taken more recently in England are similar.

The second British book, *Flying Saucers From Mars,* was written by Cedric Allingham, a Scotsman whose hobby is birdwatching and studying the heavens through a telescope. Author Allingham, who writes whodunits once in a while, was out watching birds on a moor late one afternoon and he claims, in this scientific treatise, to have seen a space ship parked some distance away.

He even surprised and photographed a Martian who, in the photo Allingham took and which is shown in the book, seems to be in a hell of a hurry to reach his ship. In his 190-page book, with nine photographs, Allingham tells of his experiences on the moor. He says he's heading for California. The two new books and the one that inspired them, *Flying Saucers Have Landed,* are exciting reading.

However, I'll reserve judgment on all these stories until I actually see a space ship land at Main and Texas some high noon, a spaceman alight and ask me personally, in carrier pigeon English, "Can you direct me, Mr. Earthman, to the office of Soapy Joe? We've heard so much about him on Mars."

All of the above, including italics, is quoted.

In England they see a lot of flying saucers, considering the small geographical area involved. However, England has always had more than its share of erratic events, as testified by the researches of Fort, Price and many others. Anyway, here is a good sighting reported by the Portsmouth *Evening News,* February 12, 1955:

—AND CIGARS OVER SUSSEX—

Three girl secretaries sat in the sunshine at their office windows in East Street, Chichester, yesterday. Just another humdrum day. Then, Miss P. Coom (18) saw something unusual.

Now, secretaries today are worldly creatures, not likely to be taken in easily. So with scorn on their faces, her two friends, Miss P. Vigar (24) and Miss E. M. Rogers (21) followed her gaze.

And there, sure enough, bobbing about above the clouds, gleaming in the sunlight, frisking like tadpoles in a pond, were six "flying saucers."

For ten minutes the girls watched. Said Miss Vigar, of 5 Graydon Road, Donnington: "They seemed to be chasing each other, bobbing round and round. They were very high and moving very much faster than aircraft. They looked like bubbles but were flat and disc-like. Obviously they were metal, too, because when the sun caught them they reflected its light. I know people will say we are crazy, but we saw them."

The saucers disappeared at speed, still juggling like tadpoles, traveling towards Portsmouth.

At East Wittering, 14-year-old John Barnard, of Rooks Nest, Barn Close, saw a cigar-shaped object in the sky. He said the object moved slowly, stopped momentarily, and then disappeared into the clouds.

"It didn't look anything like any aeroplane I've ever seen," said John.

He was with his aunt, Mrs. Emily Jones, of Marine Drive, who although unwilling to commit herself, apparently agreed with his description. "It wasn't like any aeroplane I have seen," she admitted.

At Tangmere R.A.F. Station Meteorological Office the information about the "saucers" was taken seriously. Every half-hour, the skies are scanned from there, but yesterday the observers reported nothing unusual.

A spokesman wanted a description of Miss Vigar's "flying saucers," however. He wanted to know the time they were seen, which direction they took, how many there were. Not that he believed in "flying saucers" of course. "But just in case."

On February 11, a Pan-American Airlines crew reported two strange objects of reddish green (reminds me of that iridescent silk we used to buy thirty-five years ago) which flew under their wings. The objects were seen by some of the passengers.

On February 12, a U.S. Stratojet bomber on an arctic flight, flying at 35,000 feet, exploded mysteriously. There were two survivors, who were stunned by the impact, but revived in time to open their chutes, but they could shed no light on the cause of the accident. There had not been an instant's warning.

The disappearing plane is becoming a common occurrence, as also the plane that crashes without warning or explanation. Here is another of C.R.I.F.O.'s coverages:

(Case 58, Rome, Italy, February 13, 1955.) A Belgian Airliner carrying 29 persons (four Americans) vanished a few minutes after radioing Rome's Ciampino Airport that it was preparing for a routine landing. According to radio station KGO (San Francisco) the pilot had radioed seeing a "fireball" in the sky. Next day station KCBS said the missing airliner first reported "flight okay" but four minutes later started sending another message—which broke off suddenly—NO mention of contents! Later the same day ABC and NBC networks in San Francisco told of the search operations but kept mum on the UFO. Significant and sinister, on February 14, the French African short-wave station in Brazzaville reported the search for the airliner and added that due to the mysterious "orange spot in the sky" the departure of the Italian Prime Minister and Foreign Minister (in another flight from Rome to London) had been delayed.

There is getting to be a real pattern in this disappearance business: planes approach an airport, due in four or five minutes, radio for landing instrustions—and disappear . . . *Stendec!* Chile, Africa, Rome, Calcutta, etc., *Why?* We've one coming up in the December chapter.

On February 13, 1955, according to the following Case 67, from C.R.I.F.O. another GFB (green fireball) took out over the USA from Texas, via Oklahoma, to New York and points East. Was this a part of the general fireball show? Here is C.R.I.F.O.'s account and some comments:

(Case 67, Texas, Oklahoma, New York, February 13, 1955.) As far afield as Mineral Wells to Lufkin, through Dallas to Jackson, Mississippi, the fireball soared in its eerie glare and silence. Separate reports were made in Tulsa and other parts of Oklahoma. Finally the "thing" was seen over Hallstead and Triple Cities, New York. Unconfirmed reports say the object exploded or hit the ground but no evidence has been found. (Ed.: True with all GFB's, save in finding traces of copper in the air.)

The most vivid account came from a control operator at Pounds Field, Tyler, Texas. He said, "Around midnight this light seemed to pop out of the sky directly above us. It looked like a huge electric arc. It was greenish, like the tip of a welder's torch. It was going due south. There were three of us in the tower. We had the lights on, but the room lighted up brilliantly. It was a blinding light, the brightest I ever saw. The object looked like a football with a short tail."

John Fontaine, CAA Authority at Lufkin said: "Along about midnight we felt a percussion as if from an explosion. We didn't see a flash, but it was reportedly seen in town. They said it went down somewhere between Tyler and Lufkin. Everybody in town is stirred up. Several people said, when it hit it felt like a car door slamming. Phone calls flooded the Weather Bureau in Dallas where the object's glow lit up the SE sky. (Credit: Dorothy Howarth, Mrs. McIntyre, H. G. Rovner, Mrs. W. J. Daily.)

Several Triple Cities residents in New York reported a similar fireball. One witness who was driving back from Scranton described it as similar to a Fourth of July rocket. The weather bureau at Broome County Airport said that if the Texas and Southern Tier "fireballs" were meteors, they could not possibly be the same one since rapidly falling meteors burn out quickly and are observable over a relatively small area. (Credit: F. J. Kelly.)

Sometimes, it is said, coming events cast their shadows before them and here, in the *New York Times*, February 13, 1955, there was a rather definite ripple of the satellite announcement which the government was even then preparing for release in

August. Sometimes the government reminds me of some Congo natives beating drums to frighten away evil spirits. Only in this case, it is the naughty but persistent reports of the ubiquitous UFO's.

SCIENCE IN REVIEW. A PROPOSAL
TO PLACE A SMALL SATELLITE ABOVE
THE EARTH AS A STEP TOWARD SPACE TRAVEL

Above are the headlines over a two-column article analyzing the proposal. But more was to come as the months passed.

The Waco (Texas) *Tribune-Herald,* February 13, 1955, carried the following feature article by a former citizen living in Venezuela. It is the saga of the Venezuela Saucer sighting and "little men" contacts:

EX-WACOAN IN VENEZUELA
RELATES SAUCER SAGA THERE
By Mary Louise Edgar

Boundless curiosity is unleashed whenever the words flying saucer are mentioned. What is it? Could it be a guided missile or a spy ship from Mars?

A letter recently received by Dr. and Mrs. V. A. Kelley, 1225 N. 13th Street, caused friends to wonder anew about this scientific phenomenon. The letter was written by the Wacoan's daughter, Mrs. Elizabeth Anttila, who with her husband, Earl, works at the Escuela Normal Rural Inter-Americana School in Rubio, Estado Tachira, Venezuela.

Her letter concerned "a luminous disc" which landed in a city near Caracas and its effect on two Venezuelan merchants. Although casually related, the incident attracted more than casual interest among readers.

Two men were driving along the road around 2:00 a.m., preparatory to taking goods to the market. A "luminous disc" some two meters long and one meter wide, hovering about sixteen meters over the center of the city street forced them to stop. They noticed three small men, one meter tall, around the glowing object. Grabbing a flashlight the driver ran forward. His companion was with him until he noticed one of the little men holding an "apparatus." Frightened, he ran the other way to a nearby traffic control point.

Elizabeth is secretary of the school, employed by the Venezuelan government, and Earl is an instructor employed by the Pan-American Union.

Meantime, the driver threw his flashlight at one of the men and missed. He then ran up, grabbed the little fellow, held him high against his chest and tried to take him back to the car. The little man gave him a hard blow in the left ribs and squirmed away. Drawing a knife the driver tried to stab the creature but his knife struck "a surface like stone." Immediately the three little men entered the disc which ascended and disappeared.

Later at the traffic control point the driver exposed his left side which was beginning to show a bad bruise. He said he believed the little creature was scooping up handfuls of earth which he took into the disc. Authorities reported the men had not been drinking but they were still undergoing treatment for shock and nervous collapse at the time Elizabeth wrote about the incident.

A drawing of a saucer man seen in Venezuela was received this month, but, although interesting, it was not well executed as to detail and therefore has not been included in the *Annual*.

The Riverside (California) *Enterprise*, February 13, 1955, thinks a flying saucer was seen nearby. It says: "Some object shining brightly in the sky over the mountains to the west of the valley attracted attention between 7:00 and 8:00 a.m. the other morning . . . according to those who saw it, the object was at a high altitude and moved its position only slightly before it disappeared."

That sounds almost like a sighting of the planet Venus, but not enough details are given.

The Baltimore *Evening Sun,* February 14, 1955, reported the great green flash seen over Texas, and quotes an Associated Press report from Tyler, Texas. This flash, or soaring fireball has been widely discussed in UFO literature. This is the report:

BRILLIANT GREEN FLASH SEEN OVER TEXAS

A fireball, its weird green light casting a fiery glow over three men in an airport control tower, flashed like a "huge electric arc" across the East Texas piney woods last night.

It was apparently a meteor. There were unconfirmed reports that it exploded or hit the ground, but no evidence of it has been found. Information indicated that it was first seen here and disappeared some sixty miles south, near Lufkin. But the weather bureau at Dallas got reports of its glow as far as Jackson, Mississippi, to the east, and Mineral Wells, in West Texas.

The most vivid account came from J. N. Aber, a control-tower operator at Pounds Field.

"Around midnight," he said, "this light seemed to pop out of the sky directly above us. It looked like a huge electric arc. It was greenish, like the tip of a welder's torch."

The following saucer sighting was reported in the Circleville (Ohio) *Daily Herald,* February 14, 1955. These moon-like yellow or orange objects have been reported very descriptively for several hundred years, and they are almost certainly the two objects described in *The Case for the UFO* which have repeatedly been reported by astronomers as passing over the face of the sun, or having been seen at times of solar eclipse. The reddish color is typical, and these spheres are navigable in space. Their repeated re-discovery by Tombaugh and Babgy was predicted in *The Case for the UFO.*

ANOTHER "SAUCER" SIGHTING CLAIMED

Mrs. Hilda MacNeil, of Circleville Route 3, described in calm, matter-of-fact manner Monday a strange, luminous object she saw in the sky from a window of her home north of the city.

"I guess some people will think I'm nuts," she laughed, "but I definitely saw something mighty strange in the sky, and nobody— no matter how they kid me or laugh—is going to change my mind about that."

Mrs. MacNeil's story, the latest in periodic "flying saucer" reports in this district, carried an especially strong note of credibility in the good-humored way she anticipates the skeptics. She said she is fully aware that "many people will just laugh it off and say it was my imagination, a reflection or something."

Mrs. MacNeil recalls it was about 6:15 a.m. Saturday morning when her attention was attracted to some sort of light that flashed near a corner of her kitchen window. It was still quite dark outside, and she was preparing breakfast at the time.

Her curiosity was aroused by the small reflection, she went into a darkened room and looked out a window toward the northwest. There, fairly high in the sky, she saw an object which she immediately assumed to be the moon.

With this assumption, she explained, she did not expect the object to move, and did not notice any form of motion. However, she remembers that the object was of unusual shape, being slightly of a fat, football outline—roughly that of a large saucer seen broadside. Mrs. MacNeil also noted the color of the object to be "bluish-white, and glowing."

Mrs. MacNeil thought nothing in particular about the incident until a minute or two later, she happened to glance out another window and saw the moon. The moon, she said, was seen at the time almost directly over the home of Mr. and Mrs. Wendell Turner.

The MacNeil home is a short distance north of the Turner residence. Both dwellings are on the Walnut Creek pike, just north of the city limits.

Mrs. MacNeil said the moon and the unidentified object differed considerably in shape. The moon was almost "yellowish," she said, while the object had a definite white-and-blue glow. No marking of any sort was visible on the object.

Astonished to see the moon "after I thought I had already seen it in another direction," Mrs. MacNeil hurried back to the spot where she first sighted the object. It had disappeared.

Mrs. MacNeil's husband, Norman, was shaving at the time of the incident, but his wife explained she did not call his attention to the unusual object immediately "since she just thought it was the moon."

Mrs. MacNeil related her experience to Bruce Stevenson, well-known local farmer who has described one of the most detailed "saucer" sightings on record. Stevenson spotted the "saucer" several years ago, but he pointed out to Mrs. MacNeil it was around this time of year, and on an extremely cold night.

The temperature was around zero here early Saturday morning.

On February 15, 1955, the Cleveland (Ohio) *Press* published a review of Cedric Allingham's book, *Flying Saucer From Mars*. It made very interesting reading and in a nutshell summed up the controversy and general opposition that has helped surround the UFO phenomenon with so much ridicule.

Melbourne, Florida, does well in its effort to uphold the position of its state in the UFO field. We believe they even have an open-minded Astronomical Society or club there. Readers with a good memory will perhaps recall that a great herd of whales was beached and died at Melbourne not so long ago. The Melbourne *Times* of February 16, 1955, reported a "sky mystery":

CITY HAS SKY MYSTERY

What is the cause of this "mystery in the sky" which several Melbourne residents have witnessed recently? Meteors and this type of flashes occur occasionally but they go through the sky at such a fast rate of speed that they are rarely seen by the average person

Humane Officer and Mrs. John F. Ginty reported this week that they had seen several flashes in the southwestern section of the sky over the Melbourne area this week.

The Gintys were watching television one evening when Mr. Ginty noticed a strange light in the yard. He immediately went outside to investigate the situation but found nothing and returned to his TV program.

In a short time, Mrs. Ginty called her husband and said she had seen another flash in the sky just west of the new Drive-in Theater on the Kissimmee Highway. The Gintys then became interested in the mystery and timed the other flashes which happened at 10:05, 10:06 and then at 10:25 and 10:27 p.m. Ginty stated that the flashes were on the order of a photo flash but it lit up the whole countryside. He said it was as if you were looking into the sun, only it was a bright yellow circle with a large corona around it and, getting darker red toward the edges of the huge ball of fire.

"It resembled a dying sun," stated Ginty, "and the flashes came instantly but died more slowly."

After Ginty contacted the *Times*, Nick Dean, Melbourne Airport Manager, was questioned, but he said that the flashes were probably something to do with Patrick Air Force Base as he had seen them several times before and when he inquired about the mystery the answer he received was that the base had been shooting flares over this area as some type of experiment.

Dean's information concerning the base led the *Times* to call Major S. A. Pelle, but he stated no work of this type at night was undertaken at the Missile Test Center. It was then learned that Ginty had also contacted the base and he was told that it may have been some type of aerial photography going on at Avon Park. Dean and Pelle explained that it was probably nothing to get alarmed about.

The base personnel has requested that any other persons who see things of this type should contact the base as they are very much interested in finding out the cause of the "mystery in the sky."

The **Texas Flying Saucer Research Society** is a fairly recent addition to the investigatory field. Here is a letter they wrote to the **Corpus Christi** *Caller*, and published February 17, 1955:

Editor, The Caller:

There has been considerable to-do over the subject of *flying saucers* in the past few weeks. Perhaps it would be good if a summary of events in this field might be presented here.

To begin with a number of well-known scientists have **affirmed** their belief in flying saucers. Some of the most notable of this group are: G. Duncan Fletcher of the Kenya Astronomical Society; Dr. Herman Oberth, famous German rocket scientist; Commander Justino Strauss of the Brazilian Navy; William P. Lear, inventor of the robot pilot and holder of the Robert J. Collier Aviation Trophy, and a number of others. The British Astronomer Royal, Sir Harold Spencer Jones, has stated that there is little doubt that intelligent life exists on other worlds. It is primitive and egotistic to think otherwise.

There have been several saucer sightings in the not too distant past. In several eastern states, discs have been caught in spotlight beams and observed by thousands. Priests and Ministers have sworn affidavits telling of sighting these objects. Are these people, men, of God, liars? Some people would have us believe this.

In Oregon, a number of persons at different points reported seeing a blue light moving along the highway. According to the newspaper there is no explanation for this light. Over the entire nation these objects are reported as much as five a day.

In New Zealand only a few days ago, a strange silver shape flashed overhead. The object was described as being like a cigar. It emitted a dazzling light and traveled at high speed. Seconds after the object was sighted a strange explosion shook hundreds of square miles with a terrific force. Reports of cigar-shaped objects and the explosion poured in from great distances.

This letter tells what strange things go on in the short time of a few weeks. Happenings such as these are common occurrences everyday. Those that take the time can find accounts of these events hidden away in our newspapers. It seems that things like those described above do not warrant much space. It is too bad that the wire services do not tell the public the facts about the flying saucers.

From the Charlotte (N.C.) *Observer*, February 17, 1955.

It is not news to the saucer fan who knows his Bible, that Ezekiel was looking at a UFO when he saw the "wheel." Here is a quote from the San Diego (California) *Tribune* in which the savant Menzel again douses the "wheel" sighting with the cold fluid of hallucination. But, unfortunately, not everyone can know the truth, so let us be tolerant:

ILLUSIONS?

EZEKIEL, TOO, SAW SAUCER,

SAVANT SAYS

Mankind has been seeing flying saucers and the like since Biblical times, when Ezekiel saw a wheel in the sky, a Harvard astronomer said, yesterday.

Dr. Donald H. Menzel, director of Harvard University's Solar Observatory, Climax, Colorado, spoke as a flying saucer expert.

He said he has seen them for forty years almost every day or night he looked for them. And he has a number of quite eerie photographs of them.

Plato saw them, too.

In the 1880's, strange air ships were sighted in remote sections of the United States, causing near panic.

What are they?

Among other types, there are: Ice crystals, spiderwebs, birds, milkweed and dandelion seeds and weather balloons. Temperature inversions, such as cause smog, can reflect city lights and the reflections in the sky can be seen for miles.

Menzel said he and his wife trailed such a reflection in the sky one night while driving in Colorado recently. It hovered over the road ahead of them. It came from the lights of a big truck.

The astronomer, here to address the Sigma Xi Club at Scripps Institution of Oceanography, concluded: "There's not a scientist alive who would even hint that what we see are objects from outer space carrying little men."

The *Kent Messenger*, Maidstone, England, printed the following report on February 16, 1955:

WORKMEN SEE "FLYING SAUCER"
It Was Certainly Not
An Airplane They Say

It has been said that anyone can see flying saucers—from hallucination, spots before the eyes, a drop too much, or just because they want to—but when two level-headed men, concentrating on nothing but their work, both see something at the same time, one sits up and takes notice.

This happened on Tuesday morning in Best Street, Chatham, where the new telephone exchange for the area is under construction. I met the two men who had seen it—Tom Mallion, 58-year-old laborer, of Mount Road, Chatham, and Leslie Streeter, aged 35, the foreman carpenter of Leighton Street, West Croydon, less than an hour later, while it was still fresh in their minds, writes a reporter.

The two of them were taking some levels about 11:30 that morning. Mr. Streeter using a level and Mr. Mallion holding the surveyor's staff for him. Mr. Streeter, squinting through the level, told his companion to hold the staff up level.

"I looked up at the top of the staff," Mr. Mallion told me, "and there it was."

He said "it was about as big as the palm of my hand and going like—!

"It was absolutely smooth, the underside of a plate or a saucer, white and without any wings or holes in it. There was no sound and no smoke. We only had time to say two or three words to one another before it had become so small in the distance that we could hardly see it. We called the ganger's attention, but by that time it was out of sight.

"Whatever it was, it was certainly no airplane."

According to Mr. Streeter, the object was heading directly from Rainham in the direction of London, and when he first saw it after Mr. Mallion had called his attention it was no bigger than his thumbnail and getting smaller rapidly.

Seeing it against a clear patch of blue sky, it seemed to him to be silvery and cigar-shaped, again with no projections, smoke or sound.

Used to aircraft spotting in the Royal Navy in the war, Mr. Streeter was still unable to estimate its height, because he had no idea of its actual size, but said: "It was up a terrific height and going at a colossal speed. It was only a matter of seconds before it was too small to be seen any longer."

Let the foreman on the site, Mr. J. A. Brightwell, of Shuttle Close, Sidcup, have the last word: "With a lot of people you would think they had been having a drink or were seeing things, and you would not take any notice of them. But these two chaps are intelligent and level-headed, and are absolutely convinced about what they saw."

The following is from the *Weston Mercury*, Weston-super-Mare, England, as printed on February 18, 1955. From this we gather that the British are almost as dissatisfied with their Air Force bureaucrats as we are with ours:

INFORMATION ON "FLYING SAUCERS"
IS SUPPRESSED, ALLEGES SPEAKER
Thought-Provoking Talk to Weston Rotarians

What is the truth behind "flying saucers," and why is information about them suppressed? These questions were left with members of Weston-super-Mare Rotary Club by their Friday luncheon speaker, Mr. John Armitage, a member of the Bristol Flying Saucer Bureau.

His visit drew such a large attendance that some members lunched in another room, joining the main body for the address.

Mr. Armitage began by declaring that "saucers"—"celestial crockery" as they are called in some quarters—were not a new discovery.

As long ago as the 13th Century according to records of Glastonbury Abbey, monks working on the September harvest saw bright shining discs. The religious brethren were so horrified apparently that they ran to the chapel and fasted for two days as a penance.

Logs of old ships contained many references to strange sights, the speaker continued; but it was not until after the 1939-45 War that the subject really began to attract attention.

Kenneth Arnold, a commercial traveler, who frequently traveled by air, happened one day to see five or six shining lights some miles

away. The objects were circular in shape and appeared to be following each other round the mountain tops. The speed was estimated
at around 5,000 M.P.H.

Arnold reported this phenomenon and headlines appeared in several papers. He was interrogated by the U.S. Federal Bureau of
Investigation, and the matter was pushed to one side, until practically the entire population of Mexico City saw similar objects.

An aspect of the matter which particularly interested the Rotar-
ians was the speaker's allegation that all information and photographs collected by American observers had been confiscated by the
U.S. Government and organizations broken up.

"A tremendous amount of information was obtained," Mr. Armitage said.

A similar thing happened in Australia and investigation bureaux
are not now permitted, he declared.

"Britain is the only country where there is still an organization
and perhaps that will be closed down soon," he added.

He went on to quote many instances—particularly where the
entire crew and passengers of an air liner had witnessed the appearance of "saucers." A newsreel cameraman who happened to be
among the passengers was able to take a film of the objects, but
it was confiscated by the government.

A reason given by the U.S. Government was that these reports
might lead to "mass hysteria" but Mr. Armitage believes in the
old adage, "Never believe anything until there is an official denial!"

There were many theories, he went on, and mentioned guided
missiles, meteorological balloons, and visitors from another planet.
He suggested that if they were piloted craft, someone would have
to pilot them—facts which are difficult to conceal for a long time.

Natural phenomena, such as ice-crystals and mirages, would
hardly move at the great speeds reported he suggested, and pointed
out that information gathered from all over the world revealed a
similarity in the sightings.

"The reports bear out one another," he declared.

The speaker said he considered we were "jumping to conclusions"
when we said that life was impossible on Venus. "Why should we
flatter ourselves that they should be like us?"

He suggested that the nitrogen-laden atmosphere so different from our own might have produced a quite different form of life—plant, perhaps.

The speaker was thanked by Rotarian John Widgery.

Here is another report of "something" that seems to like hovering over the Idyllwild area of California. The sighting was reported in the Hemet (California) *News*, February 18, 1955:

"THING" SEEN AGAIN IN MOUNTAIN SKIES

Don't look now, but that thing is back again. This time it appeared to Mr. and Mrs. Arthur Camp at about 3 o'clock on the morning of Tuesday of last week.

The Camps reported that they were awakened by a brilliant light that shone from a round aerial object "hovering" low in the sky in the general direction of Palm Springs. The object, they said, appeared as large as the large full moon, and shone with a shimmering blue-white glow of great intensity. The object seemed to move back and forth, the glare dimming and intensifying with each movement, they reported.

Although no one else in the Idyllwild area has reported seeing "the thing," a newspaper account the next day revealed that a couple on the desert side saw a similar sight in the direction of San Jacinto peak, some seventeen hours later.

The following account was sent to me by an on-the-spot investigator named Paul A. Hahr, 1013 Indiana Avenue S.E., Albuquerque, N. Mexico. The account is reminiscent of several others in which planes get hopelessly off course for no reason that is apparent to investigators:

A TWA Martin-404 crashed into the Sandia Mountains on February 19, 1955. (Saturday morning, approximately 7:30 a.m.) after taking off from the municipal airport. There was radio contact with the tower at the time of clearance for take-off. The plane was to follow the radio beam then report at the "turn-off" point to Santa Fe. The turn-off point is about five minutes out from the field. The flight is a regularly scheduled one. The pilot and co-pilot were veteran flyers in this area. The situation is summarized as follows:

1. The mountain and its overcast could easily be seen (as it is the highest and only peak in this area) for many miles around.
2. The pilot and co-pilot had considerable experience flying this route.
3. Indians in the area of San Domingo Pueblo heard a plane at about 7:30 a.m.
4. Only one plane (the 404) was known to be in the area at this time.
5. Radar showed a pip in the area of San Domingo Pueblo (a pip which suddenly disappeared) at about 7:30 a.m.
6. The plane crashed into the sheer west side of the mountain, about 1,000-feet below the crest and at least sixteen miles off the proper course (as determined by radio beam and visual flight). I understand the plane was not flying on instruments at the time.
7. The CAA held extensive investigations and arrived at no positive conclusions; only that the instruments had not been faulty (were they being used?) and that a pilot error was improbable (could the co-pilot also make the same error?). The cause—as far as I know—was listed as unknown.

From my observation of the mountain (which can be seen by anyone within a radius of perhaps fifty or sixty miles) that morning, a pilot would almost have to intentionally fly directly into the overcast area to even come close to the crest. Such a route would be completely off course. The radio beam is so placed that it purposely misses the mountain by several miles.

What is it that seems to disintegrate or bend radio beams at times and lead planes as much as fifty miles off course? Was it something like that which caused the five Avenger bombers to circle helplessly over the sea east of Florida a few years ago? (See *The Case for the UFO*.) Are compasses, radio and gravitation all three affected by some very mysterious new force?

The following two reports from the New York *Journal Ameri-*

can and the Miami *Herald,* February 22 and 23, serve to highlight the problem of the "angel hair." This peculiar substance seems to be associated with certain types of UFO, and has been reported in many countries and for a period of many years. Major Donald Keyhoe postulated that the peculiar, disappearing fibre is some kind of exhaust product from UFO's of the large "cigar-shaped" type. The fibre looks like cotton, is slightly radio-active, and disappears, or evaporates on being touched by human hands.

MYSTERY IS STUDIED

A grey, cobwebby and slightly radio-active substance that fell out of the sky covered a half-square mile of ground near Elmira today. Scientists who examined it said its radioactivity was "not dangerous." It was identified as "extremely short-fibred cotton" by Dr. Charles Rutenber, professor of chemistry at Elmira College. He said the radioactivity was normal in the present series of atomic tests.

"I doubt very much that the cotton was American grown," he told the N.Y. *Journal-American* on the telephone. "The fibres are much too short."

Rutenber said the substance "spread like a giant cocoon," beginning Sunday night. Its grey color came from industrial dirt which the professor said contained substances not found in any local industry.

"I believe from its moisture content that it was airborne for some time and picked up its coloring possibly hundreds of miles away," he said.

The professor said the substance was shiny, had no apparent odor and did not burn rapidly. He described the web as a "felt-like deposit made up of fibres that could almost have come from an artillery shell—if there weren't so much of it."

The above story received wide coverage in the press and aroused great interest. Some papers even printed pictures of Dr. Rutenber examining the substance.

These flashes were reported by Charles Fort and various periodicals, many years ago. They are becoming more frequent, or else we are becoming more aware of them. The following story is from the Kansas City (Missouri) *Star*, February 23, 1955:

STRANGE LIGHT OVER OCEAN
PAN-AMERICAN CREWMEN SAY
IT IS LIKE ATOMIC BLAST

An atomic-like flash was reported over the Atlantic today by crewmen of an air liner. M. J. Fuller and John Thomas, crewmen of a Pan-American clipper flying from New York to London, said they spotted the phenomenon and sent a message to London airport.

On arrival here, Fuller said: "We were flying at 21,000 feet four hundred miles west of Ireland. Thomas and I were in the cockpit and one hour before dawn we both saw a mysterious explosion. We were too high for it to have been caused by a ship. It was definitely not lightning and the sun had not yet risen.

"When the atomic bomb was exploded at Las Vegas I was flying over Santa Barbara and had been warned to look out for the flash. What I saw this morning looked very much the same."

London airport said no other planes had reported seeing anything unusual in the area.

The London *Daily Sketch*, February 24, 1955, published the following complete report of a saucer contact in its issue of that date:

A FLYING SAUCER BUZZED ME,
SAYS METEOR JET PILOT
"IT FLEW STRAIGHT AT ME AT STAGGERING SPEED"
By Flight Lieutenant James Salandin, of the RAF

I have been buzzed by a flying saucer over the British coast. It was on a Sunday afternoon while I was climbing in my 600 m.p.h. Meteor jet fighter at 16,000 feet. The sky was a clear blue.

Some people don't believe me, but it happened.

The thing looked like two ordinary saucers placed together with a bun-shaped bubble on top and another underneath. It was silvery in color and apparently metallic. It flew straight at me, more than filling my whole windscreen vision before turning away past my port side. I had taken off from North Weald and was heading out over the Thames estuary, climbing towards a gaggle of Meteors at about 30,000 feet.

When I was at 16,000 feet, and approaching Southend-on-Sea I suddenly saw two circular objects streak past the Meteors in the opposite direction. At first I thought they were Meteors too, and I turned and climbed to intercept them. But I could not identify them. One was gold and the other silvery in color and I was staggered by their speed. I estimated it to be about 1,200 m.p.h.

I watched them, fascinated, until they were out of sight high up on my lefthand side. When I turned back to look straight ahead again I got the shock of my life. There was this thing coming straight for me.

It did not appear to have any portholes nor were any jet pipes or other means of propulsion visible. It did not seem to be spinning.

After flying around for a few minutes to recover from the shock I filed my first eye-witness report by radio telephone. On returning to base I prepared a detailed report for investigation by the special flying saucer section of Air Ministry Intelligence.

I was the biggest skeptic in the squadron where flying saucers were concerned—but not any more. There was no question of balloons or clouds in this case. I am willing to be convinced by any logical explanation—but it had better be good.

Now every time I climb into the cockpit of my Meteor I am on the lookout for another saucer.

Flight-Lieutenant Salandin who is 29, and began flying with the Fleet Air Arm during the war, is by no means the first airman to report seeing a "flying saucer." Other sightings have been reported by airliner crews of both British Overseas Airways and British European Airways.

The *Columbia Basin News*, Pasco, Washington, February 24, 1955, carried the following account of a very puzzling object seen by a local woman:

RICHLAND WOMAN OBSERVES
STRANGE SKY PHENOMENON

A strange phenomenon shining with the brightness of the sun and having the shape and characteristics of both a sun and rainbow was observed in the sky over northeast Richland Friday morning by an Atomic City housewife.

Mrs. Howard Poyner, 1302 Cedar, told the *Columbia Basin News* she first observed the strange object as she was driving her husband to work about 7:45 a.m.

"It was clear at the time," she said, "and just to the north of the true sun we saw this tremendously bright ball with a vertical rainbow along one side. It hurt one's eyes to look at it. The object wasn't moving."

The housewife went on to explain that she was very excited about seeing the object as she had never viewed anything like it before nor had she observed a flying saucer. Mrs. Poyner surmised the phenomena was probably a reflection off a cloud as the object was somewhat misty. She said she believed it to be a reflection off a cloud in another part of the sky.

Officials of the Atomic Energy Commission report they had not received any calls on the object. Employees entering the administration building had been observed looking at the object.

The Weather Bureau at Spokane said the "second sun" was probably a sun dog—a complicated type of halo caused by the reflection of light through thin, almost invisible cloud.

John Philip Bessor, 6349 Walnut Street, Pittsburgh, Pennsylvania, has been a student of UFOlogy for many years. John says that different types of flying saucers tend to appear in different localities. The Harrisburg (Pennsylvania) *Sun-Telegraph,* February 27, 1955, carried a long Sunday feature article about UFO's, and gave some weight to Mr. Bessor's opinions. Among other things, they published a preliminary sketch map of the U.S.A. showing how Mr. Bessor believes the distribution was effected. Some new data since then is available, but your editor believes that distribution is a factor which should have careful attention. Here is the map.

Oval or spherical 'saucers.'
Comet- or meteor-like objects with tails.
Cigar- or torpedo-shaped objects.

Lest any casual space navigators become careless or scornful of our ability to look after our own interests here on earth, we quote the following from the editorial page of *This Week Magazine*, February 27, 1955. It seems an appropriate manner in which to close out the month of February which is otherwise noted for fireballs and mysteriously crashing planes.

WARNING

We understand that the mayor of Chateauneuf-du-Pape in Southern France is so convinced that there are flying saucers and other weird craft cruising over his bailiwick that he has issued the following decree:

"The flights, landings and take-offs of airships called 'flying saucers' and 'flying cigars' of any nationality are forbidden on the territory of the community of Chateauneuf-du-Pape."

MARCH

In opening the chapter on March, there does not seem to be anything of especial or startling significance to use as a take-off point, unless we stress the obvious significance of the continued presence of UFO's.

It might be well at this juncture to stress a warning against the two extremes of gullibility and dogmatic rejection of evidence. One is as bad as the other, as was recognized by the great French scientist Flammarian when he prefaced some of his works with a chapter on each of these two weaknesses of homo sapiens.

It is the purpose of the *UFO Annual* to *report* the events of 1955, with perhaps an occasional enlightening comment, but in general not to pass judgement on everything that is reported.

A few patterns are emerging, however, as we pass into the third month. For one thing, we are having an overflux of fireballs, and these have had an unusual amount of attention because of their number, brilliance, and the kelly-green color of some of them. There does, indeed, seem to be something queer about them. C.R.I.F.O. has gone into this in great detail, and those who are especially interested in the fireball problem would do well to obtain back numbers of the C.R.I.F.O. publication. For the record, it might be stated that the green fireball flurry did not originate in the U.S.A., but apparently in Sweden. This was a few years ago and essentially before the greatest intensity of interest in UFO or saucers. They were then thought to be Russian rockets or missiles; and to this day we cannot prove that they were not Russian. In the U.S.A. the green fireballs made their debut in New Mexico and were thought to be associated with the atomic energy experiments. Now, however, they have spread over much of North America and, frankly, we don't know what they are nor why, nor from where.

Another pattern relates to disappearing and crashing planes. Jets are taking a real beating—bombers, fighters, transports. They disappear practically at the end of runways; they explode in the air; they crash on mountain sides; and, if we can believe the reports that come to us, the jets are being kidnapped right out of the air by marauding UFO. Cases in point are the sighting by our friend Metcalf in Illinois, as told in the *UFO Reporter* (Citadel Press) and the Lake Superior case stressed so heavily by Major Keyhoe.

Your editor is not as convinced of the malicious intent of the UFO as are Major Keyhoe and H. T. Wilkins. Nevertheless, there have been some surprising incidents which give good grounds for suspicion.

As readers of *The Case for the UFO* are aware, we have looked for evidence of intelligence in the actions of the UFO's and have used such evidence to demonstrate that they are controlled objects. Control means either remote-control from a space headquarters or innate control from a self-contained intelligence.

Now, there has been one indication of intelligence which has not come up for discussion: casualness. To this we might add

D

ubiquity which means prevalence or commonness. . . . Take, for
example, the presence of birds in our atmosphere. We see them
all the time, in great numbers and much variety. Who questions
their ability to use the air as a habitat? Birds are at home in the
air, as fish are in water. We have not seen fit to question their
adaptability, for the birds have been always with us; they were,
in fact, here before we were (as the UFO may also have been).
Birds use the air *casually* as a medium for travel, but pause and
close your eyes a moment and try to imagine your feelings if
you came here from a planet where there was not enough air for
the adaptation of birds, and perhaps no water for fish. Imagine
your efforts to explain what your eyes tell you about the *casualness* with which millions of birds skim through the air.

It is this selfsame *casualness* which has made the UFO so
puzzling. They live and move in space with the same ease and
facility that birds live and move in the air and fish in the sea.
When you stop to think, isn't it the ease and casualness of movement of the UFO which have made them so puzzling?

These casual movements—appearances and disappearances,
etc.—of the UFO have been observed for hundreds of years.
UFO, whether indigenous or not, have been a part of the earth-
moon system for hundreds and thousands of years, as have birds
and fish. One thing, however, I am inclined to concede: that the
UFO do seem to have been more prevalent during the past few
years. I do not know the reason for it, but I tentatively call attention to the apparent increase in the number of bright objects
occupying craters on the moon (craters like those recently found
by your editor in Mexico). Some of the British astronomers and
selenographers have called the bright objects "bowler hats" because of their shape. The "bowler hats" were first noticed about
the time of the "incredible decade" (1877-1886) and it is possible that the "thing" which moved in and occupied the crater
Linné just prior to that time may have been the first to arrive in
the earth-moon system. Whatever they are, and from wherever

they come, they are occupying lunar craters, and their number is increasing in geometric progression indicating that their number may be doubling about every 18-20 years. Starting with one in the decade of the 1860's, there are now over 200 of them.

What are the "bowler hats"? And why is their number increasing as the numbers of our UFO increase? My forthcoming *The Expanding Case for the UFO,* will discuss these developments on the moon in detail.

The following sighting, quoted from C.R.I.F.O. *Newsletter* points up one minor thought, namely: that UFO's are seen at sea as well as over settled areas and atomic energy plants. The very fact that even a small percentage of the UFO sightings are made at sea would seem to prove the ubiquity of the UFO, and to indicate that UFO's are a part of our earth-moon system, rather than being visitors who come here merely for reconnaisance.

SAUCERS OVER PACIFIC

(Case 69, Honolulu to Suva, March, 1955.) The Orsova, of the Orient Line reached Auckland, March 4, fresh from a record-breaking run between San Francisco and Honolulu. Steaming for Suva, crew members reported sighting a bright luminous oval object darting through the sky at great speed. It appeared to swing around in an arc, disappeared behind a cloud, emerged again, then vanished into a cloud. (H. Fulton, N.Z.; C. Chapman, Australia)

Charles Fort reported some UFO's as witnessed at sea, and they were not too different from those described today.

The government would like for you to believe that the Flying Saucer issue is a dead duck, but do not be deceived by the news blackout. There is still large interest and larger activity. Here is a discussion published in the Baton Rouge, Louisiana newspaper, March 1, 1955:

COLONEL EMERSON SAYS FLYING SAUCERS
ARE OF EXTRA-TERRESTRIAL ORIGIN

The so-called flying saucers are real, and the best guess is that they are of extra-terrestrial origin, Colonel Robert B. Emerson, local research chemist and physicist told an audience last night at the Howell Park community Center.

Speaking before a sizeable group that included teen-aged youths and housewives, LSU professors and at least one physicist, Emerson said, "If we ever hope to get to the bottom of these fishy things going on around us, we're going to have to stop accepting irrational explanations and make a serious effort to find out what really is going on."

The speaker became interested in the saucer phenomenon a few years ago—expecting to find a simple solution, he said—and has since collected all that he could find on the subject. His files include hundreds of reported sightings.

Emerson said that he doesn't think the space visitors are either friendly or hostile. "I think, perhaps, they are sightseers, much like us of earth. Whereas we step into an automobile to go for a ride," he explained, "they get into a space ship and travel.

"And," he added, "they're probably afraid to make a landing. Picture yourself in a plane over the wilds of the African jungle. Would you," he queried, "consider landing in an area where you were fairly certain that there were lions and try to talk things over?"

Emerson said he felt certain that some of the universe's other planets had probably picked up earth's radio signals and had sent ships to investigate. Explaining his reasoning, he pointed out that occurrences of flying saucers and other strange objects in the sky had increased since the advent of radio on earth. He added that these increased reports might be due to improved communications on our own planet.

"Flying saucers," he declared, "are nothing new to this planet. They were sighted as far back as our history goes."

Recorded writings of other civilizations such as the Egyptians, show that similar objects were spotted in those times he explained.

Emerson said his own files included all years of the present century, all years except for three of the 1800's: all except twelve of the 1700's, and most of the 1600's, in which reports were made then of such objects being seen.

As for the possibility that space visitors might land and communicate with earth's citizens, Emerson said he didn't think "these visitors would care to divulge secrets that would allow residents of this planet to get out of hand."

"I don't think," he declared, "that they'll make any effort to communicate with us, until we're in a position to communicate with them."

During his informal discussion, Emerson cited numerous instances where "almost concrete" proof was found of space visitors to earth. In his own case, he said, he had been sent a piece of signboard from Connecticut for laboratory analysis. Another laboratory in Milwaukee, he said, was also sent fragments of the sign.

A ship, he explained, had swooped on the sign as though "buzzing it" but had crashed through. The object continued to where it remained motionless over a highway for a few moments, scaring a motorist, then shot back into space.

"A rocket," he said, "doesn't follow that kind of pattern." Emerson said he had been requested to see, through lab analysis if there were other types of metal on the jagged edges of the hole left in the sign—metals that otherwise were not in the sign.

"Strong traces of copper," he said, "were found." The Milwaukee laboratory, he added, sent in a similar analysis.

Though it didn't get into the newspapers nearly as often last year, the U.S. Air Force received an average of 700 reports of flying saucers being sighted each week, Emerson said. "Perhaps," he concluded, "the Air Force, which has acted repeatedly to discredit flying saucer reports had something to do with it."

He said Air Force officials upon investigation, found that about two percent of the reports were hoaxes; another 73 percent were passed off as conventional objects, with what he described as "often irrational explanations;" while another 25 percent could not be explained.

"It is this 25 percent that solidly leaves me to believe that there is definitely something to flying saucer reports," Emerson said. "I think that it's time for the public to roll up its sleeves and look into these things."

In citing specific instances where he said it was known that strange objects were visiting the earth, Emerson pointed to White Sands, New Mexico, where rocket and other tests are currently in progress by the U.S. government.

"At a height of fifty miles," he explained, "one of our V-2 rockets —fastest known to our military, was completely encircled by one of the ships. Its speed," he said, "was estimated at 22 miles per second. The escape velocity of earth's gravity," he added, "is only seven miles per second."

Emerson said there had also been recorded reports of the strange ships buzzing airfields, "much like the fly-happy lieutenants and colonels in our own air force."

Here is something from the London (England) *Daily Sketch*, March 1, 1955. It was accompanied by an alleged photograph of the well-known "Adamski" or "light fixture" type of flying saucer, about which many serious students of UFO phenomena have expressed some concern:

"I THOUGHT IT WAS JUST A BIRD"
BOX CAMERA SNAPS "SAUCER"
BOY TELLS OF "THING IN SKY"

Sixteen-year-old Harold Cummins, of Wednesfield, near Wolverhampton, has taken a photograph in a million with his box camera.

It distinctly shows a dark, saucer-shaped object apparently hovering low in the sky. *It could be a flying saucer.*

I found Harold at his home in Stubby Lane, Wednesfield, writes Len Smith, and this is the amazing story he told me.

"I was alone in the house one afternoon in December. I was watching at the window, watching birds which usually come into our garden to pick up the scraps which we leave out for them.

"Suddenly I saw something in the sky. It was flying quite straight and moving from left to right. I thought it was another bird. Then it stopped. It stood still in the air. I grabbed my camera and took a shot. I watched it for a second or two and then turned away for a moment, and when I looked back it had gone."

When his parents came home Harold made no mention of the *thing*. A quiet, soft-spoken lad whose hobby is building radio sets, Harold was shy about telling his story outside the family.

"I thought they would laugh at me," he said.

So Harold waited until he had finished the whole roll of film. And there it was, on the negative!

Marshalltown, Iowa, is a good solid American prairie city, and not given overmuch to runaway imagination. Here is a report from the Marshalltown *Times-Republican,* March 2, 1955:

CITY COUPLE SEES BRIGHT "LIGHT" MOVE ACROSS SKY, THEN VANISH

A strange bright light which moved slowly across the sky and then vanished after five minutes' observation was reported by a Marshalltown couple Tuesday night.

Mr. and Mrs. R. B. Avery, 407 W. Church Street, watched the object, which Avery, 78, described as being "like something I've never seen before," from near the M. S. Arney residence, 1503 Doty Street.

The Averys first spotted the brilliant whitish object about 1:30 p.m. Tuesday. Both persons had it in view for at least five minutes. They were driving west on Doty Street when the weird object was under observation.

"It went very slowly down towards the horizon," Avery said Wednesday, "it split the air and made it light—like a rocket except it didn't have any color."

"It was falling like a star, but didn't have a tail of light like a shooting star," Avery added.

After five minutes had passed, Avery said the brilliantly white object vanished into thin air, and the streak of light behind it also faded away. "It had a heavy, white 'head,' " Avery stated.

Avery said the object was traveling in a southerly direction and vanished approximately "somewhere between Colo and State Center."

Avery said he and his wife pondered whether or not the object might have had something to do with the atomic tests being conducted at the Nevada Proving Grounds. A bomb, which sent out a flash of light visible almost five hundred miles away was set off at the proving grounds shortly before noon Tuesday.

The San Bernadino (California) *Telegram,* March 3, 1955, announced an unusual sighting as follows:

S. B. MAN REPORTS SEEING OBJECT
IN SKY SECOND DAY

Over the San Bernadino Valley at 1:45 p.m. Wednesday, hung a bright object—silver and gleaming.

It was reported by Raymond Adams. "It was high, north-northeast of here. Silver, like a triple star . . . brilliant. I saw the same thing Tuesday noon or early afternoon. Thought it might be a plane, they do shine sometimes. But planes don't stand still like this object!"

A check at Norton Air Force Base proved unsuccessful in determining the identity of the object. Norton doesn't release any weather balloons, but March Air Force Base, at nearby Riverside does.

Perhaps it was a balloon from March, perhaps a plane, or perhaps it was . . . who knows?

Dr. Menzel and the U.S. Air Force ask us to believe that all of these instances are illusions, but how do they explain the simultaneous "illusions" of several good people in widely separated areas? It seems evident that there was something over the West Coast on March 3, 1955, for we have this supporting observation as reported in the *Daily Chronicle,* of Centralis-Chehalis, Washington, in its March 3 issue:

BLAZING BALL SAID SIGHTED

A strange ball of fire was reported passing west of Centralia early Thursday morning by Mr. and Mrs. R. D. Pollock, 1233 Alder Street.

Mrs. Pollock, calling the *Daily Chronicle* to learn if anyone else had reported seeing a similar object, said she noticed the ball about 3:00 a.m. "I was lying in bed awake, looking out the window when I saw this big ball of fire going along in the sky."

She said the ball seemed to be somewhere past the new Pacific highway, and was traveling north. The Pollocks estimated the ball to be about 30-feet diameter.

"It was sort of a blue-red color," she said, "and just the most wonderful sight. It wasn't until it was all over that I began to wonder what it was."

No other reports of the strange object either from residents in this area or over the Associated Press wire, had been made at noon Thursday.

Here, in the Providence (Rhode Island) *Journal,* March 3, 1955, is a reader's discussion of the "sonic boom." It has occurred to many speculators in the field of the UFO that they do not, but should, cause sonic booms, and on the arguments used by the skeptics and scoffers about the UFO's silence, little has been said. It seems, however, to your editor, that maybe some of the booms recorded in past history, as well as those which attracted much attention in the summer of 1955, may well have been caused by some type of UFO, as perhaps not all UFO's can penetrate the air silently. Also, I wonder why meteors entering the air at seven to seventy miles per second do not cause sonic booms? Anyway, here is what the reader says about booms:

WHY SAUCERS DON'T BOOM

Nelson F. G. Whipple, in the *Sunday Journal* of February 20, wanted to know why flying saucers didn't make a "sonic boom" such as jets are making these days.

The "boom" of a jet flying at or near the speed of sound occurs for the following reason: A jet, say, five miles away traveling toward a stationary observer on the ground at the speed of sound, arrives at the observer's position at the same time as all of the sound that the jet has created in that distance. That is, the sound sort of piles up from five miles away—the sound the jet makes at five miles travels along with it at the same speed and adds to the sound it makes at four miles and so on until all of the sound arrives with the jet at the observer's position in one big burst of sound or "boom."

A flying saucer, presumably, traveling at two or three times the speed of sound, doesn't do this. Assuming that it makes any sound at all, it would outrun its own sound. That is, as such a flying saucer passed over an observer, the sound it made at that instant would be the first sound that the observer would hear. Then would come the sound made some distance before its arrival and then the sound made some distance before that. If an observer could watch an aircraft of some sort flying toward him at two or three times sonic speed and if this aircraft "backfired" so that the observer would see the flash, this observer would have the strange experience of hearing first the noise of a plane passing overhead, and would next hear the sound of "backfire" that was made two miles before.

At any rate, the sound of a flying saucer of jet flying at two or three times sonic speed would have its sound spread out in time just as it is when traveling much below the speed of sound and thus there should be no "boom."

It is interesting to speculate on some of the possible effects of future supersonic aircraft.

Arizona was visited in March by UFO. Here is the report of Mrs. Lawless, taken from the Tucson *Star*, March 3, 1955, and this looks like collusion of some kind between California, Washington and Arizona—a lot of territory—if we are to believe the standardized hallucinations explanations:

HERE-WE-GO-AGAIN DEPARTMENT:

"FLYING SAUCER" SEEN

Tucson was visited by a flying saucer yesterday or Mrs. Robert Lawless, 4318 E. Whitman Street, is badly mistaken—and she is quite sure she is not mistaken. She is also certain that the crews of four planes in the sky at the same time she saw the object should have seen it. It was traveling from the northwest to the southeast, in the general direction of Davis-Monthan air force base. Mrs. Lawless, who was in her yard near 3:00 p.m. said she watched the object approaching with a "loping or rocking" motion. She estimated it was about two-thirds as high as the planes which were leaving vapor trails in the sky. That would put the object at about 20,000 feet.

The peculiar motion was most discernible when the object was nearly overhead, but slightly to her north, Mrs. Lawless said. But the motion was again noticeable after it passed. She said the object was rectangular in shape but was rounded at the ends and the color was white. She agreed her estimate of the height and size might be off, but said the object appeared to be smaller than the bombers which made the sky trails. The object was not leaving any trails.

The following Ecuadorian account from the Lincoln (Nebraska) *State Journal*, March 5, 1955, shows that activity was not confined to the United States. In fact, I know from personal research that in December 1954, for example, when there was a virtual blackout of saucer news in the United States, and practically a blockade against incoming foreign reports, that the South American papers were taking the UFO very seriously, and in some papers a large part of the front page and about twenty per cent of the inner pages were devoted to world-wide saucer news, translated from all languages.

FLYING SAUCERS GET AROUND, ECUADOR NEWSPAPER REVEALS

Reports of flying saucers have been received recently but according to foreign newspapers the objects are "visiting" other parts of the world.

Mrs. Riley Groves, 3336 R, has received a copy of a Quito, Ecuador, newspaper from her son, Arthur Wilson, which describes the sighting of two of the reported "flying saucers" in detail. Wilson is an engineer in South America.

According to the foreign newspapers, more than one hundred persons saw the flying saucers, at a height of about 8,500 feet above

Quito airport. "The objects in the blue sky shone brightly in the form of a half-orange with a cabin in the top center, and with the base of the object appearing concave. The surface of the object was of the color of white metal, as of aluminum, and reflected the rays of the day's sun," the newspaper reported.

The newspaper said the objects, which could be clearly seen with the aid of field glasses, remained in the air for more than an hour and then one moved with "incredible velocity" to the south.

The "saucers" had been seen previously in Peru, the newspaper said.

The following notice in the Portland *Oregonian*, March 5, 1955, indicates that the flurry of sightings early in March was not local, and may have persisted over a period of days. We wonder how many were not reported and of those reported how many were dropped in the vertical file by dutiful editors following the modish "scientific line"?

OBJECT IN SKY STILL PUZZLE

The fact that you are able to read this story probably indicates that an unidentified object spotted in the air by a Beaverton ground observer at 5:30 p.m. Friday was NOT (repeat NOT) an enemy bomber loaded with a city-wide knockout drop.

Just what kind of nonlethal object it was the Portland air force filter center was not reporting. "Regulations, you know."

Information given state police was to the effect that ground observers spotted "something" and that "something" also appeared on filter center screens.

The filter center reported that a Major Gettings at McChord field was the only man who could release the report on the object. Efforts to reach him by telephone turned up the fact that he was "not available."

Here is a report that is important, even though we may not know the full significance. Clothlike items have been falling for centuries as attested by many records. But so far as I know, this is the first one that burned a hole in a pavement. Or at least the first to be caught in the act. There are some characteristics to be noted: the terrible smell, the ability of the substance to burn or dissolve the pavement, the floating slowly downward, etc. The story is from the Sunday *Patriot-News* of Harrisburg, Pennsylvania, March 6, 1955:

"WHATSIT" LANDS IN FRONT STREET, "BURNS" HOLE IN PAVEMENT

Honest, here's the way it happened.

It was 9:00 a.m. and Harold Taylor of 1153 Rolleston Street, Cloverly Heights, looked out of his office window. He saw what appeared to him to be birds—like crows, he said—flapping their wings, then gliding for a while, about two hundred feet above Front Street.

Five minutes or so went by and there was another one. But this one was gliding downward and before Taylor could say flying saucer, it had landed near the top of a tree back of the YMCA.

"It hung there for perhaps half a minute and then floated to the ground, like a bird," he said. "As it hit, though, it seemed to lose its substance and became a mass. I forgot about it for a while and when I went out for lunch at noon, I looked at the spot where the 'thing' had landed. It had been depressed into the asphalt on Front Street."

Taylor, wary of telling anyone what happened, ate his lunch and returned to the office. But he couldn't keep it inside him and confided in Meade Hager, 1815 Mulberry Street.

Together they went out with a shovel and dug "it" up.

"The smell was terrific," he said, "something like the gas which escapes from faulty refrigerators. It got so bad we had to take it outside."

It turned out to be a mass of filthy, denim-like cloth and bits of it adhered to the asphalt.

A Sunday *Patriot-News* reporter and photographer took it to a metallurgical laboratory, which recommended that the State police go over it.

At State Police Headquarters, chemical analysis experts looked over the cloth and said it couldn't have happened that way. Anything which would have had enough power to burn or eat its way into the asphalt, they reasoned, would have disintegrated the cloth, the envelope in which it was carried to them, and the floor of the automobile in which it was transported.

Coincidence, they ruled.

But the odor remained unexplained, the fluttering flying and gliding objects remained unexplained. Yet, that's the way it happened, honest!

It is uncertain whether this sighting from Texas was a part of the group reported around the first to the third of March. It's from the Beaumont (Texas) *Journal,* March 7, 1955:

FLYING SAUCER REPORTED IN LOCAL AREA

First flying saucer sighted in this area in many months was reported Monday morning by F. A. Rice, who works for the Edwards News Agency.

Mr. Rice saw what he described as a flying saucer over the Nome-Sour Lake highway. The object appeared to be about 3,000 feet high, was an estimated thirty feet in diameter and six feet deep. It was saucer-shaped and silver.

The machine seemed to head toward Beaumont for a brief period, then it zoomed straight up until it disappeared, Mr. Rice reported.

The following story may actually refer to a meteor. We repeat it here for the simple reason that it is becoming harder than ever to know where artificial fireballs leave off and "natural" meteors begin. The report is from the Medford (Oregon) *Mail-Tribune,* March 9, 1955.

Please note the gradual build-up to the satellite announcement, and also the fact that this was known to various news reporters and commentators many months before the story "broke" in August. The following advance ripple is by Frank Carey and appeared in the Washington (D.C.) *Post and Times-Herald,* March 10, 1955.

The study of the artificial satellite is, of course, a part of the general UFO field, but not entirely for the reasons usually accepted by the layman. The satellite is not a logical step toward space flight as is being fully explained elsewhere, particularly in *The Expanding Case for the UFO,* due shortly.

FIVE MILES A SECOND—
STUDY ASKED OF SATELLITE'S PRACTICALITY

The American Rocket Society has asked the National Science Foundation to make a definitive study of the practicality of launching an artificial unmanned satellite into space, and its possible value.

The society coupled its proposal with the declaration that such a satellite is "technically feasible." Milton Rosen, a rocket expert for the Naval Research Laboratory, told a reporter Tuesday night how a group of experts in the society feels about the project. He said the experts believe that a rocket-propelled instrument-laden "small object" could be launched a couple of hundred miles above the earth, swing into a gradually diminishing orbit around the planet. It would serve the following purposes, Rosen said:

Get new information on the upper atmosphere.

Study the effects of outer space radiation on experimental animals carried in the "object."

Serve as a relay station for radio communication, and perhaps even furnish a means of making TV telecasts across oceans.

Help in more detailed mapping of the earth.

Furnish further information as to whether space flight by man will eventually be possible.

Get new weather and astronomical data.

Rosen said the National Science Foundation had agreed to take the proposal for a "utility study" under advisement.

The rocket man said it was deemed feasible that a satellite could be launched from the earth at a speed of slightly more than five miles a second and that when it reached an altitude of about two hundred miles, it would cruise around the earth at a speed of about five miles a second.

Along the same line is the following "planned" introduction of saucer-like aircraft, and this is (in hindsight) clearly a part of the build-up toward the Air Force announcement in November to the effect that there "ain't no such saucers till we build 'em."

This story appeared in the Palo Alto (California) paper for March 10, 1955. Unfortunately the correspondent did not send the name of the paper with the clipping:

"YOU'VE SEEN NOTHING YET" ...
HILLER PREDICTS "IMAGINATIVE" PLANES
TO BE COMMONPLACE

A "truly revolutionary means of flying" was hinted at by Stanley Hiller Jr., internationally-known inventor of helicopters, in a talk before the San Francisco Advertising Club, Wednesday.

He said for the past several months "a most unconventional lifting device" has been flying in Palo Alto, but said the public can only be given scant details at this time.

He pointed to a propellor-driven fighter which takes off straight up and to test aircraft which are supported on pure jet thrust and said, "You have seen nothing yet.

"Don't be surprised if you open your newspaper in the not-too-distant future to read of the establishment by one of the largest manufacturers of aircraft, of an anti-gravitational division," Hiller said, remarking, "This may sound as Buck Rogerish as flying rotorless helicopters."

Hiller said the unconventional flying device he referred to earlier is not "anti-gravitational" in principle. He indicated the Army might reveal the secrets within a few months.

"By 1965, we will see the equivalent of flying jeeps, staff cars and an ambulance in much greater quantity than those of few service military helicopters of today," Hiller said.

He also said that "during the late 1960's and early 1970's mass movements of troops, particularly by Army and Marines in vertical take-offs in high speed transports, should become commonplace."

East Palo Alto residents have reported seeing flights of an unusually small, helicopter-type aircraft described as little more than a "flying-cockpit." The plane creates a loud rapping sound as if propelled by some sort of a jet thrust. Small helicopter vanes over the cockpit stabilize the ship in flight, according to reports of witnesses.

Hiller said many types of aircraft which the general public regards as wild dreams of the future actually have passed the blueprint stage and are under experiment. He said more than fifty per cent of the work being done in the Hiller plant under contract with the Army is on "unconventional" devices.

Here is a story to be read very carefully. Note that it precedes the official satellite announcement of August, 1955, by several months—yet it says that the government is planning the satellite experiment for *spring of 1955*. What happened? Did the satellite disappear into far space, like some rockets we have heard about? Or was it a failure? Did the government postpone the experiment, or was it successful? Maybe some of these little basketballs are what Astronomer Bagby saw from Chicago? Note the discussion on "Aviation Medicine" or more specifically: "Space Medicine." How close are we, really, to an actual attempt at space flight? Why all this preparatory propaganda? The feature is from the Washington (D.C.) *Daily News*, March 15, 1955, written by Robert Allen, former partner of Drew Pearson:

U.S. SPACE SHIP SET FOR RECORDS

A historic space experiment is set for this spring. The Air Force is planning to test a satellite prototype that is expected to remain above the earth for at least a week, sending back coded data through special instruments.

It will be the most important U.S. experiment of this kind to date.

The prototype that will be tried out is in no sense a satellite. It is a profoundly significant development toward that end. One authority informally describes it as a "three-stage guided missile."

Pending this fateful test, the Air Force in the meanwhile is making unannounced space history of another kind. A piloted plane has made flights in excess of 100,000 feet altitude. That is twenty miles above the globe and the uppermost recorded height so far attained in the history of human flight.

Progress in space flight of all kinds is so rapid that extensive consideration is already being given to celestial hazards which are likely to be encountered. Foremost among them are flaming meteorites, most of which "burn out" at between 25 and 75 miles above the earth. The Air Force has compiled a special study on space hazards. It is titled "Aeromedical Research Implication of Space Flight," and one section deals in particular with "Problems of Movement Through the Border Zone of Space."

Following are publishable highlights from this Air Force report:

"For the first time in the history of flight, the possibility of hazards produced by meteorites must be considered . . . The bulk of meteorites burn out between 25-75 miles above the earth . . . another interesting problem, resulting from the process of movement through the border zone of the atmosphere and space, is that of the gravity-free state.

"This problem has never before been discussed in aviation medicine since man has never experienced these states except for the duration of fractions of a second. (This is an extremely significant reference. Nothing more can be said about it.)

"Further research on this problem will undoubtedly produce results of the greatest importance. In future flight, strange and novel environments will be encountered which will be better understood by considering the various functions of the atmosphere as a whole.

"A major question at the moment is protection of crews against radiation by (1) the fuselage of the airplane and (2) against rays produced within the airplane.

"A new era in the physiology of human flight has opened . . . Problems of space medicine must now be dealt with . . ."

NOTE: The Air Force School of Aviation Medicine, Randolph Base, Texas, has a special department of space medicine.

Florida is back again. There is a steady consistency about UFO reports from Florida. Very few have elements of hysteria or hoaxing as some do from the West Coast. There cannot be any doubt about the concentration of activity over and near Florida, as was so demonstrated in the summer of 1955. Here is a typical Leesburg (Florida) *Commercial* report, March 15, 1955:

"FLYING SAUCER" REPORTED SIGHTED
IN THIS SECTION

A phone call to the *Commercial* last night about 9 o'clock was answered by a reporter working late, and the caller asked if anyone else had reported seeing "flying saucers" in the last few minutes.

Gerard Tetrault unhesitatingly gave his name when a request for further information was made, and said he and a friend, Harry Boltman, had been fishing in Lake Harris and were just coming in to the landing at Venetian Gardens when they noticed the peculiar flying phenomenon.

"It looked like objects flying in a large V-formation," said Tetrault, "going very fast and too high to distinguish definite shapes. It appeared to be twenty or thirty objects surrounded by a hazy reddish glow and headed north at a high rate of speed."

Tetrault would like to know if anyone else saw the eerie flying shapes, and would like to compare impressions.

The following is objective reporting by the Dowagiac (Michigan) *News*, March 15, 1955, covering a large meeting of flying saucer investigators at Grand Rapids. It is a hodgepodge of facts, fantasy, fiction, and shows the average reader what a mess we are making of the greatest problem of the century. There is a good deal of ponderable material in this report, and it goes far toward summarizing the general state of the UFO field as of March, 1955:

SAUCERS AND SATELLITES

They say flying saucers are just a figment of the imagination, weather balloons or the like. Even Dowagiac's flying saucers were just optical illusions, according to the experts. But there are those who believe there must be such things because there are those who've seen them! One of these is William P. Lear, a noted aeronautical scientist.

Lear was converted to the corps of flying saucer observers after spotting a mysterious object in the California sky about two months ago. Head of Lear Inc., one of Grand Rapids' largest industries, Lear added a lot of weight to the flying saucer cause and these mysterious objects now are a common topic of conversation in the Grand Rapids area.

Lear is convinced that these flying saucers not only are real but they are from outer space and are flown under the direction of an intelligence of super-human caliber that has repealed the law of gravity. His opinion, based on wisdom and experience that has made him a leader in the field of aeronautical development, made a lot of people wonder if all these reports of flying saucers might not be worth giving a thought about.

In fact, nearly 1,000 persons turned out recently for a Grand Rapids meeting of the Flying Saucer Council of America but many of them probably were more confused than enlightened by the technical data. However, speakers at this meeting showed colored movies of flying saucers and backed Lear in his theory that these objects are guided by a superior intelligence from somewhere in interplanetary space.

The real lowdown on flying saucers was presented after the meeting when representatives of the Laymen's Home Missionary Movement distributed leaflets in which the exact nature of flying saucers was explained. According to the leaflet, they're "fallen angels or evil spirits who are approaching judgment day."

The saucer theories got indirect backing from dispatches from Minneapolis and Moscow enlarging on the prospects of travel in outer space. From Minneapolis in a copyrighted story by the Minneapolis *Tribune*, comes the report that a satellite the size of a basketball could be encircling the earth every few hours by 1958. The *Tribune* story claimed some of America's top scientists believe such a satellite could be developed now for about one million dollars and would "teach us to crawl in space before we try to fly."

The word from Moscow discloses that a flight to the moon would require only two ounces of uranium and concludes that space travel is "feasible, especially if we consider the rapid advances that are being made in such fields as atomic physics, nuclear energetics, radio physics and radio engineering." Meanwhile, western scientists say that the first power to set up an outpost on the moon could dominate the earth. Any volunteers for the trip?

These saucers and satellites may seem a long way in the future, but remember it hasn't been too many years ago they were saying the automobile wasn't here to stay!

Normally we do not try to use undated clips which do not even name the paper reporting, but this story serves to highlight the mounting toll of jet planes, and particularly in Illinois. The *UFO Reporter* for summer 1955, carried a story about a jet being swept up by a UFO:

IDENTIFY CREW IN PLANE CRASH:
ILLINOIS AIRMAN MISSING
IN NEW BOSTON WRECK

U.P. March 15, 1955: The Air Force today identified two officers listed as "missing" in the crash of a T33 jet trainer on a farm near here.

The plane, a two-seater, was on a routine training flight from O'Hare air base near Chicago to Colorado Springs, Colorado, when it crashed on a farm near here late on Monday.

The public information office at O'Hare said today those aboard were Major Jack Fox of Atlanta, Georgia, and Captain Robert Garrison, Cambridge, Illinois. They were assigned to the 4706 wing (Air Defense) at O'Hare, and each has a wife and two children. Both have been living in Des Plaines, Illinois.

Although parts of a human body were found near the scene of the crash, the Air Force listed both men only as missing.

A board of officers was named to investigate and an investigative team from the air base examined the scene to determine the cause of the crash. The plane caught fire in the air and exploded when it crashed on the Stewart Guthrie farm, five and a half miles from here, halfway between New Boston and Muscatine, Iowa.

Florida again! This one sounds authentic. It's from the Miami *Daily News*, March 16, 1955. The *News* is a broad-minded, objectively reporting newspaper as regards UFO news. Their Billie O'Day conducts a radio program which is very sympathetic toward saucers:

**SAUCER FLIES IN MIAMI SKIES,
THIS ONE CAUGHT IN TELESCOPE**

University of Miami Senior Robert Leventhal, 200 SW 58th Street, an amateur astronomer, was out in his yard with a telescope at 10:50 p.m. yesterday when he saw a "round, oval-shaped, bluish-white disc."

It traveled quickly from southeast to southwest in "an irregular motion in about a minute," he told police. "It was bright as a second magnitude star."

"It wasn't a plane or a meteor," he said, "and I don't have any idea of what it actually was. But it looked like something I saw in the sky about two years ago in Ithaca, N.Y., along with thirty other people."

The following is from the Waterbury (Connecticut) *Republican*, March 20, 1955, and needs no comment:

BOYS REPORT SAUCERS OVER WATERBURY

Flying saucers have again been reported over Waterbury. A breathless boy called the city desk yesterday to report that he and a friend had seen a "flying saucer" while walking along de Cicco Road in the East End.

Between gasps for breath he explained that he didn't know exactly how high they were but that "they were way up and there were just two of them and they were really traveling." He added that they were headed west and were so high they seemed "as small as fingernails."

"We ran almost a mile to a phone just to call you," he ended. The boy identified himself as David Mariani and his friend as Peter Wittke, both 11 years old.

Here again is a case of independent sightings at the same time in distant parts of the same general region, by independent observers, and reported through different press media. Surely the Air Force has to give some weight to these mutually supporting cases. This is from the Manchester (New Hampshire) *Sunday News* of March 20, 1955:

TWO LOCAL GIRLS REPORT SEEING "FLYING SAUCER"

Two 13-year-old Queen City girls reported seeing a "flying saucer" while playing in the Straw School playground at Brook and Chestnut Streets yesterday afternoon around 4:30.

Joanne Crowley, daughter of Mr. and Mrs. Bernard Crowley, 27 Blodgett Street, and "Gene" Tobias, daughter of Mr. and Mrs. Fred Tobias, 638 Chestnut Street, said they noticed the "saucer" when their attention was attracted to "a round disc with a yellow glare" in the sky.

The girls, both eighth-graders at the Straw School, agreed they saw a "shiny disc in the sky turning over and over, with a yellow glare around it."

The girls said the object was moving noiselessly at high speed and disappeared behind some distant trees after they followed its flight for several seconds.

The Madison (Wisconsin) *State Journal,* carried the following saucer account on March 12, 1955. We do not receive many accounts from that area. In fact, the area east of Idaho to the Great Lakes, seems to lag far behind the remainder of the country in sightings of all kinds:

SEASON'S FIRST SAUCER FLIES IN AT HIGH SPEED

Madison's first flying saucer sighting of the year was reported Friday night by a Lakeside Street resident.

Lawrence Grab, 714 W. Lakeside Street, reported that he and his son saw a phosphorescent object travel at terrific speed over Madison at 7:50 p.m. Friday, flying from southwest to northeast.

"Before we saw this object," he said, "we saw a brilliant flash of light." He said the object traveled at such a speed that "nothing at Truax Field could touch it." The weather bureau at Truax Field reported it had not seen the object but suggested that it might have been a meteor. The Ground Observers post atop the Belmont Hotel also reported it had not seen the thing.

Our overseas friends send us a few clips from time to time— it's one way of cracking the U.S. blockade. Here is one from the *Barrow News,* of Barrow-in-Furness, England:

AN "OBJECT" IN THE SKY AT WALNEY

What was the object seen for a few seconds passing through a clear blue sky on Thursday at lunch time by three people at Walney? Could it have been a flying saucer, or was it a freak cloud formation?

Mr. Fred Jackson and his wife, Eleanor, told a *News* reporter their story as they sat in their neat Robin Hill bungalow at North Scale yesterday.

Pointing out through a bay window which provides an extensive sky-view, Mrs. Jackson said that an object shaped like a fish came sweeping into view from a northerly direction. "I showed Fred the thing as we watched it change shape. It was traveling very fast and my husband dashed outside to call our neighbor, Mrs. E. Hebblethwaite. She had also seen the object and was in her back garden. It disappeared from sight very quickly dipping away behind the fork.

"It was very clear yesterday about twenty past twelve," said Mrs. Hebblethwaite. "The object did not seem solid but more like a cloud, or a puff of smoke. But it was twirling round and round."

At Walney Fort it was said that the only observation undertaken in the past few days was of a jet aircraft which broke through the sound barrier—but that was yesterday morning.

Iowa is in the picture again with a report in the Clinton *Herald*, March 12. Am I imagining things or does there really seem to be a cycle of about four to six days in these scattered reports?

MOTORED "SAUCER" FLIES HIGH, FAST

A flying object whose speed was estimated at 2,000 m.p.h. was spotted Friday afternoon by K. B. Hershire, 835 10th Avenue S. He reported to police.

Hershire said he saw the white oval cloud-like object about 4:15 p.m. yesterday while in the yard of his home. His attention was attracted by the sound of what he thought was an airplane engine, he said. The object, about the size of a doughnut, was moving very rapidly from west to east at an altitude of 45,000 to 50,000 feet, he said. The object disappeared while over the city. But Hershire could still hear the noise of its motors.

Georgia is close to Florida, where they see a lot of UFO's. Here is a report from the Macon (Georgia) *Telegraph and News*, March 13, 1955:

FLYING SAUCERS STILL HERE, MACONITES SAY

In case you've been wondering what became of the flying saucers, this is to report that they are still with us, snooping around up there in the upper limits of the atmosphere.

Henry E. Watson, 805 Magnolia Drive, and Mr. and Mrs. R. A. Edwards, 1605 Rembert Avenue, caught sight of one or what looked like one yesterday around 7:00 p.m. They were standing in the Sparks Motor Company lot at 811 Third Street, watching the sun sink slowly in the west, when a round, black object appeared.

As Watson described it, the object was barrelling along at a speed that would have made a supersonic jet appear to be going backwards.

"I've seen plenty of jets flying over," Watson said, "but this thing was much faster." Watson said he thought at first it was a balloon. It appeared spherical, left no vapor trail, made no sound whatsoever, and took a little more than a minute to go from the western horizon to the eastern. It was not flat like a saucer, he said.

"It appeared to be very high, and to our sight it was about twelve inches in diameter. But of course it must have measured more than that actually."

Watson said he had heard about flying saucer sightings, and had always felt there was nothing in such reports. "But I'm fixing to change my mind now," he said.

March was a very important month in the affairs of saucer investigators and fans. We have several newspaper accounts of the great meeting of the Flying Saucer Convention in California. It is not the function of this book to detail the activities of these meetings, nor to analyze the statements made at them. We do feel that the newspapers have made light of the affair in a rather unnecessary manner, however.

Here is a report from *Newsweek*, March 21, 1955. While some newspapers felt supercilious obligations to belittle this meeting, it is of some import that the national news magazines saw fit to give it coverage:

WHISTLING INTO SPACE

About 1,000 men and women, and children gathered around a massive, egg-shaped boulder in the Mojave Desert in California last week. There, safe from the sneers of skeptics, they munched sandwiches and drank pop, while they listened to stories about Mars and Venus and other planets, including several hitherto unknown to science and invisible through even the most powerful telescopes.

It was the second annual Spacecraft Convention, and the speakers were men who claimed to have visited outer space in spaceships, and what not, and to have consorted with Martians, Venusians, etc.

Among them was Daniel W. Fry, an instrument technician for the Aerojet Corporation. July 4, 1950 wasn't much of a holiday for Fry. He missed the last bus into town from the White Sands Proving Ground where he was then working. The air-conditioning in his room broke down. He was hot and lonely.

Fry went for a walk. Suddenly, a space ship landed near him. "It was just an ovate spheroid flattened at top and bottom with no protuberances, about thirty feet in diameter and sixteen feet in length; no larger," he told his listeners. Naturally, he went on board. The ship took off. In fifteen minutes it was whizzing over New York; fifteen minutes later it was back at White Sands.

Mrs. Dana Howard had quite an experience to recount, too. A space ship landed near her, took her aboard, and whisked her off to Venus. She stayed there just long enough to marry a Venusian named Lelando. She last heard from him about six weeks ago. "My body went into a violent revulsion," she declared.

Truman Bethrum, a 56-year-old construction worker from Utah, told of "eleven contacts" with a saucer-shaped "scow" from a planet unknown to science named Clarion. The ship was manned by a crew of 32 and commanded by a beautiful woman, Aura Rhanes. She had a Latin complexion, dark hair, and dark eyes, and what was more, this visitor wore "a radiant red skirt and a snug-fitting black blouse."

"Very definitely a woman, very definitely," said Bethrum, chuckling.

While the speakers recalled their travels, a slight, nervous man of 43, in a blue beanie, pink shirt, and blue slacks wandered about the crowd, distributing copies of the first issue of his tabloid newspaper, "20th Century Times." He was Orfeo Angelucci, who says he has ridden in flying discs which landed near a Los Angeles cemetery. Most of the stories in his paper dealt with his experiences, including his encounters with "exquisite personages" aboard the discs.

"Isn't it wonderful, a meeting like this?" said a middle-aged woman as the convention broke up at dusk. "Such an uplifting experience!"

Her companion replied, "Yes, outdoors, it is so spiritual and elevating."

Most meteors do not look like two-gallon pails. They do not even look like a small dinner-pail. They look like small yellow lights, sometimes brighter than the planet Venus, but more often as faint as a second or third magnitude star.

METEOR LOOKS LIKE TWO-GALLON PAIL
TO O'NEIL WOMAN

"About as big as a two-gallon pail," was the way a meteor, Tuesday night, looked to Mrs. Earl Forest of O'Neil. She was in the barn milking when she saw a light which she thought at first was from an auto. As the light did not diminish, Mrs. Forest's curiosity was aroused and she came out of the barn for a look. About that time she heard a loud sound.

"It was west in the sky," she said. "The object was colored like a huge moon and was travelling real fast, leaving a trail of sparks."

Mrs. Forest thought the meteor veered to the northwest before falling from her sight.

The March 15 *Saucer Sentinel* carried as a news release an announcement that George Adamski was fined by the Mexican Government for lecturing without a permit. The same issue noted that a flying saucer was over Coventry, England, in the year 1666, the year of the Great Fire of London. The reporter had found a contemporaneous letter which said: "A strange matter flew over the City. It was about the thickness of a large bowl and had a long blue tail which wiggled. It was not so high as the tops of the tallest steeples."

That thing was obviously a weather balloon. (1666!) No more perfect description (for Air Force purposes) could possibly be found!

This issue of *Saucer Sentinel* states some rather cogent reasons why the Mexican Saucer Landing of 1949 may be substantiated:

MEXICAN SAUCER LANDING OF 1949
APPEARS VERIFIABLE
(Reprinted from The Vimana)

Reason 1:

Ernest Gates, automobile dealer, is a substantial down-to-earth individual with an acute sense of what's going on in the world.

Returning from the General Motors School in 1949, and leaving Flint, Michigan, on a Saturday afternoon, his car radio was suddenly interrupted by a special newscast message emanating from Mexico City. The announcer then tuned to a remote control pick-up broadcast wherein an American lady reporter began describing the amazing fact that a saucer had landed in the area not too long before, somewhere on the outskirts, and now the section had been roped off, and authorities were attempting somehow to get into the craft. This reporter went on to describe how difficult it was to penetrate the hard surface of the large saucer which had landed; that blowtorches, acetylene flame, etc., were of little help. She continued by saying that it appeared that there were several "smallish" men slumped over, apparently unconscious or dead from our atmosphere. "Keep tuned in to this station" the cut-in announcer said, "and we'll keep you notified as things progress." Ernie kept tuned in, but no other saucer newscast developed.

Reason 2:

In an article in the Detroit *Times,* March 10, 1949 (INS), Ray L. Dimmick, Los Angeles businessman, is quoted as saying that he had seen the wreckage of a flying saucer which, he stated, crashed recently near Mexico City, escorted there by Mexican business associates, to this military base which was heavily guarded. Dimmick described the saucer as being 46 feet in diameter. He said that Mexican officials and some scientists believed the saucer was from Mars or some other planet. He said he was told by Mexican officials that the saucer was piloted by a "strange type of man" who was only 23 inches tall. He said the pilot was killed in the crash in hilly country only a few miles out from the Mexican capital. Dimmick added that military and government officials from the United States inspected the saucer.

(Was this the same saucer thence carefully wrapped in tarpaulins, hoisted onto huge army conveyor trucks, and with heavy escort, carted to Wright-Patterson Air base, Dayton, Ohio? Several excellent sources seem to believe so . . . stating that fields were crossed in the daytime and night so the convoy would escape going through large cities, along main traffic arteries.)

Crashes of planes, big and little, continue to daze the reading public. Their causes daze the researchers. Here is one from the Washington (D.C.) *Daily News*, March 22, 1955:

ALL 66 ON BOARD DIE IN PLANE CRASH

Honolulu (UP)—A four-engined Military Air Transport Service plane enroute from Hawaii to California with 66 persons aboard crashed and burned today. The Navy said there were no survivors. The plane, which crashed on a ridge inside the Navy's top-secret Lualualei ammunition depot about twenty miles northwest of here, carried fifty-seven passengers and nine crew.

A spokesman for the Navy air-sea rescue co-ordinating center said emergency crews had reached the scene of the crash and found no survivors. The passenger list included two female dependents, one under five years old, and two civilians. All the rest were reported to be servicemen. A Navy spokesman said the plane caught fire after it crashed in the Wainaie Mountains on the western side of Oahu Island, 2,000 yards inside the main gate of the depot and 650 feet up the side of the mountain.

The plane, a Navy version of the DC-6, was on a flight from Hickham Field to Moffett Field, California. Shortly after take-off, it tried to return to Hickham, possibly because of radio trouble. The exact cause or reason was not known. It was believed it turned back after it was about three and one-half hours out.

The Lualualei Naval Ammunition Depot and the nearby naval radio station is one of the heaviest guarded military installations on the Island of Oahu.

The Ground Observer Corps sees them too, but the ever-watchful Air Force doesn't like them to talk about what they see, and it's against orders to tell the public when bonafide UFO's are sighted. The ground force reports that we know about are mostly from the northwest, around Cincinnati and over New Jersey way. Here is a short account from the *Herald and News*, Klamath Falls, Oregon:

GOC REPORTS SKY OBJECT

An unidentified object in the sky was spotted on Monday night between 9:30 and 9:40 p.m. by observers at the Ground Observer Corps at the airport.

On duty at that time were Leveta Beard and June DesMazes, who described the object as looking very much like a household light globe when viewed with the naked eye. Training binoculars on the light which had appeared at the north, traveling southwest, the observers said it looked like an iridescent or incandescent teacup.

"The object blinked on and off and had no tail," the observers said. It was visible for seven minutes and was judged to be approximately seven miles west of the tower. At the end of that time it disappeared behind the Cascades to the west. The observers reported the incident to the filter center at Portland.

We wish somebody would get the Air Force to explain why both British and American planes are always chasing meteors, fireballs, planets, balloons, etc. Certainly we have been often enough assured that UFO's do not exist, so the jet boys are either chasing nothing at all or are burning a lot of high-octane gas trying to catch mirages, sun-dogs and what have you. Why? The implications—if we accept the Air Force's "explanations" are appalling. The following from C.R.I.F.O. needs no introduction:

FIERY RED BALL WITH RED TAIL ELUDES R.A.F.

(Case 73, England and Wales, March 24, 1955.) A Squadron of Meteor Jets, flying full speed, chased a fiery object with a tail across England and Wales. The *Daily Mail* said the blazing object, like a gigantic meteorite, zigzagged from one end of the country to the other. Hundreds of telephone calls warned police and fire stations of the onrushing object, and there were several reports of aircraft crashing, but no evidence was found. The *Daily Mail* quotes an Air Ministry spokesman as saying: "A formation flight of Meteors from the R.A.F. station at West Malling, Kent, saw the object when they were flying over Manchester toward Birmingham, just after 7:00 p.m. It looked like a ball of fire descending rapidly from above them. They were flying at 20,000 feet and gave chase, but the object made the five hundred mile trip from Land's End to Glasgow in about 45 minutes." (Credit: G. L. Menefy, N.Z.)

Would we be correct in saying that Ohio, Florida, Oregon and Southern California are the four principal areas of UFO sightings in the United States? At least that's the way they seem to be running at present. Here is another Ohio report via the Galion *Inquirer*:

THOSE "FLYING SAUCERS" SEEN AGAIN HERE

Three Galion girls reported seeing a "flying saucer-like" object in the sky above the city Thursday at 5:00 p.m. The youthful observers were Sharon Crissinger, 12, and her playmates Kathleen Nicholls, 11, and Melinda Harmon.

The incident occurred at the intersection of Carmel and N. Market Street where the three girls were playing. They all reported it to be a silver shape, about the size of a basketball, quite high and stationary. After about five minutes the object disappeared, they reported.

This was the second such experience for Sharon who saw a similar "flying saucer" two years ago while visiting in Crawfordsville, Indiana. This observation was confirmed by several other observers at the time.

SKY OBJECT ALARMS BRITAIN: EXPERTS BELIEVE FIRE TRAIL WAS CAUSED BY METEORITE

London, March 25. (Reuters) Thousands of persons all over Britain were alarmed last night by a fiery red object with a green tail which hurtled through dark skies over the country.

An air force spokesman said meteorological experts decided that the blazing object was a huge meteorite which blew up two hundred miles above Wales at it entered earth's atmosphere from outer space.

Look closely. The following item is small in format, but it may well be the most important single announcement of the year, or of the century or even the whole Christian era as far as its context is concerned. *This announcement is the first we have seen which states bluntly that the government has conquered gravitation!* If it is true, there has never been a greater discovery and we do not exclude electricity, nor even the "wheel." We think it may be true, and perhaps the first in a series of build-up announcements leading to the claim that the Air Force has been making the UFO all the time. (Would that include the silver disc over England in 1290 A.D.?)

But note throughout the year: forewarning about satellite manufacture; forewarning re control of gravitation; announcement about satellites being seen; announcement about our definite plan for satellites; announcement that there are no flying saucers but that the government is making some for us!

Anyway, here is the little item, from the New York *Daily News,* March 29, 1955. Innocuous-looking, isn't it? But . . . ?

BROADWAY by Danton Walker

Degravitation, regarded as a more important scientific contribution even than the atom bomb, has been achieved in one of Uncle Sam's hush-hush military experiments (degravitation permits an object, regardless of weight, to remain suspended in mid-air).

Cincinnati is back again. Here is a report from the March 29 edition of the Cincinnati (Ohio) *Post.* Keep Cincinnati in mind. The summer brings forth some astonishing events along the Ohio river:

WALTON FOLK SEE "SAUCERS," THEY SAY

Police Chief Herman Simmons and ten or twelve Walton citizens said they saw what they believe may have been flying saucers at approximately 9:30 p.m. Monday, the chief reported Tuesday.

Chief Simmons said first a regular plane was seen headed north-

E

east toward Pittsburgh, and a short time later two noiseless brightly lighted objects were seen heading south. One appeared to grow brighter and brighter, and then turn toward the east during the three or four minutes it was under observation.

In closing out the month of March, there is at least one thing which deserves re-emphasis: the control of gravity. Never in known history has so small an item been so cogent in terms of development of Man and his conquest of his environment.

If the government—any government on earth—has reached such an understanding of gravitation that even a small but definite step has been taken in control and use of it, then we can say, safely and without reservation, that this is the greatest discovery that Science has ever made.

Make no mistake—that is the sober truth.

If such a discovery has been made, it is of greater import than the development of atomic energy, and the two combined *could* give us space travel almost overnight! The power of the atom, combined with its use in gravitational reaction, could and would enable man to match the observed performance of the UFO.

If the government, or the Air Force, has developed such a control, it fully justifies the secrecy and deceit which have been practiced against the public—and the public is you and I.

But there is more to it than that, even!

Why has the government been handing the Atomic Energy Commission several billions of dollars a year, during the past five years, when the major research is supposed to have been completed? Isn't it just probable that a large part of this money has been secretly poured into gravity research, behind the smoke screen of atomic energy, rocket power and silly little satellites?

APRIL

There is probably nothing better with which to start the month of April than Herbert Elliston's editorial in the April 3rd edition of the Washington *Post and Times-Herald*, Washington, D.C. There is a good deal that's pertinent to our times and something of philosophy. In view of the revelations of the previous chapter, it seems safe to say that we can associate the development of atomic phenomena with those of gravitation and the UFO, at least insofar as spiritual relations are concerned.

And so, without further ado . . .

IS CHURCH GROWTH SPIRITUAL REVIVAL?

During a spell in the sickbed sometime ago I read one of those lewdish classics with a moral which the pseudo-moralists of the Comstock variety would consign to the flames along with *Lysistrata*.

This particular fable was a story by the great but cynical Anatole

France. France deals with a young lady who retained her virtue impregnably till her would-be seducer showed her a skull and used it as his text for a homily on the brevity of life. The tempter won out. The virgin surrendered. If life was so short, why not take her, fill of the fleshpots while there was yet time and opportunity?

There is ample proof, I think, that this moral has no validity as a general proposition. When you are faced with extinction, nine times out of 10 you turn not to the things of the flesh, but to the things of the spirit. Even the condemned criminal in most cases tries to make his peace with God on the way to the deathhouse. For the cosmic setting fascinates the just and the unjust alike. Newspaper lust for the exceptional fails to take account of the stories of the majority of those next door to oblivion who don't rush around seeking distraction.

However, the guardians of our temporal security used to be addicts of Anatole France's view of the human race. The theory was that if you told the people of the perils they live under, they would cease to be good citizens. It would be a case of eat, drink and be merry, for tomorrow we die. And secrecy is not limited to our country. All the governments of the free world shrink from telling the truth to the people to whom they owe their stewardship. The habit testifies to a lack of faith in democracy. Yet, as Bishop Butler puts it, "Things and actions are what they are and the consequences of them will be what they will be: why then should we desire to be deceived?"

Our own government is now getting over its reluctance to take the people into its confidence on its major preoccupation. For the facts of life and death in the nuclear age have literally blown themselves into the open. And what is the result? You can see it in the capital as well as all over the Western world—churches full, new churches going up in all the main avenues, a prayer room at the Capitol, the MRA, evangelists and revivalists in great demand.

Does this activity mean that spiritual renewal is at hand? The poet Robert Frost is said to have told Secretary Dulles that everywhere he went on his recent mission to South America, he encountered the charge that our religion is, predominately, materialism.

The church-going Mr. Dulles could not understand it. He said the Latin Americans ought to be told of the percentage of our church attendance and then they would know better.

Yet a religious revival is not the same thing as a spiritual revival. It is superficial to see in church-going the automatic sign of a spiritual life. As a matter of fact, the father of psychiatry, Jung, lumps us all in the Western world in the category of "spiritual heathen." The Western worshiper of the sacred figures may still be "undeveloped and unchanged in his inward soul" because he has "all God outside" and does not experience Him in the soul."

So the phenomenon of these desperate times to which I refer may be more of the same thing. Billy Graham's success, for instance, may be in part an illustration that there's no business like show business. The churches where attendance is soaring are precisely those where the dancing dervish would be most at home. Most of us are caught in a dilemma in this matter. We are torn between the need to experience God in our souls in company with our fellows and the emptiness of most forms of popular-style worship.

The fact remains that the religious phenomenon which is more and more evident in the Western world does represent a spiritual longing in the presence of life's uncertainty. Moreover, if, as Arnold Toynbee says, communism is a counter-religion, clearly the best defense against it and the best attack upon it is to strengthen our own religion—to fill that spiritual vacuum in our individual and community lives which Jung writes about. It is a vacuum created by the concentration for 200 years past on the scientific and intellectual man. This concentration has supplied all the answers but the main one: the one to the all-abiding mystery. It is time to give spiritual man a chance—the man, that is, with the inner-directed personality.

The aerial explosions continue, as noted here in the April 4th edition of the Los Angeles (Calif.) *Times.* No comment seems justified at this point:

TRIO REPORT MYSTERIOUS EXPLOSION HIGH IN AIR

A mysterious aerial explosion was reported yesterday by three motorists who witnessed the phenomenon from a point about five miles east of Pinon Peak in the Walker Pass area of Kern County.

John Anderson and his brother of 1835 Glen Park Ave., Pomona, and Ralph Hess of 248 West Gleason Ave., Monterey Park, reported to deputy sheriffs at Walker Pass Lodge that they had seen a burst of smoke and flame, as of a plane exploding, at an altitude of approximately 14,000 feet. They also said they saw shiny objects falling through the air and disappearing behind a ridge.

These they at first identified as parts of a plane, but later said that they could not be sure that the objects were part of a plane or possible human occupants.

The report was transmitted to Civil Air Patrol Squadron 82 at Harvey Field, Inyokern. Lt. E. K. Martin sent four search planes to comb the area for an hour. They were followed by a rescue helicopter, piloted by Lt. George Peebles of the nearby U.S. Naval Ordnance Test Station. All pilots reported no signs of any wreckage in the area.

The Case for the UFO made its debut in the thickening crowd of saucer books. The author attempted to assemble a cross-section of all past and present events which have been difficult to explain on any basis other than space flight and space intelligence. He made some rather broad hypotheses as a framework for the data, and whether or not you agree with these hypotheses you must admit that the general structure does hold together. *The Case for the UFO* confronts science with its own data, and goes far toward refuting the specious and stolid arguments of such astronomers as Donald Menzel, who has written a book full of dogmatic negatives relative to a subject about which nobody knows enough to justify dogmatics or pedantics.

The heavenly little island of Majorca, in the blue Mediterranean Sea, was finally invaded by flying saucers, as told by the

New York *Herald-Tribune*, April 5, 1955. (Personally, we feel that they will probably be a less disturbing factor than the tourists!)

FLYING SAUCERS INVADE MAJORCA

A special attraction for flying saucers seems to exist in the island of Majorca, in the Mediterranean east of Spain. No fewer than thirty-seven saucers have been "sighted" there in recent months.

A truck driver returning to Palma at night had one of the best close-ups. He saw a "solid radiancy" 800 feet from where he stood beside the truck. The object, in a field, was the size of a telephone booth. Suddenly it left the ground "with a noise like dynamite" and disappeared at the usual "incredible speed."

Even our Midwest newspapers take some interest in the doings of fireballs and UFO in England, when the news breaks through the blockade. The following is from the Tulsa (Oklahoma) *Tribune*, April 5:

STRANGE LIGHT SEEN OVER MIDLANDS
BELIEVED TO BE A METEORITE

People in many parts of Britain reported seeing a strange light in the sky last night, believed to have been caused by a meteorite which broke up over Wales just after 7 p.m. at a height of about 200 miles. Midland police were ordered to be on the alert and watch for a plane thought to have been in distress and crashed, but later the alarm was attributed to a particularly bright meteor.

A jet plane was seen over Bromsgrove, but an Edgbaston Observatory spokesman said the reports were consistent with the possibility of a bright and fairly big meteor which would have burned up on entering the earth's atmosphere.

The phenomenon was seen over a wide area of the Midlands and Wales. From the Grosvenor Hotel, Barmouth, Miss Allday telephoned *The Birmingham Post* and said that shortly after 7 p.m. she and her brother saw a large bright light in the sky, surrounded by a red glow.

From an inn near Ashby-de-la-Zouch, a motorist telephoned *The Birmingham Post* and said: "Here is a public-house full of people very shaken by what they have seen. A bright green light seemed to come down to earth. A red glow was seen where it appeared to hit the ground in the direction of Lichfield."

Mr. A. R. Stokes, of Ryland Road, Birmingham, observed the phenomenon from Sparkhill. After it went down in the sky he saw a mass of black smoke. "It was like a white-hot mass of something—probably a meteor," he said.

Staffordshire County Police said that eye-witness reports from as far afield as Stoke to West Bromwich described seeing an explosion "with something coming down in flames."

Returning to Leek from a country journey, a bus driver, Mr. R. Johnson, of Hanford, Stoke-on-Trent, reported having seen a comet. "It had a very long tail and remained visible in the sky for what seemed to be quite a few seconds," he said.

There is no serious reason to doubt the validity of the following statement about meteorites, but some of the fireballs you have been reading about are not meteors or bolides of the conventional variety. There is more than iron and stone moving about in orbits in space, and some of this miscellaneous debris does get through to the earth. Some of it may be controlled.

This is from the Washington *Post and Times-Herald*, April 4th:

ICE AND ASH FROM COMETS
SHOOTING STARS YOU SEE IN THE SKY
FOUND TO BE SIZE OF HICKORY NUTS

The shooting star you see on a clear night is a fragile offshoot of a comet about the size of a hickory nut with less than the weight of a cigarette, Fred L. Whipple, of Harvard University, today told an American Astronomical Society meeting.

Whipple said those shooting stars observed without visual aid come from comets. He said high-speed cameras reveal the comets are composed of ice and clay-like ash. As they approach the sun, the ice melts and the mass fragmentizes.

The small fragments seen by watchers on earth are so fragile they could not be picked up with the fingers without breaking, he said.

When seen, they are about 50 miles high and traveling about 18 miles a second—or about 55,000 miles an hour. They disintegrate before reaching earth.

He said they differ from the large meteorite masses usually seen in museums, which are offshoots of small planets.

The same paper came through with the following account from New Mexico, April 6:

GREEN FIREBALL WITH TAIL SEEN

A "green fireball" with a flaming tail was reported seen over several southeastern New Mexico towns at 9:55 a.m. (MST) today.

Pilots flying near Roswell and Carlsbad reported sighting the mysterious object briefly to the southwest.

Mrs. Charles Wells, a Roswell housewife, said the ball was green and a tail following it was orange, as if it was burning fiercely.

Another account of "fireballs" in New Mexico was reported in the Washington (D.C.) *Evening Star,* of April 6, from Albuquerque, via the Associated Press:

FIREBALLS FALL IN NEW MEXICO

Scientists today tried to untangle the mystery of two unidentified brilliant objects believed to be fireballs which flashed across New Mexico skies.

Dr. Lincoln La Paz of the University of New Mexico Institute of Meteoritics, said he believed the two objects were "of the same family." He said he does not think they were ordinary meteorites since it would be "incredible" for two to fall in New Mexico in one day. He added:

"We'll find nothing most likely when we try to recover what dropped."

The two objects—one brilliant green, the other brilliant white—flashed through New Mexico skies at almost the same moment yesterday morning. Observers reported they saw "dirt fly into the air" when the white one hit the ground about 30 miles northeast of Lordsburg. But they reported no sound. Observers of the green fireball heard nothing either. Dr. La Paz said meteorites make a tremendous noise.

The New York *Herald-Tribune* and the New York *World-Telegram* also carried these stories. Here is one from the *World-Telegram:*

SKY FIREBALLS ORIGIN HUNTED BY SCIENTISTS

Scientists today tried to untangle the mystery of two unidentified but brilliant objects believed to be fireballs which flashed across New Mexico skies.

Dr. Lincoln La Paz, of the University of New Mexico Institute of Meteoritics, declared that they were "of the same family." He said he did not think they were ordinary meteorites since it would be "incredible" for two to fall in New Mexico in one day. He added:

"We'll find nothing most likely when we try to recover what dropped."

The two objects, one brilliant green, the other brilliant white, flashed through New Mexico skies at almost the same moment yesterday morning.

Observers reported they saw "dirt fly into the air" when the white one hit the ground about 30 miles northeast of Lordsburg. But they reported no sound. Observers of the green fireball heard nothing either. Dr. La Paz said meteorites make a tremendous noise.

"The lines of sight on both make me almost certain these are two distinct objects," Dr. La Paz said. "But I believe they are of the same family. I don't know what they are."

The two objects had in common direct falls rather than a sweeping horizontal passage through the skies. Neither made any sound. So far no trace has been discovered of either.

The green fireball was sighted in Albuquerque and Roswell, and in the Tularosa Basin covering almost all of southeastern and south central New Mexico. The white one was near Lordsburg, in southwestern New Mexico.

As if the above accounts (which were carried in many leading papers throughout the world) were not enough, the following day a *third* fireball made its presence known, and Dr. La Paz continues to refuse to identify them, specifically, as meteors. The following account of Fireball #3 is from the San Bernadino (California) *Telegram,* April 6:

NOT BELIEVED METEORS!
THIRD MYSTERIOUS FIREBALL
FLASHES ACROSS NEW MEXICO

A third mysterious fireball flashed across New Mexico and plunged to earth at the state's southeastern corner Wednesday and a leading scientist said the chance the objects were meteorites was very small.

The scientist, Dr. Lincoln La Paz, director of the University of New Mexico's Institute of Meteoritics, could offer no explanation, however, for the objects.

Observers at Hobbs, New Mexico, reported that a fireball "no more than 12 inches across" plunged into the earth a few miles east of there near the Texas-New Mexico state line. Searchers sent to the scene could find no fragments.

Civil Air Patrol planes meanwhile searched but failed to uncover any trace of a larger object which apparently crashed and exploded Tuesday in the Burro Mountains near Lordsburg in the west corner of the state amid the glow of "intense white heat."

Meanwhile, the University of New Mexico Meteoritics Institute puzzled over a green fireball which flashed over the southeast part of the state and was seen as far north as Albuquerque, 200 miles away.

The last two mentioned were the first major fireballs sighted in New Mexico since last September. (Ed.: This twist of phraseology would indicate that fireballs are almost commonplace in that area; small fireballs, that is!)

C.A.P. Lt. Paul Mallott said those who had seen the white light here described it as "falling so fast we couldn't make out its size or its shape." But vapor tails trailed behind as it fell.

Mallott said the object came "straight down" to about the top of the mountains. Suddenly there was a "white blinding flash with no color to it at all," he said.

"There was no smoke," he said, "but a huge cloud of dust rose above the mountain when the object struck and apparently exploded."

Dr. La Paz said reports throughout the state indicated the green fireball which flashed over Roswell and the adjoining area was headed for the Tularosa Basin east of White Sands Proving Grounds, where rocket tests are conducted.

La Paz said he had only one clue: The fact that neither object emitted sound led to belief they were the "same type of objects."

The fireballs of New Mexico continued to hold the attention of the public, and the controversy over the mystery continued throughout the day in most major presses.

The following day, April 7, found still another fireball speeding its way across the New Mexico skies, defying description, almost, and certainly defying absolute identification. Dr. La Paz had his hands full! He declared flatly that these were not normal meteorites—a statement to be reckoned with when issued by one of the foremost authorities on meteorites—and it would appear that their silences and other puzzling characteristics tend to put them in the UFO class.

Here is a brief report from the Long Beach (California) *Independent,* with reference to still another:

FOURTH FIREBALL SLAMS INTO NEW MEXICO AREA

A fourth mysterious fireball plunged to earth in southern New Mexico late Wednesday, and a University of New Mexico scientist said he was sure it and three earlier fireballs were not meteorites.

Dr. Lincoln La Paz, director of the University of New Mexico's Institute of Meteoritics, said a meteorite fall seldom spreads itself over more than 10 miles. He said chances of two falls in the same area about the same time are "infinitesimal!"

The following account is of a bonafide comet. Nothing but the most powerful of telescopes would disclose it, and even then it most likely could only be seen by photographic methods. 17th magnitude is very faint. A 16th magnitude object is about two and one half times as bright as a 17th; a 15th is about two and one half times as bright as a 16th, etc. The faintest object visible to the average human eye, unaided by lenses, is about 6th magnitude.

Here is the notice as published in the Washington, D.C. *Post and Times-Herald*, April 7th:

NEW COMET FOUND OF 17th MAGNITUDE

A new comet has been discovered by astronomers at the Mount Palomar Observatory, the National Geographic Society said today.

The comet is of the seventeenth magnitude and cannot be seen with the naked eye. It was discovered on March 22, by Dr. Robert G. Harrington and Dr. George O. Abell while they were making a photographic sky survey, the society said.

The Washington *Post and Times-Herald* of April 7th contained the following article by staff writer Nate Haseltine. These so-called radio signals do not signify intelligence per se. They do deserve further investigation, however, and one does not forget the great red spot that appeared during the incredible decade of 1877-1886, and the number of times when there have been too many satellites over Jupiter, and when there were more shadows of satellites than there were satellites to cause shadows. There seems to be something besides inert methane gas in the Jupiter system.

JUPITER'S RADIO WAVES INTERCEPTED HERE

Radio astronomers here have intercepted bursts of radio static which may have originated in monstrous thunderstorms around the planet Jupiter, it was reported yesterday.

"This is the first recorded instance of such waves being received from one of the other planets of our solar system," said Dr. Kenneth L. Franklin, research fellow of Carnegie Institution of Washington.

Dr. Franklin joined Dr. Bernard F. Burke, a member of the Institution's Department of Terrestrial Magnetism, in reporting the event yesterday at Princeton, N.J., to the American Astronomical Society.

The radio waves from Jupiter were received at the Institution's huge 96-acre network of radio telescopes at nearby Seneca, Md.

Jupiter is mammoth in comparison to the earth, and if the radio bursts do originate in thunderstorms there probably no life has felt the fury. The planet's atmosphere, calculated as thousands of miles thick, is believed to comprise gases deadly to life.

The largest solar planet, Jupiter is 88,700 miles in diameter at its equator, in comparison to earth's diameter of 7,927 miles. And despite its great mass, Jupiter rotates much more rapidly than earth, once every nine hours and 50 minutes to the 24 hours it takes earth to make a complete rotation.

The waves observed through telescope receivers at the Seneca installation were described as having the short random bursts of static characteristic of thunderstorm interference heard over radio broadcast receivers. They were regularly observed about one day out of every three during the minutes Jupiter came within the narrow beam of the special radio telescope antenna.

Their apparent location from outer space, the radio astronomers reported, was observed to agree with that of Jupiter, and changes in the position of their course paralleled the normal movement of the huge planet over a period of several months.

During the first week of April, your editor received a letter from Mr. S. Bloomwald and Mr. Sidney Ginsburg of Dorchester, Mass., describing some experience they had with a UFO.

It appears that they were walking through Franklin Field, in Dorchester, when they noticed a light in the sky above them. At first they thought it was an airplane light, but its motions were not those of a plane." It "headed downward," and after dropping a bit another light "from out of nowhere" came from the same direction as the first (from East to West), and circled around the first. Both were noiseless and seemed to move without effort; the circle seemed to be completed in a very short time, described as about "one second flat." In any case it was too fast to be a plane. Mr. Bloomwald says it was as rapid as you can make a circle in the air with your finger, which is pretty quick. Mr. Bloomwald thought that the second light seemed to repower the first, after which the second returned in the direction from whence it came, and the first continued its course in a westerly direction. Here is the most startling part of the performance: "But while we were watching it in its course across the open field, it suddenly changed shape like that of a star and it went bobbing or fluttering across the sky, reminding me of a pebble when thrown into a lake."

These men have had more than their share of UFO's. About a week later, they say, they were again walking in the field when they saw a huge orange-colored light that looked like a ball of fire. It was heading toward the ground near them and they ran over to it "half scared, half curious." It was now about three feet off the ground and they approached within about five feet of it. They say: "When we were about to approach it, it disappeared into thin air. It was a huge ball of light." Further correspondence with Mr. Bloomwald did not obtain much more detail, except that the ball of light was perhaps the size of a basketball and made little if any noise. So far as your editor is aware, this is the closest approach ever to be made to one of the orange-colored UFO fireballs, and it is regrettable that more such contacts cannot be reported so that we can get some close-up information.

The strangest experience of Bloomwald and Ginsburg, however, was yet to come. Mr. Bloomwald was lying in bed when he got a hunch that he might see a UFO if he looked out the window, so he arose and raised the shade—sort of joking with himself the while: "So I pulled up my shade and what I saw I shall never forget in my whole life. Even to this day I can't make myself believe that I saw this fantastic object. There, up in the sky, was this huge (about the size of the Moon) *pinwheel* rolling along in the sky. It was orange; orange of the same intensity of the ball of fire in Franklin Field and it rolled as if it was on tracks. The next day I saw an item in the paper about a woman in a different town who saw the same thing at about the same time I did. It was really frightening and reminded me of a huge monster." Mr. Bloomwald sent a rough sketch which looks a bit like a four-petalled daisy, or a four-blade propeller with a large hub. What sort of UFO was this?

The following account of three objects was prepared from personal observation by a staff writer of the *Flying Saucer Review* (Seattle, Washington). The sightings took place at Plattsburgh, New York, where observation has been more than usually keen, particularly by the Ground Observer Corps, and where more UFO's have been seen than the average of points in the New York-New England area:

THREE UFO's IN ONE DAY ...

On April 9th, 1955, I was with a member of the Office of Civil Defense, Ground Observation Corps, when we made a very accurate and detailed sighting that we reported to the Albany Filter Center, U.S. Air Force. The Air Defense Command was extremely interested in the sighting. I took pictures of the object with a fixed-focus, but not one photo came out for us.

The roll of film was developed by a local press photographer. The odd thing about the roll was that not even the frames of the pictures came out on the negatives. The entire roll was milky-white, and blank, except for an indefinable fringe area on what we think was the first shot. The pictures were taken from a good height—nine stories up, on top of Physicians Hospital, where the O.C.D.-G.O.C. Observations Post is maintained. At the time I made the shots, the sun was just beginning to light the horizon.

The first sighting made on the ninth of April, 1955, was at one thirty one a.m. At that time we observed a rust colored light, round in shape, and covered with, or surrounded by, a misty cloud . . . moving away from our post. It was very low, perhaps about 1,500 to 2,000 feet up. The thing moved slowly out over Lake Champlain, headed in the direction of Grand Island, Vermont. It banked to the left, and we could see that whatever it was, it was shaped round. It seemed to diminish in brightness, and went down behind the ridge of mountains on the Vermont side of the lake.

We figured that the unknown object touched land in the area of Grand Isle. I checked with the Vermont State Police and called the Civil Defense Office in the general area of Grande Isle, but no one reported seeing the thing.

The second in a series of the three separate sightings of UFO's that day, April 9, 1955, was made at 3:34 a.m. This time we watched an odd vapor trail stretched across the sky, and traced it to an odd thing that just hung in the sky. It was shaped like a pencil or cigar. It gave off green light around the edges, and glowed bright gold, or yellow, in the middle. The object was visible right until the sunrise.

The third, and most spectacular sighting, was made at 4:10 a.m. This time, we had signed out the post with Albany Filter Center, and had waited around due to a strange glow off to the north-east, as if there were a fire on the horizon over in the Vermont area. There was no fire reported, or plane crash, or anything else unusual. We checked on them later. But, to get back to the sighting at the time —the other observer called to my attention an unusually bright object that was entirely motionless in the sky to the east, over the Grand Island, Vermont area. I told him perhaps it was a star. But he said in all the hours he had been on watch, he had never seen the object. We watched it, and played a pair of binoculars on it. We then saw that it was beginning to change color. It changed from incandescent white, to greenish-white, to a pinkish color, to red, then to a sort of blue, and then back to white. I could have had more witnesses if I had called someone on the phone on the next floor down, which is open to public use, but at the time, neither of us thought of this.

We observed the object as it changed colors, and then it began rising straight up. We put the post back into operation, and described the object to the filter center down-state, and they told us they wanted to connect us with the Radar Station the U.S.A.F. operates in St. Albans, Vt., but we couldn't hear what they were saying. The telephone lines from Plattsburg to the Burlington areas (where the filter center is located) were staticy for some unknown reason. The person on the other end couldn't hear us, and we couldn't hear him.

We stuck with it, and waited until the sun came up—at which time the object had risen to about 60,000 or 70,000 feet. The sun then blotted out the object. But while we watched it through the binoculars, we got a good picture in our minds of what it looked like. We watched the thing for over an hour as it hovered and rose about four miles from us.

Through binoculars, the object was shaped like an inverted dessert dish. It glowed deep red on top, had flanged rims along the bottom. It gave off a green vapor in a series of eight exhaust-like trailings underneath and gave off a brilliant yellow light underneath that obscured other distinguishable features in the underside. There were three apertures near the top of the dish. No noise was heard during its first visit—or its last.

To compile a true "annual," one must attempt to collect and publish all activities of the year which pertain to the phenomenon of UFO. Sometimes even the humorous is important, or at least is a necessary and integral part of the full year's picture. Our compilation would not be representative without including samples of all kinds of press notices, for it is our sincere desire to reflect the entire picture, and eventually, perhaps, our collections will form the basis for the only extant résumé of the full picture . . . *before!* Who knows?

The Ventura (California) *Star Free Press,* April 10, announced the formation of a local welcoming committee for the reception of spacemen. We recall that David Kletter, of Miami Beach, Florida, has assembled a similar committee. Both Florida and

California seem likely places for such clubs to function for they are two of the most active centers for UFO.

The account:

FRIENDS OF FLYING SAUCERS
AIM TO MAKE SPACE VISITORS WELCOME
IF THEY COME HERE

Calling all space men! Come down, come down, wherever you are!

Free parking space can be had from "a certain good-hearted lady" who is offering her 500-acre upstate farm "for landing purposes for the flying saucers only."

This intelligence comes from the just-published April issue of the New York organ of the flying-saucer cult, the "Flying Saucer News."

The 16-page publication also makes a generous offer of its own in one item of its "service department" column.

"Attention—a one year subscription to Flying Saucer News will be sent free to any interplanetary visitor. He or she is welcomed to visit this shop first."

The editor of the publication, James S. Rigberg, who also sells crystal balls, ouija boards, seems inclined towards the poetic, for he has included, in his publication, the following:

> Up where good folks always go;
> And there an angel, in mid-air
> Awaited me to share her love,
> I honestly declare . . .

The rest of the edition is prose, albeit lilting prose. There's an article by Gilbert N. Holloway, Ph.D., pointing out that "the saucers are interdimensional." Holloway explains that many, if not all, flying saucers are "from another dimension of the universe."

This, he says, accounts for their strange "habit of disappearing and reappearing so easily—they do not fade into nothing, they

simply raise their frequency levels or vibrations and slip into another dimension."

The following news feature is from Palo Alto, California, dated
April 10th. The prime service such articles serve to the astute
UFO researcher is to prove, beyond doubt, that strange and heretofore unrecognized means of "flight" *are* possible and are actually being "toyed" with by our armed forces. It might be going
too far to suggest that such "flying platforms" might well be
prototypes of eventual "flying saucers," but there is always the
intriguing question of gravity control and how such a "gadget" as
this seems to be destroying, optically at any rate, some of our
preconceived notions pertaining to gravity.

"FLYING PLATFORM" EASY TO PILOT

A flying machine that defies gravity without rotor blades, wings,
tail or ordinary propellers was shown here today. (Ed.: By the
Navy) At a distance it looks amazingly like an airborne man-hole
cover. . . .

Although it looks as if it could easily be tipped over, experts say
the platform has an inherent stability.

The first man to go aloft on the platform was Phil A. Johnston,
a World War II fighter pilot who downed two enemy planes. He
says he found the platform simple to fly. . . .

Work (on the platform) got under way in 1954. Arthur Robertson, an aeronautical engineer who had designed planes for Lockheed
and once worked on a flying automobile project was placed in
charge.

Mr. Robertson said that, in addition to the thrust of the fans,
lift was provided by the flared lip of the platform, like the edge of
a pie tin. The fast flow of air through the sieved platform by the
sucking action of the fans reduces the air pressure over the flaring
lip, making the pressure under the lip relatively greater.

He also said the counter-rotating fans acted with a gyroscopic
effect, producing stability.

A problem remaining is emergency protection against engine fail-

ure. If either engine conked out now, the platform would drop like
a brick. . . .

(Ed.: This "flying platform" was actually invented by Stanley
Hiller, Jr., whose own life story reads like a real-life Tom Swift!)

One issue of *Collier's Magazine*, in 1955, devoted it's feature
space to this fascinating "Flying Platform."

Again, in 1955, the mystery of the moving boulders of Death
Valley was revived, this time in Walt Disney's "True Life Adventures," a kind of believe-it-or-not cartoon series. In the April
11th edition of the Washington, D.C. *Evening Star*, three illustrations of these strange stones were evidenced. Some of the large
stones weigh as much as a ton, and they *actually move* around on
the floor of Death Valley. They have no apparent source of
power, but they leave deep, deep groves in the sand and rocks
over which they move. *Yet no one has ever seen them in motion!*
The tracks and traces of their movement are there for everyone
to see, and still their source of power, or the actual moving force,
remains a deep mystery.

Suddenly we remember the great megaliths of Nasca and
Mexico. Some of the marks left by these boulders resemble those
markings in Death Valley, and all are without explanations. Some
of the marks are complex and indicate sudden changes of direction by the meandering megaliths.

Could these stones be being moved by forces from space?

As the Disney column put it:

TRUE LIFE ADVENTURES:
THE RIDDLE OF THE ROCKS THAT MOVE!

None of Nature's mysteries is more puzzling than the strange
trails of boulders weighing as much as a ton, gouged in the floor of
a dry lake on the western edge of Death Valley.

Nobody knows whether the rocks were pushed by the wind, carried by flood waters, or impelled by some unknown force.

No one has ever seen the rocks in motion . . . only the markings
of their mysterious movements.

The two reports following appeared side by side in the Washington (D.C.) *Daily News,* April 14th.

First, as to the metal disc: we have had some discs and hand-worked metal in UFO lore ere this time. Where do they come from? And why do we raither naively assume all the while that a state of radio-activity is a sort of sine quo non in proving space origin? Second, about this disappearing barn. That is far from being the first time such a thing has happened. Exploding roofs have been recorded before, also. And it seems that this is a characteristic peculiarly centralized or concentrated in the mid-Atlantic seaboard states.

Well, here are the items, as they appeared under the general heading "Oddities in the News":

CENTRAL CITY, COLORADO

Central City AEC officials admitted today they were unable to identify a small but highly radioactive metal disk found in a gulch south of this historic mining community.

The mysterious metal disk, measuring two inches in diameter, and about a quarter-inch thick, also had baffled the FBI, U.S. Geological Service, state health officials and veteran mining men as to origin or use.

A Geiger counter reading of the strange "button" showed it registering more than 20 per cent radioactive.

Morris Steen, 30, a millworker for Cherokee Uranium, Inc., found the disk in Lake Gulch a mile south of here. He said he spotted what he thought was a chunk of lead and pocketed it without further investigation.

The millworker said when he was removing the lead to make fishing weights yesterday he discovered the mysterious disk inside. Officials said the lead apparently was a shield for the object.

The disk has a small glass window on one side and a white, powdery substance which glows in the dark is visible inside the window. On the reverse side, the object has a clasp similar to a clip used to hold objects on trouser belts.

Also on back is an inscription reading: "UNDARK" at the top. At the bottom it reads: "22M-TTR58 USRC" then "poison inside."

LUMBERTON, NORTH CAROLINA

Puzzled police and firemen called in an explosives expert today to try to solve the mystery of the vanishing barn.

Fire Chief Ed J. Glover said the tobacco barn, located just inside the city limits, "simply disappeared in a sort of explosion" last night, but a preliminary investigation indicated there had been no explosion.

There was some speculation that the barn might have been the victim of a freak tornado which hit the earth in only one place, but the U.S. Weather Bureau at Raleigh discounted that.

The bureau said no severe storms had been reported in the state and that atmospheric conditions in the Lumberton area were not right for a tornado.

Authorities said they did not believe the barn could have been destroyed by an explosion such as dynamite because all of the destruction was in one direction, upward and to the north.

They called in an explosives expert to examine the scene where only the foundation of the barn remained. Parts of its tin roof were found 25 feet from the ground in a tree about 50 yards northwest of the foundation. All other wreckage was found 20 to 100 yards north of the foundation.

Cecil Davis, who lives nearby, said he heard a "tremendous roaring noise," then a sound like a muffled explosion and saw sparks flying from a power line hit by pieces of tin.

The Wallowa (Oregon) *Record* of April 14th gave an excellent account of a blue light seen by several people. This blue-light type UFO is definitely new in the UFO field. It has been seen very few times. In one or two localities it has been seen several times in the same general area, however. We are beginning to associate kelly-green with fireballs; orange and yellow glow with round objects about the apparent size of the moon; and a mixture of green, white and red lights with high-speed saucers and cigar-shaped ships. The data accumulated thus far allows for such general classifications. The blue lights, however, are far too rare, as yet, to provide much basis for classification. It is urgently requested that everyone report, to your editor, any and all sightings of such lights (and of *everything!*) so that next year's *Annual* can be more personal and can include the largest number of sightings and personal accounts possible.

BLUE LIGHT SEEN BY THREE LOCAL PEOPLE ON MONDAY

"It was very interesting and I wasn't a bit scared."

That is the way Roy Leverenz of Lower Valley described his feelings Monday evening as he witnessed an aerial display of light which he describes quite unlike any of the flying saucer phenomenon reported the past several years.

The object was a bright blue light, quite large, quite low down and quite near. Mr. Leverenz saw it for several seconds, watched it drift slowly and disappear into the dusk at 7 o'clock. Had the strange light occurred after dark he believes it would have lit up a large area.

Mr. Leverenz took especially close note of the direction in which it stood from where he was watching it. He could see the mountains beyond it, so he knew it must be within the valley, perhaps as close as six or eight miles. It was almost due south from the Leverenz home, a little west of south.

He described the sight as being about the size of an average room. It was round, or somewhat oval in shape. There seemed to be something resembling smoke, apparently coming from the object.

During the few seconds Roy was watching it, a smaller bright blue light dropped off the bottom and glowed separately for an instant. Roy would say that if the main light were the size of a baseball, the small light would be the size of a grain of wheat.

(Ed.: The account tells, too, of the same sighting by two others in the area, at the same area and at the same time. Their descriptions tallied to perfection.)

The following clipping shows one of the typically erratic paths taken by some types of UFO. The object made a swoop down and then up, sort of the shape of a festoon, then made an abrupt turn of more than 90 degrees. Motion of this type is not "natural," for bodies moving freely under the unmodified laws of nature.

The account was in the *Shelton Mason Co. Journal* (Shelton, Washington) April 14:

SHOWS STRANGE OBJECT'S PATH

Route of the mysterious object she witnessed in the sky late Tuesday of last week is pointed out by Mrs. D. A. Smith, Mt. View housewife. Her report of a large, brilliant blue-white body streaking westward followed several in New Mexico telling of similar strange bodies, possibly fireballs. Mrs. Smith drew the line taken by the fast moving body, showing how it started to make a circle then shot downward, behind trees and out of sight. Photo shows her seated before front room window through which she glimpsed the object.

(Ed.: A photograph showed the path sketched on a large sheet of paper, the sighter pointing the line drawn to indicate the path of the UFO.)

In the cartoon called "Scott's Scrap Book" appearing in the Harrisonburg (Virginia) *Daily News-Record,* April 15th, there is a description of a comet. It says: "A comet is said to be a 'dirty iceberg' of space—a mass of frozen water, ammonia, methane, and similar substances in which are imbedded iron, calcium, chromium, nickel, sodium, aluminum, manganese and magnesium."

Now, if comets *do* contain such an assortment of debris, why are astronomers so loath to accept that ice and other volatile materials fall from the sky? Why do they deny space origin to everything but their pet items of iron, nickel, or stone meteorites? And why did it take hundreds of years to bring them to admit even those massive materials as coming from space?

The Long Beach (California) *Independent* is one of the newspapers that tries to be fair minded about UFO. In its April 16th edition, it carried a long feature regarding mentions of Flying Saucers in the Bible, written by Elise Emery, Staff Religion Editor. Of especial importance and interest was the forecast from the second chapter and thirteenth verse of the seventh Book of Moses, saying that "In the slow passage of the eons of years, the works of the world shall be governed by the inhabitants of Marsalia who shall bring peace for a thousand years to a troubled world, thus ending wars and rumors of wars."

We shall not publish, here, the entire article. It was lengthy and detailed, but it would serve no real purpose at this time, particularly in view of your editor's own research into this most fascinating aspect of UFOlogy which has hitherto been totally neglected.

One or two passages are of titivating interest, and Dr. Paul A. Hunt was quoted as saying:

"They (Flying Saucers) know all about us and the petty things we go to war about. Sightings have been reported from all over the world, but are tremendously increased during wartime when cannonading, artillery fire and barrages are under way. The space people don't like war and bloodshed."

"They have been watching us from ancient times and if they meant us harm would have taken action before now. In South American and in the Ankor Vat ruins in Cambodia we have evidence of ancient civilizations. It is possible the space creatures settled here, then abandoned earth."

Quoting provocative passages from the Bible, editor Emery included the following interesting items:

II Kings, 2:11 And it came to pass, there appeared a chariot of fire, and horses of fire, and parted them both asunder; and Elijah went up by a whirlwind into heaven.

Psalms, 18:10 And he rode upon a cherub and did fly; yea, he did fly upon the wings of the wind.

We shall all be hearing more about UFO and the Bible!

Of late—the last few months or years—there has been a great deal of to-do about some scientists, like Drs. Urey and Shapley, saying that statistically there is every probability that there are billions of inhabited planets in the known universe. There is nothing new about such assertions. Some current writers are making much of these statements, inferring that this is something new in astronomical concepts. Your editor can assure you, from perusing hundreds of dusty tomes in the Library ot Congress, in Washington, D.C., that astronomers have been saying this for at least the last one hundred years! However, it must also be admitted that they were strongly opposed by entrenched religion, and by a large percentage of their own kind who simply refused to open their eyes to the possibility of *any* intelligent race but Man—anywhere, anytime.

The following item, from the Washington (D.C.) *Post and Times-Herald,* April 19th, quotes Dr. Urey as saying that "the Earth is unique, *so far as we know,* in having a great free oxygen supply." (The italics are ours)

What was omitted was the information that we don't know enough about any other planet, particularly in the billions of systems outside our own solar system, to even speculate whether or not they have oxygen. The same statistical reasons which postulate the possibility of intelligence in other systems would lead to the conclusion that there are about an equal number of planets with oxygen. No valid reason can be conjured up to oppose this assumption.

LIFE ELSEWHERE PROBABLE—UREY

Dr. Harold C. Urey, head of the University of Chicago's Institute for Nuclear Studies, said today it is "exceedingly probable" that there is other life in the universe more intelligent than ours.

He said the earth is unique so far as we know in having a great free oxygen supply on which life depends. But he said the absence of oxygen would not necessarily mean the absence of life, explaining: "There are animals and plants on this earth which live without oxygen."

(Ed.: Dr. Urey might also have said that there is every possibility that a living and intelligent race could be based on compounds of silicon, under conceivable planetary conditions, as opposed to our own dependence on carbon. The two elements have several items of similarity.)

Unexplained aerial explosions, although recorded for generations, seem to be currently on the increase. They are not confined to any special location in the U.S.A. We only get a few reports from overseas, but there seem to be some recorded in England and at the antipodes in Australia and New Zealand.

The United Press carried, on April the 20th, a story which was carried by many leading papers throughout the nation:

EXPLOSION JARS PART OF STATE

A sharp explosion, preceded by a brilliant blue-white flash in the heavens, jarred parts of North Carolina today.

Scientists and weather observers believed the blast occurred as a meteor from outer space that entered the earth's atmosphere. Apparently no particles from the explosion hit the earth.

Some observers reported a second explosion shortly after the first.

The flash illuminated the skies from Virginia to Florida and was visible to airline pilots as far west as Cheleston, West Virginia, and Bristol, Tenn., and as far south as Jacksonville, Fla.

Authorities at Greensboro-High Point and in nearby Burlington reported the explosion rattled windows and jarred homes.

Police switchboards were flooded with calls. At Burlington, desk Sgt. Johnny Dupree said the first call was received at 2:08 a.m. EST.

Scientists said a meteor entering the earth's atmosphere begins to burn at a height of about 75 miles above the ground as its downward speed compresses the air before it. It glows and burns rapidly in its descent at a speed of about 21 miles per second.

A. F. Jenzano, manager of Morehead Planetarium at Chapel Hill said a meteor disintegrating might cause a loud explosion and that it probably would have disintegrated about 40 miles above the earth's surface.

Residents here and in Burlington reported to police that they were awakened by a "loud cracking" explosion and the sound was such that it rocked their houses.

Ripley's "Believe It Or Not" in the Washington (D.C.) *Post and Times-Herald* of April 20th, shows a drawing of some very peculiarly shaped stone houses. It is said that four thousand of them were constructed in Sardinia, without cement of any kind, and that they are at least 2600 years old and still in excellent condition.

There are two observations of interest here:

First, stonework put together without cement is not uncommon *in structures whose age is definitely more than 2000 years.* Witness the Pyramids, Sacsaguaman in Peru, the platforms of Easter Island, the megalithic structures of Baalbek, etc., and there is no doubt about the existence of an archaic civilization of worldwide scope which built structures of this nature.

Second, these houses bear a remarkable resemblance to many descriptions of UFO sightings; i.e., they have a cupola on top and a flaring, bell-like bottom. They are, in other words, "flying saucer houses!"

At this point in April, we find another hint of the government's thinking, and perhaps its progress towards saucer construction. The Philadelphia (Pennsylvania) *Inquirer,* ever on the alert to pick up morsels of information relating to space flight and similar subjects, reported the following on April 21st from a conference of engineers:

FLYING SAUCERS ON ORDER

Opinions expressed by military authorities at the spring meeting of the American Society of Mechanical Engineers in Baltimore that "flying saucers" must be developed if the United States is to have first rate air defense shows that the public rumor can sometimes be as far ahead of progress as a Jules Verne yarn.

For if flying saucers don't exist already, as their devotees have so long insisted, it appears that we can now take odds that they—or reasonable facsimiles—soon will. The Navy has revealed its flying washtub, its pogo stick; the British have hooked two jet engines in tandem and have caused them to rise, fly and hover at will—without wings. But this is the first time military men have come right out and described what they are aiming at.

Spokesmen both for the Navy and the Air Force are emphasizing that our fast fighters and bombers should be dispersed over wide areas, impossible so long as they are dependent on a few over-long runways. As it is, the planes (and our runways) might be wiped out in a single blow or two. What the military people want their designers to do is create the "completely integrated spherical aircraft," in which power would be drawn from the engine to provide lift, direction control, acceleration and deceleration, irrespective of speed. In other words—a flying saucer. Moreover, they expect to get it.

So don't scoff any more at people who see flying saucers. They may only be gazing into a crystal ball with remarkably accurate prophetic powers.

On April 24th, the astute and conservative New York *Times* carried a story on Dr. La Paz' attempts to solve the quandary of the continuing fireballs over New Mexico. This is far more than a mere record of more sightings; it points up the serious nature of the fireball problem and, in a sense, would indicate that many informed sources give more credence to these sightings than they would like to have us believe:

FIREBALL SHOWER BEMUSES SAVANT
METEORITE EXPERT INVESTIGATES REPORTS
OF BRIGHT OBJECTS BURSTING IN SOUTHWEST

If anybody ever catches up with the mysterious fireballs that are reported frequently over the Southwest, it's a good bet that Lincoln La Paz won't be far behind.

What are the fireballs? Nobody knows for sure. And nobody wants to know more than Dr. La Paz, who runs, at the University of New Mexico, the only Institute of Meteoritics in the United States.

Dr. La Paz feels that there has been enough documentation of the fireballs to warrant a thorough investigation.

This spring brought a new rash of the reports, which over a period of years have been made by ranchers, bus drivers, airline pilots, state troopers and others.

During the week beginning April 3, five fireballs were reported in New Mexico and two in Northern California. April 5 brought many reports, but Dr. La Paz said it was finally concluded that only three objects were involved. This, he said, was a record.

Descriptions vary so widely that they could be applied to almost anything from an exploding star to a runaway traffic light.

They come by day and by night. Most often the fireballs are reported at night as yellow-green. But various other colors including white, blue and red, creep into the descriptions.

During the April 3 week, for example:

Three men working on a derrick near Oil Center, N.M., reported an object which appeared to be about twelve inches across exploded soundlessly only a few feet away. They found no fragments, but an airline pilot who reported seeing apparently the same object said it "definitely" exploded.

Four Albuquerque residents said they had seen an object streak across the evening sky and disintegrate; one witness described it "as big as a street light."

Tower crewmen at Oakland (California) International Airport reported an unidentified object so bright that a pilot thought it was a flare from another plane.

Near Hobbs, N.M., a housewife reported a fireball burst, and in the Tularosa basin of south-central New Mexico an Air Force sergeant reported seeing a yellow fireball with a red trail, going down fast.

Dr. La Paz has found it hard to apply the hard, cold logic of mathematics, in which he holds a doctorate of philosophy, in seeking to track down the reports.

"There is no definite way to measure the size of the fireballs," he says. "There's nothing to compare them with side by side, the distance they are from the observer is unknown and no remains of any have been found."

One theory is that the fireballs are a form of meteorites, but Dr. La Paz says he's sure they're not normal meteorites because they are not accompanied by sound.

"If you saw a falling meteorite the size of most of these fireballs the noise would scare you to death," he says. "And meteorite falls are a long way apart. You don't have showers of them!"

He says he has no definite theory as to what the fireballs are.

Air Force planes have occasionally been sent to search areas where fireballs were reported. So far they have found nothing, but a spokesman at Biggs Air Force Base, El Paso, Texas, says the matter "is by no means closed."

That he found no trace of the objects was particularly frustrating, for Dr. La Paz collects fragments from orthodox meteorites and ships them to various scientific organizations.

He dates his preoccupation with such matters all the way back to his boyhood, when a meteorite exploded over his home in Wichita, Kansas.

The British Government made a study of UFO and Saucers similar to our own "Project Bluebook." The following article, from the London (England) *Sunday Dispatch*, April 24, indicated how it was handled.

Your editor does not feel that a comment should be necessary. This strange situation speaks for itself:

FLYING SAUCERS REPORT IS KEPT SECRET

Air Ministry chiefs have been shown a full report of the R.A.F.'s five year probe into Flying Saucers. To the great question, "Do Flying Saucers exist?" the answer is *understood* (Ed.: Italics mine) to be "No." But the public are not to know the details.

Ten weeks ago the *Sunday Dispatch* knew about this report and pressed for publication in the public interest. Yesterday the Air Ministry stated that a senior officer had ordered that the report is *never to be made public*. (Ed.: Again, the italics are mine)

Fear of scepticism is one of the reasons that induced the air-marshals to have the report filed away. They feel that the findings cannot be explained without revealing top-secret facts and that without a full explanation there would be a nation-wide controversy over the truth of the report.

On April 29, the Miami (Florida) *Herald* carried an INS report from Chicago about the United States Government having already launched an artificial satellite. This may well have been "planted" by the government publicity offices as a part of the studied build-up towards the satellite announcement which came later in the year. It may also have been carefully directed towards the Soviet Union in an effort to establish priority of announcement.

U.S. JET 'SATELLITE' SPEEDING AROUND WORLD AT 16,000 M.P.H.?

A magazine suggested the United States has launched an artificial satellite which is now hurtling through space at the rate of 16,000 miles an hour.

The magazine stated the man-made satellite may be an experimental "space platform" circling the earth on its own momentum some 800 miles out in space.

Popular Science, in its May issue, declared "reports have reached

F

us persistently from independent sources that they even took place months ago, possibly at the Banana river rocket range in Florida."

At the rate of speed estimated in the magazine, the satellite would be spiraling around the earth 13 times a day, or once every one hour and 51 minutes.

The magazine offered these points in making its case:

1. The late Secretary of Defense James Forrestal announced the United States was conducting satellite rocket tests in 1948.

2. Experts say "a manned satellite could be launched into space within 10 years, a rocket to the moon in a not much longer time."

3. A rocket "on the loose" today would be the final stage of a "multiple-step rocket fired experimentally—the implication is that this was an experiment that worked too well."

The magazine also suggested that an atomic warhead missile could be put on an orbit circling the earth under control of coded radio signals which would pinpoint it at a given time on a given target.

April, therefore, has given UFOlogists much food for thought!

MAY

In the May 1, 1955 issue of the Toledo (Ohio) *Blade,* there is a longish article by Professor Charles A. Maney, head of the department of Physics at Defiance College. Dr. Maney has been studying UFO for years and, for a scientist, is well versed in the subject of UFOlogy. This brief but general account will serve to introduce newcomers to the subject. Much as we hate to admit it, there may still be a few underprivileged folk who haven't been inculcated with the facts of life about UFO's. We think this article is a fitting way to start the month of May:

SCIENTIST FINDS SOME "SAUCER" REPORTS
STILL TO BE SATISFACTORILY EXPLAINED:
MYSTERY YET CLINGS TO AERIAL OBJECTS
WIDELY SIGHTED OVER EIGHT-YEAR PERIOD

The subject of flying saucers has from time to time engaged the attention of the American public since the summer of 1947. On

June 24, of that year, a businessman, Kenneth Arnold, flying in his private plane over the Cascade Mountains in the state of Washington, reported observing a chain of nine disc-shaped objects flying with tremendous speed.

The objects sailed over the peaks in a manner resembling the skipping of flat stones thrown across the surface of a pond. Mr. Arnold described the unidentified objects as "flying saucers." The story of his fantastic experience captured the fancy of the public. Since that date literally thousands of reports of strange aerial phenomena from all parts of the world have been reported by the press from week to week.

It would take volumes to describe in detail all the phenomena said to have been observed in the skies over this planet during the past eight years. There are historical records going back into the remote past giving isolated instances of strange unexplainable aerial occurrences. But starting in 1947, the number of such reports suddenly increased a thousandfold.

In spite of all the material available to the serious student of these phenomena, very little is definitely known. Controversy still rages between those who doubt the reality of these sightings and those who declare that they are definitely what they appear to be, actual fast-moving material objects seemingly intelligently manoeuvered.

The Air Force Technical Intelligence Center at Wright-Patterson Field, Dayton, maintains a continuing investigation of such reports. The Department of the Air Force recently issued a statement on this subject which can probably best be summarized as follows:

"The Air Force would like to state that no evidence has been received which would tend to indicate that the United States is being observed by machines from outer space or a foreign government. No object or particle of an unknown substance has been received and no photographs of detail have been produced."

Only one American institution of higher learning has sponsored research in this field. Ohio Northern University undertook such a study in August, 1952, under leadership of a former dean of that institution, Dr. Warren Hichman. The project was closed two years later voluntarily because of inability of those in charge of the study to obtain sufficient cooperation from other agencies elsewhere similarly engaged, to share information.

Quoting from a report of this university: "Project A is closing merely because we possess no means of obtaining further information with which to make a study." The work at Ohio Northern did lead, however, to the statement of a definite conclusion arrived at by the group in charge. This reads in part as follows: ". . . a sizeable fraction of the sightings throughout the country were sightings made of material objects . . . not standard aircraft . . . possessing ability to manoeuver at extremely high speeds."

Very few American scientists have as yet committed themselves publicly as believing that these unidentified flying objects actually do exist, although a number have expressed doubt as to the reality of the phenomena. In this connection it might be interesting to note an extract quoted from a directive issued by an Air Force officer a short time ago: "At this time we are experiencing renewed reporting of unidentified flying objects by ground observer personnel. This information is invaluable to the Air Force in evaluating the situations surrounding the sightings of flying objects."

One prominent aeronautical specialist expressing himself on this topic is Major Donald Keyhoe, former chief of information for the Aeronautics Branch, Department of Commerce, author of several books on the subject. Major Keyhoe states positively his belief that these objects originate from outer space.

Dr. Maurice A. Diot, a leading aerodynamicist in the United States and a prominent mathematical physicist, is quoted by *Life* Magazine as declaring: "The least improbable explanation is that these things are artificial and controlled . . . My opinion for some time has been that they have an extra-terrestrial origin."

A few aeronautical engineers of other nations have definitely given expression to their convictions on this subject. These include Dr. Walther Riedel, now in the employ of the United States Government, formerly chief designer at the German rocketry laboratory at Peenemunde, who says: "I am completely convinced that they (flying saucers) have an out-of-world basis."

The *American Weekly* of October 24, 1954, quotes Professor Hermann Oberth of Germany, an internationally known authority on guided missiles and whose technical writings were said to be of vital importance in the development of Germany's famous V-2 rocket, who argues: "It is my thesis that flying saucers are real and that they are space ships from another solar system."

The London *Sunday Dispatch* quotes British Air Chief Marshal Lord Dowding, commander-in-chief of the Royal Air Force and one of Britain's foremost aviation experts as saying: "I have never seen a flying saucer, and yet I believe that they exist."

The material presented in this article covers one type of these strange occurrences which recently have attracted quite a bit of attention among those interested in the study of the subject. One of the most interesting happenings took place not long ago in Ohio.

This occurred last October 22, some fifteen miles northwest of Columbus, Ohio. The pupils of Jerome Elementary School had been granted an extra recess that afternoon as a reward for good behavior. As described by one of the two teachers of the school, Mrs. George W. Dittmer, "It was one of those glorious warm fall days and the whole sky was a clear blue."

The attention of the children became directed toward a strange object in the sky circling high above the school. The object was dazzling bright and ciger-shaped. The children watched the object a while before thinking to call their principal, R. R. Warrick. In response to their shouts Mr. Warrick came out to the fire escape in time to observe the object at that moment hanging high and motionless in the sky. Then the ship made off at tremendous speed, disappearing from view rapidly.

Mr. Warrick called Mrs. Dittmer, who at once came out on the fire escape too late to observe the object but in time to witness a most beautiful scene. For, as the object darted away there appeared another strange sight. The air as high and far around as the teachers and children could see was filled with "the most beautiful soft white-looking tufts of cotton slowly floating to the ground." Mr. Warrick said it was almost at once as the object disappeared that this material began to show in the sky. For about 45 minutes they watched this fibrous material floating downward. The children brought up pieces of it to the fire escape for Mr. Warrick and Mrs. Dittmer to examine. In the words of Mrs. Dittmer "the substance had long fibres very much as if someone had taken strands of 'angel hair' and pushed some in bunches toward the middle or end, leaving a trail of fibres attached to it. It was very fine and soft to touch. It did not stick to our hands, but when we held two ends and pulled, it stretched without tearing. Where it stretched it had a shiny appearance. The part we held between our fingers very quickly seemed to go to nothing."

"However, we could roll it between our fingers into a very, very tiny ball. In a short while our hands had a green stain on them. I soon washed my hands in warm water and the stain rinsed off quickly. Mr. Warrick said he was leaving his on his hands to see what happened. He later said his hands became clammy and finally the color disappeared of its own accord."

Mrs. Dittmer goes on to say, "When we left school, we noticed it clinging to the grass, flagpole and some on the cars. I believe the thing that impressed me even further was what we saw as we drove the three miles to the Columbus road. The telephone wires were completely woven shut, as if hands had carefully spread 'angel hair' out very evenly. Not only this, but the telephone wires were connected to the electric wires on the other side of the road, so that it was like a canopy over the road for three miles. No more seemed to be coming down by this time."

One of the issues of *Flying Saucer Review* (Seattle) contains a staff report on a saucer sighting. It is short, but it is first hand reporting:

GRAFENWOHR, GERMANY

"On Sunday, May 1, 1955, I saw a flying saucer. I observed this UFO for about ten minutes. At first I saw a bright light almost due north at about five hundred feet up. If you would hold your head at arm's length, three fingers span would just cover it.

"The only form that I could observe was spherical. It made no noise that I could hear and had no tail or exhaust that was visible to me. The UFO made four horizontal passes at a slow (100 m.p.h.) speed. It hovered occasionally, finally it slowly started up in a northeast direction. It picked up speed and soon was traveling up and away from me at a great speed. Soon it looked like a star. However, if you observed closely you could see it getting smaller and smaller and traveling in a very slight, almost minute, spiraling motion. If it ever changed color from its bright white, I did not observe it.

"I have two reliable witnesses beside myself, and they were not believers in UFO's. They are not talking about it. It seems as though they do not want to believe what they saw. But they did see it.

"There is no chance of it being an airplane or a helicopter because we are only a few miles from the Russian sector and there can be no flying at night over this area.

"This all happened about one hour after sunset. The town of Grafenwohr is not too far from Weiden, a larger town than Grafenwohr. I can say now that I believe there are UFO's."

There have been a few sightings on Long Island, and one or two very puzzling disappearances and crashes of planes. Here is a small report from the Garden City (Long Island) *Newsday*, May 2, 1955:

FLYING SAUCER SIGHTED?

Glen Cove—Here's a little item of interest to all those flying saucer fans.

At noon, on April 27, I saw what I believe to have been an extra-terrestrial flying machine. While walking along West Glen Street I suddenly noticed a strange, green object, circling above Glen Cove firehouse tower.

As I came nearer, I saw that the thing was oval in shape, and had peculiar appendages around it. It was completely silent. After a few seconds, the crab-like machine ceased manoeuvering, and flew off in the direction of Long Island Sound.—Marion P. Kuczabinski.

On Tuesday, May 3, 1955, two members of the staff of the Bismarck (N.D.) *Tribune*, each with his wife, made separate and independent reports of sighting a UFO. It was moving westward over Bismarck about 8:45 p.m. Monday night. Neither the Air

Force filter center at Bismarck, nor the local radar station had any other reports of the object. No planes were known to be in the area, and the radar revealed nothing . . . it was a bright light, apparently circular in shape, and traveling at a high rate of speed a little north of west. In a matter of seconds it vanished in a cloudbank near the horizon. There was no sound at all. The altitude was estimated at less than five thousand feet, and the speed at least that of the fastest jet plane.

The attempt to analyze the data on fireballs continued through May, according to an AP report from Albuquerque, New Mexico, dated May 12. This onslaught of green fireballs continues to baffle the best meteoritic specialists available to us. Dr. La Paz brings a great experience to bear, but as he says, these green fireballs are a new phenomenon. We agree that the matter is not closed.

The Hartford (Connecticut) *Times*, May 13, contains a feature story by Edwin M. Kent, about a local UFO sighting. The account is fairly detailed and we believe that the data is worthwhile:

MYSTERY FLYING OBJECT REPORTED IN TERRYVILLE

The sighting of an unidentified flying object by three Terryville residents Wednesday night is being studied today by the Air Technical Intelligence Center, Wright-Patterson Field, Dayton, Ohio.

This was disclosed by Major P. C. Hunner, director of intelligence, Roslyn, L.I., Air Force Base, base of operations for the 26th Division of the Eastern Air Defence Force, which covers this area.

Major John W. Anderson, commanding officer of the Air Defence Filter Center, New Haven, said that a check through "routine" channels failed to disclose the nature of the object sighted.

Although official sources remained otherwise close mouthed about the affair, Mrs. Robert A. Nelson of Terryville, one of the people who saw it, said she was told after reporting the incident, that planes and radar were to be used Wednesday night in an effort to track the object.

The other witnesses were Mrs. Nelson's husband, owner of a Bristol service station, and her father, August D'Andrea, Farmington tailor.

"My husband and I first noticed the object when we were out walking, about 9:45 p.m. Wednesday," said Mrs. Nelson. "It looked like a regular star until we saw it move.

"We were a little frightened because it looked like a planet that had suddenly gone crazy. It seemed to be large, like Venus, and it had a definite bluish caste to it. It moved fast and in a very funny pattern.

"First it went straight up and then it came down in an arc. It set there a few seconds and then it went up at an angle and about double the distance it did the first time. Then it moved almost straight to one side and then straight down.

"That was about 10:00 p.m. We didn't notice any movement after that until close to midnight, although there was a period of perhaps half an hour when we didn't watch.

"Twice when planes approached it became agitated and moved in irregular patterns. Then about midnight a third plane approached. This thing that was sitting there made a huge arc across the sky in the direction of the plane. It seemed to move a tremendous distance but, of course, it was difficult to judge height and distance and speed."

She added, "The object seemed to be perfectly round. Once, just before it made the big arc in the sky toward the plane, it seemed to flip over on its side. Then it looked flat."

Reuters reported from Helsinki that there was a sizeable fall of worms at the Finnish town of Kinomaeki.

Two self-nominated scientists made a farce of a TV discussion May 16, 1955. What was billed as a sensible serious panel discussion turned into a childish riot based on some dogmatic assinities.

The May 17, 1955 issue of the Marshall (Michigan) *Chronicle* details a sighting of a flying saucer. Sightings are less numerous in this area than elsewhere:

FLYING SAUCER REPORTS BACK IN THE NEWS

"Did you see an object resembling a flying saucer, Monday, May 17, 1955?"

L. J. "Jake" Shreve of Marengo township, sighted a mysterious object at 8:30 a.m. that morning and he wonders whether any other persons in this area did.

While driving on the Townline Road, north of Marshall, one and one-half miles east of U.S. 27, he heard a whistling sound. Looking out of his car window, he spotted a sparkling, bright object, "five hundred to a thousand feet" in the air. He states, "It was very pretty, and sparkled like a morning star; however, it was so big, that I realized it couldn't be a star."

He sighted the object for from three to five seconds, and then it turned and "shot to the left angle through the air."

He said it was out of sight in less than a second. He estimated the object was from 3½-4 feet in size. Shreve stated "I held back reporting this, thinking some others might have seen it and said something. However, now I'd just like to know whether anyone else saw the object."

An engineer in Canada takes UFO seriously, and recently told the Canadian Parliament some of his theories and ideas regarding the possibility of UFO's causing radio interference and other phenomena. Since his long experience has convinced him that UFO are thoroughly real we believe his opinions worth reading. The report was in the Ottawa (Ontario) *Journal*, May 18, 1955, as follows:

RADIO MP'S STARTLED BY EXPERT WITNESS

With a straight face, an expert witness yesterday told the Commons Radio Committee that while flying saucers were not accountable for television interference they could be blamed "for a lot of other things."

The expert witness was William B. Smith, the engineer-in-charge of the Broadcast and Measurement Section of the Telecommunications Division of the Department of Transport, and he came before the committee to explain some of the technological complications of radio and television.

But flying saucers were still close to his heart, and he still believed, as he has for some years, that there are such things.

A tall, dark and intense-eyed young man with an iron-grey brush-cut, he was giving the committee the technical explanation for the interference aircraft set up in telecasting when Jean Richard, Liberal MP for East Ottawa broke in to ask: "Aren't you the Smith who operated the Transport Department's Flying Saucer Sighting Station at Shirley Bay?"

"That's right."

Mr. Richard hesitated a moment, then asked if Flying Saucers accounted for some of the interference that fluttered across television screens.

"No," replied Mr. Smith evenly, "you can't blame flying saucers for TV interference, but you can for a lot of other things."

Mr. Richard neglected to follow up the intriguing possibilities this answer might have offered.

The resulting silence was broken in a few seconds by Donald Fleming, Conservative MP for Toronto-Eglinton, who wanted to know why Mr. Smith had been "watching flying saucers."

The Saucer Sighting Station had been operated by Transport from August, 1953 to the late summer of 1954 "to gain knowledge."

Mr. Fleming wanted to know why it had been closed after only a year.

"We were getting nowhere," reported Mr. Smith.

George D. Weaver, Liberal MP for Churchill, attempted to follow up the inquiry, but Committee Chairman Dr. Pierre Gauthier Liberal MP for Portneuf, ruled him out of order.

The Commons Radio Committee had been assigned the job of looking into CBC radio and television enterprises, he reminded, not to conduct an inquiry into the Transport Department's investigation of flying saucers.

While the committee chairman had ruled out flying saucers, Mr. Smith was quite willing to discuss them with anybody who had the interest and took the trouble to ask.

He still "believed."

"I am convinced there are flying saucers," he said as the Committee rose for the day, "but I'm in the unhappy position of the police chief who knows who robbed the bank but can't prove it in court."

And when he had told the committee the saucer research had been "getting nowhere" he had been speaking for the Transport Department, not for himself.

Personally, he had felt further investigation was imperative since there had been one morning when the instruments at the Shirley Bay station had produced what Mr. Smith termed a "wiggle." This could be explained by no known atmospheric phenomenon.

"I didn't know then what caused that strange and fascinating instrumentation," he recounted, "and I don't know now . . . but the possibilities are interesting."

After a year's operation he had advised the Transport Department that the research should be full and complete with all possible facilities made available, or it should be dropped altogether.

"There was the choice to go all out or get out," he said, "and the department decided that the investment in terms of personnel, laboratory facilities and equipment would not be warranted, particularly in the light of the opinion that a great many people held flying saucers in ridicule."

Still with a straight face, this telecommunications engineer, who enjoyed the confidence of former Transport Minister Chervier, confided as he left the committee hearing that while he "believed" there were flying saucers, he didn't know precisely what they were. They could be space vehicles, he said, and then again they might only be some unknown type of "celestial fireball."

The committee after shyly asking a few more shy questions of Mr. Smith returned to the more familiar subjects of television and radio operating licences and the procurements of these highly prized assets.

But before they had finished with him, the committee got back to the question of aircraft and TV interference.

The interference, explained Mr. Smith, was first set up by the TV transmision itself. Some TV waves rippling out from the transmitter strike passing aircraft and are bounced back to the transmitter and so out on the television signal to the viewers' screens.

Here is another California case reported by C.R.I.F.O.

A CLASSICAL CASE OF CONTRADICTORY CLAPTRAP

(Case 88, Los Angeles area, May 1955) A covey of jets returned to Norton AFB after a "fruitless search" for three silvery disc-shaped objects that entertained numerous people over a wide area, including Mt. Wilson, between 7:15 and 8:15 p.m. Lieutenant John Elliot of the Pasadena Police, who went to investigate after phone calls began pouring in, said he could see the objects "changing formation as if playing tag in the sky." Another witness said the objects seemed to be "leaping over each other." In Montrose, the Sheriff Station's deputies reported seeing the objects clearly and said that from Montrose they appeared to be over the La Canada area and very high. Most observers, however, reported the objects as "silver and disc-shaped."

Ohio manages to keep pace pretty well with California and Florida in the number of sightings of UFO reported. The Elyria *Chronicle-Telegram* of May 19, contains a good report:

"FLYING OBJECT" STILL IS MYSTERY

A report on an "unknown flying object" otherwise known as a flying saucer, came to light last night at a meeting of the Elyria Ground Observer Post.

This saucer looked like an airplane—but not enough to satisfy the two watchers who spotted it Friday afternoon, May 6, Mrs. Dorothy Parsch, 120 Lafayette Street, a veteran observer, and Mrs. Kathleen Turner of 119½ W. Bridge Street.

The silver-grey object streaked across the sky from east to west, disappearing in the sun's rays, five times between 1:56 and 3:00 p.m. Always it appeared just after a multimotor jet or another multimotor airplane had disappeared from view although it did not necessarily follow the route of the other craft.

Speed, and the fact that both women looked at the object without the aid of binoculars, probably accounted for a variation in their descriptions, post officials said. Mrs. Parsch said it resembled a very squatty airplane with especially squat wings and that it appeared to have numerous propellors. Mrs. Turner thought its projections were more like antennae. She described the object as "egg-shaped."

Mrs. Parsch believed the object was about 4,000 feet above ground, but Air Force officials, hearing her description thought the altitude was more likely twice that. Reports of unknown flying objects were received at Canton from two other GOC posts about the same time. Elton Becker, supervisor of the local post, said he understood that radar facilities were unable to pick up the object and, as a result, it was impossible to send Youngstown-based Air Force jet planes out on a scramble for it.

Mrs. Parsch said the object whizzed over at such terrific speed that each time the women raised their binoculars to get a better view of it they lost track of it and had to find it again without binoculars. There was no sound or smoke from the object, according to Mrs. Parsch.

Jackson, Michigan, was the locale of a sighting by a man who patiently kept up a persistent watch from 1947 to 1955. The Jackson *Citizen-Patriot*, May 20, 1955, published the story:

SALESMAN SEES FLYING SAUCER OVER JACKSON

John C. Potter, 33, of Lansing, makes a living selling door to door: and he covers Jackson.

But he keeps an eye peeled for other things, too, when he's making his rounds. He has been on the lookout for flying saucers since 1947. "I take a lot of kidding about it," he says, "and now I'm going to get some more of it, I suppose."

He says he saw a flying saucer over Jackson Wednesday.

One of his women customers, in whose Hill Street backyard he was standing at the time, backs up his observation. "This thing was very high up and came from the northeast, from the direction of the prison," Mr. Potter says.

It was visible for about thirty seconds, he says, and was soundless and had no vapor trail.

According to the Lansing man, the object "was shining white, but was more like a light than a reflection." He said that when it slanted on its side, he observed that it was elliptical in shape.

"I'm sure it wasn't a jet airplane, because it had no tail or wings at all," Mr. Potter says.

This phenomenon, at Freeport, New York, was reported by the Washington *Post and Times-Herald,* May 20, 1955. Any astronomer or meteoritics expert can tell you this is a completely abnormal event. Meteors just do not come down and set fire to things, as reported in this case:

FIREBALLS RAIN DOWN ON CITY

A storm of miniature fireballs rained down on the city today, setting fire to three parked cars and four boats in a canal.

Here is another piece from *Two Worlds* (May 21) and this time it is about a world-famous British astronomer: Dr. H. P. Wilkins (not to be confused with author H. T. Wilkins).

Dr. Wilkins made a tour of the United States. The gist of this article is that Dr. Wilkins actually saw a UFO while in flight in a commercial airplane in this country. The account is of especial interest because of Dr. Wilkins' views regarding life and intelligent activity on the moon. He comes as near as a conventional scientist dares to in saying that there is intelligent activity on the moon, in his excellent book, *Our Moon.* All serious students of UFOlogy would do well indeed to get a copy of this book from the library and read it carefully. It is well-written in a popular and non-technical style. Here is the article:

The latest flying saucer story comes from one of Britain's leading astronomers. He is Dr. H. P. Wilkins, director of the British Astronomical Association Lunar Section.

In his latest book, *Mysteries of Time and Space,* he says he was a firm unbeliever in flying saucer stories until he took a flight from West Virginia to Georgia in June of last year. (1954)

His attention was caught by "two brilliant, oval, sharp-edged objects hovering apparently suspended or hovering above the tops of two masses of clouds." They were of a yellow color "like polished brass or gold, and looked exactly like polished metal plates reflecting sunlight." They moved slowly northwards in a direction opposite to which the clouds were moving.

A third similarly-shaped object appeared. This was dull and greyish, "presumably because it was not in the sunshine." Within two minutes the objects had disappeared from view.

He calculated that each must have been nearly five hundred feet across. They were rectangular in shape. Four such objects had been seen in the air over West Virginia within five years.

After studying a large number of reports of sightings, says Dr. Wilkins, and making allowances for practical jokes and "cooked photographs," there was a residue "which may be accepted in the sense that something was undoubtedly seen. The point at issue is what these 'somethings' were."

The C.R.I.F.O. *Orbit* Vol. II, No. 4, passed along the following about another mysteriously disappearing jet plane:

(Case 91, near Madison, Wisconsin, May 22, 1955.) CAA officials at Truax Field said the two F-80 jets left Fort Wayne, Indiana at 2:28 p.m. on a training flight to Duluth, Minnesota. Flying at 35,000 feet at 350 mph, the F-80's entered bad weather. The pilot of one turned back over Janesville and returned safely to Fort Wayne, the other disappeared *without leaving a single clue.* During the extensive search, a fisherman in Lafayette County reported seeing a flash and hearing an explosion, *but nothing was found in that area.*

There were a few really exciting items of UFOlogy which broke into print in 1955; and a good many which didn't because of the "brownout." We believe the one that caused the greatest general stir is the report which appeared in a very large number of U.S. newspapers on or about May 23, cabled from London by Miss Dorothy Kilgallen of the New York *Journal-American.* Miss Kilgallen needs no introduction. Her reputation for authenticity is highly respected. It is difficult to believe that there is anything of fabrication in this story about a crashed saucer in England, which contained "little men." Yet, after the wide release of the story in the United States there was an outright denial by British authorities. Is this denial part of the "conspiracy" so aptly portrayed by Major Donald Keyhoe?

This story touched off a chain reaction in my mind, the results of which can be read in the forthcoming *Expanding Case for the UFO.*

Here is Miss Dorothy Kilgallen's story as it appeared in the *Journal-American,* from the international News Service:

SAUCER REALLY FROM OUTER SPACE

I can report today on a story which is positively spooky, not to mention chilling. British scientists and airmen after examining the wreckage of one mysterious flying ship, are convinced that these strange aerial objects are not optical illusions or Soviet inventions, but are actually flying saucers which originate on another planet.

The source of my information is a British official of cabinet rank who prefers to remain unidentified.

"We believe, on the basis of our inquiries so far, that the saucers were staffed by small men—probably under four feet tall," my informant told me.

"It's frightening but there is no denying the flying saucers come from another planet."

This official quoted scientists as saying a flying ship of this type could not have possibly been constructed on earth. The British government, I learned, is withholding an official report on the "flying saucer" examination at this time, possibly because it does not wish to frighten the public.

When my husband (Richard Kollmer, Broadway producer) and I arrived here for a brief visit, I had no premonition that I would be catapulting myself into the controversy over whether flying saucers are real or imaginary.

In the U.S., all kinds of explanations have been advanced. But no responsible official of the U.S. Air Force has as yet intimated the mysterious flying ships had actually vaulted from outer space.

The interest of all believers and many scoffers was aroused by this release and clippings poured in to all UFO writers, from all over the U.S.A.

Strangely enough, the Kilgallen announcement was accompanied by a front page story about a tremendous UFO actually photographed over the heart of the city of New York. We include, herewith, the complete record as published on May 23rd in the *World-Telegram* (New York):

IT'S THE FLYING SAUCER SEASON AGAIN
SPHERE IS ONE OF THOSE THINGS
TV TECHNICIAN TAKES PICTURES

The flying saucer season, usually as unpredictable as an oboe player's moods, has arrived in New York at last.

So quietly, indeed, did the season arrive—Sunday, May 15, at 4 p.m., if you're interested in making a note of the time—that it might well have gone unnoticed had it not been for the alertness of a young television technician named Warren Siegmond and an attractive French girl, who as it turned out—well, there's no point in going into that.

What happened was simply this: Mr. Siegmond rented an English reflex-type camera for $1.25 on May 13 and bought two rolls of films to make pictures of the attractive French girl, whose name is Jeannine Bouiller and who works for the French Government Tourist Office.

On the Sunday afternoon when the flying saucer season opened they were in Mr. Siegmond's apartment at 7 W. 15th St. when he suddenly said the only decent place to take pictures was on the roof. Up they go. Mr. Siegmond began making pictures of Miss Bouiller, he clicking, she smiling, when she gasped and cried out, at the same time pointing.

There in the skies above the familiar water tanks, grimy roofs and angular structures of the Union Square neighborhood was a spherical object without markings. It moved rapidly. Obviously it was in the hands of a skillful pilot, and a daring one, moreover, since the risks of saucer flying in the Union Square area are so well known. (Apparently familiar with police regulations against low flying, the pilot kept well above the legal limits, indicating to Mr. Siegmond that he was a disciplined flier.)

Mr. Siegmond, himself a well-disciplined young man—he served from 1943 to 1945 as a gunner in an anti-aircraft battalion in England—shifted his camera quickly and began taking pictures. The strange aircraft wheeled, its sharp metallic glitter faded, it became a blur and vanished.

Dazed but gallant, Mr. Siegmond helped Miss Bouiller downstairs and had the film developed at a drugstore. Then he brought the negatives to the World-Telegram and Sun.

The pictures were shown to an Air Force officer familiar with the inquiry into flying saucer reports. "Whatever it was, it was moving," he said cryptically. Moreover, that was all he'd say.

To get a less austere reaction, a W-T & Sun reporter showed the pictures to Mrs. Margaret Rigberg, president of the Flying Saucer News Club, an organization of people who watch the skies for flying saucers.

Mrs. Rigberg runs a little bookshop at 1597 Third Ave. where books on metaphysics, occultism and spiritualism are prominently displayed.

Mrs. Rigberg looked at Mr. Siegmond's pictures and said, "Ah-h-h." Of course, they weren't the first photos of flying ships she has seen. Man over in New Jersey has some; sells them at $1 each.

As the owner of the largest bookstore to deal in flying saucer material, Mrs. Rigberg spoke with authority. Her husband is vice president of the club. Mrs. Rigberg has never seen a flying saucer, probably because she is too busy with her books.

But her husband saw one last month. About 6 in the evening as he was leaving a small eatery where he works as a daytime counterman. (This would place the arrival of the season earlier than May 15, but Mrs. Rigberg didn't care. Let somebody else claim the credit if he wants to.)

This is one case where your editor had an opportunity to talk at length to the sighter and photographer. Warren Siegmond is a fine young man who saw something which he thinks is of value to mankind. He not only saw it, but he had a witness, and he photographed the object.

Siegmond came to my apartment and brought some of his photographs. Fortunately, Siegmond retained a few of his original films which were not turned over to the Press. It is our very great pleasure to reproduce one of these hitherto unpublished photographs in the UFO Annual for 1955. It is with equal pleasure that we extend our thanks and appreciation to Mr. Warren Siegmond for bringing them to us.

I state, unequivocally, that I believe completely in Mr. Siegmond's honesty and sincerity.

The *Western Mail* of Cardiff, Wales, published the following notice of a sighting on May 26, 1955:

WE SAW A FLYING CIGAR, SAY AIRMEN

The crew of a Portuguese Air Lines Skymaster aircraft claimed on landing at London Airport yesterday that they saw a long cigar-like object without wings while flying between Epsom and Dunsfold on their way to London.

The radio officer of the aircraft, J. O. A. O. Almeida, said that the object "was traveling at a terrific speed. In nine years of flying I have never seen anything like it.

"It was long and slim and seemed to be revolving as it flashed under the nose of the aircraft.

"It looked as if it was made of aluminum." The pilot, Captain Durval stated, "I do not know what it was."

Flight-engineer Jose Eliva said, "The object seemed to approach from the port side and pass right under the nose. To me it looked like a silver cigar. There was no smoke-trail coming from it."

An Air Ministry spokesman said, "I can't suggest any explanation."

In the past more than 95 per cent of similar reports had turned out to be attributable to some ordinary object such as airborne meteorological equipment, he said.

Plattsburgh, New York, has had a considerable number of sightings this year. Here is one account which is from the Plattsburgh *Press-Republican,* May 28, 1955. It is a good sighting and the effort of creating a report is well worth while:

"FLYING SAUCERS" PUZZLE OBSERVERS

Most people think Plattsburgh is a pretty dead place at two or three o'clock in the morning.

But the people who man the Ground Observer Corps tower atop the Physicians Hospital roof are anxious to be assigned to the graveyard shift, because that's the time of day when the flying saucers start appearing.

The idea of flying saucers may be silly to some citizens, but the existence of unidentified missiles in area skies is a serious matter to a group of Plattsburgh people who say they have seen the objects.

The picture (accompanying the article) was taken by James Roddy, Radio Station WEAV newscaster, who was one of four people to spot an unidentified object Saturday morning.

"I'm firmly convinced the Air Force knows something exists, but they are not telling the public what is going on," Roddy said. He has seen the strange objects on several occasions and at some instances Air Force jet planes have appeared and buzzed the objects, as though to study or chase them.

However, he said, the Air Force will not even admit that its planes have been out.

The Saturday morning phenomenon was observed by Roddy, Post Supervisor Lester Giverson, local dentist Dr. Alfred Dittmar and Arthur Einhorn, a student at the State University Teachers College at Plattsburgh. The four men were watching for aircraft as part of the Civil Defence program.

Roddy said they thought at first the object was a star. It was bright red, and was first seen over northern Vermont. After a few minutes it began to move and at the same time it changed color from red to a brilliant orange. It moved over Vermont, Roddy reported, across the lake and settled over the Plattsburgh Air Force base.

The observers got an excellent opportunity to see the object which was flat-bottomed with a rounded top. It was thought to be from two hundred to three hundred feet in diameter. When it left the Air Base it went off northwest, moving at from 250 to 300 mph, and disappeared.

Seconds after the object had disappeared into a cloudbank, the viewers said, a jet plane sped after it going in the same northerly direction.

Roddy further thinks he has spotted the mother craft to the discs that have been observed in the area. He was driving along Route 9 last week when he saw a cigar-shaped object circling over Point Au Roche. The object disappeared into cloudbanks occasionally, but fled when an Air Force jet appeared and began to buzz it.

This sight was also observed by Mrs. Arthur Pierce who was a patient in the Physicians Hospital at the time. Roddy is keeping a comprehensive log of the sightings he and others have made.

Here is a report, sent to me by Mr. Aden R. Major, of Dracut, Massachusetts:

Stockholm, May 3, 1955 (AP): Four missing Swedish jet fighter planes were discovered today to have crashed in close formation through the melting ice of Lake Glottern.

An Air Force officer said, "The four planes all fell in a line about twenty yards long."

The Swedish-built aircraft disappeared yesterday soon after their take-off from a base at Norrkoping, fourteen miles south of the lake. Each carried its own pilot.

The Air Force could not explain the accident. The formation had just received and acknowledged permission to pass through clouds that should have sent them upward.

Wreckage on the lake ice showed the planes were in the water below. Divers found more wreckage at the bottom. The lake is in a rugged area of steep mountains and dense woods.

UFOlogy is an infant science. As it stands today it is 90 per cent collecting of data (meaning sightings and observations of all kinds) and ten per cent asking questions. He who proposes dogmatic conclusions is a fool. It seems fitting to close out the eventful month of May with the following editorial from the Augusta (Georgia) *Chronicle*. This editorial is a pleasure to read, after some of the supercilious and specious diatribes one encounters. True, the editor betrays an element of healthy skepticism, but if everybody would take as fairminded an attitude and get down to basic research instead of smirking over the expression, "There ain't no such animal," we would all be a lot happier and we would get this problem solved before the Air Force could say "blackout"!

FLYING SAUCER SEASON?

Is there a reason for flying saucers, just as there is one for polio, or gnats, and heat waves?

One is inclined to think so as one reads again recurring reports of strange things seen in the skies.

From New York City comes the story of the young couple who went to the top of a tall building to take pictures of themselves and came down with photographs of a mysterious object hurtling through the sky over the city.

In London, the crew of a Portuguese airliner reported last week, on arrival from Lisbon, that they had seen a "long cigar-shaped object without wings traveling at a terrific rate of speed" as they approached London.

What are these strange objects in the sky?

The question is plaguing the people everywhere. They are no longer quite able to believe that reports such as the above are based on imagination, or the way sunlight fluctuates, or on weather balloons, or any of the other vague explanations that have been offered.

There is too much detail in the descriptions. One feels also that trained airmen do not usually make mistakes in sky observations.

It remains to be seen how many more of these reports of "flying saucers" will be coming in. Certainly they should not be dismissed as unimportant, merely because the authorities are obliged to admit ignorance about them.

It would be better to speed up watchfulness and work out methods of getting needed information. Knowing more about these strange objects in the sky may mean the difference between safety and disaster for the nation.

JUNE

In spite of the clamp-down by the press, wire services and Air Force, there continued to be a steady, though curtailed, flow of saucer sightings throughout the month of June. There were no announcements as spectacular as the famous Kilgallen story, nor any sightings so well recorded as Siegmond's, but the activity around Plattsburgh, New York, was considerable, and the evidence incontestable. Metcalf's sighting of a UFO sweeping up a jet plane in flight is a remarkable event.

On June 1st, the London (England) *Evening Standard* reported a block of ice falling in a garden at Loughton. Though the article said ". . . believed to have fallen from an airplane. . . ." to the occasional reader who has not been introduced to the vagaries of falling ice, let it be here said that ice has been dropping from the sky for centuries. It is not hailstones. Some localities get more than others, which is indication of selective dumping. Falling ice is one of what is called "fortean" phenomena: that is to say, unexplained physical events. The relationship of falling ice to UFO has been explained and examined in considerable detail in my book *The Case for the UFO*, but this early June report makes it clear that such phenomena are continuing, and since these chunks of ice come in quantities, and come from the sky, and defy ordinary accountings—need we say more?

The June-July issue of *Flying Saucer News*, published by James Moseley, Box 163, Ft. Lee, New Jersey, contained the following readers' comments anent the Navy's "flying platform." These comments serve to clarify further the true nature of the device, which is definitely, it would now appear, not in the UFO field unless it contains a secret lifting mechanism which has been successfully concealed from the public and from operators, which does not seem to be the case.

READERS' COMMENTS ON THE "FLYING PLATFORM"

The Navy's circular "flying platform," revealed on April 11th, deserves attention by Saucer students. A good friend of mine, who visited the Pentagon recently, reports that the Air Force officer in charge of issuing public statements on the UFO "investigation" admitted that he had not known of this Navy device before it was made public! This shows how valueless are the Air Force's denials that the U.S. has any secret devices which the public reports as "saucers."

Another U.S. device which the Air Force knows nothing about, I'll bet, has a code name which paraphrased would be X9-XL-Apple. This craft has an even more fantastic appearance than the circular platform revealed. . . . When this one is publicly announced, even skeptics will have to admit it resembles another type of UFO in shape and behavior. Moral: Pay no attention to Air Force denials.

Dr. L. D.

White Plains, New York

Information regarding the U.S. Navy's Palo Alto Flying Platform, initially free-flown on January 27, 1955, is not exhaustive. Certain facts regarding the basic structural components of this simple-looking aerial contraption have not been revealed.

It is alleged that wreckage parts obtained from accidentally-landed UFO's, plus still saucer photographs, disc movies, and wordy descriptions of close-range ball-craft sightings have all contributed formidable knowledge to our armed forces.

Even since Pilot Kenneth Arnold spotted a covey of flying saucers over the State of Washington in 1947, our Navy has evidently worked feverishly to duplicate the extraordinary aerodynamic features of these so-called interplanetary airborne machines.

This writer has observed that the Navy has openly admitted that its novel aerial platform is a long way from the finished product, and the fact that it has but reached the Kitty Hawk stage. In other words, the present vehicle is not a real flying saucer. Unlike the genuine flying disc, it is awfully noisy most of the time. It is a slow-moving apparatus, capable of 35 miles-per-hour top speed. Its present altitude range is eight feet; its flight duration is but twenty minutes. It is not a safe device. Its engine belts are actually over-size rubber bands; should one of these snap, the machine would go completely out of control.

The question now arises: Is the Navy Flying Platform the true answer to the pertinent query, "Is the Flying Saucer of American construction?"

Unless our armed services are holding back some very vital information involving a first-class disc-shaped flying machine, this writer is inclined to answer in the negative.

Dr. Benjamin Benincasa
Buffalo, New York

We have not heard very much about UFO over the state of Arkansas. Reporting from the area is not very good, but one or two residents have said that they were contacted by space people. Those were not stories of 1955, however.

The following is from the Paragould (Arkansas) *Press*, of June 1, 1955. We believe the children are just young, innocent and naive enough to tell the truth about what they saw:

NO WISHING STAR, OBJECT SOARS BY

"Star light, star bright . . ."

That's the beginning of a childhood verse made just for wishing. But three young Paragould girls have a different version to tell today.

The girls are Deanna Harrison, 11, granddaughter of Mrs. Olive Keelor of 1007 West Court; Patsy Williams, 11, and Peggy Williams, 8, daughters of Mr. and Mrs. Odis Williams of West Court.

Playing a bit of softball near their homes early Tuesday night, Deanna stopped long enough to make a wish on the "first star she saw that night." But Deanna insists it wasn't a star at all—and she was so sure she forgot to make her wish.

With the other girls nodding approval, Deanna reported the "first star" she saw really was some sort of object high in the sky, zooming southwest at a rather high altitude. It was noiseless—at least to the girls—and was a sparkling V-shape.

"It was all lit up like a star. V-shaped like the corner of a star. But was much larger and was moving," Deanna said today. The girls said they stopped playing and watched the object until it went out of sight. It happened at about 7 o'clock, they said, but they weren't too certain of the exact time.

Flying Saucer? Well, maybe so, and maybe no, but Deanna missed making her wish, whatever it was!

Your editor desires that you read this report from Plattsburgh carefully. This state of affairs is more or less typical of the experiences of a number of G.O.C. (Ground Observer Corps) posts in various parts of the country. Ohio is especially blessed with sightings.

You are not being told of these sightings, for they are restricted by Air Force edict.

The significance is this: the number of saucers, whatever they are, wherever they may originate, is *increasing!* The blackout is suppressing the news, but not the UFO.

Again it seems desirable to stress the casualness, or the free and easy manner of the UFO's, for—they act as if they "feel at home." There does not seem to be any nervousness about their action, and they treat us and our jets about the way we, in turn, treat the nuisance of gnats or mosquitoes. There may be no connection with the apparently stepped up activity on the moon, but there is enough indication to justify making enquiries.

Here is the Plattsburgh report, as printed in the Alben (New York) *Times Union*, June 3rd:

MANY FLYING SAUCERS SEEN IN PLATTSBURGH AREA

Allen Roberts, a spotter for the Ground Observer Corps in Plattsburgh, was taking a ribbing around town for his yarns about flying saucer phenomena during his midnight vigils. James F. Roddy, news director for WEAV, resolved to find out for himself what Roberts was seeing. He took to sitting in with him at the GOC post atop Physicians Hospital.

Now skeptics are asking Jim Roddy what kind of hootch he drinks. During the past few weeks, he has seen enough to convince him that spacecraft are flying missions over the north end of Lake Champlain, that they give special study to the progress of the new Plattsburgh air base, and that one of them actually landed on Vermont soil.

Reports on a series of such sightings have come in from the Plattsburgh GOC to the Albany Filter Plant.

The most recent one of a spectacular nature took place on May 21 with four witnesses besides Roddy and Roberts. They sighted the bright "saucer" at 2:15 a.m., got its pictures on Tri-X film, and kept a log on its movements until 2:31 a.m., when the entry says: "USAF jet plane is heard coming from East. Plane gives pursuit. Object is seen to suddenly spurt ahead. Lost to view of all six men."

Roddy tells us they have seen Air Force jets take off in pursuit frequently, but the "saucers" dart away as if the jets were standing still. He remarks with some logic: "Six men can't imagine the same thing at the same time. The Air Force doesn't send out jet fighters or interceptors to chase something that isn't there."

On April 9th, at 1:31 a.m., Jim Roddy was dozing in his chair when Allen shook him, pointing to a bright object drifting overhead. Roddy dashed out on the roof to try to pick up a sound. It was noiseless, and "just seemed to coast through the air." He describes it as rust-colored and "definitely round." It headed down over the lake and they think it landed on the Vermont side.

Now wide-awake, they kept eyes peeled, and at 2:34 a.m. spotted a "cigar-shaped object" hanging very high in the sky. (This is the kind of thing Adamski has described as being the mother-ship of the saucers.)

The big thrill came at 4:08 a.m., and they watched it through field glasses until 5:45 a.m. when it ascended out of sight. It was "a glaring, brilliant, incandescent white; round on the top and flat on the bottom, much like an inverted dessert dish." A stream of eight green lights, which they took to be gas or vapor, pointed downward from its bottom. Directly underneath "a bright yellow-white flame or glow, very powerful, was emitted."

"In this sector," Roddy declared, "the sightings are coming fast and furious. We counted over 36 small-sized circular craft whizzing over our observer post on May 28."

For the seasoned UFO researcher, even apparently unrelated incidents demand scrutiny and thought. Whereas it would be impossible to include each and every such item, the following snippet gives some idea of the frequency of strange and unexplained incidents which constantly take place, which are constantly printed and published and discussed, and which are constantly ignored by too many researchers. Your editor begs you to watch for such items and to keep your ears alerted to such stories coming from your locale, and he would appreciate receiving any and all information. One can never know from what source a true key to the puzzle may emanate, and we wish to make the next *Annual* as representative and all-inclusive as is

humanly possible. The United Press carried the following story
from Montreal, Canada, June 3rd:

SPACE MICE EAT AUTO WINDOW

Hugh McGlynn, 23, reported today "space mice" shattered his
auto's rear window.

He said he heard a crack, turned around and saw the window was
"cracked all over. Then it began to disintegrate and crumble in
small bits and pieces," he said.

" 'Space mice' are what scientists believe are tiny organisms called
micrometeorites."

(Ed.: Notice that in the actual reporting of this item, the
person who actually wrote the little story took a rather tongue-in-
cheek attitude; however, we discover, at the end of the article,
that there is scientific basis for the use of the term "space mice,"
and it is precisely this terminology which might mislead many an
otherwise interested and/or intelligent reader. It is common for
mankind to fear the unknown, and history is full of tales of the
masses laughing at the few—and history records all too frequently
how "the few" were eventually proved to be right. They killed
Socrates, but who amongst us can name his accusers, his jailers,
etc.? No—it was the man whose insight and wisdom and courage
and intelligence and fearlessness brought him to this condition
who lived!)

Your editor thinks that the government is completely wrong
in its attitude that "The Public" will panic if it is told the truth
about UFO.

What would be the nature of this panic? Who is going to flee
to where? What will he do when he gets there?

In other words, the universality of UFO, and their omniscience
and omnipotence—relative to our own state of progress—makes
flight patently absurd.

It is my firm belief that an announcement to the effect that

Chief Littlejohn with mysteriously fallen dead birds. Charlotte Ob-server, *September 28, 1955. {Observer Staff Photo—Osborne)*

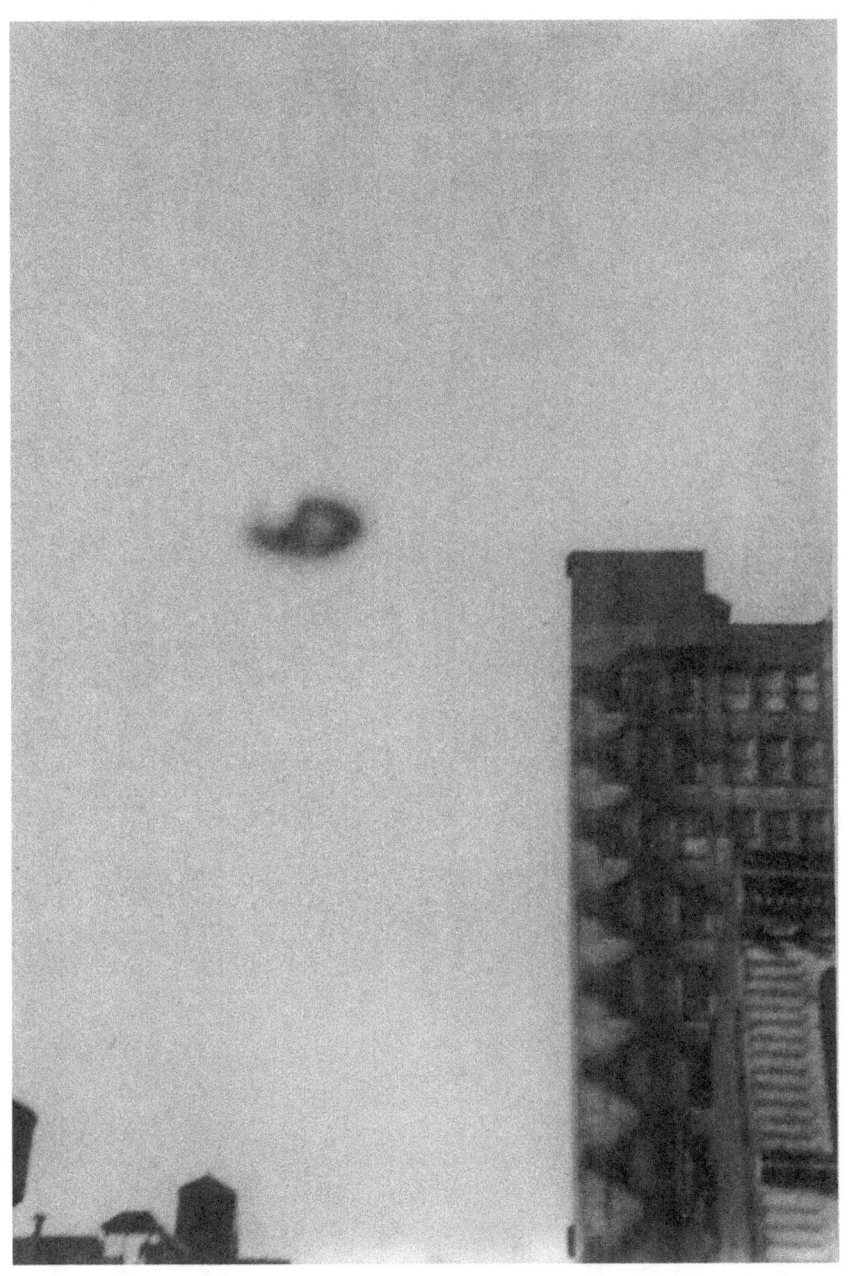

Photograph taken by a young television technician on the roof of a New York City apartment house. New York World-Telegratn & Sun, *May 23, 1955. (Warren Siegmond)*

These armored phyllopods mysteriously turned up in Bicycle Lake near Camp Erwin, Los Angeles Examiner, September 19, 1955. (International News Photo)

George Brinsmaid displaying a fish which smashed his windshield on the streets of the nation's capital. Washington Evening Star, *December 22, 1955. (Star Staff Photo)*

Designed by Rene Cousinet, this engineless model of the French aerodyne has a diameter of almost 27 feet. It will be powered by three 135-horsepower engines and the turbojet reactor visible on the underside in the lower view. Philadelphia Inquirer, July 5, 1955. (World Wide Photo)

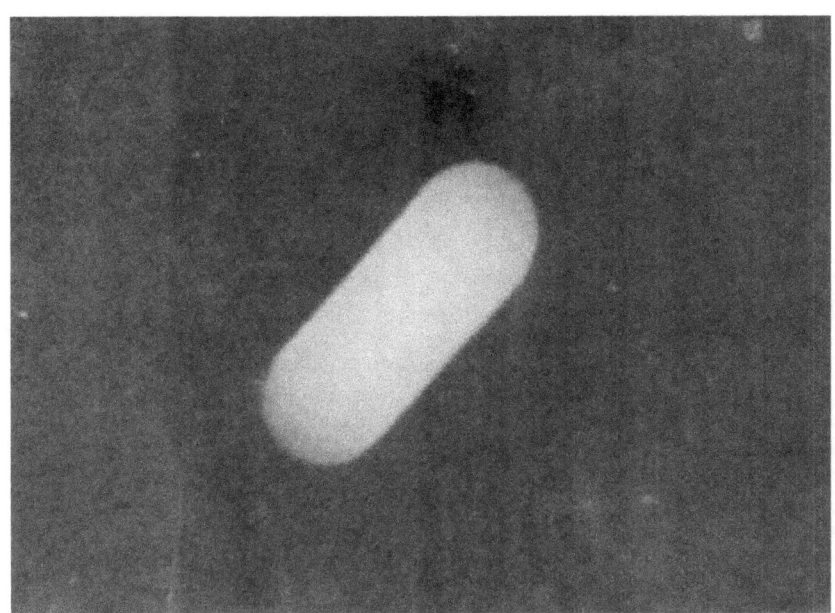

This strange light in the sky was caught by a newspaper photographer. Above: this is how it looked when he first saw it. Below: the camera registered this 'change 15 minutes after the first exposure. Plattsburgh Press-Republican, *September 19, 1955. (Photos by John Lonergan)*

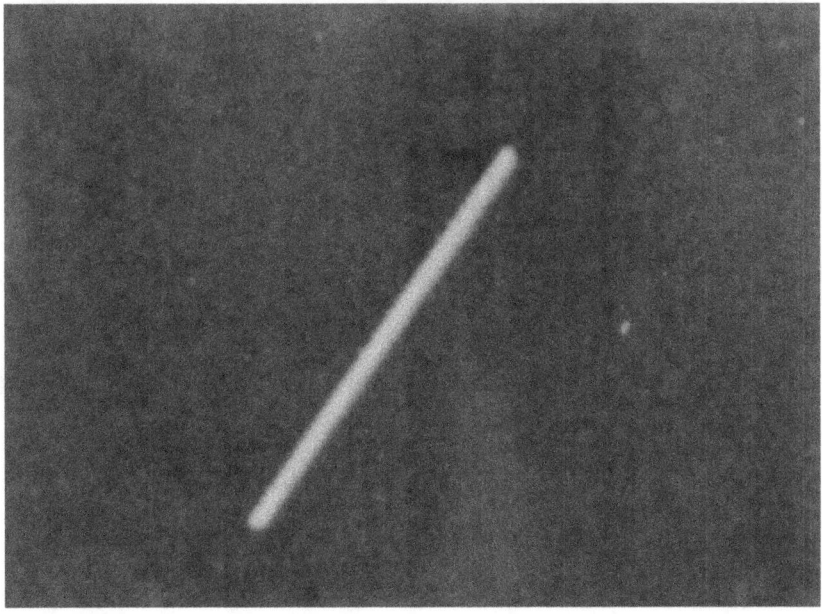

This strange, gray, cobwebby substance fell out of the sky and spread over an area a half-mile square at Horseheads, New York. An Elmira College chemistry professor identified it as radioactive, heavily damaged cotton fiber, but no one could say where it came from. Miami, February 23, 1955 {World Wide Photo)

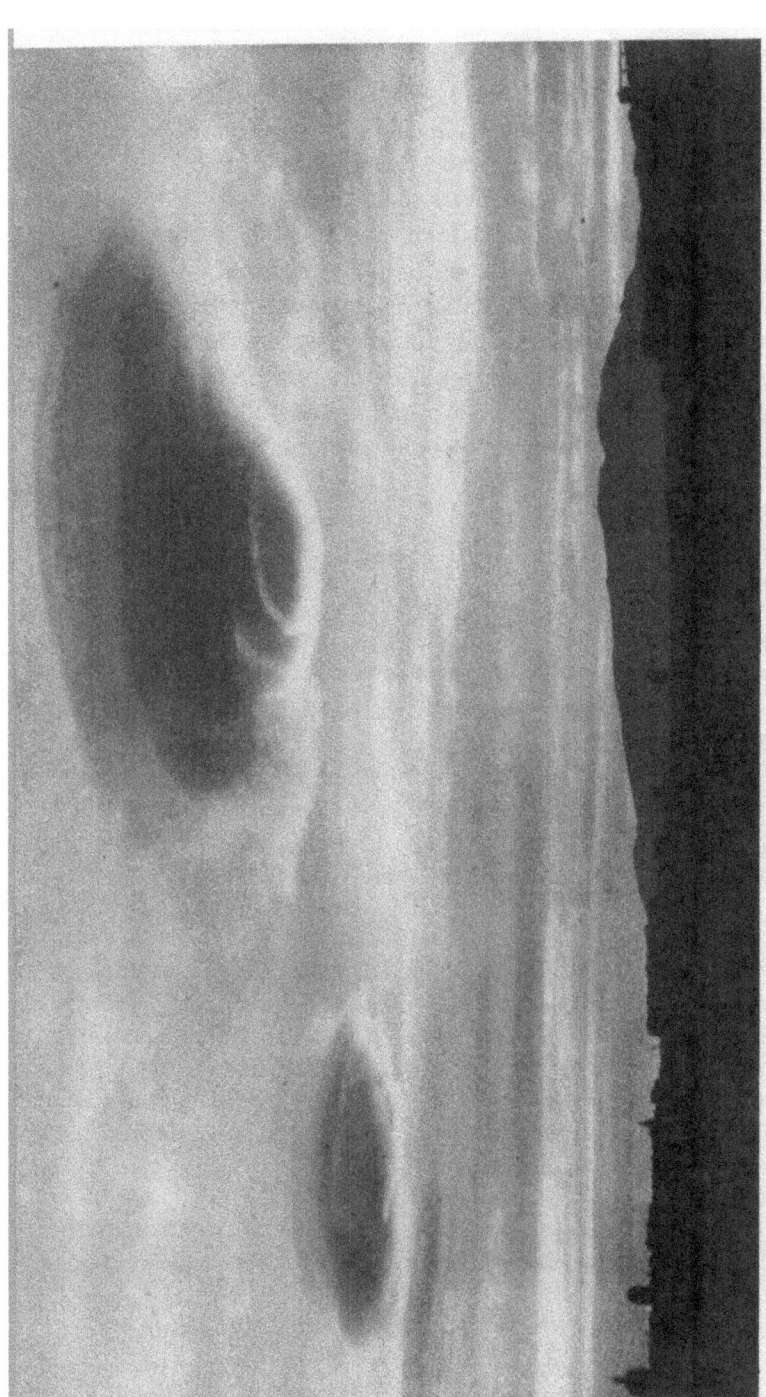

The United States Navy released this photo, which they say shows an "unusual cloud formation over the city of Marseilles, France." The Navy gave no indication as to why they released the photograph. New York Times, July 3, 1955. (World Wide Photo)

flying saucers are here and are from outer space could have but
one ultimate effect: a world-wide sobering, a re-adjustment of our
present standards of value, and "peace in our time."

The Cincinnati (Ohio) *Times-Star* conducted an "Inquiring
Reporter" street interview which, while skimpy, is something
of a cross-section. There is not the slightest hint of hysteria in
these interviews, although made in Cincinnati where there have
been more important sightings than almost anywhere outside of
California or Florida. These five statements were published in the
June 3rd issue of the *Times-Star,* and we reproduce them here as
indication that the American People can take the UFO, like anything else, in their stride.

(Ed.: We regret that we are unable to reproduce the photographs of these people: it is a handsome collection of fine
American faces!)

TODAY'S QUESTION:

WOULD YOU BE SCARED IF FLYING SAUCERS EXISTED?

Miss Kitty Barnhart, 3773 Hutton Avenue, Linwood, student:
"I don't think I'd be too scared. There have been too many reports
about them lately. I don't think they would be from Mars or any
other planet. They'd be something to do with the defense of the
country—or something like that. The Government has a little more
information than we have about them, but if everything known
about them was told, a lot of people would be too scared to come
out of their houses."

Norman Lew, 722 Gholson Avenue, Avondale, accountant: "I
wouldn't even be surprised, because I've thought all along that they
did exist. I've seen a lot of pictures of what is supposed to be flying
saucers. I wouldn't be surprised, shocked, or scared. I just take all
the stories about them for granted. There is no reason to doubt what
people have said about having seen them. Some stories could have
been imagined, but not all of them."

Jim White, 114 North Ft. Thomas Avenue, Ft. Thomas, Kentucky, accountant: "I wouldn't be scared. I've always thought that
they did exist! We've been hearing these reports for a couple of

G

years now. There was a picture in the paper the other day of what was supposed to be a flying saucer. I wouldn't say it's a fact, but they might exist. Personally, I don't think anyone knows whether they exist."

Carol Brefeld, 2700 Arbor Avenue, Hyde Park, student: "I'd be surprised! I could hardly believe it if they would announce that they were actually men from another planet. It wouldn't be hard to believe if they were from Russia. But I don't think the Russians are that far advanced. There really are no flying saucers, though. For one thing, if they did exist, why haven't they taken a picture of one? I would think they could do that!"

Miss Ruth Pollard, 309 West Fourth Street, Covington, stenographer: "Naturally I think I would be frightened temporarily because people get scared of things they know nothing about. Once they were told more about them, the fright would be gone. Flying saucers are coming probably sooner than anyone thinks. Anything is possible. They're bound to be man-made, but it's conceivable that they're made by men from another planet."

Here is another G.O.C. report, this one from Ohio. The Loveland (Ohio) *Herald* of June 4th brings it to our attention. Several other efforts have been made in the past to air the sightings of the G.O.C. observers. We remember one such try in *Fate* Magazine a few years ago in which a G.O.C. observer told of the many times she had seen UFO. These observers are on the watch all of the time, and they naturally see more UFO than other people. Why does the Air Force keep these sightings from us?

PLANES SENT UP TO CHECK OBJECTS REPORTED
BY OBSERVER WITH LONG EXPERIENCE

On Tuesday, May 24, at 7:48 p.m., according to the log which is kept of the flights of planes reported at the Ground Observer Tower on Lebanon Road, four flying saucers flying in formation passed over and were reported to Columbus by the observer on duty. They were flying in a northeasterly direction and when reported to

Columbus planes were sent out to identify them. No public report ever came back to the tower, but this is regular practice and none was expected. The observer on duty at the time was Mrs. Frank Whitecotton. She has served more hours in the observation tower than any other person and was said to be thoroughly qualified in plane identification and reporting.

"This may come as somewhat of a surprise to some of the skeptics, but now that flying saucers have been identified here by one of our own workers, let us not be lulled into a sense of complacency," a CD official said. "Keep the watchtower occupied at all times. The very moment it is left unmanned may be the time the enemy will strike. Join the G.O.C. today. It will be a pleasant place to spend a few hours each week this summer."

The Pueblo (Colorado) *Chieftain*, June 7, published a debunking story on a "sighting." Their "debunk" however has boomeranged, for I firmly believe that such stories are a great contribution to our research. This may seem inconsistent, but upon scrutiny and thought you will probably agree.

The point is, we are very happy to know of these balloons. *We do not want faked or false or misconceived sightings, and everything possible must be done to prevent erroneous conclusions. We're after truth!*

It is with that thought in mind that we happily reprint the story of these balloons.

(Ed.: It should be pointed out, however, that pear-shaped, bell-shaped and bulb-shaped objects have been reported for several hundred years!)

AIR FORCE BALLOON OVER CITY
CAUSES "FLYING SAUCER" FLURRY

For several hours Monday afternoon it appeared Pueblo was experiencing a rash of flying saucers, indistinguishable cigar-shaped objects and mysterious flashes of flame in the skies.

The U.S. Air Force allayed the consternation, curiosity and confusion by admitting the spherical object which excited local residents undoubtedly was one of its balloons being used in a meteorological project.

The object was spotted here moving in a westerly direction and apparently at great altitude. Observers were curious because prevailing surface winds were in an easterly direction.

Arthus Montez, 309 S. La Crosse, first reported sighting a "strange white object" high in the sky south of Pueblo at 4:45 p.m. He could not distinguish motion.

Mrs. Leonard T. Walsh, 310 West Pitkin, next reported seeing it. She trained Hensoldt 8x24 binoculars on it, and said "it bounced around noticeably." She described it as looking like a "transparent plastic electric light bulb."

Bradley Senger, 1517 East Sixth, also viewed the object. He said it appeared at times to have distinguishable sides, but that it was too high for him to be certain.

Harold D Myers, 231 Quincy, also reported seeing it. He said an Air Force B-36 circled it, then flew away as he watched it.

The 1110th Air Support Group, Lowry Air Force Base, Denver, is releasing a total of 25 such balloons during May and June as part of a joint research project.

The devices, the largest 130 feet in diameter, carry 200 pounds of instruments including a radio transmitter that sends signals enabling ground receiving stations to plot its course and retrieve the instruments after the balloon descends.

The balloons stay aloft for an average of two days and are designed to operate at altitudes above 40,000 feet.

Your editor has had several letters from Mr. Eugene Metcalfe, of Paris, Illinois. We regret the "flash-back" element in the procedure we have decided to adopt, but it seems to be the most advantageous for the presentation of this exciting situation.

Under the date of June 7, 1955, Mr. Metcalfe wrote:

Dear Mr. Jessup:
After reading *The Case for the UFO*, I have been scanning the skies more than ever with my three inch stellar telescope, mostly at the moon. You are right about the small planets between the Earth

and Moon. I found this to be true on June 3, 1955. There are at least four such planets that are visible to the eye, but you have to look through a 'scope to see they are so near! I saw four shadows crossing the Moon and watched them from 8:30 until 11:30 p.m.

Hope you got my letter of May 19th sent to Citadel Press!

Well, Mr. Metcalfe's letter was unaccountably delayed, but when it arrived, it was probably the most startling letter received by your editor during the entire year. The casual, matter-of-factness of his report is as remarkable as the information it contained. We are left almost gasping, and all we can think of to say is, "Air Force, how long has this been going on?"

It is true that we cannot vouch for the accuracy of Mr. Metcalfe's report, but we have his signed statement, which was published in the *UFO Reporter* during the summer.

Here is the now famous letter, reprinted without further comment:

Paris, Illinois
May 19, 1955

The Citadel Press
222 Fourth Avenue
New York, New York

Re: *The Case for the UFO*
by M. K. Jessup

Dear Sirs:

I have finished reading the above book and I would like to say I found it most interesting.

Many, I presume will say—a book of fancy, or a good book on the impossible.

However, I can say that Mr. Jessup knows what he is writing about . . . (and I can say it) *from my own experience!*

For the past three years or so I have noticed a strange airborne craft in the sky—it was shaped like the top of a call bell—it also could move faster than any plane I have yet seen. I have seen it at a time when the darkness was almost night and when it would start to move there would appear a stream of green sparks—just like the old electric street cars used to make on a high joint on the power line.

Now here is my story—strange but true.

On March 9, 1955, I saw the above mentioned craft take a Jet propelled plane out of the sky and, believe it or not, this plane has never been found. This happened, you might say, in my own back yard. It was all in plain view. I plainly saw both the plane and this craft. It scooped the plane up as easy as a hawk would a chicken —then disappeared.

I sent letters describing this action to the following: The Chicago *American* newspaper: Comment, none. *Newsweek:* comment, would like to print letter if room was found; Civil Air Patrol, comment, first said was American craft, then said they didn't know. Who does? Federal Bureau of Investigation: they thanked me for my information, so maybe some one of them will get their eyes opened some day!

If possible, forward this letter to Mr. Jessup; however, even he might think the same as the above mentioned.

Again I say the above book is full of nothing but the truth, and I firmly believe time will bear it out.

> Respectfully Yours,
> (signed)
> **Eugene Metcalfe**
> R. R. 1, Paris, Illinois

Further correspondence was received from Mr. Metcalfe, but strangely enough it was received incomplete and only with some difficulty. First of all, a letter said to contain photographs of this strange UFO was returned from the editor's New York apartment with the notation "Not At This Address," despite the fact that your editor was at that address continuously throughout the period during which Mr. Metcalfe attempted to communicate. Next, Mr. Metcalfe wrote and posted a registered letter. When received, it had been opened and re-sealed with scotch tape, and was forwarded through my publisher. This letter was supposed to have contained the photographs from the previous mailing—but they had been removed!

A June 9th report of a falling object near Mt. Hamilton indicates that there is more in the air than the Air Force cares to admit, and this certainly was not a balloon!

FALLING OBJECT TOUCHES OFF AERIAL SEARCH

A brief but intense air search of the Mt. Hamilton foothills east of Milpitas was made yesterday afternoon, after an aircraft spotter told of seeing a falling metallic object.

W. J. Everett, on duty at the Jail Farm observation post, said he saw a piece of metal falling slowly "about four miles east of Milpitas."

Everett said the object exploded and fell to pieces. He estimated the altitude of the explosion at "four or five thousand feet."

His report to the Air Force filter center touched off a search by a Coast Guard helicopter and planes sent by the Air Force, Coast Guard and Navy.

No wreckage was found, but the Coast Guard said it would be back for another look today.

(Ed.: And no further information has been made public!)

From the Enid (Oklahoma) *Eagle*, June 9, we learned that four Enid people reported seeing a flying saucer over the area about 9:30 p.m. John Pash and grandmother, Mrs. Annie L. Dixon, 220 West Park, noticed an apparently bright object cutting fancy turns and swooping in one direction and then another.

Two fishermen were coming in about the same time from the North and thought what they saw was a hail cloud, and slowed down so they wouldn't drive into it.

The commander of the weather detachment at Vance Air Force Base speculated that it is very possible that the object was nothing more than an unusual cloud formation in a heat area, reflecting the rays of the Sun.

(Editor: How stupid is the observer supposed to get? What connection is there between a bright object cutting fancy turns and a hail cloud? And since when has the advancing head of a thunderstorm [hail cloud] been "an unusual cloud formation in a heat area, reflecting the rays of the sun?" At 9:30 p.m.?

Is this not one of the better examples of the "controlled" or "purposeful" storms? Was the bright object "cutting fancy turns" supposed to be the same as this cloud? Or was it the control center for a created storm?)

On June 9th, the Sunburst (North Carolina) *Farmer* reported the sighting and hearing of a large group of UFO's. We have already commented on the increasing number of sightings in which swarms of UFO's appear. This is one of the more puzzling events of 1955, but it points up the increasing number of multiple sightings:

HE SIGHTED SOME OBJECTS

A farmer reported sighting a flock of strange aerial objects flying in and out of formation over the Western North Carolina mountains today.

Allen Jones of Sunburst said he was fishing on Lake Logan near here when he sighted the objects in the rosy light of early morning.

"I heard a noise like a swarm of bees," he said. "I looked up and saw these five objects about 1500 feet up. They were rusty brown color."

From Jones' position on the lake the objects appeared "about the size of the inside of an automobile tire" and apparently were small. He said the objects "definitely" were not jet planes, although they moved very rapidly in and out of formation.

They swept off in an easterly direction toward 5,794 foot Mt. Pisgah, he said.

Under the date June 10th, we received a letter from Mr. Norman C. Caum, of Del Mar, California, reporting a sighting as follows:

". . . On 1 July, 1950, at midnight, at Flathead Lake, Montana, I, with my brother-in-law, observed a light which at first we thought was a falling star. But the falling star, instead of disappearing at the end of its arc, made a left angle ascending turn and disappeared in the eastern sky." The following day newspaper and radios stated that at that moment the object had been sighted by the Spokane, Missoula, Kalispell and Whitehall air and weather observers. The object appeared to be an incandescent ball with a glowing orange "rear-blast."

I did *not* report this to any authority."

Note that no meteor ever takes a zigzag or angular course across the sky. This "thing" must have been controlled. The description is typical of sightings reported for several hundred years.

Flare and blast. Flash and blast. Unaccounted explosions. These mysterious explosions have been known for centuries, but their number has apparently increased within the last five years. This account is typical, and appeared in the Chicago (Illinois) *Tribune*, June 11:

FLASH NOTED BEFORE BLAST IN LAKE BLUFF

Further mystery was added yesterday to an explosion which shook a mile wide section of Lake Bluff Thursday night. Mrs. Edward H. Finch, 123 Woodland rd., Lake Bluff, told Police Chief Christian Elfert she saw a large flash of light west of her home just before the explosion. It appeared to come from Skokie rd., she said.

The explosion was felt in a belt extending from near the lake to about a mile west. It appeared to be centered at Green Bay and Rockland rds. Damage was negligible.

Some persons theorized the blast could have been concussion from a shock wave of a passing jet plane. A spokesman at Glenview Naval Air station conceded this possibility, but said no planes were aloft.

Some readers will perhaps demur over the inclusion of an item relating to the antiquity of man on earth. Actually, your editor believes that this is most pertinent to the UFO problem, for he believes that man has been a cultured creature on earth for thousands of years more than is accredited him by conventional archaeologists. Your editor thinks that this archaic civilization may very well have discovered the principles of gravity control which resulted in space flight, and that this discovery was more accidental than the result of physical research.

The gravitational astronomy built into the structure of the Great Pyramid of Giza is almost a self-contained proof of such a postulate. The following dissertation on the antiquity of man represents contemporary thinking and research. It appeared in the New York *Times*, June 12th:

23,800-YEAR CLUE TO MAN IS FOUND;
ATOMIC 'CALENDAR' INDICATES NEVADA
DISCOVERIES ARE OLDEST FOR CONTINENT

An archaeological find in Nevada indicates that men lived there at least 23,800 years ago, the Southwest Museum revealed today.

Until recently, the oldest established habitation on the continent was 10,000 years old. In 1953 evidence was reported that the "Sandia Man" had lived in New Mexico 20,000 years ago. Human remains in Lebanon in the Near East dating from about 75,000 B.C. were reported by a 1948 Boston College-Fordham University expedition. The Nevada discovery consists of the bones of mammoths and other ancient animals bearing distinctive marks of human processing. Mixed with them was charcoal, presumably from camp fires. The charcoal was dated by measurement of its content of carbon 14, a radioactive form of the element. Carbon 14 enters living matter from the air. When the matter dies, the carbon 14 starts disintegrating very slowly. The degree of disintegration provides a "calendar" that scientists say is extremely accurate.

The Nevada charcoal was unearthed only last month by museum scientists. It was tested by Dr. Willard F. Libby at the University of Chicago, one of the pioneers in carbon 14 dating. He reported, the museum said, that it was at least 23,800 years old—as far back as its instruments would measure.

The ancient deposit was found near Tule Springs, about twenty miles north of Las Vegas. The site was discovered by Fenley Hunter of the American Museum of Natural History in New York more than twenty years ago. He dug there in collaboration with M. R. Harrington, curator of the Southwest Museum, in 1933.

Some of the objects from that expedition were submitted to the University of Chicago when the carbon dating system was perfected as an outgrowth of recent atomic research. The indications of age were so remarkable that as a check the museum organized another expedition this year. The participants included Ruth D. Simpson, assistant curator, and several other California and Arizona archaeologists.

The findings are from the fourth or "Wisconsin" period of the Pleistocene ice age, Miss Simpson said. At that time the Las Vegas area was covered by a lake that may have been as much as forty miles long and twelve miles wide. Its edges are strewn with remnants of ancient habitation.

One of the major finds of the latest digging was a four-foot section of a huge mammoth bone, and part of a mammoth tusk. That was ten feet or more long. There were also bones of camels, bison and horses.

Some of the camel bones bore marks of human scraping, the museum said. Other bones plainly appeared to have been split by human hands, although no tools were found close by.

The museum plans to do more excavating with heavy equipment next fall.

The antiquity of the "Sandia Man" was reported in 1953 by Dr. Frank C. Hibben, an anthropologist of the University of New Mexico, at Albuquerque.

It was established by carbon 14 analysis of a mammoth tusk. The tusk had been found among flints and other man-made debris in Sandia Cave, near Albuquerque, in 1937. The analysis was made by Professor H. R. Crane of the University of Michigan.

While the "Sandia Man" heretofore has been acknowledged as the oldest North American finding, several discoveries have been made since then for which greater age was proclaimed. These assertions have not had general acceptance, according to Dr. James A. Ford, associate curator of the American Museum of Natural History here.

The one receiving the most intensive check, Dr. Ford said, was the discovery off the coast near San Diego, California, reported by Dr. George Carper, Professor of Geography at Johns Hopkins University. Dr. Ford said that most of the archaeologists didn't think the items turned up were artifacted. The other "discoveries," Dr. Ford declared, "were not taken very seriously."

(Ed.: Another fascinating article appeared on the same date in the Miami (Florida) *Herald*. Entitled "Earth Yields Clues to Old Civilization," it is worthy of the attention of all students of UFOlogy who are particularly intc.ested in researching this particular phase of the problem. Though too lengthy, and perhaps too esoteric for our purposes, to be quoted herein, your editor is sure that the newspaper would gladly sell back-copies of that particular issue should anyone care to study this particular column.)

And we are then brought abruptly to another sighting. On June 17, the Waterbury (Connecticut) *American* announced the following sighting. The combination of lights is somewhat unusual for a UFO, and certainly abnormal for any known type of terrestrial aircraft:

12-YEAR-OLD BOY SPOTS FLYING SAUCER

An aircraft of the flying saucer class was sighted last night from Waterbury, according to a 12-year-old boy who said astronomy was his hobby.

The boy, Joseph Lamontagne, of 28 Dixie Avenue, said he was sure the object he saw was not an optical illusion, nor a conventional airplane.

Joseph related he was outside his home scanning the sky with a four-inch diameter telescope, when the noiseless object moved into his view.

Carrying four yellow lights on top, and one green light below, the aircraft seemed to be oval shaped, the boy said. He reported the object, in view about two minutes, moved fast from the south and disappeared over the western horizon.

Asked if he could have mistaken the yellow and green lights for recognition lights on a military aircraft, Joseph reiterated that he did not think the machine was of conventional type. He said his mother could see the lights after the location was pointed out.

A pupil in the seventh grade at Washington School, the boy has been studying astronomy to the point where he can pick out 15 of the 90 known constellations.

The Fremont (Ohio) *News-Messenger*, June 18th, announced another Ohio sighting. Aside from the fact that Ohio, and most especially the southwestern quarter, produces far more than its pro rata share of UFO sightings, there is generally a ring of authenticity and matter-of-factness about Ohio reports. (And let us not forget that the Air Force's Wright and Patterson fields are located in Ohio!)

There is a lot of food for thought in the number of Ohio sightings and their patterns as to size, shape and color.

IT'S FLYING SAUCER TIME AGAIN!

An unidentified object seen in the skies from out Christy road way was observed by several residents of that area Sunday night . . . The glowing object seemed to hang motionless in the sky and later just disappeared . . . Those who saw it did not say it was a saucer, but added it definitely did not appear to be an aircraft of any kind because of its motionless position.

Here is a report from the Nashville (Tennessee) *Banner*, June 20, which bears careful study:

LARGE METEOR OBSERVED FLAMING ACROSS CITY SKIES

A flaming ball of fire zipped across the skies here last night.

Dr. Carl Seyfert, director of Vanderbilt observatory, said he failed to see the phenomenon but that it was apparently "an unusually large meteor." He said he was basing his conclusion on calls he received. Seyfert says he's hopeful of finding fragments to study.

The pilots of separate military aircraft reported to the Nashville Civil Aeronautics authority tower they sighted the meteor around 8:45 p.m. One reported he saw an explosion north of Nashville.

Dr. Merrill D. Moore, director of the executive committee of the Southern Baptist convention, said he also saw it. "It was by far the largest I ever saw," he said. "It looked so close I could distinguish the colors blue, red and white. It traveled to the north and just went out."

Dr. Carl Seyfert, whom we "met" in the previous clipping, again made the press on June 22nd, this time directly on the subject of UFO. His clear-mindedness and obvious sincerity give us reason to consider his cautious words carefully.

The following is from the Nashville (Tennessee) *Tennessean,* June 22:

FLYING SAUCERS, IF TRUE, NOT EARTH'S, SERTOMA TOLD

Flying saucers—if they exist—don't come from the earth.

This was the only concrete point agreed on in a verbal battle about the space objects in a "they is and they ain't" discussion at the Sertoma club yesterday.

But there was a heated discussion for both sides of the question.

Joe Thompson of Northwestern Mutual Insurance maintained that all the qualified people such as airplane pilots who have seen the flying "somethings" couldn't be so far wrong. John DeWitt president of WSM Inc. said he would have to see part of such an object before he would believe it, and Dr. Carl Seyfert, Vanderbilt University professor, the other negative speaker, said IF they are and IF they do what they are supposed to be doing, then the objects are not from the earth.

Thompson's argument hinged on the fact that pilots, accustomed to watching for objects in the sky and instantly recognizing regular objects, have seen the so-called flying saucers.

"These qualified men with thousands of flying hours know what they see and don't see," he said.

Dr. Carl Seyfert scratched his head as he told the luncheon meeting of the club he didn't know if they existed or not.

He said that 90 percent of the sights can be explained away. "It's that other 10 percent that bothers us."

DeWitt said it was not possible to prove they do not exist, but "suppose they do, where do they come from?" he asked as he continued the negative argument.

"They have to have a base. It's not the U.S. or Russia or Germany, for scientists are not that advanced, so that excludes earth," DeWitt said.

Coral Gables, Florida, is a lovely area adjacent to Miami proper, and the whole area is very "saucer sensitive." Sightings are quite common. Many of them were listed in the UFO Reporter which I prepared following the publication of *The Case for the UFO.*

The following account resulted from an interview with Norbert Gariety, a businessman of Coral Gables, who is personally known to your editor. Mr. Gariety is a conscientious investigator and reporter of UFO phenomena, and has given dozens of fascinating lectures all over the Miami area.

The following is taken from the June 23rd Coral Gables (Florida) *Riviera Times:*

"SAUCERS" ARE REAL, GABLEITE SAYS:
HAS FACTS FOR PROOF, ALSO THEORY

Most people regard flying saucers one of two ways—many think they're nothing but a lot of crazy talk and unfounded rumors; a small minority of "lunatic fringes" come up with stories wild enough to come near justifying the first group.

But there's also a group who take the saucers seriously, and who adopt a calm, sane attitude to the whole affair.

One of these is Norbert F. Gariety, of the LeMans photo studio in Coral Gables. Gariety believes in the saucers, he has definite theories about them, and he can back up his ideas with names and dates, something that "saucer bugs" can't do.

He has seen only one saucer himself, and can produce witnesses who also saw the same UFO, or Unidentified Flying Object, as the saucers are scientifically classed. Gariety saw what he describes as a "round, luminous object, very bright white," flash across the sky last December 21 at 7:30 p.m.

"It was a cloudless night with a full moon," he says, "and the object, though smaller than the moon, was brighter. It took about 15 seconds for the object to cross the complete sky, from West to East. There is no way of knowing how high it was, but even at ground level, it would have had to be traveling 5,000 miles an hour."

It could not have been a meteor, Gariety says, because of its course, which was parallel to the ground. Meteors only fall.

Francis R. Gallegher, a winter resident, was out driving with his wife that evening, and they saw it too. When they stopped for a stoplight, they asked three occupants of another car if they had seen the same object. They had.

"That incident," according to Gariety, "got me interested in the saucers. I started giving talks on them to groups like the Lions, Kiwanis, and others. Wherever I went I met people who had seen saucers but never said anything because they were afraid of being ridiculed."

What are the saucers?

"Here's where my ideas seem to get a little bit wild and woolly," Gariety admits, "but that's only on the surface. I think they're spaceships from another solar system."

Many people, he says, think that the earth is the only world that can bear intelligent life. But the great telescope at Mt. Palomar, in California, shows literally billions of stars. If only one star in twenty has planets, that still comes to several hundred million solar systems in the universe. And if only one solar system in twenty bears intelligent life, that still makes five million intelligent races.

"Of all these intelligent life forms," Gariety argues, "there must be many with scientific development comparable to ours. And a look at current newspapers and magazines will tell you that we are on the very verge of space travel.

"I do not believe that God would have created this whole great universe and then left it all empty and uninhabited except for the one tiny planet where the human race lives."

As for the purpose of these space-visitors, Gariety thinks that they are explorers. "Some of the mysterious disappearances of history may have been these visitors taking earth-people home with them," Gariety continues. "This does not necessarily mean that they are unfriendly. Remember, Columbus took several Indians back to Spain with him after discovering America."

That, according to Gariety, is the saucer story. And, fantastic as it is, it makes sense when you put aside preconceived notions about Buck Rogers and little green men.

The whole story will be told only with the pasage of time.

Is there a connection? Is the "snowman" a visitor from space?

Datelined June 23rd, London, England, the following comes to us via the Washington (D.C.) *Post and Times-Herald*, June 24:

RAF CLIMBERS REPORT DISCOVERY
OF BIG FOOTPRINTS IN HIMALAYA SNOWS

The Air Ministry announced tonight that British explorers in the Himalayas have found heavy tracks of "an exceptionally large animal" believed by native guides to be the legendary "abominable snowman."

An official Air Ministry announcement said RAF climbers found tracks of a two-legged, five-toed creature with feet 12 inches long and a weight so great the footprints sank 11 inches in snow that a man's foot compressed only one inch.

The reported discovery of the tracks gave one of the biggest official blessings yet bestowed on the legend that an "abominable snowman" roams the Himalayan heights.

Native Sherpa guides have long insisted that a hairy half-man half-beast creature which they called the "yeti" lives in the mountainous regions.

The Air Ministry said the tracks were found by three members of an RAF Mountaineering Association expedition in the Kulti Glacier valley, some 12,375 feet above sea level.

"There were many prints, each measuring about 12 inches by six inches and indicating that the creature who made them was two-legged with five toes a quarter of an inch wide on each foot," the ministry said.

The Air Ministry said the RAF mountaineers reported discovering the tracks on June 12. It said one of the men, Squadron Leader L. W. Davis, had spent six seasons in the Himalayas and is of the opinion the footprints were "far larger than those of any bear."

Note, in the following, how the article is slanted to indicate that this was, "beyond doubt," a meteor. Note too, friends, that the "meteor" went *across* the sky!

At the moment we do not wish to state definitely whether these huge fireballs are really meteors. Suffice it to say that we must watch vigilantly for further reports, and perhaps with a world-wide survey during the present year we shall be able to discover some common denominator, some element of repetition which may be another missing link in the UFO puzzle.

From the Lowell (Massachusetts) *Sun*, Friday, June 24th:

KING SIZE METEORITE SEEN BY THOUSANDS IN THIS AREA
SPECTACULAR SHOW IN THE HEAVENS
SHORTLY BEFORE 9 O'CLOCK LAST NIGHT

Thousands of Greater-Lowell residents were amazed at the sight of a ball of fire zooming across the heavens last night and as a result the offices of The Sun were flooded with calls as to what the flaming object was.

It wasn't a "flying saucer burning up," as some excited residents thought. Astronomers today theorized that it was a meteorite.

Webster's International Dictionary defines a meteorite as "a stony, or metallic, body that has fallen to the earth from outer space."

When parts of the meteorite are found they usually show a pitted surface with a burned crust, caused by the heat developed in their rapid passage through the earth's atmosphere.

The meteorite did not fall to the earth last night and astronomers at the Harvard Observatory in Cambridge theorized that it disintegrated off the southern New Hampshire coastline at a height of about 30 miles.

Callers to The Sun office, from all parts of Greater-Lowell, described the flaming object as about three feet long, shaped like a tube with a red tail of shooting sparks.

The meteorite was visible for a few seconds and appeared in the heavens of this area at 8:58 p.m.

Some observers saw the meteorite as a pear-shaped object of a greenish-blue color.

In addition to observers in Greater-Lowell, reports of the flaming meteorite were received all the way from Stoneham to Bar Harbor, Me.

Ira Cruckshank of Stoneham, a General Electric Co. executive, said "if it was a meteor, it was a big one." He said it was brighter than meteors he had seen before.

Lester Higgins, a farmer whose home is in the Granite Hill section of Augusta, said the object he saw "was along the general lines of a meteorite, but much brighter."

He said it was reflected against the sky and was the size of "two or three Zeppelins," such as he had seen shot down in Europe during World War I.

The Civil Aeronautics Authority said it had received similar reports from Bar Harbor and Old Town.

Radar observers at air bases throughout the northeast tried to spot and track the object.

Are you beginning to get a feeling for the "sensitive" areas?

Here is another announcement of a UFO light moving over the state of Washington. The story was in the Bremerton (Washington) *Sun*, June 25:

STRANGE LIGHT SEEN MOVING OVER BREMERTON

An unidentified flying object that "certainly wasn't a plane" was reported seen over the city early this morning by a West Bremerton resident.

Mrs. Leo A. Davis, 2914 17th Street, said that between 1:30 and 2 a.m. while returning home from a drive-in theatre with her husband, she sighted a bright light in the sky, "larger than any star," and it was moving slowly southward.

"It was not over a mile high," Mrs. Davis said, "and there were no red and green blinking lights on it like those on an airplane. But it suddenly disappeared after watching it for at least a couple of minutes."

The local ground observer post atop the Enetai Inn could cast no light on the subject as there was no one on duty there at the time, it was reported.

At the same time there was another bright UFO light in Southern California. It is getting to be a little remarkable how many times these reports come in pairs.

June 25, from the San Bernardino (California) *Sun:*

STRANGE, BRIGHT LIGHT BURNS THURSDAY NIGHT

Mr. and Mrs. Conway Brightwell of Rt. 1, Box 242-A, Verdemont, were sitting on their front porch Thursday night when they noticed a brightly burning light over Rialto.

They said they watched the light, which was "brighter than a star" for nearly an hour.

It would burn for several minutes, then disappear. Sometimes it hovered at tree-top level, other times it circled to an elevation of about 1,500 feet.

Norton Air Force Base said it had no planes over the area!

Another short report comes out of South Africa via the New Orleans (Louisiana) *Times-Picayune*, June 27:

FLYING SAUCER SIGHTED

Albert Ashworth and his 17-year-old son reported sighting a flowing, purposeful, sausage-shaped object traveling over the sea near Port Elizabeth, South Africa.

The following letter, dated June 28th, comes from one of the most solid and active UFO observer units in the United States. The letter explains something of the nature of study-group purposes and activities. Your editor would like to see some kind of national headquarters or clearing house established for the assembling and classification and appraising of UFO material and any and all related "oddity" data. We consider this essential for the most coordinated and effective effort, and careful consideration is being given to several plans which have been suggested.

Your editor would welcome further suggestions and/or comments:

1309 Forest Glen Drive
Cuyahoga Falls, Ohio
June 28, 1955

Mr. M. K. Jessup
Author, "The Case for the UFO"
c/o Citadel Press
222 Fourth Avenue
New York 3, New York.

Dear Mr. Jessup:

After reading the suggestions made in your excellent book about saucer enthusiasts forming observation groups, I decided to write you. We have had a group very close to what you described in operation for a year. We are composed of amateur astronomers, radio hams and saucer enthusiasts. Last summer we had no planned observation program. We would just try to spend as much time out at night as possible with the necessary equipment. The telescopes that are most used are small three inch reflectors. These telescopes are small enough to be easily movable and yet are very sturdy and offer sufficient magnifying power. One member has an eight inch reflector but, unfortunately, it is not portable.

Over half of the thirty reports in this area last year were made by members of our group. We are also very friendly with the local G.O.C., which not only verifies our reports but also tells us if the objects have been identified by the local Air Force Filter Center. We make sure that all of our reports can't be explained by any known natural phenomena. The information from the Filter Center aids in this, and we are also very friendly with several astronomers at the Warner and Swasey Observatory that don't have a closed mind on the subject. These astronomers have been very helpful in checking the more important reports for all possible causes, and also help us if we get into a technical problem.

During the winter we do a little observing, but not much. We use this time of the year to do research work with only the reports that we gather. This cuts down greatly on reports that might be hoaxes or that have explainable causes. Light beam communication equipment is being constructed and plans are being made to build any other equipment that might help us. What is your opinion about light beam communication equipment, and how does its future look to you? There is a possibility that a radar set might be in use this summer. It belongs to a boy in Cleveland who built and entered it in the Northeastern Ohio Science Fair and won first place in his division. We have a place selected for setting up an all night observation station. It is located in the country away from city lights. Only two things limit our work. They are lack of people to help us in our work and lack of enough money to build research equipment.

You are not alone in your idea that observation groups should be formed. These groups would contribute much information that would PROVE what flying saucers are. Do you know of any other groups similar to ours, or the kind described in your book, that have been formed? In the "Astronomical Scrapbook" section in the June issue of "Sky and Telescope" two objects were reported. These were explained as "merely ordinary Fireballs," but they actually sound like good reports of U.F.O.'s.

Yours truly,
Fred Kirsch, Director
U.F.O. Research Organization

The following item is reprinted from the San Antonio (Texas) *News* of June 29th:

FLYING SAUCER REPORTEDLY SEEN NORTHWEST OF CITY

A "flying saucer," shaped like half a sphere with the flat side down, flew at 10,000 feet or more two miles northwest of San Antonio about 6:30 p.m. Tuesday and disappeared into a cloudbank.

At least that's what Fred Hites, city waste disposal department timekeeper, reported Wednesday.

Hites, a licensed pilot, was cautious about his claim and said his wife saw the "saucer" too.

"I'm no flying saucer fanatic and if it were just me seeing it I would think it was an optical illusion," he said.

He said he and Mrs. Hites saw the saucer while watching a jet plane flying west. As they watched the jet, they saw the bright silver "saucer" flying northeast above the jet.

While Hites dashed into his house to report to the U.S. weather bureau at San Antonio International Airport, Mrs. Hites kept her eye on the "saucer."

When Hites returned, Mrs. Hites told him the object had disappeared into the cloudbank. They didn't see it come out, Hites said.

"North East" is the name of a town in Pennsylvania. They have a newspaper called the North East *Breeze*, and with that combination of names they are most assuredly entitled to at least one UFO per year! And in 1955, they reported one in the June 30th issue:

FLYING SAUCER

The flying saucers are back again!

This time one flew over the Findley Lake area at 11:15 p.m. on Friday, June 17th. It was spotted by Mrs. Ben Sweet and Pat Culver on the Francis Spencer farm.

The saucer swooped low, seemed to be suspended momentarily and then disappeared over the trees. Lighted, the saucer startled its observers. In fact, Mrs. Sweet almost ducked it seemed to come so low.

In Texas, it would seem that everything is double or nothing, UFO's being no exception.

Consider the following, from the San Antonio (Texas) *News*, June 30th:

TWO "SAUCERS" SEEN IN FLIGHT

A report that one "flying saucer" soared over the San Antonio area Tuesday is incorrect, a man identifying himself as R. A. Mathews of 907 West Rosewood Avenue telephoned San Antonio News Thursday.

There really were two, he said.

Fred Hites and E. M. Viliarreal, both employes of the city waste disposal department, reported Wednesday they had seen a round-shaped craft at about the same time although both were at their homes 15 miles apart.

Mathews said he and his wife were driving on Hwy. 281 about 15 miles north of San Antonio Tuesday when they saw two objects "shaped like silver dollars" flying east at a high altitude. One was something higher than the other, "as if in formation," Mathews said.

Mathews said he felt he should report what he saw although "I have been reading about those things and I don't believe it much."

And June ended with an interesting letter on June 30th, from the always interesting Bill Raub, of 10390 Capitol Avenue, San Jose, California. He said that he had talked to Robert Gardner, who lectured on saucers in the San Jose Auditorium, and on being pinned down, Gardner is said to have stated that he talked to several men, including doctors, who actually examined "little men from the cracked up saucers in Mexico."

Mr. Raub has been most helpful with news items and personal sightings. He reported personally to your editor that on April 7, 1955, at approximately 9:10 p.m. he observed the moon through 7 x 50 binoculars. The moon was at first quarter. On the dark side, near the edge farthest from sunlight, he saw a light which he describes as "much brighter than one of Jupiter's moons." He watched it for several minutes, and then, suddenly, it was gone.

On the same day, Mr. Raub and Leo Denny saw two black objects traveling very fast in the sky. Jets were nearby, and were of entirely different shape. Also, the jets left vapor trails, which the objects did not.

The UFO's disappeared when they got near the sun, but the jets were seen in silhouette against the sun.

JULY

July and August more or less combine into what we might call the "Satellite Months." The government's monumental extravaganza was announced at the end of July, and the furor took place in early August. So, we'll coast along through July with just the routine and commonplace of the UFO: Mere sightings by mere people, who do not have the weight of bureaucratic omniscience backed by bureaucratic omnipotence, and who, therefore, can only report what they actually see, and be laughed at for their efforts.

The C.R.I.F.O. *Orbit* carried the little note quoted below about another multiple jet disaster. Like C.R.I.F.O.'s editor, we will limit our comment. We would just like to inject the one word . . . *why?*

(Case 93. Coimbra, Northern Portugal, July 1, 1955) Eight jet planes of the Portuguese Air Force, part of a formation of twelve, crashed on Carvalho Mountain—the cause, bad visibility or a mid-air *collision*, military authorities were not sure. The aircraft were taking part in Air Force Day celebrations, which were cancelled after the crashes. Military authorities closed the crash area to reporters.

Another sinister incident reported in C.R.I.F.O. from N.B.C., June 17, minus details, involves the simultaneous crash of five U.S. jets in a western state, two pilots rescued. Still another *admittedly* "million-to-one" disaster occurred during NATO atomic air maneuvers over Germany. Here, an American Sabre-jet rammed a four-engined British bomber five miles up. All six crewmen of the British bomber were killed, while the U.S. pilot parachuted to safety. Said the pilot, "I can't remember a thing about what happened."

While (as we have noted constantly) mysterious aerial "bangs" have been recorded for some centuries, their origin has never been established. The following account is from the Associated Press, datelined July 5, London, England. It appeared in a Boston paper. These "sky-quakes" are often of such violence that they are thought to be earthquakes. Yet the Air Force, wherever possible, asks us to believe they are "sonic booms" caused by jets:

TREMENDOUS BANG SHAKES SOUTH ENGLAND:
COULD HAVE BEEN METEORITE OR U.S. JET PILOT

A tremendous bang (double) shook up a big stretch of southern England early today. And as big as the bang itself was the mystery of what caused it.

London newspapers favored two theories: 1. A meteorite had exploded on contact with the earth's atmosphere. 2. Some exuberant U.S. jet pilot topped off Independence Day celebrations by crashing the sound barrier.

The bang, which came fourteen minutes after midnight, rattled windows from London's northern suburbs to Maidstone, forty miles to the south.

Thousands rushed out into the streets in nightclothes asking, "What was it?"

Scotland Yard and newspaper offices got hundreds of inquiries. Fire trucks rushed out after an emergency call reported acrid smoke fumes spreading from a South London building. They found fumes in plenty—and a notice saying: "Smoke issuing from this building is due to bacon smoking in progress and there is no cause for alarm." Six hours after the bang, Scotland Yard said: "It's still a mystery. We've no report of damage on the ground, so it must have come from the air."

The weather office said it definitely wasn't thunder and pooh-poohed the idea of a meteorite. So that left the sound barrier. The Air Ministry said no British planes were in the area. A spokesman at U.S. Air Force Headquarters said: "We don't know a thing about it."

The Jefferson City (Missouri) *Post-Tribune* published a very excellent account of saucer sightings on July sixth. The good story follows, and once more we timorously ask: How many people are *you* going to accuse of illusion, hallucination, or hoaxing, before you accept the plain-view sightings of others?

REPORT STRANGE AERIAL OBJECTS SIGHTED IN JEFFERSON CITY AREA
AT LEAST NINE CAPITAL CITIANS VIEW OBJECTS ON FRIDAY, SATURDAY NIGHTS

"Flying saucers" visited Jefferson City Friday and Saturday nights, according to the earnest declaration of several Capital City witnesses making one of the first reports of the strange aerial objects in this area.

The witnesses were Mr. and Mrs. Harold R. Herron, 1102 St. Mary's Boulevard, who saw the unidentified object from Highway 50 near Washington Park; Mrs. T. J. Herron, Seven Hills Road, who was visiting at a residence on West Main Street; Elmer

Schmutzler and three other members of his family, who saw the object from their home on St. Louis Road; and Mrs. Dean Wilson, Seven Hills Road, who saw from her home what apparently was the same object but saw it Friday night instead of Saturday night as did the others.

"My husband and I were at a root beer stand on the highway near Washington Park Saturday night at about 8:00 p.m.," Mrs. Harold Herron told a *Post-Tribune* reporter. "I happened to glance out of the car window at the southern part of the sky and saw this object. It was white with a greenish glow, with a sort of white tail or afterglow behind it. It was traveling at a slant toward the earth at a high rate of speed. It looked about the size of a street light, if you were standing right under the street light.

"I pointed it out to my husband and we watched it for about three seconds until it disappeared behind some trees."

Mrs. T. J. Herron, a sister-in-law, said: "I was visiting at the Baldwin residence at 2508 West Main Street when I saw the object from the terrace there between 8:00 and 9:00 p.m. It was going in a straight line at high speed, apparently in an easterly direction. It was bright green with a fuzzy reflection on one side. It was bigger than an airplane usually looks. My niece and I could see it for about ten seconds, then it suddenly seemed to vanish like it had turned off the lights or something."

Mrs. Dean Wilson, Seven Hills Road, said she saw what appeared to be the same object as to size and color Friday night "flying in an arc" across the sky. "It looked about the size of a large grapefruit," she said. "And it was definitely green."

Elmer Schmutzler said the object was witnessed by himself, his wife, his son and his daughter Saturday night between 8:30 and 9:00 p.m.

"It looked like it was traveling in a southeasterly direction," he said. "It traveled in a sort of arc. It was bright green, moving very fast, I thought at first it was a meteor, but I never saw one that close and bright. We watched it for about ten seconds until it went behind some clouds. It was so bright we could see it through the clouds for a little while after it went behind them."

Of great interest is an excellent and careful report sent from Washington, D.C. postmarked July 6, 1955. It is from Mrs. John C. Jackson, 1500 Massachusetts Avenue, Washington 5, D.C. She says:

Last night, July 5th, about 10:30 p.m. my husband and I were sitting on the roof of our apartment building. I noticed a perfectly round black spot about the size of a silver dollar, stationary at the very center of the moon. It remained stationary for about two minutes. There were small clouds scattered west and southwest in close proximity to the moon. During the two minutes interval, as I watched, these clouds consistently moved farther away from the moon in a WSW direction. Not so the spot. When it moved all of a sudden, it moved slowly in a northwesterly direction! The whole incident took only three to four minutes.

This object was almost certainly in space, and not close to Washington, although we cannot be sure.

Ohio continues to hold its own. The Circleville *Herald,* July 6, 1955, gives an unusually lucid and detailed account of a sighting with human interest overtones:

TWO LOCAL FISHERMEN SEE MYSTERY LIGHT:
CHUCK RIHL, DICK BUSKIRK KNEW STORY
WOULD TOUCH OFF RIBBING

Shrugging off with grins the good-natured jibes of their friends, two Circleville men today were standing firm in their story of a strange, "square" light seen among the trees near Circleville waterworks.

Chuck Rihl, 332 E. Union Street, confirmed how he and Dick Buskirk, E. Mound Street, had seen the light while in that area one night last week. They had gone there to fish. Rihl explained he and his companion, both employees of the local General Electric Company plant, had anticipated the ribbing their story would attract.

"We just didn't say much about it," Rihl laughed, "because even as it was, they were kidding us plenty at the shop. Somebody said we had seen a flying saucer and boy, that did it!"

Rihl emphasized that he and Buskirk saw only a "square and glowing light," which otherwise had no particular details or pattern. Rihl added, "It was a mighty bright light, though—brighter than anything I've ever seen before."

Rihl said the light he and Buskirk saw glowed with an unusually brilliant "bluish" glare. He said he and his companion first sighted the phenomenon after they had finished fishing and were walking back to their car, parked some distance away. It was about 10:15 p.m., he said, and "real dark." The moon, he explained, was just beginning to rise and had yet to make an impression on the deep gloom around them. Buskirk carried a flashlight. The men said they are positive no other fishermen were in the area. And the moon, they recalled, was in a position where it could not possibly have been responsible for the mystery light.

They first saw the light directly ahead of them while they were crossing a clearing and approaching the waterworks. It was well off to the right of the waterworks structure, motionless, and roughly at tree-top level. Almost as soon as they noticed the light, Rihl said, it began to dim steadily and in a moment disappeared. The men, both able to claim more than average knowledge in the field of high-power lighting, stressed the fact that "the light certainly didn't snap off suddenly—it dimmed, and very shortly went out altogether."

When they first spotted the light, Rihl estimated, they were at a distance of approximately one quarter mile. Made curious by what they had seen, then hurried forward but failed to find any sign of explanation for the light at the spot where they figured it had been. There was a dim light burning in the waterworks plant itself, Rihl recalled, but no sign of activity.

Standing in the vicinity where they figured the light had appeared, Rihl said he and Buskirk were then puzzled by a noise in the trees overhead. He said, "It's hard to describe that noise we heard. It was sort of like a big rustling of the trees, or like a whole flock of birds were fluttering around among the leaves. I honestly can't describe how it sounded. Believe me, it gave a fellow a strange feeling. As for Dick, he said: 'Let's get out of this place!' And I certainly was willing to go."

Rihl said it would have been virtually impossible to have seen an object, even if of any great size, if it had been hovering overhead. The trees are fairly close together at the location he explained and the foliage is dense.

The Hartford (Connecticut) *Courant,* July 9, 1955, had the following about a local saucer sighting:

"FLYING SAUCER" SEEN IN NEW BRITAIN SKY

A local resident, James Carey, of Leona Lane, told the *Courant* he saw a "flying saucer" over the city about 9:00 p.m. Friday "at great height and tremendous speed."

Carey, who lives near the A. W. Stanley swimming pool, in the extreme northern section of the town, said he was sitting on his front terrace gazing at the stars, when a disc-shaped object, light orange, almost yellowish, swooped in from the southwest.

He said he followed its path for about thirty seconds and reported it headed northeast, then turned abruptly due north. "It came back in a southeasterly direction," Carey declared, and headed toward the northeast again, disappearing in the general direction of Hartford.

Here is another one from Oklahoma. The Bartlesville *Enterprise,* published it on July 11:

DEWEY MAN THINKS HE SAW SAUCER

A Dewey man said Monday he has seen what he thinks is a flying saucer. M. B. Killian said he saw a "round, silver" object flying at great speed about 15,000 feet over his house at 300 North Creek in Dewey about 9:30 a.m. Saturday.

Killian said the object was flying a north-northeast course, made no noise, discharged no smoke, and he described it as being about fifty feet in diameter and having no wings.

Killian added that it stopped its course, circled twice and then esumed the course again after picking up speed. Another Dewey resident, who requested that he be unidentified, corroborated Killian's story and said he saw the object about the same time.

The 796th AC&W radar station west of the city said it had no report of any unidentified aircraft in the area at that time.

From the Santa Ana (California) *Register*, July 11, 1955:

SAUCER SKIMS CHANNEL, SO SAY FISHERMEN

Now cigar-shaped flying saucers have been spotted over the Cataline Island Channel.

Robert I. Parker, 1725 Plaza del Sur, Balboa, and five other fishermen aboard a Huntington Beach sport fishing boat yesterday told the Coast Guard of seeing a strange cigar-shaped craft fly over their vessel.

Parker said the craft was pale blue on top and aluminum colored on the bottom and was flying about one and a half miles off the Camar II when they spotted it. It seemed to be moving at a moderate speed and medium altitude before it disappeared, he said.

The sighting was made at about eleven o'clock in the morning. On Saturday, a group of fishermen from Newport Beach, according to the Coast Guard, reported seeing a "conventional" round-shape flying saucer over the channel traveling at speeds described as "preposterous."

San Bernardino (California) *Sun,* July 12, 1955:

MAN DESCRIBES OBJECT SEEN OVER CHANNEL

The sighting of an unidentified object in the sky was described more fully by George Washington, San Bernardino accountant and tax consultant, at his home Monday.

Washington, whose office and home is at 503 Mountain View Avenue, sighted a round "cylinder-like" object in the sky while cruising with his family towards Cataline Island Saturday afternoon. His radio report to the Coast Guard at Long Beach brought Air Force jet interceptors blasting into the area almost immediately, apparently in hot pursuit of the object, he related.

H

Washington said the chase was short lived, as the object shot off into hazy clouds in the direction of San Diego, leaving the jets "far behind."

The accountant, who said his wife, Elise, and young daughter Maria, first sighted the object floating about 2,500 feet above the boat, described its shape as "a round cylinder, greyish and white, turning rapidly within its own axis."

He said it was surrounded by a "haze of fumes" apparently blowing out from the object. Washington observed it through binoculars for several minutes before deciding to notify the Coast Guard, who asked him to keep an eye on it until he could get planes into the air. He was under way at the time, having throttled down his engines when his wife and daughter called his attention to the object's presence. Washington said it maintained its position above him as he moved through the water.

He described the object's movement after the appearance of the planes in the following manner: "It zig-zagged upward with more fumes blowing out its sides and then suddenly zoomed away into the hazy clouds above to the south."

Asked about its speed, Washington said, "If the jets were going 600 mph, then it must have been going 6,000 mph."

The object's dimensions "are very hard to determine . . . maybe sixty feet in diameter, which may be right or wrong," he said. "I don't believe in flying saucers and that sort of thing, but the only conclusion I can come to is that it is something neither myself nor my wife have ever seen before."

At the time of the sighting, the accountant in his $15,000 22-foot boat, was about nine miles west of Newport, headed for Avalon Harbor, thirteen miles away. Sunday he was interrogated by Coast Guard officials and numerous press and radio correspondents concerning the sighting.

"It was fascinating," he concluded. "My only regret is that all that time I had my camera in the boat with me and didn't use it."

The Springfield (Massachusetts) *Morning Union,* July 13, 1955, presented the following sighting:

FLYING SAUCERS REPORTED SEEN OVER BLANDFORD

Flying saucers have arrived. Seven children picnicking in the backyard of the Lee Wyman home today, suddenly yelled to their parents, "Flying saucer, flying saucer." By the time two astonished mothers ran out of doors, however, the saucer had indeed flown, but the children—all seven—were able to give a good description of the round silver object that had suddenly appeared high in the sky above the Sven Anderson home on Birch Hill, then flown over the Leonard Mason home and off across the workmen on the Robert Mason farm toward Tarrot Hill where it disappeared.

Civil Defense spotters see more UFO than most people, but seldom are they allowed to tell about it. Here is a report of some of their sightings in California, as printed in the Riverside *Enterprise:*

C.D. SPOTTERS SEE FIREBALL IN HEAVENS

Authorities theorized yesterday that a ball of fire reported to have flashed across central California skies Monday night, must have been a meteorite.

The Sacramento Air Defense Filter Center said Civil Defense ground observers hundreds of miles apart reported that the fireball swirled through the air and appeared to crash somewhere to the east.

In Oakland, a spokesman for the Civil Aeronautics Administration said the weird object apparently was a meteorite or some other celestial phenomenon. He added that it was difficult to determine from the scattered reports where the fireball crashed but that it apparently went down somewhere near Tonopah, Nevada, 170 miles southeast of Reno.

Officials at the Sacramento Municipal Airport said incoming pilots reported seeing a flaming ball in the sky headed eastward over the Sierra at about 40,000 feet.

The filter center said it received its first report at about 8:30 p.m. and that the reports continued coming in until approximately 10:00 p.m.

Palmdale, California, had a good working over by UFO's. Here is the account from the *Southern Antelope Valley Press*, July 14, 1955:

SILVERY "FLYING SAUCER" OBJECTS
SIGHTED IN MANEUVERS OVER PALMDALE

Three silvery triangular objects soared over Palmdale in plain view of observers early Tuesday evening.

First to spot the mystery "things" at about 8:15 p.m. was Bob Jones, 14, son of Mr. and Mrs. Isaac Jones, 1540 Palmdale Boulevard, who said the object first looked to be long, thin and silvery. As he watched, the long shape appeared to split into three shiny triangles which darted over, under and around each other, sometimes standing almost still and then suddenly darting away at great speeds. Bob called his dad who operates the control tower for Civil Aeronautics Authority at Palmdale Airport. The elder Jones, after viewing the strange objects, telephoned Palmdale Airport where William Kane was on duty as tower operator. Kane leveled high-powered glasses in the direction of the objects, southward from Palmdale, and confirmed that there were three of them, silvery looking, and triangular in appearance. Jones said the objects appeared to be at about 20,000 feet, were clearly visible, and were not airplanes. Mrs. Jones, who witnessed the phenomenon, was emphatic in stating the objects were not airplanes; that they were made of metal; that there definitely were three rectangles in the sky.

Tower operator Kane said he watched the objects off and on for some time, and that he could not identify them. He said they might have been weather balloons, but did not act like balloons.

The objects were reported seen by Vincent Fire Station south of Palmdale and also by guards employed by Convair and Lockheed Air Terminal at Palmdale Airport.

California was taking full advantage of the summer weather. Here is another report, this one from the Vista (California) *Press:*

MYSTERY OBJECTS SEEN IN SKY
BY SEVEN VISTANS

Anyone see a flying saucer last Friday night? Well, at least seven Vista people did. It was viewed in the western sky around 7:30 p.m. from Nevada Avenue and between 8:00 and 8:30 p.m. it was seen in the west and north sky from Cypress Drive on the opposite side of town.

The object was first discovered by Mrs. E. N. Starr, 221 Nevada, who called her neighbor, Mrs. R. J. Marcotte. They described a shiny, tapered object, larger in front, which was traveling north and south. It appeared to be going somewhat slower than a jet, but faster than a blimp.

It finally turned and traveled out of sight and from the back it appeared to be round, the two women said. They watched it for several minutes.

While the sky was still light, but just beginning to get dark, Mrs. T. M. Cox, her mother and three other persons on Cypress Drive saw a similar object. At first they thought it was a comet but then after watching it for twenty minutes, thought otherwise.

It was described as being round-nosed with a light at the front, tapering to a tail which glowed like the moon. It moved around, made arcs and at times stood perfectly still, Mrs. Cox said. Finally it seemed to head towards the earth, turned pinkish and disappeared in the denser atmosphere of the murky, near-dark sky.

Nevada is so sparsely settled that there are not many people to be looking for UFO, and perhaps for this very reason there may not be many UFO over the region, although there have been some unconfirmed reports of UFO using the Nevada Mountains as hideouts. Here, however, is a report of a Nevada sighting as taken from the Las Vegas *Review-Journal:*

FLYING SAUCER REPORTS
STIR LAS VEGAS SECTION

Belated reports from Las Vegas brought flying saucers closer to home today.

George Griffiths, 418 Pleasant Road, Las Vegas, notified the *Review-Journal* Wednesday that he saw "something" Monday night, coinciding with reports from Lovelock, Tonopah, Cedar City, Bishop, and Sacramento. At the same time, the *Review-Journal's* John Romero and Miss Denece Jolley, 1260 South 8th Place, Las Vegas, said they saw an aerial phenomenon Monday evening.

Griffiths said he and his wife saw "a glowing white light with a tail that seemed to hang in the sky, then disappear," about 8:30 Monday night.

"The light headed toward the Charleston Range," Griffiths said. "My wife and I watched it for quite some time. It was a very bright light, and seemed to have a long tail of some kind. It appeared to stop and hang for a while, then the light vanished and the tail remained, then it broke up."

Miss Jolley said she saw a strong white light moving in erratic fashion toward the Charleston Range about 9:30 the same evening. "At first I thought it was a shooting star," Miss Jolley said. "It appeared to come straight down, then levelled off and proceeded across the sky toward Charleston. Later I saw some jets in the vicinity and their wing lights were clearly visible at a high altitude. The other object seemed to be one steady strong light."

Romero verified Miss Jolley's description of the object.

The same evening, watchers in Cedar City and Lovelock reported glowing lights. United Airlines pilots flying over Bakersfield and the Hollywood Hills reported they saw a "red cylinder with a vapor trail."

A rancher at Tonopah reported a "cylinder glowing red that plunged out of the sky and exploded in a shower of flame," and at Sonora Angels Camp, and Clements, California, people saw a bright flash accompanied by a smoke trail.

Wallowa, Oregon, must be in one of the "sensitive spots" of the Northwest. Here is another report in the Wallowa *Record*, July 14, 1955:

FLYING SAUCERS SIGHTED HIGH ABOVE WALLOWA

Flying saucers, ten or a dozen of them, were sighted high over Wallowa Tuesday morning about 10:30. The two reputable witnesses who saw them are going to be hard to convince what they saw were not in fact fast-moving objects at extremely high altitudes.

O. W. "Shorty" McKenzie and Ralph Pease, who was painting the McKenzie home, witnessed the spectacle. At first, Shorty said, he saw four of them close to the sun. "Oh, just dandelion thistles," he said in a joking way.

Then he watched more closely and saw them move. They must have been traveling at a high rate of speed, he said.

Then he saw more of them in other parts of the sky, until he and Mr. Pease had counted ten or twelve. They appeared to be very high, to be made of aluminum and to be spinning very rapidly. Recalling that the sky watch program has urged observers to report unusual aerial phenomena, Mrs. McKenzie called the Wallowa sky watch tower. Finding no one was there, she called Mrs. Aneta Goebel, who called the filter center at Bend directly, reporting what had been seen.

Returning from the house where he had gone to have Mrs. McKenzie phone, Mr. McKenzie took his high-powered glass and focused on the aerial objects. "They looked like an extremely bright star," Shorty said, "except that they moved, going as fast or faster than a high-speed jet." The "saucers" were in view a total of between two and three minutes.

Mrs. Ike Steele reports that the evening previous she saw a lone aerial object travel across the sky. Her description tallies closely with that of Mr. McKenzie and Mr. Pease.

Since this is the kind of news story which copy desk men on the *Observer* delight in lifting for a front-page position Saturday, the editor hereby wishes to inform his fellow scribes that Mr. McKenzie operates the Wallowa Cash Market and is a partner in the McLean Theater at Wallowa. He is a veteran of World War I, and enthusiastic sports fan, and definitely not given to fanciful imaginations.

Pennsylvania is back in the news with this report from the Hazleton *Plain Speaker*, July 15, 1955:

FOUR CLAIM THEY SAW "SAUCER"

Anthony Kotarski, 19, of Swoyersville, and three friends, who were with him several days ago at Meshoppen are convinced that they saw a flying saucer.

"We were walking in a field Monday night, between 8:00 and 8:30," Kotarski said, "when, looking up into the sky in a north-westerly direction, we saw this shining object. It moved in a straight line, then got smaller and smaller and eventually we lost sight of it as darkness fell."

"If the object was a balloon," he said, "it would bob along and it had none of the features of a plane." The strange thing, according to Kotarski, was circular-shaped and appeared to be metallic. "It changed colors probably from the sun's rays," he stated.

Kotarski claims he got a good view of the object because the air was clear and the sky cloudless.

Many newspapers open their reports on UFO with wisecracks to the effect that the "saucer season" is with us again, implying that it is some sort of "silly season." The fact that people spend more time out of doors and looking at the sky, especially at night in the summertime, is overlooked. And, it may just be that there *are* more UFO during the months of July and August. Here is one from the Cleveland *Press*, July 15, 1955:

RESIDENTS SIGHT FLYING SAUCER

The flying saucer season has arrived.

Paul Webbe was peacefully working his acres along route 306 in Kirtland when he heard a noise overhead. He looked up and saw a shiny, circular object. It had a shady center section and a hole in the center.

It was spinning east and at the intersections of routes 6 and 306, it turned right along 306. It was up about 5,000 feet, stayed in sight for thirty seconds, he said.

John Andrisin, 13, often gazes from his yard at 3802 Park Drive, Parma, in the evening, to watch for flying saucers. Last night he saw one. He and some pals watched for about five minutes before the object, which had a light on a pole sticking out of the center, disappeared behind some trees.

And the following is from Idaho, via the Lewiston *Tribune,* July 15, 1955. Surely there is significance in the multiplicity of sightings from one end of the country to the other during the past few days?

FLAMING OBJECT FALLS FROM SKIES

A flaming, comet-like object soared over Lewiston early this morning to crash to the ground—seemingly in the vicinity of Lewiston.

Lewiston and Clarkston residents who called the *Tribune* shortly before 1:00 a.m., described the object as a "big ball of flame, with a long tail—much bigger than any falling star I've ever seen."

At Clarkston, it was reported to have apparently fallen to the ground "north of here"—with estimates as near as five miles away. At Lewiston, a resident reported the object—apparently a meteorite —"looked like it hit the ground a little west of here."

The object was, residents reported, "about as big as a small airplane, with a long tail shooting sparks."

There can be no doubt about it: Florida and New Mexico get more big, spectacular fireballs than the law of averages can account for. The Miami *Herald,* a reasonably conservative paper, published the following report on July 15, covering one of South Florida's most important visitations:

BALL OF FIRE HURTLES ACROSS EVENING SKY

A bright ball of fire flared briefly and silently across the skies Thursday night, and it was described by authorities as a meteorite or a comet.

But dozens of Miamians who saw it flash high overhead insisted it was a ship of some kind.

The object was reported by airplanes as far away as Houston,

Texas, and San Juan, Puerto Rico, the control tower at Miami International Airport said.

"It was just an especially bright meteorite," said Paul Hannum of the weather bureau," a big hunk of rock that busted loose from its moorings up there somewhere."

Clyde Cohron, senior controller at the airport tower, said the object was probably a comet because it followed a path straighter than that usually described by meteorites.

Both Hannum and Cohron agreed that the fireball could not have been a plane or a guided missile. Some of the 125 callers who flooded the *Herald* switchboard in the forty-five minutes after the object was sighted at about 10:15 p.m., insisted the fireball wasn't a natural phenomenon, however.

Most agreed it was red-orange with a long white tail and travelled from east to west. Estimates of its height ranged from tree-top level to thirty miles. "That was no meteorite or comet, that's for sure," said Hank Demorsky, 1615 NW 15th Street, who was fishing from a seawall on S. Bayshore Drive, when he saw the object.

He said it was a ship with an elongated body and a dome on top; with this idea being substantiated by several other callers.

Bill Bayer, news editor of WITV, saw the object as he was driving in North Dade. He timed it at seven seconds. A few others like S. T. Fecho, 5526 NE Second Avenue, reported seeing two balls of fire, one a few minutes after the other, while others said the object eemed to be lighted from within.

Most witnesses agreed the object was traveling at about 1,000 to 1,500 mph, but Cohron, the tower controller, said the speed must have been much greater if it went from horizon to horizon in a few seconds. He also pointed out that the object must have been higher than earth's atmosphere to be seen as far away as Houston, Texas, and San Juan, Puerto Rico.

The Palm Beach *Times*, July 15, 1955, also has a brief account, in which an expert in saucer investigation takes part:

METEORITE SEEN THURSDAY NIGHT

A flash of light that moved swiftly from east to west over the city, about 10:15 last night, also appeared over Miami and Key

West, according to reports received by Jack Giddens of the CAA control tower at PBIA. A number of excited persons telephoned the Palm Beach Post that the light, ranging from white to dark red, swept in from the ocean and was visible for three or four seconds before disappearing in the west.

Gene Hutchinson of the PBIA Weather Bureau said that, although he hadn't seen the light himself, from the reports he had received, he believed it was "apparently a meteorite."

An airman fishing at the Palm Beach had a different story to tell, though. Informing bystanders that he had had experience in saucer investigation, he described the light as dark red and flat like the side of a sardine can, traveling about 1,000 mph and at an elevation of 30 degrees. He said it was not a meteor, although it did have a tail.

The Philadelphia *Enquirer*, July 16, 1955, reported a piece of ice weighing six pounds, and measuring four by six inches, fell during a storm at Brampton, Ontario. Where do these chunks of ice come from?

The Northwest again, with a report of a blue ball of fire from the *Spokesman-Review*, Spokane, Washington:

BLUE BALL OF FIRE WITH TAIL SIGHTED

A large bright meteor appeared to fall north of Spokane early yesterday, July 16, Earl Strawn, E3304 Fairview, told the *Spokesman-Review*.

Strawn said he was walking in the Minnehaha area about 1:00 a.m. when he sighted the object. He said it was a blue ball of fire with a long orange tail. "Comparing the moon to the size of a basketball," he said, "this was about as big as a grapefruit."

He said the object traveled from west to north at a speed too high for an airplane and that it made no sound when it appeared to hit the ground. It lit up a large area of the ground, he said.

The Salem (Oregon) *Capital-Journal* came up with this little item on July 19, 1955:

FLYING OBJECT SEEN

Sweet Home—Three Sweet Home residents are wondering what
the strange object seen in the sky was, as they approached Salem
from Portland, last Friday night. The thunder and lightning storm
was raging and as they looked to the sky to watch the lightning
they were startled to see a round object hang motionless in the sky
then take off at terrific speed. After they watched it for a while it
again hung motionless, then disappeared in a burst of speed. The
time was 8:50 p.m.

Wilkes-Barre (Pennsylvania) *Times-Leader-News,* July 20,
1955:

The residents of Red Rock Mountain area continue to sight flying saucers, one of them reported today. Davis Kittle said he recently viewed two of the elusive airborne objects from Fred Kittle's
store, Mooretown.
The first, sighted some weeks ago, a "silver object in the sky"
was above Mountain Springs. Mr. Kittle said it stayed motionless
for a time and then turned quickly in the direction of Harvey's
Lake. Last week he sighted the second similar object in the same
vicinity, which remained motionless for fifteen minutes before slowly
disappearing in the direction of Mountain Springs.

The Sterling (Illinois) Gazette, July 21, reported another
object with bluish-green light. These seem to be more common
than they used to be. Here is the story:

STRANGE OBJECT WITH "BLUISH-GREEN" LIGHT
REPORTED SEEN HERE

A strange, bluish-green light was seen near the A. L. Stewart
farm, northwest of Sterling last night.
The incident occurred between 11:00 and 12:00 p.m. when the
Stewarts were sitting on their porch. A strange object with a blue-
green light was sighted "sliding" along in the sky. Suddenly the

object took a dive and landed in a ditch just north of the Stewart house.

It kept bobbing up and down on the ground following the small ditch, never ceasing to glow. Then, suddenly, as quickly as it had come, it disappeared into the east. The entire incident took only two or three minutes, the Stewarts estimated.

They thought at first that it was a balloon because of the way it seemed to bob along. The Stewarts were unable to determine the size and had no chance to investigate until this morning in the ditch. They found nothing to give any clue as to what it was they had observed the evening before.

Back again to Kenneth Arnold's home base; the *Idaho-Statesman,* Boise, Idaho, published a saucer sighting on July 21, 1955:

AIR WATCHERS SIGHT STRANGE OBJECT IN SKY

The Boise Filter Center Wednesday night reported that observation posts throughout the area reported seeing a "silver object" that was identified by watchers as everything from a weather balloon to advertising signs of an amusement company.

The center said that the forest service at McCall thought the object seen there at 5:40 p.m., 20,000-feet high and drifting west, looked like a weather balloon.

An Indian Valley spotter saw the object, silver and round, drifting slowly at a high altitude. Cambridge reported that it was pear-shaped and was blue on one side and red on the other.

Payette reported at 8:00 p.m. that it was a drifting balloon and Council skywatchers said it looked like a balloon at five hundred feet. There were other reports from Ustick and Willow Creek.

Some thought it was advertising something and others thought it was a weather balloon, the center said.

The Scotia (Nebraska) *Register* also reported a sighting on the 21st. It was going in a northwesterly direction and may have been the same object as was seen at Boise and La Grande:

"FLYING SAUCER" NEAR SCOTIA

The youngsters at the Laverne Jess home south of Scotia report seeing a "flying saucer" at about 4:00 p.m. yesterday (Monday) afternoon.

The object described by the children as being "round and shiny" was about the size of a B-36 but was going three or four times faster. The "saucer" was traveling in a northerly direction at the same time that a B-36 was heading in a southeasterly direction, both in good view of the youngsters.

A number of large planes have been seen in the skies in this vicinity lately, but this is the first "flying saucer" report. Did any others see the round shiny object Monday afternoon?

On July 22, 1955, another report came from the northwest; this one from Oregon, via the Hood River *News*. The note was brief:

A round object was observed in the sky above Hood River at about 11:30 a.m. Thursday. The object apparently reflected light and was almost in line with the sun.

Now, when an object, or group, or series of objects get reported over as wide an expanse and by as many independent observers as this object or group, it is useless for the Air Force to say "it wasn't there," merely because everyone who saw it didn't have a sextant or theodolite in his pocket so as to make triangulation sightings!

On the 22nd, the *Oregon Statesman* of Salem reported as follows:

LIGHT FLASHES OVER SALEM

What appeared to be a meteor was sighted about 10:45 p.m. Thursday by several people out driving on Salem's outskirts.

To some the fiery ball with the fuzzy tail seemed to be moving westward south of Salem. To others it appeared as a bluish-green flash that lit up the entire sky.

Among those who reported seeing it were Stanley Fagg, Salem Route 6; State Policeman Henry H. Helper; Gary Doty, 3857 Hollywood Drive; Al Whitaker, 1959 N. Church Street; Henry Martin, 1245 Hoffman Road; Maxine Warboise, 1063 Hoffman Road.

More about the fireball in the Puget Sound area was published in the *Oregon Journal* of Portland:

"BALL OF FIRE" OVER CITY

A ball of fire skimmed over Oregon about 11:00 p.m. Thursday, giving numerous Portlanders a momentary thrill but confusing them about its actual shape, color and direction.

It was seen as far south as Medford and as far north as Tacoma. Some callers to the *Journal* described the ball as blue-white; others saw it as fiery red. One woman said its glow lasted for about twenty seconds as it tore west over Mount Scott.

The ball was presumed to be a meteor. Wednesday night a similar astral display was provided in the Puget Sound area—a sight seen by so many that McChord Air Force Base finally sent out air searchers to investigate the possibility that a plane had crashed. But observers are now convinced that a meteor was responsible.

In its editorial column, "Science Notes," July 23, 1955, the New York *Times* made the following announcement about Russia's seriousness as to space flight. There was also a statement about the estimates of the age of the earth which tends to stretch out all of the time scales having to do with human history and development. Here are the notes:

SPACESHIPS

Soviet Russia takes interplanetary communications so seriously that the Astronomical Council of the Academy of Sciences has created a permanent commission to coordinate and direct all research on problems that have anything to do with travel in space. L. I. Sedov is the chairman. Kapitsa is a member of the commission.

One of the first tasks is the planting of an artificial satellite between the earth and the moon.

AGED EARTH

Dr. G. J. Wasserburg (University of Chicago) and Dr. R. J. Hayden (Argonne National Laboratory) have made a new estimate of the earth's age and published it in the British Scientific weekly *Nature*. The two measured the amount of radioactive argon-40 present in a meteorite. The measurement indicated that all the elements in the universe were created five billion years ago. Not only this, but the earth and the meteorites were probably formed at the same time.

The following was sent to the *Annual* by Charles P. Boatwright, 542 Orme Circle NE, Atlanta, Georgia. The date is July 24, 1955, and it is from the Atlanta *Constitution:*

A strange "glowing" object that traveled across the sky with "fantastic speed" was reported seen by at least forty residents of the East Lake section, Thursday night.

Startled Atlantans who called the *Constitution* agreed the "thing" shed a phosphorous-like light, seemed to revolve and left a jet trail. They differed slightly on whether it was round or oblong.

"I'll never forget it if I live to be 90!" one caller said. "It stayed in the same spot for half-a-minute then, phfft! Out of sight in two seconds."

A woman, who had her neighborhood water-melon cutting interrupted by the object's appearance, said she was positive it "wasn't a light from the ground, because clouds came between it and partially blocked it off for a while."

Atlanta Municipal Airport authorities said the object could not have been a commercial airliner, as none had been over that area lately.

Mr. Boatwright said: "I was standing directly beneath it and it appeared to me to have two jet exhausts! I could be mistaken.

Sir! I believe that thing was at least two miles high and at least one hundred feet wide."

Boise (Idaho) *Statesman*, July 24, 1955:

Mrs. Velma Hacker, 4111 Kootenai Street, said Saturday she and her three daughters had seen a strange object in the sky while driving home from Twin Falls Friday night, and surmised that "we have seen our first flying saucer."

"It shot up from us very fast, disappeared and then reappeared again," Mrs. Hacker said. "It wasn't an airplane, nor a meteor, and was flat on the bottom and curved around the edge. It was so easy to see that we watched it for fifteen minutes.

"At one time it had fire on the bottom, but later the fire went out. While it didn't shine, the lights from the city reflected on it in such a manner that the bottom side could be seen, and also one side."

Now here is something, the significance of which escaped the writer, and probably escaped most of the readers. The point is twofold: first, the object is known to have fallen from the sky. Second, it fell slowly, without exploding or making a crater in the ground, and it is not ordinary meteoric material of the conventional iron or stone variety. No bunch of school boys is going to hack a "standard" meteor to bits while it is cooling off. This thing is no normal meteorite. What is it? The *Annual* would like to have a follow-up report on its analysis and what the astronomers and geologists said about it. The account, as follows, was taken from the Chicago *News*, July 26, 1955:

VISITOR FROM SPACE HACKED UP BY KIDS
FIERY METEORITE FALLS AMID
PLAYING LYONS TOWNSHIP YOUNGSTERS

A whizzing fireball snorted into the earth near 7121 Joliet Road, Lyons Township, Monday night, but it didn't last long.

Excited kids whacked up the interplanetary visitor with an axe. They thought it was a message container dropped by a flying saucer. The ghostly chunk appeared to be nothing more than an old-fashioned meteorite, however. There were no little men with coon-skin puttees riding its ridges.

The thirty-pound hunk from upstairs landed about fifteen or twenty feet from Paul Gutillo, 12, and his cousin Dominick Gutillo, 15.

They were playing volley ball in a field but this was one volley they didn't expect. Four other Gutillo youngsters were nearby. "It could have killed them," said Paul's father, James, 40. He is assistant superintendent of the House of Correction prison farm. He and his wife Lena were sitting in the yard when . . . zoom!

"I said, 'Look at that,'" said Gutillo.

A blue thing with a yellow tail streaked through the sky. It looked like a boiling mushroom when it landed.

Paul came rushing over and said, "It's a message from a flying saucer."

"I said, 'You've been reading too many comic books.'"

The youngsters ran for an axe and the Gutillo's dog, Blackie, charged the sizzling grey object. Blackie thought better of it, however, and contented himself with a few feints and growls. If he got a message, he wasn't saying.

Gutillo's children broke the fireball into pieces and brought it to him, smoking on a shovel.

He said it seemed to be porous when it landed but quickly turned harder and brown in spots. "It looked like molten rock and metal and blended together," observed Gutillo.

When the chunks cooled off, Gutillo decided to use one for a doorstop. He said he will keep the pieces as souvenirs.

A reporter took one chunk to Adler Planetarium. (The Gutillo children, apparently, were able to stand the heat of molten "rock" and handle it!)

The Liverpool (England) *Evening Express*, July 27, 1955, reported:

A dock worker, Mr. H. Jones, saw a cylindrical object over Liverpool. He called some colleagues and they watched the object hover over the city for eight minutes. . . . The same evening a retired headmaster from Ellesmere Port saw a mysterious object in the sky. He and neighbors watched for five minutes. A ball of fire was seen over the Irish sea the same night.

Astronomers who do not see these magnificent fireballs find it very easy to pooh-pooh the idea of their being anything but conventional meteors. Nevertheless the objects are peculiar and puzzling. Here, from the Miami *Herald*, July 28, 1955, is a statement of how puzzling they can be to an open-minded expert:

NAVY CELESTIAL EXPERT PUZZLED BY "STREAK"

A navy celestial expert said Wednesday the *baffling bright object streaking across the skies July 14 was not a meteorite, hinting broadly it was a man-made machine from outer space.*

Captain Curtis H. Hutchings, 42, of Key West, said the glowing tear-shaped object was "not made on this earth," and said he computed its speed at an estimated 63,000 mph.

"It's the first thing I've seen in the skies I couldn't explain," he said.

But he refused to guess exactly what it might be. Yet he said it "was not a star, planet or airplane or rocket."

Hutchings is a commander of the Navy's super-secret air development squadron at Key West, and an authority in astrological sciences. During the war, he was head of the Navy's navigation training section and wrote publications dealing with star tables.

Hutchings, driving his wife and three children home, spotted the object on the night it was seen throughout South Florida. By scientific computation, Hutchings said the object was eight hundred feet in diameter and about forty miles above the earth.

But, curiously enough, Hutchings said, he believes the object was stationary. "It's interesting to note that the earth's orbital velocity is about 64,000 statute miles an hour. Hence, the object probably was a 'fly-by' which the earth passed."

He pointed out that the object passed in a straight line, with no visible "tail" such as seen on comets.

"I can't commit myself on the thing," Hutchings said. "I've heard of flying saucers all my life, and suddenly here's something different than anything I've ever seen. I'm reluctant to say what it was."

Official government meteorologists have not identified the object, nor have they expressed opinions about its appearance.

Wallowa again. This time it's the *Wallowa County Chieftain* of Enterprise, Oregon. The jets came out again. Why?

"FLYING OBJECTS" ELUDE JETS

"Unidentified flying objects" have been sighted lurking over nearby towns. Even though they don't zip or streak or whiz by but just hang there, the Air Force is having trouble with them. On Wednesday, July 20, the Weston post of the Ground Observer Corps reported to the Bend Filter Center that a round object of silver base color was in the sky over the town.

A jet was sent up by the Portland Air Base but his maximum altitude was only 55,000 feet. The object went to 65,000 feet. A second jet was sent out, this a higher altitude job that could go to 65,000 feet. The object, however, remained elusive and went up to an estimated 95,000 feet. And there it stayed.

No further contact was made and the jets went home.

A week earlier similar objects were reported over Wallowa. The Filter Center was notified but it was too late to make aerial contact with them.

Anyone spotting any flying objects is asked to contact the nearest Ground Observer post immediately.

Norbert Gariety, of Coral Gables, Florida, sent in the following account, among several others, of a bonafide and authenticated sighting by a personally-known businessman, on July 29, 1955. This emphasizes the fact that Florida gets far more than the average number of sightings. There has to be a reason other than chance or hallucination for these "sensitive" spots:

Joseph Murphy, Coral Gables lawyer, who lives on Key Biscayne, awoke at 4:30 a.m. on July 29, 1955, because his nine-month-old daughter was crying.

While in the process of awakening and before turning on the lights, he heard a faint humming noise coming from outside the house. This humming noise, he had heard several times before, always in the early morning hours and after hearing it the last time, he decided that the next time he heard it, he was going to get up and investigate. The hum, he says, he can best describe as being like the hum of a fluorescent light, only louder and more intense.

As soon as he turned on the light in his bedroom, and the little girl's room, the hum started to fade away as though it were moving away. Leaving the little girl for his wife to see to, he went out into his living room which faces the east and the Atlantic Ocean, and looked out into the night sky.

There, he saw all the stars shining in the sky, but one of them looked different than the rest. Because it looked different he stood and looked at it for a while, and suddenly, this bright object, which had been stationary, moved very fast, straight sideways. Before disappearing from his view toward the left, it stopped and stood still again. After standing still for a few seconds, it started back again to the south.

It accelerated very rapidly, and as it picked up speed, he could hear the hum again, which increased in intensity, as the speed of the object increased visually. As it went by (he estimated it to have passed over the beach, six blocks away) it seemed to bank, so he saw the underneath part of it. Rotating in a counter-clockwise direction, on the outer rim was an orange-red ring of fire, and inside this circle of fire was a glowing blue light. He called to his wife.

They both ran outside to the yard, but by that time the object had completely disappeared. However, his wife had heard the humming noise as the object accelerated and left for parts unknown.

This lawyer was previously a skeptic and had never heard a description of the underneath of one of these visitors. Yet his description was exactly the same as the sighting by Art Gray, who saw one over Key Biscayne two years ago. He watched his for seven minutes through binoculars, and then it disappeared—straight up.

The San Bernardino (California) *Sun,* July 29, 1955:

An Upland man and his wife reported Thursday they sighted what appeared to them to be an orange-yellow ball of fire heading from the Ontario area toward San Bernardino. Names are withheld by request. The man arose about 2:45 a.m. to investigate a smell of smoke. He went outside to the yard and looking up toward the roof saw the ball of fire. He said it seemed to be traveling in a predetermined direction. In the skies over southeast Ontario it made a half-circle and then headed toward the northeast. It made no sound, and shed no sparks.

Objects were seen again over the area around Salem, Oregon, as per the *Oregon Statesman,* July 31, 1955. Here is the article:

THREE OBJECTS SIGHTED OVER SALEM AREA

Three cloud-colored objects, size and shape undetermined because of their height, were sighted going from south to north over Salem shortly after 2:00 p.m. Saturday by a resident of the area nine miles south near Highway 99E.

A high-flying plane was seen traveling in the opposite direction on a similar line a minute or two later, "but it wasn't anything like the other three things which were in V-formation and alternating between going extremely fast and considerably slower," he said. The informant said the formation was in sight about sixty seconds.

Thus ended sightings for July.

JULY—AUGUST

The Philadelphia *Inquirer*, which always has good coverage of important events, contained one of the most complete and thorough of all announcements of the artificial satellite in its July 30, 1955, issue. The announcement had obviously been planned by the government over a long period of time and very carefully. Hints had been "leaked" for months. The following are taken from the *Inquirer:*

U.S. TO LAUNCH EARTH SATELLITE

PLAN OKAYED FOR SPHERE

TO CIRCLE WORLD 200 MILES UP

All Nations to Get Data Collected by Man-Made Planet

The White House today unveiled a "world of tomorrow" project to launch earth-circling satellites into the outer atmosphere as possible forerunners of space ships of the future.

Scientists present for the dramatic announcement said the unmanned satellites, about the size of basketballs, would whirl around the world 200 or 300 miles in space at speeds of 18,000 mph.

The immediate purpose would be to explore the ionosphere for information on cosmic variation and other scientific data. But in the long run the satellites may advance the ultimate scientific goal of human travel in outer space.

The fantastic project was explained to reporters by a group of scientists from the National Academy of Science and the National Science Foundation. A White House spokesman said President Eisenhower gave his approval to the plans today.

Under these plans, the world's first artificial satellite will be blasted aloft by rocket between July 1957 and December 1958, with the launching site still to be selected. If it is successful, others will follow, a foundation spokesman said.

The satellites will be designed to spin around the earth at gradually diminishing altitudes and speed until they finally hit the inner atmosphere and disintegrate.

Scientists can now only guess at how long they will stay aloft. Estimates range from a day or two to possibly weeks. At full speed, they could circle the earth every ninety minutes.

Speaking for Mr. Eisenhower, Presidential Press Secretary James C. Hagerty emphasized that the project would be entirely scientific in nature. Data collected in the experiment would be made available to all scientists throughout the world, including the Russians.

The scientists said they hoped the "bird" as they called it, will provide invaluable information on such things as air density, atmospheric conditions, affecting radio transmission, and the dangerous effects of cosmic radiation from the sun.

An even more exciting prospect is that the observations made possible by the satellite will one day enable man to share in the outer space experiences now being described in the pages of "science-fiction."

The statement released by the White House said the satellite would "indicate the conditions that would have to be met and the difficulties that would have to be overcome if the day comes when man goes beyond the earth's atmosphere in his travels."

Dr. Allan T. Waterman, director of the National Science Foundation, was asked whether the project was a forerunner of an effort to reach a specific planet. He replied that it was an effort to get an object "to behave like the moon" at an observable distance from the earth.

The plans were announced jointly by Waterman and Dr. Detlev W. Bronk, president of the National Academy of Science. Others who took part in the conference were all top men in their fields.

The project will be part of this country's participation in the international geophysical year which takes place between July 1957, and December 1958. The initial cost was estimated at $10,000,000.

First news of the plan reached here from Belgium even as reporters were being briefed at the White House. It came from Professor Marcel Nicolet, executive secretary of the special committee of the geophysical year.

Nicolet said the satellite would be launched from somewhere in the United States and would be in the form of a three-stage rocket. He said atomic energy would not be used in the launching.

The first stage will take the satellite twelve to fifteen miles high and the second stage on up to about 180 miles. There it will begin an orbit around the earth and receive a third boost to maintain its course the Belgian scientist said.

He estimated that in seven to ten days gravity would begin to pull it back to earth. Eventually, he said, atmospheric friction would destroy it, just as it does "shooting stars," some thirty miles above the earth's surface.

The program has been under study by various units of the government since 1949. Mr. Eisenhower's action today gave it the official go-ahead.

The scientists said that because the first satellite still was in the planning stage, it had not been determined whether to send up a solid object or one containing instruments that could automatically radio observations back to the earth. If instrumentation is used, scientists of other nations will be notified of wave-length on which the instruments will be broadcasting. Scientists of other nations will be informed when the object is launched and be kept constantly aware of its orbit.

The scientists said very valuable information could be obtained even if the satellite carried no instruments.

Waterman pointed out that telescopic observation of a solid object in the upper atmosphere would give scientists an unprecedented opportunity to study air density. He said, "We now have no very good idea of the make-up of air in the 200-300 strata. At that altitude there is still some trace of atmosphere, but it is exceedingly thin."

Asked whether they expect to be able to go on to the construction of a man-carrying satellite of "military importance" the scientists agreed that the present project was only the start of the experiment.

"You want to crawl in space before you can fly," one said.

Waterman, commenting on man's lack of knowledge of conditions in outer space said, "It is as though we are in a depth of the ocean and can't see above us. And now we will send out this bird which in turn can tell us about conditions far above."

It has not been determined where the first satellite will be constructed. Waterman said this decision would be reached after recommendations from scientific groups all over the country.

The scientists emphasized that the only connection the Defense Department would have with the operation would be shooting the satellite by rocket to the upper atmosphere.

To the suggestion the satellite might be launched from one of the polar regions, Waterman said this was a decision to be reached later.

When plans for the International Geophysical Year were drafted at a Rome meeting of scientists last year, all nations were encouraged to consider satellite projects.

Russia was among those represented. There have been recent dispatches from Moscow telling of the formation of a satellite program in the Soviet Union.

Item No. 2, from the New York *Herald-Tribune* News Service:

SATELLITE OPENS WIDE NEW VISTA

The man-made moons announced by the White House yesterday could usher in a fantastic era of space travel very soon.

Instruments inside the basket-ball sized globes 200-300 miles up could radio back to earth information about conditions there.

Launching even such a small object to that great distance will acquaint rocket scientists with the technical problems needed to put a permanent space station outside the earth's atmosphere. From such a station space ships could take off to the moon and other planets.

Here are some of the things scientists could do with the smaller, temporary moon now proposed to be launched by 1957 or 1958:

They could make delicate measurements of cosmic rays without interference of the atmosphere. They could, with the construction of special telescopes, make observations on distant stars now also obscured by the atmosphere.

They might be able to establish a relationship between disturbances on the sun—sunspots and solar storms—and the weather on earth.

They could use it to make accurate distance measurements on the face of the earth by sighting its position from different locations. They could reflect television and radio beams from it to test the feasibility of permanent moons as relay stations.

They could load small animals into them to test the effects of long periods of weightlessness in gravity-free flight.

They could make important measurements on atmosphere pressures and the condition of the ionosphere, that layer of air that reflects ordinary, but not high-frequency, radio waves.

And they could examine some of the problems of the northern lights—the aurora borealis—and other earth phenomena, like gravitation and magnetism.

Not all these things could be done in one satellite, but several could be done and are quite feasible because of the existence of transistors, those tiny bits of germanium and silicon metal that can be built to behave like radio tubes.

So the scientists can build many miniature instruments· radio transistors, solar batteries, Geiger counters, pressure measuring devices, biological test facilities and temperature recorders. All could be built into a 100-pound satellite, the size the proposed globes are said to be.

How will the moon get up there? The scientists propose a three-stage rocket.

A permanent space satellite could be put at 22,000 miles above the earth's surface. At that height the speed would just equal the earth's rotation and it would maintain a fixed position above the earth. This could be useful as an intercontinental radio and television relay station.

Permanent satellites could also be used for air navigation, for the launching of intercontinental missiles, and for many scientific purposes.

The heavy atmosphere that overlays the earth protects human life from the bombardment of the ultra-violet light from the sun and from cosmic rays. The latter are high speed particles from outer space.

But this same protecting layer makes scientific investigation difficult. The giant 200-inch telescope at Mount Palomar, Calif., is used at only ten per cent of its efficiency because of the atmospheric filter.

There were many newspaper comments in reaction to the satellite announcement of July 30. There were far too many of them to reproduce here. Since the satellite is hardly to be considered as even a stepping stone toward UFO's we will omit most of the general statements, but here, from the Philadelphia *Inquirer*, July 31, 1955, is one discussion pertinent to the field of UFO research:

SATELLITE REVIVES "SAUCER" MYSTERY

President Eisenhower's action in giving the government's official blessing to a projected "earth satellite," to be launched within two years, has given rise once more to a question often debated and never satisfactorily settled:

Have at least some of the so-called "flying saucers" sighted in the last eight years actually been experimental devices, sent up by government scientists in their efforts to develop a "workable" satellite, and so hush-hush that even the U.S. Air Force had to deny their existence?

The fact that scientists, sober and reputable ones, now talk

calmly of putting a satellite project into actual operation within
two years argues that the experiment already is far beyond the blueprint stage. How, except through the use of pilot models sent into
outer space, it may be asked, can the National Academy of Science
and the National Science Foundation have convinced themselves of
the practicality of such a venture?

In the summer of 1952, when the furor over the sightings of "flying saucers" was at its height, a shrewd and reputable columnist,
commenting on the lack of excitement in official Washington, had
this to say: "Manifestly, whatever is up there does not seriously
alarm us. The Defense Department itself is only perfunctorily disturbed. It has ordered our jets up to chase away whatever it is, and
for the rest has left the worrying up to the people who are experts
on saucers.

"This aplomb on the part of our security officials suggests to
some that the things that go blip in the dark area over Washington
are our own secret devices, which we cannot admit to, and thus must
'investigate' and pretend to drive away with the jets."

Some of the public's aplomb, it is obvious, has been due to the
assurances by the Air Force itself, many times repeated, that the
"saucers" are merely free-floating weather balloons, cloud formations, spotlights on clouds, radar mirages, and the result of so-called
air inversions.

Nationally known astronomers, including Dr. Donald H. Menzel
of Harvard University, and Dr. I. M. Levitt of this city's Fels
Planetarium, have shown how optical illusions, the bending of rays
of light by unusual atmospheric conditions, can account for the
great majority of saucer-sightings throughout this and other countries of the world in recent years.

Their experiments and demonstrations do not explain away however the 20 per cent of sightings which the Air Force, after sending
up jet planes to investigate at close range, has had to mark for its
files: "Conclusion: Unknown." These instances include a number in
which experienced pilots, men not given to hysteria, have sighted
mysterious flying objects at such close range as to preclude any
possibility of optical illusion.

Scientific predictions made last Friday that the earth-circling satellite would travel at a speed of 18,000 mph, bring within the realm of reason the reports by Air Force pilots who encountered UFO's that they tracked them on their radar screens at speeds of better than 7,000 mph. The reports were made back in 1952 and 1953.

The Air Technical Intelligence Center, at Dayton, Ohio, which is responsible for investigating and reporting the probable explanation for such unusual occurrences, classifies much of its data as secret, so that even if it were able to identify some of the UFO's as experimental devices looking toward an artificial earth-satellite, the public still might not know the fact.

Arguing the likelihood that experimental satellites were responsible for the rash of "saucer" sightings two and three years ago are these factors:

For reasons of safety and secrecy, such devices would have to be kept well away from the routes of scheduled airline flights, while the reputable pilots who have told of sighting UFO's have sometimes described how the objects followed or "buzzed" their planes.

All plans made to date for an artificial earth satellite contemplate an unmanned type; the UFO's described by airline and Air Force pilots gave every appearance of being manned by intelligent beings.

In view of the fact that Russia within 24-hours of President Eisenhower's action, announced it, too, was planning an earth satellite, Air Technical Intelligence cannot dismiss the possibility that some "saucers" sighted over this continent came from sources beyond our control.

As one ATIC officer put it, "Our job is to detect any weapon that might be used against the United States. In the future, a weapon that 'probably was a meteor' may prove to be a global rocket."

Although the public was first made aware of the Saucers in 1947, the ATIC has been studying similar phenomena for at least two years previously.

This takes the matter back into the closing days of the Second World War, when German rockets were still bombarding London from secret launching sites along the coast of north Europe. These rockets, the most effective that Germany's admittedly superior technicians in the field could produce at that time, had a maximum range of less than 100 miles, although they traveled faster than the speed of sound.

Thus there is a serious question as to whether any device similar to the projected earth satellite, which is to be rocket-launched, was responsible for the sightings under ATIC study a decade or more ago.

There is nothing better to start off August than H.R. 7843. On August 2, 1955, H.R. 7843 was introduced into the House of Representatives by Mr. Karsten, of St. Louis, and referred to the Committee on Rules. It can hardly be coincidence that this bill was introduced at almost exactly the same time as the announcement of the planned satellite. Nor is it likely that this bill is a casual whim. The very introduction belies the Air Force's protestations that there are no flying saucers or UFO. In part, the bill reads as follows:

To Create a Joint Committee on Extraterrestrial Exploration

Be it enacted by the Senate and House of Representatives of the United States of America in Congress assembled. That there is hereby established a joint Committee on Extraterrestrial Exploration to be composed of nine Members of the Senate to be appointed by the President of the Senate, and nine Members of the House of Representatives to be appointed by the Speaker of the House of Representatives. In each instance, not more than five members shall be members of the same political party.

The joint committee shall make continuing studies of the activities and problems relating to the development of *extraterrestrial exploration and travel*. All bills, resolutions and other matters in the Senate or the House of Representatives relating to this subject shall be referred to the joint committee . . .

The italics, of course, are our own. By all means note carefully the wording of the bill. Note that it says nothing at all about the satellite although the satellite *may* be implied as a means of extraterrestrial exploration. Note the inclusion of the word *travel*. Certainly this is not mere satellitery. In my opinion this is clearly a recognition of the reality of space flight, and an admission that such flights are imminent for mankind.

Fireballs continued to be prominent in the news in August. Here is a report from the Richmond (California) *Independent*, August 2, 1955:

MYSTERY SKY FIRE BALLS SPOTTED BY PAIR HERE

Mysterious balls of fire—this time in triplicate—were seen today flashing over San Francisco Bay by two Richmonders.

James Dodd, 16, a student and Jerry Gilbert, 20, a member of the Air Force, saw the white ball about 3:08 a.m. They had just returned from a movie and were in front of Dodd's house at 146 West Bissell Avenue, talking.

Dodd particularly remembers the time because he checked the clock in the auto in which they were sitting. He said the white ball was equipped with red, white and green lights. It was going east at about a 45-degree angle upwards.

"At first, we thought it was a plane," Dodd reported. "Then as the lights began to fade out, it split into three parts. Each part was a white ball of fire and went in a different direction. Then we knew it wasn't a plane."

The youths telephoned Daniel Artegea, chief observer of the Richmond Ground Observer Corps. He said the post was closed last night so there were no reports from the sky-watchers. The reports of Dodd and Gilbert were forwarded to the Oakland Filter Center.

The following story of a weather observer who saw a UFO, appeared in the Fresno (California) *Bee*, August 2 or 3, 1955. It is worth noting that the objects mentioned were checked with powerful instruments:

WEATHER OBSERVER SIGHTS
STRANGE OBJECT OVER CITY

It would appear that the flying saucer season has arrived, following two reports of unidentified objects sighted in the skies yesterday, one by a trained weather observer with 17 years experience.

The last person to see an object flitting through the atmosphere over Fresno was Warren Langer, a weather observer briefer stationed at the Federal weather bureau at the Fresno Air Terminal.

Langer said the object he saw was round, silver colored and moving through the skies at a regular rate of speed.

Early yesterday morning an International News Service photographer reported sighting a mysterious speeding light over Fresno.

Langer added he has been a weather observer for seventeen years and while he has seen other unidentified objects this one caused the greatest question in his mind.

A. A. Lothman, the chief of the Fresno weather bureau station, said Langer is one of his most reliable observers. Langer said he believes in the stories of so-called "flying saucers" because "too many good observers have seen them."

Langer explained he was making observations of a weather balloon at about 1:30 p.m. when the object passed through his field of vision against the wind.

"I was sighting through a theodolite at a pilot balloon," he said, "when the object passed close by the balloon." He declared the balloon was at 30,000 feet.

He explained a theodolite is a low-powered telescope used for sighting on balloons and determining wind velocities aloft and other weather data. "I followed the object for twenty to thirty seconds," he added. "It moved away at a regular rate of speed.

"I had no way of estimating its distance but it must have been up somewhere near the balloon. It appeared about one fourth or one third the size of the balloon, which is six feet in diameter.

"I don't know what it was but it was sharply outlined against the sky."

I

Although headed "The Cracker Barrel," the following is a serious column. Written by Jonathan Yank, in the August 3, 1955 *Herald and Express* of Los Angeles, the column poses some questions that would be embarrassing if the Air Force and other official spokesmen felt obliged to make a candid and objective answer.

Eagle Rock, California, August 3: On December 15, 1954, President Eisenhower told a news conference that to the best of his knowledge there are no flying saucers coming from other planets. Since it is a matter of military record that "unidentified flying objects" buzzed Washington on the night of July 20, 1952, one is inclined to wonder if the mysterious craft do not have their homes on this planet. George Klein (former German minister of munitions) who now lives in Switzerland, reports that Hitler's Reich produced a pilotless remote-controlled saucer that, on February 14, 1945, soared to a height of 40,000 feet in three minutes, over Prague. His disclosures, recently published in Switzerland, state that one top rocket expert, together with a working model, fell into Russian hands during the closing days of the war. Four other top saucer scientists, he says, are now working for the United States government. Klein goes on to state that saucers developed since 1950 by the Avro Corporation of Canada have been inspected by Marshal Montgomery and have attained a speed of 1500 mph. James W. Mosely, commenting on all this in *Fate Magazine,* says (without giving his authority for the statement) that American pilots now have orders not to approach or fire on the saucers. Can it be that *America and Russia already are inspecting each other's defenses?*

Here is another sighting, this time from the Midwest. It was reported as follows in the August 4, 1955, edition of the East St. Louis (Illinois) *Journal:*

WAS IT A SAUCER?

RESIDENT REPORTS FAST "SHINING SPECK"

A pair of housewives spotted the season's first flying saucer.
The women, who live on Outer State Street, saw the object sta-

tionary for fifteen minutes. Then it streaked off eastward, "faster than any jet," one of the witnesses said.

She said she and a neighbor were chatting on her front porch and went down the steps to see a pair of jet planes roar past. As they looked up, her neighbor spotted the object, "just a shining speck" in the sky.

At first they thought it was a weather balloon, she said, but its metallic appearance and the speed with which it disappeared ruled that out.

Others joined them until three men and three women were in the yard craning their necks. She added, "A couple of the men weren't able to see it."

Her neighbor finally ran to her home to get a pair of binoculars but by the time she returned and focused them, the object shot away.

The women reported another neighbor had spotted something Wednesday night.

"I hadn't asked what it was, but I'm going to now," she said. "I was sitting on my porch and I heard them say 'there it is now, over the housetops.' If I find out they saw the same thing or if I see it again I'll tell you my name. I don't want to now, though. Somebody might think I'm crazy."

No matter what the eventual outcome and truth of the flying saucer "craze" may be, it has done more to awaken the world to the true nature of its environment than any set of conditions since the birth of Christ.

Here is a newspaper notice about a proposal, which appeared in the New York *Journal-American,* August 4, 1955:

ASK SPACE PROJECT AGENCY
RIGID CONTROL HELD NECESSARY

The American Association for the UN proposed today the creation of a special agency for coordinating experimentation in outer space projects such as the launching of earth satellites.

The proposal was accompanied by a warning that any "race" developing over coming years in establishing "artificial moons," and effecting interplanetary travel can become extremely dangerous.

Clark M. Eichelberger, Chief of the association, pointed out that a precedent for the creation of such a UN agency already exists in the proposed formation of a specialized "atoms-for-peace" agency.

In presenting his proposal for UN supervision of interspace launching and development programs, Eichelberger said: "We cannot help but be reminded that our greatest rivals—the Russians—announced sometime ago they are striving to set up a space satellite for experiment leading to interplanetary flight."

There can be no clearer evidence of the blackout, or brownout, on UFO news than that presented by the mysterious events at, and around, Cincinnati in the first week of August, 1955. Thousands of very reliable people saw the UFO over Cincinnati. It is a matter of record that jets from nearby Ohio air bases were scrambled to intercept the UFO, yet the startling and momentous event did not make the press wire services. True, the sightings did make minor headlines in the Cincinnati papers, and front page in one or two editions, but so thinly was it reported that the service to which we subscribe did not even send us clips from the Cincinnati papers.

Regardless of what the Air Force says or does, we are convinced that this was a major sighting, and that the problem must be taken seriously.

Here is a quotation from the Cincinnati *Enquirer*, August 6, 1955:

HALLUCINATION FROM HEAT, OR "SAUCER" OVER CITY?
NO METEOR, EXPERT SAYS

If it's as hot in outer space as it is in Cincinnati, there could be an explanation for the unexplained phenomenon reportedly seen over the city last night. Our solar neighbors could have been out for an evening's ride.

What was the phenomenon? Although descriptions vary, many

Cincinnatians and Northern Kentuckians saw it, shook their heads, and looked again. It was still there.

The thing's presence over the city was reported to the *Enquirer* by residents of Walnut Hills, Mt. Washington, Madisonville, Hyde Park, the East End, and Fort Thomas. They began telephoning about 8:45.

One man described his vision as being pear shaped, having a tail and glowing with colors such as green, violet and white. To him, it appeared to be between two and three feet long, and eight to ten inches in diameter. Everyone on the street saw it, he said.

A woman saw it from in front of her Columbia Parkway residence and was afraid it was going to hit a house. Someone told her it probably was a meteorite, and she was greatly relieved.

The Weather Bureau was called by some, too: but weathermen were at a loss to explain the vision.

Leonard H. Stringfield, 7017 Britton Avenue, Director of C.R.I.F.O., said he had an "excellent view" of the thing from his yard.

"It was not a meteorite," he emphasized, "but an 'extraterrestrial, propelled device,' better known as a spaceship and facetiously referred to as a flying saucer."

He explained that it was "perfectly round in the frontal area, tapering into a tear shape and having a blue tail."

Furthermore, Mr. Stringfield continued, it traveled too slowly to be a meteorite and traveled without trajectory (curvature) as meteorites are known to do. It left no streamers or debris in its wake as meteors do, and, moreover, there are no meteor showers present at this time, he concluded.

Anyway, whoever or whatever the thing was, certainly was bound to be cooler at 10,000 feet than we are on the earth. Wonder if it was air-conditioned?

Private George D. Fawcett, of Panama Canal Zone, wrote me as follows, on August 7, 1955:

At the present time, I'd like to give you a saucer report from Panama of this year, word for word, as it occurred in the papers here. It was taken from the *Panama-American,* an independent newspaper here in Panama City, dated April 25, 1955, as follows:

"A British farmer, who is a resident of Juan Diaz in Panama City, claimed today he saw a flying saucer of some nation of this world hover over the new race track Saturday for about four hours. The farmer, A. D. Huckerby, said he was one of a hundred eye-witnesses who watched with fascination while a big round ball hovered from 2:30 in the afternoon until 7:00 p.m. when it suddenly took off. He estimates that it was about three to four thousand feet up in the air . . . at first, Huckerby claims, it looked all one color: a silvery-blue. However, when several bystanders scrutinized it through binoculars, they would differentiate the saucer was red on top, an aluminum white in the center and blue on the bottom. It looked big as a house. The farmer said: "I didn't believe in these things before —but I do now.""

This is a valuable report, and we thank Mr. Fawcett heartily.

Forthcoming events in interplanetary travel and exploration are already casting their shadows before them. The problem of legal possession of the moon has to be settled and may very well be the bone of contention that sets off World War III with spatial overtones. The following notice from Copenhagen, August 6, 1955 appeared in the New York *Post,* of August 7th. Evidently the U.S. government's announcement about the proposed satellite was timed for the Copenhagen meeting:

WANTS WORLD TO SHARE MOON'S WEALTH

A Dutch aeronautical engineer said today the nations of the world should agree to share the wealth of the moon—if it has any.

Simon van Munster of the Aviolande Aircraft Factory, Papendreckt, The Netherlands, said the combined research efforts of all nations would be needed to get the first space ship to the moon. Therefore, he said, anything of value found there should be divided "among the world's people."

Van Munster said cooperation on research and a share-the-wealth plan conceivably could be worked out through the UNESCO organization. Van Munster is here for the meeting of the International Astronautical Federation. He said in an interview the IAF already has made contact with UNESCO concerning a program of world cooperation on research.

Saying it would be possible to reach the moon by 1980, the engineer added: "If we are to go outside the earth, we must realize that we must all work together to solve the problems of space flight. No one nation can solve these problems of getting out into space and of living there. There must be cooperation in research by all nations."

He said arrangements should be worked out beforehand so that the pioneer moon explorers would turn over to UNESCO for world wide distribution anything of value found there.

"There might be some material on the moon that would differ, say, from either coal or the iron found on the earth, but which might have value," he said.

Krafft Ehricke, an aeronautical engineer for the Convair Aircraft Co., San Diego, California, said in an interview that "it appears realizable to land a manned vehicle on the moon some time during the 1990's."

He said the lunar flight conceivably could be made with present-day chemical rocket propellants but that there is a need for working out "new types of propulsion systems," especially for any ventures beyond the moon.

Ehricke said that among theoretical concepts suggested as alternates for chemical propulsion are: An "electrical rocket" in which radioactive material would give off electrically charged atoms, or ions; these would be accelerated inside the core of the rocket by a device utilizing some of the principles of a cyclotron until they attained energies sufficient to give a thrust to the rocket.

A type of propulsion in which a mirror would focus the rays of the sun on some solid material, heating it to the point where it would be converted to hot gases. The latter would be expelled providing propulsion.

But before there is any trip to the moon, Ehricke said, it will be necessary, first, to establish a manned satellite in the outer atmosphere—as take-off point for the lunar "special."

The St. Petersburg (Florida) *Times* of August 9, 1955, printed a photo of an eleven-year-old lad holding a small object which fell from outer space. The material was *not* of the "conventional" meteoritic kind, and furnishes ample proof that other substances than iron and stone meteorites fall from space. Here is the caption:

An object from outer space plummeted mysteriously onto the lawn of T. A. Scott, 226 10th Street, early Sunday morning and was found by his son. Dennis, 11, examined the "meteor" with scientific interest. It is about the size of a baseball and very light in weight. Scott said it was obviously burned at a very high temperature and had no odor at all. He plans to contact the Smithsonian Institute to find out the composition.

August 12, 1955: The November issue of *APRO Bulletin*, states that on August 12, 1955, Vice-Admiral F. S. Low, Commander of the Western Sea Frontier, issued a request to operators of thirty-one steamship companies to report all UFO's in the air *and on the surface of the sea*. Question to the U.S.A.F.: Since there are no UFO's, what is it the Navy expects to find?

The following, rather caustic discussion about the "satellite" appeared in the August 12, 1955, edition of the Apalachicola (Florida) *Times*, and helps to bring the current "satellite" hysteria down to earth a bit:

MORE ABOUT NOTHING

By E. Ralph Damon

Of all the gimmicks I have ever read about is the one that the government expects to send up into the stratosphere sometime late next year, about the size of a football and propelled by rockets and will travel about 18-humpteen miles an hour or go around the world in nothing flat!

They say it will be used to gather data and will be shared with the rest of the world. For the life of me, I can't understand what sort of data a thing like that . . . no bigger than it is . . . could gather . . . especially going at that speed.

In the first place there will be very little use for the upper stratosphere especially 200 or 300 miles up . . . for a good many years . . . unless they have already drawn the plans to put up a series of half-way stations to the moon . . . to be used as rest stops for the very, very daring persons that will make this trip.

Could be that the scare of flying saucers of some years ago is something to contend with and the government is preparing something that will out-run . . . out-wit . . . and out-manoeuver the "things" the government said did not exist . . . but at last have awakened to the fact that maybe many persons who witnessed these contraptions were not nearly as addle-brained as some of the "heap of help" in the Pentagon.

Here is another Nebraska sighting, as noted by the Grand Island *Independent*, August 13, 1955:

FLYING SAUCERS ARE SEEN BY ANSLEY RESIDENTS

Flying saucers were observed here Wednesday night by several persons.

Faintly luminous discs were seen crossing a segment of the sky to the northeast, sometimes two together, but mostly one at a time. They could not have been reflections from car lights as they passed at intervals of 25 seconds. There is no airplane beacon closer than forty or fifty miles, so far as is known. The phenomenon lasted for several hours; in fact no one knows how long, as it was still in progress when those watching tired and went to bed.

Denison, Iowa:

Several Crawford County citizens have reported seeing what looked like flying saucers.

They are reported as white, flat objects traveling in the air at a high rate of speed. One observer reported a large cluster of them.

Ravenna (Ohio) *Record*, August 15, 1955:

A fast-moving green object with a fiery tail was spotted in the sky Sunday night by Edna Schumm, 705½ S. Water Street. Miss Schumm said she was driving south on Hudson Road near Kent at 10:30 p.m. when she spotted the object. It disappeared within a few seconds. Other persons reported seeing it and it was considered too low in the sky to be a meteor.

We thank the Hamilton (Ohio) *Journal*, August 15, 1955, for this little item about a sighting:

PHENOMENON VISIBLE IN HAMILTON SKIES

Several persons in the Hamilton area today reported seeing what appeared to be a "great ball of fire" in the skies Sunday night at around 9 o'clock.

The AP said Walter Todd, of airport traffic control at Lunken Airport, Cincinnati, who was on duty at the time, described the phenomenon as a "possible meteorite."

He said it was visible for about two seconds, was seen about fifteen degrees above the earth and was headed southward. He described the object as similar to a drop of water flying horizontally through the air.

Judging from this tiny note in the Cleveland (Ohio) *News*, August 16, 1955, the personnel in the flying trade don't exactly uphold the official edicts of the Air Force regarding the reality of UFO:

Cleveland Air Force members mention it only in voices below their voice—more than seventy per cent of all flyers believe that flying saucers exist and that they come from outer space.

Noted by the Mount Dora *Topic*, Florida, August 18, 1955:

Miss Elmira Lodor and Miss Alice Bukey, Grand View Hotel residents, have more flying saucer company now.

The Alfred W. Johnson family on Old Eustis Road is ready to join them as believers in these strange invaders from the sky. They saw them last Friday night, playfully flitting about the northern horizon.

First to see them was their son, Alfred, 14, who was out rowing in Lake Gertrude with a friend, LeRoy Meshler, about 10:00 p.m. He spotted the lights in the sky—lights that glowed big and bright and then faded to a deep red. They would go up and down, dart to and fro, then stand perfectly stationary.

Going ashore, the boys called adults to witness them too, and for several minutes the family watched the apparent playtime of saucers—or whatever they were—in the sky northward. Then they disappeared.

Formation flying by saucers is becoming more popular. Is there a UFO factory in one of those vast formations that have been seen on the moon? This time it's the Bremerton (Washington) *Sun*, August 18, 1955:

FLYING SAUCER FORMATION
SIGHTED OVER CITY BY BOYS

Report of a formation of eight flying saucers sighted high over this area shortly before midnight last night has been made by two teen-age boys.

"We were in sleeping bags in our back yard, and I guess we both noticed them at the same time—about 11:30," Kenneth Parolini, 15, told the *Sun*. With young Parolini was Nicholas Ahlfs, 14. The youths described the sight as a formation of eight lighted circles that moved out of the southwest, made a gentle arc high in the sky and disappeared in a westerly direction.

"I guess they were over us for about six seconds before they faded from view," Parolini said.

They flew in a triangular formation, Ahlfs said. "I've seen meteors before and this was definitely not one of them," Parolini emphasized.

They did not appear to change formation as they moved across the sky, and Parolini stated he was able to make out lines encircling the sides of three of the objects. "It couldn't have been a reflection. They appeared to fly in a tight formation as though actually being maneuvered," Parolini said.

The youths state that they heard no noise as the circles moved above them.

Nebraska is doing right well this year with its sightings. This report is from the *State Journal*, of Lincoln, Nebraska, August 19, 1955:

FLYING SAUCERS SIGHTED BETWEEN OXFORD, ORLEANS

The UFO's apparently were spotted here.

This time twelve of them, UFO's, were sighted by a Lincoln man between Oxford and Orleans.

And Gerald Merritt of 1965 B, is sure that cluster of lights he saw moving across the sky late Thursday night wasn't anything as commonplace as an airplane.

"I know doggone well they were saucers," he insists.

For the record, Merritt says the saucers looked like a cluster of white lights. They weren't airplanes, he says. There were too many of them, and they were arranged in a circular pattern.

They were flying low, but just how low Merritt couldn't estimate. They were moving slowly from west to east. They were in sight maybe three or four minutes.

Merritt isn't the only one sticking to the flying saucer story. He says two companions saw the same thing he did—and insist they were flying saucers, too.

Oregon again. The Hillsboro *Argus,* August 22, published the following:

FLYING SAUCERS BACK IN THE NEWS

Flying saucers are in the news again—or yet.

Carol Robbins, 18, and Ricky Booth, 12, reported watching dimly lighted objects flying over Hillsboro for about two hours early Saturday morning as they were watching meteors in the back yard of their grandparents. They said the objects appeared faster than jets, made no noise and left no trail. They circled in various directions and seemed circular in shape, the watchers added. Both said it was a "frightening" experience.

Kansas City (Missouri) *Star,* August 23, 1955:

Saginaw, Michigan, (AP)—A flashing luminous object was sighted in the sky over Central and Western Michigan last night by civil defense ground observers at the observation post at the Saginaw fairgrounds. A report was sent to the air filter center in Grand Rapids. A similar object was sighted from the ground observation post at Cutlerville near Grand Rapids.

The famous story of the Sutton family in Kentucky is reported herewith, from the New York *Journal-American,* August 23, 1955. The Sutton phenomenon is only one of several similar events in the Kentucky-Ohio area in August:

WEIRD STORY OF "GREEN MONSTERS"
KENTUCKY FAMILY FLEES "SPACEMEN"

The J. C. Sutton family at Kelly, Kentucky, today fled from their farmhouse home in the Blue Grass Country and headed for Evansville, Indiana, after they told neighbors the "little green men from outer space" paid them a return visit.

"They just upped and left town," Chief of Police Russell Greenwell of Hopkinsville, told the New York *Journal-American* by telephone.

"They beat it shortly after the spacemen they said they saw Sunday came back early yesterday and started to climb over the trees and roof. Nobody else saw the little fellows, but the Suttons said it was too much for them—and they had run out of shotgun shells anyway."

The Suttons had told the chief that the three-foot-tall creatures were indestructible. "Besides," said Chief Greenwell, "it looked like they outnumbered the Suttons two-to-one, and that's counting four children in the farmer's family."

Chief Greenwell was asked if he believed the Sutton's story of the "spacemen."

"I don't know what to believe," he said.

The Suttons said they first saw the eerie visitors Sunday night when a "spaceship" glowing like a ball of fire and shaped like a washtub, landed in a field behind the farmhouse.

"Told me there were fifteen of these little monsters," Greenwell continued. "They were jumping on the trees and roof and peering into the windows.

"The women said they were especially frightened seeing these pumpkin-sized heads with eyes like saucers glaring at them through the curtains."

The chief said he and his men went to the farm and checked for three hours without finding a trace of the "spacemen."

"But the place was all shot up," said Greenwell, "and I know there was no drinking of hard stuff going on there. Moonshine's outlawed in these parts, you know."

This item is from the Marysville (Ohio) *Journal-Tribune*, August 25, 1955:

LOCAL PEOPLE SEE FLYING SAUCER

Spotting of a flying saucer was reported today by a Marysville couple. Dale Gardner, 111 E. Seventh Street, told the *Journal-Tribune* today that he and his wife saw the disc-shaped object last evening while sitting in their yard.

Gardner said it appeared to be about eight or ten feet in diameter and was going "at a terrific rate of speed" in the general direction of Milford Center.

He said there were no outside lights on the object like there would be on a plane but that it was "all lit up like lights inside an automobile." He described the color of the light as having a reddish cast.

Gardner said the time was exactly 8:29 p.m. as he checked his watch on his wife's request. He said they were able to see the flat-shaped craft only about ten or fifteen seconds before it was out of sight.

In reporting the incident, Gardner said he was doing so only to learn if anyone else in the vicinity had seen the object.

He said he had never been a believer in flying saucers and had always considered such reports as a "hoax."

But he added, "I've almost got to say there is such a thing now. My wife and I both saw it."

The Staples (Minnesota) *World*, August 25, 1955, published the following sighting:

OBJECT SIGHTED BELIEVED TO BE FLYING SAUCER

With the thought of being ridiculed by friends, and accused of suffering from hallucination, a summer resident at Ottertail Lake and his guest have kept silent on a story that may or may not be important. The story, loaded with interest, is released by the parties this week, with the understanding that names be withheld.

The story started out, "I'm just as sure it was a flying saucer, as I am sitting here in your office." With this, they tell of the following incident:

While the resident and his guest were returning to the cottage from a fishing trip on Ottertail, their attention for some unknown reason, was attracted skyward, and they sighted a brilliant object suspended in the sky. As they came along in the boat, they continued to watch the object, and jokingly remarked, "They won't believe us, but we can say that on this night, at twelve minutes to eight, July 14—and—sighted their first flying saucer," and continuing in lighter vein wondered if they would have their names in the second book when it was written on flying saucers.

About fifteen minutes later when they docked their boat, the object was still visible, but had moved to another quadrant. Calling to his family, the resident told one of his children to get his binoculars, as he wanted to get a better look at it. The entire group watched it for another possible fifteen or twenty minutes.

In explaining the object, they state it appeared to be somewhat like an elongated balloon, squashed together, and seemed to be standing perpendicular. When it was first sighted, it was about 75 or 80 degrees to the east, and later moved into a south quadrant.

"Whatever it was, it wasn't affected by wind currents, for clouds moved around it, and there was no drift to it—it just stood still," said one of the men.

With the aid of the binoculars they could make out what appeared to be a row of windows, or portholes along the side of the object something like on a train coach. On what they thought was the underside, was a "V" which appeared to run from about the center off to the front. "It was whitish," is the way the color was explained, "maybe something like aluminum in the bright evening sun, but it was so bright it was hard to tell, it just looked 'whitish' is the best way to explain it."

The object was estimated to have been at a height of 25,000 feet as near as they could determine from the cloud structure and it appeared to be about "half the size of the moon."

When the object started its departure, they said it moved from the south slightly east, against the direction of the clouds, and then in a sort of sweeping arc started its perpendicular climb and disappeared into the south, passing through two thin layers of cloud.

Said one: "I have never discounted the possibility of flying saucers, but I was always in hopes I could see one to verify it in my own mind—and now I can," and then went on, "I can't help but feel it was somebody up there making an observation, for it stayed there so long."

This story has been passed on to the 739th AC&W at Wadena, belated as it is, and request is made, "if any people ever view such an object which can't be identified as a conventional aeroplane, if they will get all data possible as to shape, color, and where viewed, and notify them immediately. Their phone is 940—Wadena Pioneer-Journal."

In a letter dated August 26, Mr. David Bell, of Linden, California, sent me the following small clipping. It is dated Las Palmas, Canary Islands, August 20, 1955:

(UP) Hope was abandoned today for ten men aboard an inter-island steamer which flashed an SOS Thursday. Searchers could find no sign of the 238-ton Guadarrama.

For the end of August we have a final little item from the *Trentonian*, Trenton, New Jersey, August 31, 1955:

FLYING SAUCERS AROUND AGAIN

Three UFO's paid a surprise visit to Lawrence Township last night and created quite a stir before disappearing in a northeasterly direction.

The UFO's were described as "oblong" and were a reddish-white in color. Witnesses said they were flying at a height of two thousand feet.

The objects clearly were visible from Lawrence Township police headquarters.

SEPTEMBER

Was September just another month for UFO?

There was nothing spectacular to report—no government announcements, no outstanding disturbances comparable to August's in Cincinnati—all-in-all "just another month for UFO"

. . . *unless you consider a few dozen visits from outer space and hundreds of dead birds falling to earth extraordinary!*

Some of the sightings are too nebulous and lacking in verification to report; however, there is enough to report to show that the world of our environment is just a bit more complex than smug dogma has been willing to admit for some few decades!

From the Trenton (New Jersey) *Trentonian*, September 1st:

VISIT FROM SPACE!

Three UFO's paid a surprise visit to Lawrence Township last night and created quite a stir before disappearing in a northwesterly direction. The UFO's were described as "oblong" and were a reddish-white in color. Witnesses said they were flying at a height of 3000 feet. The objects were clearly visible from Lawrence Township police headquarters.

The following account from the Washington (D.C.) *Post and Times-Herald*, September 2nd, is not, strictly speaking, UFO news per se. It is, however, news from space, and as such it is of definite interest to students of UFO phenomena. The report of new stars forming in the Orion Nebula (about 600 light-years distant from earth) shows that the condition of space is not static. Events in space, however, are conducted on a time scale which is so vast that it is almost imperceptible to mankind:

TWO NEW STARS BELIEVED BORN IN ORION NEBULA

Dr. George H. Herbig, Astronomer in the University of California's Lick Observatory here,* raised the possibility today that he had detected the birth of two new stars, a unique event in the history of astronomy if confirmed.

"Our understanding of what is taking place," Dr. Herbig said, "could hardly be more incomplete, but it may be that we have witnessed the opening phase of an episode in stellar evolution."

Astronomers' use of the words "recent" and "birth" is, of course, relative. The actual birth of the two new stars would have occurred about 600 years ago, the time it takes light to travel from the Orion Nebula to the earth.

Dr. Herbig suggested that his findings may provide important support for the idea of a continual birth of new stars, and may help to explain how these stars are formed.

Dr. Herbig based the possibility that he had detected the birth of two stars on two types of evidence:

* Mt. Hamilton, California.

1. Two photographs, taken seven years apart, of the same point in the Orion Nebula, the first showing three stars and the second, five stars. All were embedded in a dark cloud of dust and gas.

2. Evidence accumulated by astronomers for years indicates that stars so embedded in gas and dust have been formed recently out of the condensation of material in the gaseous streamers.

The following United Press release, quoted from the San Bernardino (California) *Sun*, September 2, appeared in many papers throughout the nation:

NEW ASTRONOMICAL OBJECT

Radio astronomers, at Ohio State University, think they may have discovered a new type of celestial body. The object is characterized by rapid changes in strength of radio waves it emits. Dr. Jones D. Kraus, director of the Ohio State Radio Observatory, said that although the University's radio telescope has discovered several hundred celestial sources of radio signals since 1952, this is the first to show such fluctuations. It is the "most spectacular object yet recorded at Ohio State," said the three Astronomers who first discovered it. They have been studying its erratic behavior since it was first noted in January.

Dr. Kraus said the signals are often too faint to register on the radio telescope's. sensitive receiver, but even when observed clearly the peculiarly rapid variations were noticeable, he emphasized.

Dr. Kraus conceded that the source might be associated with the solar system, but believed that it was more likely a "radio star" outside of our system.

"Whatever the new source ultimately is found to be," the radio astronomer said, "its behavior suggests that it represents a new type of astronomical object."

Ed.: Radio Astronomy is a comparatively new science. It is an outgrowth of the study of radio-atmospheric disturbances (static) as connected with Sun-spots, a study which began about 1930. There are many peculiar areas in the distant heavens from which come radio-receivable rays or vibrations, and these tend to lie in a belt, as does the Milky Way. Whether these beams come from "new types" of celestial objects is debatable. They may be merely newly discovered types of radiant energy traversing space, but in any case they open up new channels for studying the universe. It is possible that they may throw some light on the habitability of space and of other planets. It would be interesting to put these signals on tapes and vary the speed of the tapes to see whether intelligible signals may be involved, which are too fast or too slow to be perceived directly by human ears.

The following editorial from the New York *Times*, September 4th, is background material for UFOlogy. It is essentially astronomical in import, but it is one small element in our understanding of the world in which we live. The more we comprehend of the universe and its size, and the time scales involved in universe phenomena, the better we are equipped to evaluate the field of UFOlogy. The concept of an exploding universe is thirty years old, and it is something like the viewpoint of an inhabitant of an atom in an expanding and drifting cloud of cigar smoke!

IS THE UNIVERSE EXPLODING?

Though they are not unanimous in its acceptance, cosmologists find the Friedman-Lemaitre conception of an expanding and exploding universe convenient. It enables them to estimate the distance of remote nebulae with the aid of what is known as the "red shift." The whistle of a locomotive that is speeding toward us seems to howl up and then, as it recedes, to howl down. So it is with these nebulae. Their spectral lines shift slightly toward the red, so that they are howling down, thus indicating that they are rushing away from us. The greater the distance the greater is the recession and the more pronounced the shift. In one of the outermost clusters of stars, which is about 700 million light-years away from us, the red shift corresponds to a recessional speed of nearly 40,000 miles a second.

The late Dr. Edwin Hubble, who first interpreted the red shift in this way, began to doubt, before his death, if the increase in shift with distance would hold good for nebulae farther and farther out. At Dublin last week Dr. Walter Baade of the Mount Wilson and Palomar Observatories presented some reason to believe that the rate at which the universe is expanding is slackening rather than increasing on the frontier of the visible universe, thereby confirming Hubble's doubts.

If the rate of expansion, as Hubble determined it in 1929, steadily increases with distance, this universe must have been a clump of matter which started to explode 3,500 million years ago. Until recently, the earth was supposed to be about four billion years old. A new estimate adds another billion years. A universe that is younger than the solar system? No wonder the cosmologists are worried. Here is an anomaly that calls for explanation.

It is easy to understand how the late Sir Arthur S. Eddington, an authority on relativity, could dispose of the problem in this fashion: "The theory of the exploding universe is in some respects so preposterous that we naturally hesitate to commit ourselves to it. It contains elements apparently so incredible that I feel almost an indignation that anyone should believe it—except myself!"

And again from the somber New York *Times*, September 4th, we have this report which is of great import to UFOlogy:

RADIO TELESCOPE
HARVARD WILL BUILD BIG ONE
TO CATCH SIGNALS FROM SUN

The sun is a colossal radio station. Its signals are picked up by specially designed stations in various parts of the world. Harvard announces that it will build one just for studying solar and terrestrial relationships. It will be mounted early next year at the Upper Air Research Laboratory on Sacramento Peak, New Mexico.

The sun's radio waves probably originate in the corona, which is visible during a total solar eclipse. When a sunspot appears the waves are much stronger than usual, indicating that sunspots or the regions around them also send out waves. When sunspot activity is high a tongue of hydrogen flares up for a few minutes. The effect is felt on the earth for days. Transoceanic radio communication is sometimes impossible for an hour; the earth's magnetic field is disturbed; the auroras are more brilliant than usual. Though Harvard is not especially interested in practical results, it is plain that the telescope will enable astrophysicists to collect much information which will probably be highly useful to communications engineers.

Like its counterparts in other parts of the world, the new radio telescope ("dynamic spectrum analyzer" is its technical name) is nothing but a big radio receiving set. Radio waves may be regarded as light waves that are too long from crest to crest for our eyes to see. Light rays can be collected with a paraboloid mirror. So this radio telescope will have a paraboloid "mirror" twenty-eight feet in diameter, which will be made of open-work wire so that it will not look at all like a mirror. It will be much more sensitive than any similar instrument so far used in the United States.

Harvard will bring over Dr. Alan Maxwell of the Jodrell Bank Experimental Station of Manchester, England, to serve as astronomer-in-charge of the new radio telescope. At Jodrell Bank the University of Manchester has built the largest radio telescope in the world. Its paraboloid mirror has a diameter of 250 feet.

Dated September 5th, the following letter was sent to your editor, and it is a pleasure to reprint the observation of such an alert UFO investigator. The letter speaks for itself:

> Barracks #3
> Arlington Bks. USNRS
> Columbia Pike
> Arlington 8, Virginia

Mr. M. K. Jessup
c/o Bantam Books
25 West 45th Street
New York 36, New York

Dear Mr. Jessup:

In April of 1953 I was stationed at NATTC, Norman, Oklahoma, a Naval Air Station. The buildings are spread far apart and are built low on that base. One clear night, at around 11 p.m., I was crossing one of the large lawns between the PX and the post library with a friend, Patrick Kelly. I have this friend's address if, by chance, you wish to substantiate this report.

About half way across the lawn, I pointed to a light just about as brilliant as the stars, and seemingly as far away, that appeared in the sky in front of us. I noticed that it was moving in an oblique, downward path. I told Kelly to look at the falling star. We stopped and watched it.

The object fell slowly. So slowly that I began to have my doubts concerning its being a meteorite. I mentioned this to my companion. He agreed, and said that it was probably a plane. I said no, a plane has, in addition to a single white light, blinking colored lights on its wing and tail.

The object continued in its downward path for some time. At last it began a very sweeping and long horseshoe turn to the left. At this point I knew damned well it was no meteor. I've never heard of one turning! The light continued steady and unblinking until it had completed its turn. We watched until it disappeared into the darkness over the station library.

Further, having served aboard an aircraft carrier for some time, I have seen the blips you speak of in radar on apparently cloudless days, while, at the same time, over the phone circuits, information has come that there are no aircraft in the vicinity.

Yours sincerely,
(signed)
Lewis Turco

The following account is from the Arcadia (California) *Tribune*, September 5th:

FLYING SAUCER SPOTTED DRIFTING OVER FOOTHILLS

An Arcadia couple, and verifying Arcadia police, on Friday night had a case of the "Flying Saucers"—or at least spotted an unidentified object drifting in the Northern skies.

Mrs. Clarence A. Bunnell, 47 Woodland, first reported the object, which was described as longitudinal, with a red light at one end and a green light at the other. She said the lights appeared to be blinking but the object itself standing still.

She and her husband verifying their initial look with binoculars, first saw the object just over the rim of the mountains. Then it rose slowly into the sky.

Arcadia Police saw it, too. When they found the object, Virgil Maine and Martin Resteria began checking. Resteria called the Temple City Sheriff's Station, International Airport and the Civil Aeronautics Administration—but the object remained unidentified.

And now—more mysterious blasts!

They are obviously not the private property of Florida and Southern California, and this report is from the New York *Herald-Tribune* of September 5th:

MYSTERIOUS BLAST IN OCEAN
IS HEARD NEAR SANDY HOOK

A mysterious explosion in the Atlantic Ocean, one mile east of Sandy Hook and three miles west of Scotland Lightship, touched off a fruitless air and sea search for more than three hours yesterday by the Coast Guard.

The explosion was heard by the crew of a forty-foot Coast Guard boat patrolling the area and by persons on a number of private motor and sail boats. But search parties found no trace of wreckage, clothing, oil, or dead fish.

The Coast Guard discarded an early theory that a boat with a gasoline motor had exploded, but it was unable to offer any other explanation.

The Coast Guard also ruled out any possibility that the explosion had been caused by a derelict mine or depth charge. One small boat, which identified itself by radio as the Joyce B., said the explosion occurred 100 yards astern in an area where there had been no other boats. The Coast Guard said that a depth charge or mine would have caused damage to a small boat at a distance of 100 yards.

The explosion took place at the entrance to South Channel, which roughly parallels Ambrose Channel, used by ocean going ships coming into New York Harbor. South Channel is used only by small boats because in many places the water is only twenty-five feet deep.

The Coast Guard received the first report of the explosion at 10:32

a.m. The Coast Guard boat reported its crew heard the explosion and then saw "bluish-grey smoke" some three miles from its position.

The Coast Guard immediately dispatched two eighty-three-foot boats and a helicopter from Floyd Bennett Field in Brooklyn.

At 10:45 a.m. the Coast Guard picked up a radio message on a frequency of 2670 kilocycles, standard for water boats, saying the Joyce B. had seen an explosion 100 yards astern in an area where no other boats had been sighted. The Coast Guard was unable to contact the Joyce B. for further details, but the radio message confirmed the Coast Guard's own report.

When the Coast Guard was unable to find any wreckage, they questioned persons on other small boats in the vicinity. A number of these reported hearing the explosion.

The helicopter returned to its base at about 11 a.m. Two of the Coast Guard boats were ordered to return to their regular patrol duty at 12:15 p.m. and the third boat gave up the search at 1:48 p.m.

On September 6th, Wallace E. Honson wrote a most interesting letter to your editor. It reports a sighting worthy of inclusion in the UFO *Annual* for 1955:

5201 Suffield Terrace
Skokie, Illinois

Dear Mr. Jessup:

At approximately 10:15 p.m., on June 17, my wife was sitting in a neighbor's yard facing in the general direction of south. She noticed a glare in the sky over the trees toward the southwest. While speculating on the cause of the glare, an object passed through the sky in the west from the south toward the north. The general area traversed was probably near the large public and military as well as numerous private airports in this vicinity.

The object was low in the west, just over the trees, and passed from sight very quickly, before a neighbor could turn her head to look. The object glowed and in addition shot sparks like from fire works. It was cigar-shaped, generally, and about two or three diameters of the moon in length.

After the passing of this object, a large number of jet planes took to the air and seemed to patrol the area for probably 45 minutes. The jet planes were from the military airports nearby.

Because of the large number of airports in this vicinity, we are quite familiar with the appearance of both military and public transport planes, and it is inconceivable that any such plane could have taken the appearance of the object seen by my wife.

Sincerely yours,
(signed)
Wallace E. Johnson

The following is from the Buffalo (New York) *Courier-Express*, September 7th:

SLOW-MOTION METEOR TRULY COLORFUL SIGHT

Sky-watchers last night got a long look at Western New York's most luminous meteor.

Niagara Falls Municipal Airport's tower identified it as a meteor after a jet pilot flying over Lockport had called attention to the phenomenon.

But William Fleming of South Freeman Road, of Orchard Park, saw it cut such a slow arc through the atmosphere he thought it must be a falling flare. He even had time to call his wife from the basement.

Local observers generally disagreed over its color. One tower control man and Fleming called it blue. The jet pilot and a second tower man described it as red.

(Ed.: Maybe astronomers *do* try to make out that all of these gliding objects of flaming brightness are meteors of stone and iron composition; however, astronomy has, for generations, been faced with "slow meteors," and astronomy has yet to come up with explanations of how these "things" can be set aflame by slow motion or sustain themselves in the upper atmosphere at such low speeds.)

A most interesting letter was received, on September 7th, from Mr. George Reeves, of 1119 Eleventh Street, Golden, Colorado, and Mrs. Reeves has obviously been doing some exceptionally fine research. He particularly went through some volumes of *The American Journal of Science and the Arts,* in the early years around 1860 to 1880. He found some interesting references to the "Obscuration of the Lunar Crater Linné." This is a matter of the utmost importance to the science of UFOlogy, and I have given it careful and detailed attention in my own research since the publication of *The Case for the UFO.* I expect to use it and treat it extensively in *The Expanding Case for the UFO;* therefore, we shall not go into detail at this time. But Mr. Reeves is to be congratulated for his courage and perception, and we need more work like his to bring UFOlogy into proper focus.

Mr. Reeves has also cited a fascinating reference to carbonaceous matter in meteorites, and he quoted the following from page 130 of the *Journal* mentioned: ". . . analyses have shown that certain meteorites contain substances . . . resembling the last residues of organic substances of terrestrial origin."

This is very significant in the general development of any theory of the origin of organic materials in space, and possibly with the origin of space flight as exemplified by the various types of UFO.

Several articles were published at this point which "debunked" flying saucers and UFO's, and pointed out examples of "sightings" which were later proved, conclusively, to be weather balloons.

This no doubt happens. Where is the man who has yet to commit an error?

And while speaking of "debunking," your editor feels it might be well to warn observers and UFOlogists against mistaking the planet Venus for a UFO. In the daytime, it is occasionally possible to see Venus as a very tiny moon in the sky. It never appears as a full moon, for at that phase it is on the opposite side of the sun and therefore invisible to us. Daylight views of Venus are most easily had when there are some thin cirrus clouds drifting past it, and its appearance of being stationary behind the clouds draws it to observers' attention.

On the other hand, there are times of the year when Venus appears as a great blazing light of golden color in the western sky at sunset. Some of our friends have mistaken Venus for a UFO because they watched it drifting slowly downward in the western sky, not realizing that all stars and planets drift downward in the western sky due to the rotation of the earth.

Parenthetically, it may be that some of you are a bit surprised to learn that Venus passes through phases just as the moon does, and may be seen in both gibbous and crescent phases. This is true, also, of Mercury. Any planet appears to undergo such phases when viewed from another planet farther from the sun than itself.

The following interesting letter came from Roy A. Marshall, 1008 North Third Street, Richmond, Virginia. Mr. Marshall is one of those observant and alert persons who saw UFO's years before Arnold's historic observation of 1947 brought forth almost national hysteria. Starting in 1926, Mr. Marshall has not only seen UFO's, he has even constructed models.

Here is his September 8th letter:

". . . Therefore, my data is sketchy, not that I have lost interest, but in the five fortunate sightings beginning with the fall of 1927, when the air mail was inaugurated under Wilson's administration, I was constructing beacon towers on the Atlanta, New York run.

This first sighting took place from the top of a 75 foot tower at Paris, near South Boston, Virginia, at about 4:30 in the afternoon. The object was coming almost straight toward me at an altitude of approximately 500 feet. The shape appeared to be a flying wing. Its flight was level but the absence of propellers or apparent control surfaces drew my keenest attention. There was an almost inaudible or high pitched whine, similar to a steam turbine. There was no trail and the object passed over too rapidly to even guess the speed. It was approximately 100 feet from tip to tip and crescent shape.

None of my fellow workers saw this object because I was the only one on the tower and they were packing tools to quit for the day. I made sketches of this observation and later models that I flew.

My second observation was from tower location Atlanta-Chicago 15, 5 miles from Hillsboro, Tenn. I had my camera and tried to get a picture of two objects that passed, but they were so far away they did not register in print. These objects were different from the ones I sighted first, and not close enough to be very definite about their shapes or size, but they appeared to be black and moved very fast and made no sound.

The third sighting convinced me that these objects changed direction without actually turning, i.e., their forward movement stopped and direction of flight changed without turning, at high speed. I saw this one execute two almost right angle 90 degree *turns* before it was lost to sight at high altitude, probably 60,000 feet. It left a decided vapor trail and appeared to shine from reflected sunlight.

I have witnessed in my sighting, three definite shapes, two apparent colors, black and reddish silver, hovering, terrific acceleration, unbelievable maneuvering and the absence of sound, jets or propellers. I have not seen the objects slip or move up and down in flight. They seemed to be supported by counter gravitational force of some kind. I know there is not enough accumulated power on earth to produce a beam to do this. Therefore, I assume that internal reactors produce this type of levitation and drive. We know that gyroscopes regress. What if they could be forced to progress! . . ."

The Santa Ana (California) *Register* is very faithful in reporting saucer phenomena, and they have our sincere thanks for doing so.

On September the 8th, the *Register* printed the following:

"SHIMMERING THINGS" EXCITE FOUR COUNTIES

Anxious callers flooded military, police and newspaper switchboards late yesterday with reports of "shimmering things" in the skies over Orange County Beaches, Riverside and San Bernardino, and Los Angeles counties.

Some observers speculated that the object sighted might be the giant 25-story-high balloon which ran away from scientists in International Falls, Minnesota, seven days ago.

Although the experimental balloon, carrying mice and guinea pigs, was thought by the scientists to be somewhere over Canada, scores of residents in Southwest Colorado have reported they saw it passing by. The scientists said this couldn't be. (Ed.: A mirthful reversal!!)

An observer using binoculars in Laguna Beach about 6:30 p.m. yesterday said that she and friends watched a giant balloon bounce around in the sky for nearly an hour. The woman, Suzette Dabney, of 1320 Carmelita Street, said the balloon had something dangling below it.

Miss Dabney said there were airplanes circling the balloon when she spotted it; however, El Toro, March Field and Norton Air Base Information Officers said that no planes had been dispatched from those fields.

Calls also came in from residents of San Juan Capistrano and Newport Beach that either "flying saucers or weather balloons" were circling over the beaches. (Ed.: Have you ever seen a balloon *circle?*)

Norton Air Force base information officers said that they had received many calls concerning objects in the sky, but they doubted that weather balloons from that base could be spotted from the ground as they are too small. They also said that no planes were dispatched from that base late yesterday.

Information Officers at El Toro Marine Air Base also said that they had received many calls concerning objects in the sky, but they had no idea what they could be.

Officials at March Field Air Force Base also denied knowledge of what the objects could be.

On September 10th, your editor received the November issue
of the APRO *Bulletin,* wherein, on page three, there is a most
interesting discussion of "Sonic Booms." Mention was made of a
"boom" which severely rocked the town of Thornton, Colorado,
a suburb of Denver, on September 10th. As usual, an attempt was
made to blame it upon jets—but without success, *for there were
no jets operative in the neighborhood at that time!*

APRO points out that Los Angeles has experienced many of
these booms, and only a few are explained by the action of jet
planes, particularly since the Air Force outlawed the voluntary
production of the booms near populated areas. In some instances,
it has been shown that sonic booms produced by jets are not
felt over so wide an area as are these mystery blasts.

UFO's?

September 10th seemed to have been "publication day," for
another intriguing publication, *The Psychic Observer,* was received and from it I wish to quote a most unusual piece:

WHERE THERE'S SMOKE

Mount Shasta

The area round Mount Shasta, California, has been the source
of many legends, stories and books. It is said that the "Mystery
People" who lived there (and may still be doing so) resent intrusions
by outsiders, and have often used their mystic powers to turn away
visitors.

Several reports state that a light has flashed before a motorist,
the electrical system of his car has ceased functioning, and did not
work normally until the car had been pushed down the road 100
feet or more.

Also it is claimed that when forest fires have approached this
region, a strange fog has risen from the ground to form a wall which
the fires never penetrated. In evidence, visitors are shown a hard
line, outside of which trees are burnt, but inside of which tall trees,
of great age, are without sear or blemish.

Local inhabitants say they have seen strange cattle, unlike any others in America, emerge from the woods, suddenly take fright, as though they had sensed an invisible signal, and immediately run back to where they came from.

Flying "cigars" are another reported phenomenon in the area. These not only fly through the air, but can land and move on the ocean, as well as dive in the same. Hundreds claim to have seen these peculiarly shaped boats or "cigars" as far as the Aleutian Islands, and land on Pacific islands.

In 1931, "a group of persons playing golf—near the foothills of the Sierra Nevada Range (exact location not named) saw a silver-like vessel rise in the air, float over the mountain-tops and disappear—there being absolutely no noise emanating from it."

The theory is that Mount Shasta is inhabited by survivors of the lost continent of Lemuria. Their city is constructed within the mountain itself. On rare occasions they emerge for their tribal celebrations. It is said they have a tunnel through the eastern base of the mountain, leading to their city, from which heat and smoke can be seen rising from the crater.

There are similar records that in Mexico, other descendants of Lemurians live in an extinct volcano.

There seems enough "smoke" here to intrigue someone to go and make a thorough investigation.

And here is a feature article by Donald Foxvog which appeared in the Washington (D.C.) *Sunday Star* of September 11th.

In connection with this piece, your editor offers no comment. Each man must decide for himself:

GENEVA SUMMIT MEETING

Zion, Illinois—It was only some 25 years ago that this Northern Illinois city on the banks of Lake Michigan achieved national attention when Wilbur Gleen Voliva and his Zionist followers staunchly insisted that the world was flat.

There is still a handful of oldtimers here who cling to that conviction, but another group with a strange new belief is now in the limelight.

K

Today the Illinois dunes, the sandy shores of Zion, are used as the site for dead-earnest "saucer sightings" expeditions by a group that is just as firmly convinced that flying saucer people from other planets have already landed on earth as the Zionists were convinced the world wasn't round.

This new group, known as the Great Lakes Unidentified Flying Objects (UFO) Club, is one of some 65 such organizations now flourishing in the United States and, for its size, it is probably the most active group in the Nation. Other prominent flying saucer clubs may be found in Chicago, Detroit, Los Angeles, New York and Philadelphia. Still others exist in England, France, Italy and South Africa.

The basic belief seems to be that soundless flying saucers are zipping around the earth almost all the time. Thousands are seen, millions more unseen. The saucers are "known" to come from Mars, Venus and Saturn in our solar system and there is one "recorded" visit from a saucer which "obviously was from another solar system."

How does one see flying saucers? Well, some just happen to come into view, other times you go looking for them and sometimes they look for you, especially if you are a "plain simple person" with an "open mind."

Jack Maynard, president of the Great Lakes UFO club, proudly says he has had 17 "sightings" since 1949; "12 with witnesses." Maynard has trained himself to "look up" so he won't miss any that just happen to whiz by.

The Great Lakes UFO Club goes on frequent "saucer sightings" at night at the Illinois dunes, and Maynard said his group saw a saucer make "three passes" one night last fall. Checking further, it was learned that about a third of the group did not see it and others "confessed" they weren't sure they saw a saucer but they didn't want to disappoint Maynard and other friends who immediately saw it.

Maynard explained that since the spacemen have equipment in their saucers which tells of the presence of "open-minded" and receptive earthlings, they can arrange to be seen by people who will make favorable reports about their experiences. The saucers people quite obviously want favorable publicity, as do the UFO'ers.

When this reporter promised to record his exact experiences while "saucer sighting" it was thought that the spacemen might take advantage of the vow and make their presence known. But they let this golden opportunity slip through their fingers . . . or perhaps weren't tuned in when the promise was made.

The night we went saucer sighting Maynard reported seeing one brief, strange, unaccountable movement of light in the heavens, but said he was not sure enough to call this a "suspicious," much less a "definite," to use the technical terms. Unfortunately, I didn't see even that much.

While saucer sighting Maynard carried a huge flashlight which he frequently flashed off and on. He assured me that he was not sending code to his friends in outer space but was only seeking to attract the attention of handy saucers.

The Great Lakes group believes that in at least 60 cases Martians, Venusians and Saturnians have landed and talked to earthlings, and the Great Lakes UFO club imports speakers who calmly relate that they have engaged in such conversations.

How are such conversations possible? Simple. Saucermen from any planet have IQs superior to yours and mine. In addition to having a language of their own, they speak any earth language. They also have telepathy down pat and thereby know what earthlings think.

You can converse with a Saturnian, for example, by just thinking. The Saturnian may answer in your language, English perhaps, or he will just put his answer into your brain. The latter method avoids noisy, turbulent conversations.

At least two visiting saucer experts have told the Great Lakes UFO group that they have been favored with rides on flying saucers. Thus history (Earth History, that is) can record that the first rides into space took place in the middle of the 20th century. (Unless, of course, some human in a previous century received a ride and kept mum about it for fear he wouldn't be believed. There seems to be no fear today.)

One earthling was whisked from New Mexico to New York City and back (about 8,000 miles) in a half hour, but time was lost while the space ship hovered over the city so the earthling could be sure of where he was.

However, this venture was next to nothing compared to the trip taken by "Buck" (shades of Buck Rogers?), a 65-year-old Missourian who refused to give his full name. (The check for his lecture fee had to be made out to cash by the club.)

Buck reported that after four earlier visits from the saucer people he persuaded them to take him for a ride on their fifth visit. And what a ride! From his Missouri farm to Mars, Venus, the moon and back in three days!

So Buck is the first known earthling to travel to the moon and other planets!

Readers may wonder why they have not read news stories about this epoch-making, interplanetary trip—certainly one of the greatest stories in our recorded history. Jack Maynard has the answer.

Air Force Intelligence has "ordered" the press associations not to publish such stories, and newspapers "go along."

"How about freedom of the press?" Maynard was asked. Answer: "They all go along for reasons of national security."

Air Force Intelligence, and even the FBI, you see, know all about the visits of the flying saucer people. They have this information locked in their files and they are determined to keep it there.

And not only that, just why do you suppose the heads of the United States, the Soviet Union, Great Britain and France met at Geneva recently? If the answer isn't obvious, it was to discuss flying saucers.

Like Senator McCarthy (though for different reasons) Maynard is confident that President Eisenhower in no way revealed what was really discussed at Geneva. The Great Lakes UFO group knows that the President is not without personal information on saucers.

One dark night, Maynard reports, the President and Secret Service agents slipped out of Washington for a prearranged rendezvous with spacemen from a neighboring planet. The saucermen felt obligated to warn Eisenhower about the dangers of atomic warfare and the President assured them that he would do all he could to prevent it. Another reason for the Geneva Conference!

Do you recall what followed on the heels of the Geneva Conference? It was the announcement that the United States would have satellites revolving about the earth in the '50s. These satellites are to gain information about the flying saucers, as if you didn't know.

Maynard feels that people are somewhat naive when they ask, "Why all the secrecy? Why is Air Force Intelligence, the FBI and the President withholding all this information?" To Maynard the answer is crystal clear:

"They don't admit that flying saucers are arriving from other planets because there would be chaos! People here (on this planet) would be all upset! Some would jump out of windows!

"No one could go on living his present, everyday life if he knew that the earth was only one of many inhabited planets!"

He was asked, "Why not?"

"There would be economic upheaval. War would positively be prevented if the Government would release the flying saucer information, and our whole economy, based so heavily on military preparedness would suffer."

The saucer people themselves, according to all who have seen and talked to them, are gentle, kind and beautiful. It is good to know they include both sexes. Space people mean no harm to earthlings and would like to help us if we would but believe.

Perhaps a brief, but accurate summary of the saucerites and the earthlings who believe in them is that they are good and against evil. It would seem that we need not panic, after all!

From Kansas, Illinois, dated September 12th, Miss Mary Kirkham wrote a most engaging letter in which she raised some points worthy of note.

". . . I am one of those people who find it entirely plausible to think beings from other worlds than ours could walk among us on city streets and never be noticed by ordinary citizens. I try to read all possible information on this subject and find myself thinking more and more in terms of the possibility of inhabitants of other planets being more highly developed than we are. Perhaps there is much that we might learn from our neighbors of other worlds that would help us."

And Miss Kirkham went on to ask if we could not arrange to publish a directory of clubs and/or people or persons, or both, as a kind of UFO directory, an attempt to unify UFOlogy and establish a UFO headquarters through which all sightings could be screened and sifted and evaluated.

Suggestions will be warmly welcomed.

From the Santa Barbara (California) *News-Press,* September 13th:

FLYING SAUCER SIGHTED

H. Harper Forrest, of 122 Skyline Circle, said that he and his wife went out last night to view the fire on the mountains—and saw what looked like a flying saucer.

"We saw something streaking across the sky like a shooting star," Forrest said, "but it went right across our vision out to sea, and then up into the Milky Way. It was too fast for a jet plane, and it was not a shooting star, because it went up and not down. Dots of fire were shooting out from it. I won't say it was a flying saucer, but I don't know what else it could have been."

Dorothy Kilgallen made a sweeping statement in her column of September 14th (published in countless newspapers throughout the country):

". . . A new series of flying saucer headlines are in the making. Behind them—a group of scientists who have been investigating reports in the southwest."

As this volume goes to press, we have heard nothing and seen nothing to justify such a statement. Our conclusion is *not* that Miss Kilgallen was in error!

Will we ever learn what her source of information was—or what happened as a result of the investigations?

The September 16th issue of Collier's presented a comprehensive review of recent naval developments of "The Flying Barrel," and the article would be of interest to those who have repeatedly said, "But such a thing just couldn't be!" Well, it could be—and it is!

In the same issue, Collier's printed an editorial of some length, with artist's illustrations, on the artificial satellite.

The Pasadena (California) *Star-News* carried the following significant account on September 16th:

BLUE FLASH PRECEDES LOUD BLAST
MYSTERIOUS EXPLOSION SCORCHES LAWN

An Unidentified Object flew out of the sky in a blue flash and exploded in front of her home last night, Mrs. Rose Modica told officers.

They found a scorched hole in the lawn, the grass burned away from an area about 5 inches in diameter. The hole was about an inch deep.

Whatever landed disintegrated completely. Police said there were no metal or paper fragments such as a manufactured explosive device would have left. Nor any rock particles that might be residue from a meteor.

Mrs. Modica said several neighbors saw the flash and heard the explosion, which she described as "very loud."

We are constantly faced with the readiness of officials to ascribe anything and everything to "balloons."

It is the fear of your editor that such willy-nilly "ballooning" on the part of papers and officials must, inevitably, silence a good number of reputable citizens who see strange objects and do not report them. We must make every effort to combat such offhandedness and demand that complete and thorough investigations be made. If they *are* balloons—let's know it: let them prove it!

And if they are *not* . . .

From the Bell Gardens (California) Review, September 18th:

MYSTERY OBJECT SEEN HERE

A mysterious object floating at high altitudes over Bell Gardens remained unidentified last week.

The object first appeared on the local scene about 3:15 p.m. and was described by Mrs. Norman Roberts, 6326 Adamson Street, as a "white balloon type object filled with something."

"It appeared about the size of a beach ball when it first came over," Mrs. Roberts said.

Although the East Los Angeles sheriff's office had no explanation, (Ed.: *Note bene!*) it was believed that the object was probably a weather balloon.

The best and most complete accounts of UFO sightings and phenomena come from the "saucerzines." This, we suppose, is to be expected, for the public press hardly dares to fly in the fact of providence by wholeheartedly espousing the UFO theme. "Providence," in this case, being the conventionally regimented advertiser who has been told that he doesn't "believe in UFO" and accepts the dictum.

The following is from the C.R.I.F.O. *Orbit*, and covers Case #104, an event of September 3rd at Cincinnati:

METALLIC BALL LANDS IN YARD
DEPARTS ON SOUND OF VOICE

Driving slowly over dark Boomer Road, west of the city, Frank Flaig and wife were startled to see through the windshield, a round airborne object, appearing metallic gray, descending slowly before them. Awe-struck, Flaig stopped his car for a better look. Reflecting the moonlight, the spheroid had no protruding parts or lights. Its downward vertical course although slow was constant and free of swerve, flutter or suspension. Flaig desperately tried to follow the object, but it dropped out of sight behind an unlighted house, about 125 feet away. Leaving his car, Flaig then went to the side of the house to investigate and to his surprise *found the object suspended about a foot above the ground*. About this time, his wife, alone and frightened, called out. At that very instant, according to Flaig, the spheroid began to rise, and, making no sound, continued its upward flight at a 45 degree angle. The object, Flaig estimated, was about four feet in diameter. The Flaigs told the writer that they thought at first that the object was a balloon, but the absence of attachments and its singular behavior ruled out that explanation.

And now we come to one of the most exciting items yet received. Here it is, from the Plattsburgh (New York) *Press*, September 19th:

**WHAT IS THIS STRANGE LIGHT
IN THE SKY OVER LAKE?**

Press-Republican Photographer John Lonergan was called from his comfortable bed at 4 a.m. Saturday morning to witness a strange phenomenon in the sky.

Standing in the Elks Club parking lot at 4:40 a.m. Lonergan saw this object as he looked eastward across Lake Champlain.

Lonergan makes no claims. He just took the picture. He used Royal Pan film with an eight minute exposure.

"The object was very bright and white. It appeared to be motionless in the sky. I watched it for 15 minutes, photographed it and left. I don't know how it got there or where it went afterward, if it did go. I haven't the faintest idea what it is."

Three people saw *It*. . . .

(Ed.: I saw three "somethings" like this in the summer of 1954 while driving homeward from Washington, D.C., to Virginia, at sunset one evening. Two of the objects were very low in the sky, not more than one degree above the horizon, and were very near to the setting sun. They were beyond cirrus clouds and so must have been high in the sky and many miles away. One

pointed upward to the left and the other was practically vertical.
They were not over ¼° in length, and shaped like a small
medicine capsule. They were of amorphous, or smoke-like appearance and slowly changed shape, but were too short to be
vapor trails. The third one was higher in the sky, about 20
degrees up, along the ecliptic [path of the sun across the sky],
and was of the same shape. It slowly twisted and disintegrated
and looked as though made of smoke. It was visible at least an
hour, and had a very "artificial" appearance—"organic," in fact.
It was impossible to conclude that these were ordinary meteorological clouds of water vapor. These photographs taken by Mr.
Lonergan are the only similar objects I have yet seen!)

John Philip Bessor, of 6349 Walnut Street, Pittsburgh, Pennsylvania, published a cleanly devised and lucidly written account
of a subject which is especially interesting to your editor, and
which has marked bearing on broader aspects of UFOlogy. With
his permission, we reprint "UFO's and Levitation," from the
August-September *Flying Saucer News:*

A REPORT ON THE UFO'S AND ON LEVITATION

One would think that, by now, the Air Force would have received
sufficient data on the subject of flying saucers to once and for all
end the controversy by issuing a report to the public that flying
saucers exist. Indeed, in the late spring of 1949, it *did* issue a report
stating "Flying Saucers are not a joke, but don't worry." Somehow,
this little announcement came out at about the same time that Sidney Shalett's "What You Can Believe About Flying Saucers" appeared in a national magazine, the whole effect of which was to play
down the phenomena as the product of mass hysteria, poor observation and sky-hook balloons.

Shalett's piece was supposed to have had the backing of Air Force
Intelligence personnel. Apparently one faction of Intelligence wishes
the public to know the facts, and another, completely bullheaded,

wished the public to rest under the delusion that the flying discs were sheer poppycock. The vocal faction of the Air Force still insists on hoodwinking the public! Recently, Air Secretary Talbot denied that his plane was pursued by a silvery disc over California, and General Nathan Twining growled "Baloney!" upon being asked by a Harrisburg newsman what he thinks the flying saucers might be.

At the risk of being disrespectful, I will say to these gentlemen one word, "Baloney!" They might well fool the masses with their misleading statements, but they are not fooling for a minute those of us who have spent years studying every facet of the flying saucers and related phenomena. In 1947 I made a bet with a friend that the Air Force would *never* tell the public the truth about the flying saucers, as it would never admit, publicly, their fantastic nature and origin, exactly as the Vatican would not acknowledge the reality of reincarnation (which was a Christian tenet till suppressed by the Church Council of Constantinople in 553 A.D.!).

Considerable space has been wasted on the controversy relating to alleged landings of "little men." I cannot emphasize too strongly that for over two years (from June 24, 1947 to August 19, 1949)— when two desert prospectors told newsmen they saw two little fellows hop out of a landed saucer—there was not a single mention of "little men" as saucer crewmen. This 1947 report, although believed to be a publicity stunt, started a veritable avalanche of "little men" tales. The mythical Dr. Gee (Whiz) added fuel to the flame. Adamski elaborated on it. The "little men" grew taller and became benevolent, soft-spoken "guardians" from Venus Etheria, or seductive damsels from Clarion. A unique type of flying saucer, the "Adamski model, 1952" came into being, complete with port-holes and pawnshop triple ball landing gear. It whizzed over to fertile England and gave birth to the "Coniston saucer."

Later, a fiction writer named Cedric Allingham took a solitary stroll, and was favored by a visit from a gangling, six foot tall saucer pilot from "Mars." Eager Leonard G. Cramp, falling hook, line and sinker for Adamski's version of what flying saucers look like, wrote a very technical book, holding up Adamski's saucer as a model, or nucleus, for his theories involving the principle of the nullification of gravity. His theories should appeal to our rocket technicians. Mr. Cramp adheres strictly to the mechanical. We could call his nullification of gravity theory a form of levitation.

I have before me an account of levitation from the London Evening News, January, 1955. The writer, A. Dhar, of Windermere Avenue, London, N. 3, relates his visit to the sacred mountain spring of Gudar, in Kilgam, Kashmir. Near the spring a group of men stood around a huge boulder. One told Dhar that an eleventh person was needed to complete the team. He joined them and they all stood in a circle around the stone. An aged man told them to touch the boulder with their forefingers, to hold their breath, and repeat the word "eleventh" in Kashmiri. They obeyed, and the stone rose about three feet in the air. It remained in the air while they held their breath, and then fell, with a thud, to the ground. They tried again with ten people, but the stone did not move.

Ripley's "Believe It or Not" book carries an item concerning levitation of a huge boulder in India. I have read of another instance of a boulder being kept in the air over a sacred Hindu shrine by the constant chanting, or singing, of several people. Perhaps India is one of the last of the ancient cultures which has not quite lost the art of levitating rocks. Desmond Leslie's highly interesting chapter on ancient Hindu aerial ships indicates that levitation was the force employed to propel them.

Recently, a form of levitation or teleportation occurred in Minia, Upper Egypt. A 90-year-old Sheikh had just died. As his coffin was being carried out of the house, it wrenched itself free from the grasp of the six bearers, smashed through a door and sailed in the air, making a crash landing two miles away! Since then, it has been reported that other flying coffins have been seen, some having made even longer flights.

Did such ships once sail over Britain and engage the defenders of the ancient "vitrified forts" in mortal combat? Did blasts from these aerial ships scorch the earth of such islands as Crete? In a recent conversation with a Greek friend, I learned that vast areas of Crete, *approximately 15 feet beneath the surface, are mysteriously burnt!*

The sudden appearance of sea-going shrimp in a desert mud-flat in the far west really leaves science with its postulates down.

May I call your attention to the sections of *The Case for the UFO* in which teleportation or dumping of low-grade marine life from space ships has been explained, or at least hypothesized.

"Orthodox" explanations are weak indeed!

This is such an interesting and, possibly, important event that we are reproducing two reports: The first is from the September 19th Los Angeles (California) *Mirror,* and the second from the Los Angeles (California) *Examiner* of the same date:

SCIENTISTS HATCH DESERT EGG PLOT

Desert caviar which may produce interesting food for biological thought is being hatched in the laboratories of Los Angeles State College.

Drs. James P. Welsh, Arthur Lockley and John Reardon brought back hundreds of tiny red eggs from a flooded dry lake bed at Camp Irwin, where recently small shrimps were found for the first time in the memory of man.

Welsh, believing the eggs to be 100 years old, plans to hatch some in water and some in dry mud taken from the lake and then baked.

He and his colleagues also brought back four tanks of the tiny fairy shrimp, a fresh-water species akin to the king crab, yet fitting no known category.

The lake where the specimens were gathered was dry until last August 23 when thunderstorms suddenly deposited a foot of water and washed out the bed the Army had been using as a landing field at Camp Irwin.

The camp is near the California-Arizona border.

As far back as anyone can recall—100 years or more—the lake has been dry. Welsh theorizes that the eggs have lain dormant during that period and were hatched by the water.

The investigator says there is no other source of water close enough to have brought in the tiny eggs or the shrimps. They are from one to two inches long.

Welsh is positive the creatures are a fresh-water member of the shrimp family. The question is: How did the little specimens get so far away from all water and manage to stay fertile?

Developments in the Los Angeles State laboratories may not, as one of Dr. Welsh's assistants thinks, "make evolutionary history," but they should be of interest to many biologists and zoologists.

EVER SEE A PHYLLOPOD?

HERE THEY ARE BEING STUDIED ON LIFE HABITS

Eggs from armored phyllopods, mysterious one-inch long animals found in Bicycle Lake near Camp Irwin, yesterday were deposited in a variety of hatching plants to determine their growth under different temperature conditions.

Dr. James P. Welsh, assistant professor of zoology at Los Angeles State College, said the creatures are definitely "scavengers, but little is known about their habits."

He explained that the phyllopods reproduce without mating, and the females outnumber the males by about 5000 to one.

Dr. Welsh said there is no explanation as to how the animals had been deposited in Bicycle Lake, a deserted, almost dry body of water in the desert.

The following is paraphrased from the Kansas City (Missouri) *Times,* September 26th:

There has been much interest in increasing reports of UFO activity in France this year. There is often excitement and terror in the reports. There have been more reports than ever during this summer and autumn. And not all the objects were "Saucers," many "cigars" were seen.

"Intellectuals," says France-Amerique's Paris correspondent, "are arguing about the mysterious objects. One of these is Prof. Hermann Oberth, astronautical pioneer and builder of the German V-2 rocket. This German scientist is however quite silent about the motive power of the UFO. He has discussed their 'crews' at some length and suggests that the pilots are plants endowed with reasoning powers. He named them *uranides* and says that they are thousands of years in advance of terrestrial mortals. He suggests that these *ura-*

nides may come from planets where oxygen does not exist in gaseous form, but in liquid state, and he supposes that the plant beings may absorb it through their pores."

(Ed.: This upsurge of sightings in France surprises nobody except the benighted citizen of the United States where it has been "unfashionable" to report UFO news for two or three years. While our press has been pedantically telling us that the sightings of UFO have fallen off greatly, people go right on seeing them and, in other countries, they are reported. But Professor Oberth should somehow make up his mind. Never forget that he is holding down an excellent job, on American tax money, while he promotes artificial satellites and the development of bigger and better rockets—neither of which is a firm step toward space travel. And how is it that the professor, knowing nothing of the craft itself, can so casually postulate about the crew and its home base?)

The following excerpts are from a letter dated September 21st, a most intelligent and profound epistle altogether. Its author, Miss Isabel K. Hagglund, 1065 Runnymede Street, Palo Alto, California, expresses—succinctly and effectively—views held by many. Let's let her words speak for themselves:

. . . There is a nightmare quality about the UFO situation and it stems, not from the UFO's or anything they have done, but from the deadly silence of all official and conventional mediums of communication. Newspapers, radio, magazines—silent on the subject almost without exception. A stunning display of mysterious lights are seen in the skies of Ohio in August—and I read about it weeks later in a tiny "saucerzine." Numerous people report encounters with small unknown beings—and the radio and press are silent about it. It is a ghastly, suffocating, unbelievable state of affairs. It is like one of those nightmares where you scream at the top of your lungs but no sound emerges; nobody hears; nobody sees. . . .

Three days after reading one of the little magazines devoted to

UFO news, or reading your book *The Case for the UFO,* or Keyhoe's book, the average person looks around, sees everything going on as usual, hears the same stuff on the radio, reads the same old stuff in the papers—and concludes that the book or little magazine he just read was written about some other world, not this one. It must have been some other Ohio in some other United States on some other earth where it all happened. It seems to me that if the moon were to float down from the sky and impale itself on the Empire State building and fifty little men were to disembark, neither the press nor radio would mention it—and presumably all the persons who witnessed the event would be gagged and/or carted off and drowned. What *does* happen to the alleged thousands of eye-witnesses to UFO phenomena? Going back over my files to the year 1947, it is apparent that these thousands may well be above the million mark by now; where are they? who are they? is there any way to compile a directory of individuals who have witnessed UFO's?

(Ed.: And here, again, we meet the need for a directory, a central filing bureau and a Central Office for the Evaluation and Dissemination of UFO Lore!!)

As for the increasing crop of mystics, psychotics and outright charlatans who are taking over the flying saucer field, it is to be deplored but hardly wondered at. The pall of silence thrown over the most momentous development of our age is certainly enough to unhinge the minds of the already unstable, and also provides perfect immunity for the ridiculous claims of the mountebanks. If our interplanetary visitors have invasion in mind, I doubt if they'll have any more difficulty taking over the earth than Cortez had in taking over the country of early "Indian" people. There is no more unity or brotherhood among the nations of the whole earth than there was between the numerous tribes that once peopled this continent. If our visitors are motivated simply by friendly curiosity, it seems we have everything to gain and nothing to lose by reciprocating with friendly curiosity. Instead of maintaining the deadly pall of silence and pretending nothing is happening!

A directory of fans, interested parties and UFO witnesses would be most welcome. . . . If thousands of us could make contact with each other, perhaps the gruesome shroud of official silence can be ripped to shreds and the good clear sunlight of fact-facing and truth be made to shine.

Sincerely yours,
(signed)
Isabel K. Hagglund

On September 27th, reports came in and the United Press carried stories of a missing plane, with eleven men aboard, including a reporter and photographer from Canada, Alf Tate and Doug Cronk of the Toronto *Daily Star*. The plane was last heard of as it approached the hurricane Janet after having taken off from Jacksonville, Florida, and a heavy sea and air search was carried out, but not a trace of the ship or crew has ever been found.

This area, as readers of *The Case for the UFO* and the *Reporter* will recall, is noted for disappearing planes and ships and crews. Where are they going? Why? and *how?*

September closed with a notice which was particularly gratifying to your editor. An amazing number of individuals have criticized me for including "Falling Dead Birds" in a book on UFO, for they maintained, and I feel confident that they were being completely honest with me and with themselves, that they had never heard of anything of the kind and that it just *couldn't* be true. They argued that if a bird or two had been found, they must have died from natural causes and then been discovered. Upon my saying that people had actually seen them falling by the score, they scoffed.

Well, 1955, September 28th to be exact, brought hordes of dead birds falling in Charlotte, North Carolina.

From the many local articles which covered the event, let's look at a smattering of quotes: "The dead birds were identified as members of 15 different species, mostly vireos and warblers. All the species are now migrating south each night." . . . "The birds were found Monday at the Police club near the airport,

but reported to City police only yesterday." . . . "Police Chief
Frank N. Littlejohn, himself a bird lover, investigated immediately, discovering that hundreds of birds had been picked up by
his club employees." . . . "hundreds of birds (were) found
near the police club." . . . "operators at the airport control
tower have seen the same thing from time to time." . . . "Last
year hundreds of birds were found dead under similar circumstances near Greensboro, North Carolina, Raleigh, North Carolina, Charleston, South Carolina, and Savannah, Georgia." . . .
"Like the deaths this year, these were reported in early autumn,
at the height of the bird migration, when thousands of birds are
flying over each night."

And, to climax this strange event, let us point out that some
local savants maintained that these mass deaths had been caused
by "the ceilometer, a mercury arc lamp . . . with 25 million
candlepower." Used by the weather bureau, it was claimed to
have attracted droves of the birds and "hypnotized them," like
moths around a flame, until they were exhausted and fell to the
ground, dead.

We are indebted to Mr. Fred A. Taylor for sending us much
fine information on this particular phenomena, and he also supplied us with the most fascinating information of all, especially
pertinent to the so-called "explanation" by the weather bureau
and the omnipresent savants who claimed the ceilometer was responsible.

"A like occurrence, when birds fell out of the sky Sunday
night near Troy, North Carolina (Ed.: Troy is about 50 or 60
miles north of Charlotte), is unexplained by the ceilometer theory.
There's no ceilometer in Troy!"

OCTOBER

October 1955, as far as UFO's are concerned, is noted particularly for the Air Force's widely heralded announcement during the last week of the month, that it had investigated almost five thousand sightings and fifty thousand eyewitness accounts of flying saucers, and found them all to be hallucinations and without substance.

(Apparently, according to the Air Force, we have more than our fair share of hoaxers and liars and just plain idiots, in these United States!)

The Kansas City *Star*, of Sunday, October 2, 1955, carried one of the most interesting newspaper features to come out in 1955 relative to any phase of UFO activity. Unfortunately the feature article is too long to reproduce here. It covered the existence and unexplained activity of a mysterious "spook light" which has taken up permanent residence near Joplin, Missouri. The account was sent to me by a thoughtful writer named John L. Homes, who is so modest that he did not give me a return address.

It seems that the light has been observed in the neighborhood for the last forty years or more. It moves upward, forward, or recedes. It flashes off and on. It changes color from white, or bright yellow, to red. It is a well-known tourist attraction in the area, and people drive for miles around for a glimpse of the "spook light." It appeared a number of times in the course of an evening, the *Star* staff observer reported.

We have already mentioned the interest of British Air Chief Marshal Lord Dowding in the field of UFO. This outstanding British military executive, certainly has access to information equal to, or even superior to that of the U.S. Air Force, and it is interesting to note that he is a big enough man, and honest enough to tell the truth where truth so desperately needs to be told. This little note appeared in the New York *Post*, October 4, 1955:

FLYING DISCS REAL THING TO RAF CHIEF

Air Chief Marshal Lord Dowding, 73, says he believes there are flying saucers from other planets, though he has never seen one.

The wartime boss of the British Royal Air Force fighter command, a prominent spiritualist, declared in a lecture Sunday, "the evidence is overwhelming."

He added, however, he doesn't expect flying saucer operators to land and tell their secrets to earthmen "until we have learned better manners."

The following item is from the New York *World-Telegram*, October 4, 1955. It shows a trend in aircraft design which leads us to suspect that the major governments are using UFO data to guide them in aircraft development:

"FLYING BOTTLE" TESTED BY SOVIET

Eyewitness reports reaching Kabul, Afghanistan, said today the Soviets were testing a revolutionary bottle-shaped aircraft at a secret base in the remote and mountainous regions just north of Afghanistan.

More than a thousand residents of the Afghan corridor—a finger of land jutting eastward toward Red China—reported seeing the strange craft which they first said looks something like a flying saucer.

The description of the eyewitnesses was almost identical. They said it was shaped like a neckless bottle, about twenty feet high, with "pins" extending down from the bottom edges, apparently similar to the new U.S. "Flying Platform."

Fire appeared to be shooting out of the top and from the bottom and there was a big wind which officials took to be the downward thrust of air at high speed. The craft had a blue band around the middle and portholes, the witnesses said. The aircraft was seen twice.

The Uhrichsville (Ohio) *Chronicle*, October 6, 1955, described the experience of two local women who witnessed the appearance of some flying saucers:

TWO WOMEN HERE REPORT SEEING FLYING SAUCERS

Flying saucers! That's what two local women say they spotted above rural Uhrichsville last Sunday.

Mrs. Albert Fanty, 314 Packer Street, Uhrichsville, said yesterday that she and her mother observed the fast-flying objects on two different occasions from the vantage point of the latter's home. According to Mrs. Fanty, the day's happenings began early in the morning when her mother spotted seven of the disc-shaped aircraft bunched at a high altitude.

Mrs. Burroway, mother of Mrs. Fanty, later described the phenomenon to her daughter who had arrived for a visit at about 1:00

p.m. As the two women and Mrs. Fanty's 8-year-old son, Kenneth searched the sky, "three or four" of the flying saucers reappeared and then vanished several seconds later.

The saucers were described as seeming to have a silver coating as they whirled through the air. Mrs. Fanty said they followed each other in an irregular line and traveled at a high rate of speed—as if they had been shot from something. They were visible for only a few seconds, she said.

Almost immediately after the saucers disappeared, the air became filled with "fine silken-like silver cobwebs which floated everywhere," Mrs. Fanty said.

A spokesman at the Aerial Phenomenon Section of the USAF base at Wright-Patterson Field, Dayton, said he was unauthorized to comment on specific situations.

A letter on October 9, 1955, from Edward Lindemann, brought out some good points. For one thing, he has contributed a very worthwhile discussion of the moral and social obligations of writers in the field of UFOlogy.

Of more immediate interest is Mr. Lindemann's comment on gravity and magnetism. He posed the question of whether gravity and magnetism are related in such a manner that, when you translate from a small hand-type magnet to a vast one the size of the earth, do you perhaps undergo a qualitative change wherein the great terrestrial magnet becomes a gravitational magnet. In other words it appears that what he suggests is that magnetism on the grand scale becomes gravity. I am not inclined to agree since the earth's magnetic field seems to be quite distinct from its gravitational field, and the characteristics of both are manifest. However, it is a thought worth remembering, and we have to admit that Einstein's last work was directed toward showing that both fields spring from a common basis.

Here is another report of mystery blasts in the area of San Francisco Bay, taken from the San Francisco *Call-Bulletin*,

October 12, 1955. These blasts have plagued citizens and officials alike for months. So far, nobody has come up with a suitable explanation, although the Air Force has made considerable efforts to soft-pedal the series of incidents:

MORE BLASTS IN BAY AREA

Three more blasts—unexplained, but believed to be sonic booms from jet planes—were reported last night in the Bay area. No damage was reported.

The first noise was heard in the Martinez-Concord area at about 8:15 p.m., and was variously described by residents there as sounding like "a howitzer going off" and "a blast of dynamite."

The second and third disturbances were heard in the Palo-Alto Menlo Park area where police said blasts were reported at 11:25 and 11:50 p.m.

Hamilton Air Force Base and Alameda Naval Station said they had no jet fighters in the air at the time.

The *great fireball* of October, in the South-Central U.S.A. was discussed in many newspapers throughout the country, and created the stir which its magnitude deserved. Here is one report as taken from the Wilmington (California) *Press-Journal:*

FIREBALL STREAKS OVER TEXAS

More than a dozen persons and weather bureaus of at least three cities reported today seeing a flaming ball sweep across the sky in the lower Rio Grande Valley about 10:30 a.m. (CST)

At about the same time, the sheriff's office at Anahuac, Texas, said it had a report of a jet plane exploding and crashing "somewhere in the county."

Residents along the seawall at Galveston reported seeing a "long trail of fire" over the Gulf of Mexico. They said it exploded and disintegrated in black smoke.

The mysterious flaming object was reported seen by weather bureaus in Galveston, Brownsville and Corpus Christi.

It apparently was traveling at extremely high altitude, making it visible over a large section of the lower Rio Grande Valley.

Residents of towns from Edinburgh to Brownsville in the valley reported seeing what they described as a ball of fire.

This fireball deserves close attention. It deserves more than one comment. In the report from the Montgomery (Alabama) *Advertiser,* the following quotation is attributed to air-pilot Roger Harlan:

At first we thought it was a flying saucer . . . *your mind is conditioned to that sort of thing.* . . . It came along right off our left wing at a tremendous rate of speed, began to slow down, and then exploded in a shower of flying sparks and shrapnel in the air . . . then we realized it was a meteor.

Harlan further described the object as an orange ball of fire, etc. The above statement is the important one. Now, no meteor pulls up "right off our left wing" and then slows down, unless it is controlled by *something.* Meteors just do not slow down like that if they are of the ordinary, heavy stone-iron variety. Here seems to be evidence of control, remote or otherwise, such as we have discussed in many phases of UFO. We do not necessarily say that it was not a meteor, but if it was a meteor, it was something very special—and we have had a surfeit of "specials" in 1955.

The New York *Post,* October 16, 1955, brought us another account of radio signals from space. Many of these signals have been heard for two generations—ever since radio began, and they have been brushed off under the general category of "static." The development of the "radio telescope" has given engineers an opportunity to localize the direction from which the signals proceed, and in this way various signals have been assigned to specific parts of the heavens, and therefore, to specific sources, such as the planet Jupiter.

Now here is one of those classic examples of scientific confusion which we have tried to high-light in *The Case for the UFO*. It is one of those cases where a tremendous mass of confused data is scrambled into one category (static, in this case) and disregarded as perhaps accidental.

Yet, when we have developed techniques of segregation and classification we find that some parts of the great scramble are susceptible to analysis, and systematic origins can be assigned and studied in detail. Gradually, characteristic categories can be sorted out and whole new fields of research ensue.

That is exactly what we are trying to do in the UFO field. We are trying to find logical, acceptable explanations, to sort out the scrambled hodge-podge of unexplained data. We believe we are succeeding slowly, in somewhat the same manner that the radio astronomers are segregating meaningful segments of the atmospheric static which have annoyed us for decades. Here is the article:

AUSTRALIA PICKS UP JUPITER SIGNALS—
DOES LIFE EXIST IN OUTER SPACE?

Melbourne, October 15 (Reuters). Australian radio astronomers, with receivers tuned in to signals from space, believe that if developed civilizations exist on other planets, man will hear them.

They already have listened to signals from the planet Jupiter. But the astronomers say these signals were certainly not made by any form of intelligent life—"little green men or their equivalent."

Jupiter, 500,000,000 miles away from earth, is dead and cold. The shiny planet probably has an atmosphere of hydrogen, helium and marsh gas, with a pressure, on the ground, a million times that of earth.

Yet, about once a week, from a white spot on its atmosphere radio signals crackle through space and are picked up in Sydney.

One day last June the signals first came through. Checking back on records, the scientists found that they had been picking up the signals for some time without knowing what they were.

Further investigation pinpointed a white spot on the planet as the source of the signals. The white spot, they theorized, could be the outpourings of a mammoth volcano, or a giant bubble in the atmosphere; spinning gases were generating radio signals.

The Australian scientists at the radio-astronomy station at St. Mary's use what they call a "Mills Cross" to listen to these space "broadcasts." This is a white-painted aerial with arms 1,500-feet long, in the shape of a cross, which owes its name to one of the two scientists who invented it in Australia, in 1953. It is the cheapest, simplest form of radio-telescope.

A larger Mills Cross will come into use shortly. Meanwhile, in Britain and the U.S., scientists are working on focusing radio-telescopes, giant searchlight-like basin aerials made of steel, which will be an improvement on the crosses.

The Australians say that when these come into use, they will detect any powerful radio transmissions made by any form of intelligent life existing in the solar system—if life exists.

The radio-telescopes work in a way similar to ordinary telescopes, except that they use radio waves instead of light.

Using them, scientists have made important discoveries about radio signals in space and have discovered dark stars which emit radio signals, but cannot be "seen" any other way.

The next item is a sighting reported in the *Pacoima Post*, Pacoima, California, October 16, 1955. This is a very complete and well-detailed sighting. This is one of those UFO events which convinces you that the Air Force is dissembling when it says there are no UFO's:

Lee Owings has been an employee of the California Water and Telephone Company for the last six years. At present, he is employed in the company's offices at San Fernando.

The company considers Lee to be a reliable employee. Lee drinks very, very seldom, and in talking to him you get the impression he is a level-headed young man. In his late 20's, Lee is a member of the Sierra Club and a very active hiker.

Why all this attention to Lee Owings? Well, it's very simple. Lee has seen what some people might call a flying saucer. Lee doesn't call it anything—he doesn't know what to call it. But, there's no doubt about it, Lee and a hiking companion saw something.

Here's the whole story: About a month ago, Friday, September 9, to be exact, Lee and a hiking companion, both members of the Sierra Club (a conservation club to encourage hiking, rock climbing, etc.) left Hollywood about 10:00 p.m. for a weekend of hiking along certain ranges on the California-Nevada state line.

Their first objective was the top of "Boundry Peak" which they reached about 5:00 p.m. that Saturday evening. Although it was starting to get dark, they decided to rest awhile and continue the climb to Montgomery Peak which is only a short distance from Boundry Peak. They reached this second peak by 7:00 p.m.

To get back to their starting point, it was necessary for them to retrace their steps and again cross Boundry Peak.

About 1:15 a.m. the next morning, which was Sunday, they had reached a low point, or saddle, after reclimbing Boundry and were almost back at camp.

It was at this point they both noticed a strange flicking light in the sky. They made mental note of the time because it was much later than they had thought. This flicking in the sky attracted their attention and they noticed it came from five or six tiny points in the distant sky.

As they continued to watch these flicking lights, they noticed what appeared to be beams of light coming from these pinpoints in the sky. From this same area in the sky a yellow light suddenly appeared and lit up the heavens. There was no moon and the light was very clearly seen.

Suddenly this yellow light shot towards them and as it did so, it changed in shape to form a sort of wavy line of light with no particular head. Its main body was in the form of a long streamer.

At approximately five miles distance from where they stood, this bright wave of light stopped its motion and changed into a crescent with both tips pointing towards the ground.

Lee says when this happened, two beams of light came from the object. One, a broad lamp-like beam illuminated the floor of a nearby canyon, the other, a narrow beam, played near the top of Boundry Peak.

This object moved towards them once again and they did not see it for a few minutes. But when they again saw it, the points of the crescent pointed towards the sky and the entire figure was just about a mile away, standing still except for a slight jiggling.

At this point, Lee and his companion decided to take cover behind some trees, at the same time moving to higher ground for a slightly better look. In so doing, they lost sight of this "thing" temporarily.

But then they saw it again and Lee says "At its closest, it was just a yellow-orange glow with a definite outline. Looking at it, we were plenty scared."

Not knowing what to expect, they again decided to take cover behind some trees. From this position they could not see the object at all. The area just beyond their vision on the other side of the ridge was suddenly lit up three times. They could tell this by the way the ridge was so brightly silhouetted against the sky.

However, not knowing what might happen next, they decided to stay out of sight of the object they had been watching and they did not see it again. When we asked Lee if he thought it was a flying saucer, here's what he had to say. "I never seriously believed in flying saucers. But after seeing what we did on that mountain, I'd be receptive to almost any new idea."

The week-end after this happened Lee and some friends went back to this same spot in the mountains. This time, completely equipped with all kinds of cameras. But all they got for their trouble was to get caught in a snow storm.

Was it a flying saucer Lee and his friend saw? Who knows? You talk to Lee and you're sure he saw something. His own words sum it up best. "It may have been some government experiment, but it sure looked like something out of this world to us."

Here is a "leak" which foreshadowed the Air Force's announcement that there are no flying saucers except those that the Air Force has been constructing from 1500 B.C. until it brings some more out in 1956, just to keep us all happy! This item appeared in *Newsweek*, October 17, 1955:

Flying saucer enthusiasts will be doused with cold water in a few weeks when the Air Force releases "Project Bluebook." It's an exhaustive study which reports that 97% of the saucer sightings can be explained by such known facts as weather balloons and atmospheric conditions. In the other 3% of the cases, the observers didn't report enough facts to justify any definite conclusions.

Really!!!

Here is an account about the interest of clubs in hearing lectures of flying saucers. This is from the Nashville (Tennessee) *Banner*, October 18, 1955:

FLYING SAUCERS MAY BE REAL, THOMPSON TELLS EXCHANGE CLUB

Think you've seen a flying saucer? It's entirely possible you did. Nearly twenty per cent of the authenticated reports of UFO's whizzing overhead remain unexplained, insurance agent Joe Thompson Jr., told Exchange Club members today.

"It is still a matter of conjecture, but there is more than a possibility that those objects are interplanetary," Thompson said. "I am convinced Pentagon officials are concerned over the unexplained sightings and are anxious that the information reach the public on an unofficial basis," he said.

Thompson, an amateur saucer enthusiast, first became interested in the subject when he commanded a squadron of reconnaissance planes in Germany during W W II.

He said his interest was aroused when he and his squadron sighted a strange flying object on a mission over the Rhine valley in 1944. None of his men, trained in the art of identifying all types of aircraft, was able to name the object, Thompson said.

He said his interest was intensified when flying saucer reports increased in 1948 and when the Air Force organized "Project

Saucer" in 1951 to study the thousands of reports. Between 1500 and 2000 sightings were authenticated by the Air Force team, Thompson said.

Though Thompson drew no conclusions, he punctuated his talk with examples of reports taken from secret Air Force data released to the public in the early part of 1954.

The most convincing of these, Thompson said, was the appearance of unidentified and yet unexplained returns on radarscopes in the Washington area in the spring of 1953.

"These were not temperature inversions or weather phenomenon," Thompson said. "Pentagon officials were so concerned about it they brought top experts to Washington and it occurred again while they were there."

Thompson said the Air Force reports state the objects circled Washington at speeds of from 2,000 to 3,000 mph.

Other reports touched on by Thompson included one by two airline pilots on a run from Virginia to Miami and verified by a group of aircraft manufacturers aboard the plane. The sighted object was similar to a large cart wheel, the report stated.

Another, in July of 1952, was reported individually by five airline pilots landing at Indianapolis and thousands of the city's citizens. A nearby Air Force radar station claimed to have picked up the object on its scope traveling at about 1,700 mph and appearing much larger than a B-36 aircraft, Thompson said.

Another mysterious "flash"—it dripped something red! The account was in the *Sun*, of San Bernardino, California, October 23, 1955:

SCORES VIEW MYSTERIOUS FLASH IN SKY

A brilliant flash in the sky at 6:15 p.m. Saturday puzzled scores of San Bernardino County residents.

Civil Defense observers at Lytle Creek Observation post on Riverside Avenue, in North Rialto, said it lighted the entire sky and lasted about three seconds. They placed its location "a few miles north" of San Bernardino and said they spotted what appeared to be "drippings of red."

The observers thought it was possibly an exploding meteorite. Sheriff's officers advanced the theory that it might be a battery of big guns at George Air Force Base, with red tracers. They said similar sights have been traced to them in the past.

Another "meteor"? or are we overworking the meteoric theory? This report was in the Santa Ana (California) *Register*, October 23, 1955. It does not sound much like the previous sighting:

GLARE CALLED METEORITE

A trail of red and white fire, possibly from a meteorite, was seen from widely spaced points throughout Orange County at about 6:20 last night.

An officer in the El Toro Marine Base field control tower said the fiery object was traveling at a very high rate of speed to the northeast and left a trail of fire much like a meteorite.

At first it was thought that the light was from an emergency red flare dropped from an aircraft in distress, but the control tower operator said it definitely was not a flare. The operator said there were no plane engines sounds or blinking running lights.

The light was spotted by a resident near Crystal Cove who told sheriff's investigators it was over the hills behind El Morro Beach. Another resident on the coast said it appeared to be a bright shooting star.

The San Francisco *News*, October 25, 1955, reported as follows on another mysterious and unexplained blast in the Bay area. The sky blasts remain a mystery:

"BLASTS" JAR EASTSIDERS

At least four sharp and unexplained explosions were heard by homeowners in a wide area of East San Jose last night.

The blasts rattled windows in some houses along King Road. They were so loud that some householders thought their water heaters had exploded.

A sheriff's car sent into the area to investigate had been unable to find any source for the blasts at a late hour.

There were no reports of fires, dynamiting or other damage. Reporting parties timed the first blast at shortly before 8:00 p.m. and the last about 9:00 p.m.

Saucer sensitive New Jersey is back in the news. The following was recorded in the *Jersey Journal,* October 24, 1955. Note the comment on the 1952 sightings. In spite of the most elaborate denials of the Air Force regarding sightings over Washington. D.C., in July 1952, we were confronted with a general deluge of similar sightings all along the Eastern Seaboard. Mass hallucination, no doubt, but peculiarly coincident as to time and locale. Here is the lady's story:

WOMAN SPOTS SAUCER-LIKE SKY VISITOR

An unidentified object which may have been a flying saucer was reported this weekend over Jersey City.

Mrs. Kathi Hyll, 126 Irving Street, called this newspaper within minutes of having seen . . . "a very large, round, shiny thing, flying exceptionally fast . . ." She spoke calmly and described the incident in detail.

Mrs. Hyll said the object was at a greater distance overhead than planes ordinarily fly. It was so bright, "I thought at first it was a shooting star," she said. The day was bright and clear Saturday. The time was minutes after 11:00 a.m.

Exhaustive checking with Jersey City Civil Defense and Military agencies showed no unidentified object spotted in the New York-New Jersey area.

Mrs. Hyll described the object as slightly larger than most four-engined planes, flying in a northwesterly direction at extremely high speed.

She said it was not a jet (several jets were spotted by official observer posts). It sounded more like the engine of a conventional plane, "but much much louder," she said.

This was not the first time "flying saucers" have been spotted in Jersey City. A national furor resulted in July, 1952, when the Jersey City ground observer post reported an unidentified craft with the typical round, glowing form linked to saucers. A plane spotter caught a picture of it which added fuel to the then ever-increasing controversy.

One more indication that clever bureaucracy is moving in on the UFO field, is the following announcement that the Air Force will soon fly a "saucer plane." This was announced, among other places, in the following quotation from the New York *Daily Mirror* of October 26, 1955:

AF WILL FLY A "SAUCER" PLANE

The Air Force served notice Tuesday night it will soon begin flying aircraft which may be mistaken for flying saucers by the public. But Secretary Quarles added that the Air Force, after a study started in 1947 and covering thousands of alleged "sightings" still has found nothing to confirm the existance of saucers which some people thought might have come from outer space.

Another mystery blast and another burned lawn are reported in the Fresno (California) *Bee,* October 26, 1955:

POLICE PROBE MYSTERY BLAST ON LAWN

The police are attempting to determine the nature and origin of a small object which exploded and burned the lawn on the east side of the home of Grace Kimble at 2414 Thomas Avenue at 8:40 p.m. last night.

Patrolman D. O. King said Mrs. Kimble and a neighbor reported they heard an explosion and then saw an extremely bright fire burning on the lawn.

King said a hole about six inches in diameter was burned in the grass. Because of the distance from the street King said it is not likely the object was thrown from an automobile. He said an airplane was circling in the vicinity and the object may have dropped from the aircraft.

Small fragments which he gathered at the scene are being studied in an attempt to identify the object.

L

Maybe the press and Pentagon know there are no saucers, but
—do the saucers know it? Here is a sighting reported in the
October 27th issue of the Rittman (Ohio) *Press:*

OBSERVERS REPORT SKY PHENOMENA LIKE SAUCER

Reports have been received of a sky phenomenon similar to a
flying saucer which several Rittman residents saw last Friday night
around 10:30 p.m. in the western and south-western skies.

The object appeared to be round and was moving in a circular
rotation like a cork screw. It appeared to be coming from the direction of Sterling and moved in a south-westerly direction and disappeared over the horizon south of Rittman.

The object appeared to be going in a circular path at a high rate
of speed. It completed each circle in approximately two or three
seconds and all the time it was moving in a south-westerly direction.
It was not as bright as a star but it had a fluorescent glow of about
the same color of a star.

It was slightly less brilliant than the moon. It could not have
been the reflection of a high powered searchlight because there was
no beam of light from the earth.

This sky phenomenon was reported to the press by Mr. and Mrs.
George Alesander and Russell W. Frey. Others who might have seen
this particular phenomenon are asked to phone the press office.

The Greensboro papers of October 27, were not far behind with
the following:

SAUCERS AGAIN

A former Air Force observer and 120 students and teachers reported sighting about ten flying saucers here today as wisps of
"angel hair" fell from a cloudless sky.

The "angel hair" fits the description of similar material found at
Burlington on October 10. The Burlington material later was *identified as spider webs carried by the wind.*

There was no immediate explanation of the saucers. The control tower at Greensboro-High Point Airport said there was considerable jet plane activity over the area today, but most of the planes were at 20,000 feet or higher.

H. D. Lambeth, principal of Whitsett School and an aerial observer during World War II, said the saucers were visible between 2:45 and 3:10 p.m.

The italics above are mine.

Most of us are so regimented and so imbued, from elementary school training, with the idea of the honor and infallibility of the government, that we do not dare to voice aloud any doubt in the paternal omniscience of the Great White Father. Not so with Major Donald E. Keyhoe. Keyhoe is the champion of the flying saucer and of the legions who have actually seen a flying saucer in action. He is one of the few who have the courage to speak up and denounce the Air Force for what appears to be outright deception. He has the documentation to back up his statements, else he would be subject to arrest for sedition and slander. Here is his protest against the Air Force denial of the existence of UFO, as it appeared in the New York *Times*, October 28, 1955. It was a United Press release and appeared in many other papers:

"SAUCER" REPORT SCORED

AUTHOR ACCUSES AIR FORCE

OF CONCEALING FACTS

Donald E. Keyhoe, former Marine Corps officer who has written several books on flying saucers, accused the Air Force tonight of a "deliberate attempt to conceal facts from the public."

Mr. Keyhoe criticizes a report issued Tuesday by Secretary of the Air Force, Donald A. Quarles, which said flying saucers were imaginary and that only three per cent of this year's sightings were unexplainable.

Mr. Keyhoe called the report "an insult to the hundreds of experienced pilots in the Air Force, Navy, Marine Corps and airlines who have been secretly reporting saucer encounters at the Air Force's own request."

The author said the Air Force "still cannot explain hundreds of the most dramatic reports that took place from 1947 to 1955."

He challenged the Air Force to deny that armed jets still "scrambled" to pursue every "saucer" that can be tracked by radar.

Here is another sighting. This one is from Whitsett, North Carolina, dated October 28, 1955. These "steel balls" look pretty solid to be illusions:

"STEEL BALLS" FLY OVER FIBER FALLS

Civil Defense officials investigated today reports from an elementary school principal that he and over a hundred pupils watched objects "like steel balls" dart through the sky yesterday for twenty-five minutes, while "angel hair" fell among them.

H. D. Lambeth, Jr., who flew 46 combat missions as an aerial observer in World War II, said he watched the objects through a pair of binoculars while his students scattered around the school yard collecting the falling "angel hair."

He described the material as a light colored whispy stuff, similar to Christmas decoration or cotton candy. Most of it, he said, was in two and three inch strips.

Recently reports of similar "angel hair" came from nearby Burlington. It was described by some as spider web.

Lambeth said he was in the school when some children called to him. He said he caught sight of one of the "steel balls" and followed it with glasses. "I called to one of the teachers and she timed one of them from directly overhead until it reached the horizon. It took a minute and a half."

Another sighting of the long bar, or rod-shaped device was reported in the Santa Ana (California) *Register*, October 29, 1955, as follows:

FLYING CIGAR SEEN IN SKIES

A mysterious flying object over Orange County was reported to Orange police early yesterday evening by two Orange men, police said today.

Reported by Tim Peterson, 25, of 533 Harwood Street, and Ted Peterson, 18, of 288 N. Olive, the object was seen about 5:00 p.m.

It was described as "long, a large bar or pipe shape; with a ball underneath, flying at about 5,000 feet in an easterly direction," according to the report.

Mount Shasta is, indeed, a region of mystery. The San Francisco *Examiner,* October 30, 1955, featured the discovery of some gigantic foot prints found by a mountain climbing expedition. The prints are of very large size, and have only three toes. They are almost big enough to be compared to the tracks of the fabled "Yeti," or "abominable snowman" of the Himalayas. When will we ever have enough proven data to piece all of this tremendous jig-saw together into an integrated whole? Here is the story:

MOUNT SHASTA FOOTNOTE REKINDLES LEGEND

Old Big Foot has been trampling on the wild flowers of Mount Shasta again, and rekindled legend is leaping like a forest fire.

Big Foot is not content with just leaving a minor mystery of footprints behind him in the mountain mud of time. He leaves a print with only three toes.

Such discoveries give great excitement to amateur archaeologists, and a cynical pain to University of California experts.

Big Foot should be warned that he is going to be trailed, and if caught, he is one day going to have to toe the mark.

John W. Chamberlain, a Yreka newspaperman when he isn't off in the wilderness spotting spoor, is the latest to discover tracings of Big Foot's strolls. Chamberlain and his fellow expeditioners, J. J. Brown and Robert S. Sanders, have a ready explanation.

Big Foot is a Lemurian.

This is a cross between the Old Man of the Mountain and the Oldest Race on earth. Nobody knows which arrived first.

The Lemurians lived in the mountains, loved salt and were something of showoffs. They would drop in at the country store and pay for a box of salt with a big gold nugget.

Refugees from the lost continent, the Lemurians supposedly got swallowed up by great Pacific Ocean floods. This story is consistent with their taste for salt.

Chamberlain has estimated Big Foot's weight at 450 pounds. The footprints are fifty inches apart, and fifteen inches long.

Such a stride is a little awesome, because a big man like Saunders can manage only thirty-three inches. Using a slide rule, Ely Culbertson's bridge rule of ten, and advanced mathematics, Chamberlain has come up with Big Foot's weight quicker than a carnival guesser.

Chamberlain believes he has found traces of the existence of another race—perhaps the one known as *The Old Ones*.

"Many researchers have said that ancestors of the ancient tribe were natives of Lemuria, the lost continent, which long ago was inundated by floods," he recalled.

"Stories current in some areas have mentioned mysterious persons, the epitome of nobility and regal bearing, who have from time to time made purchases, especially of salt, at stores in the vicinity of Mount Shasta. The visitors left gold nuggets as payment without accepting any change."

Legends build upon legend. Some residents of the Mount Shasta area note that the area now is the headquarters of the "I Am" religious group. Its followers believe that the "ascended masters" live inside Mount Shasta.

The Philadelphia *Inquirer* published the following letter October 31, 1955, from an irate Moorestown (New Jersey) reader, dated October 26. He makes a real squawk about the lack of truth in UFO affairs. Just by way of a sort of left-handed support of his position, let us ask the Air Force just what is this thing that lit on the crater Linné, on the moon, and obscured it, in the 1860's, and which seems to have doubled every twenty years since that time? Here is the letter:

To the Editor of the *Inquirer*:

"Eight-year study scoffs at saucers"—well! After eight years of research and study, the government's setting up a special division called project Blue Book with all information labeled "Top Secret." Three per cent of these flying objects still cannot be identified, but the Air Force scoffs.

I believe the majority of the public is anxiously awaiting the truth on flying saucers and we have a right to know. If other planets have conquered space travel why should the public become panic-stricken? Aren't we trying to conquer space and are we intending to be hostile? Of course not, we are intelligent human beings, and want to be regarded as such.

The "cosmic age" is just ahead of us, and we are ready to be part of it.

We will not attempt to quote the entire editorial that appeared in the Springfield (Ohio) *Sun* of October 31, 1955, entitled "End of the Saucers?" Much of it is similar to other editorials. We just point out that the editorial cites the fact that the Air Force has 50,000 eyewitness accounts which it has negated and brushed aside as unsubstantiated. *Fifty thousand* eyewitnesses, all of whom were having hallucinations! *Fifty thousand!* Count them: fifty thousand good Americans who haven't sense enough to know that they don't see what they see. Tragic, isn't it?

Note this letter carefully. It appeared in the Dayton (Ohio) *Journal-Herald*, October 3, 1955, from a reader:

FLYING SAUCER NEWS

Editor of the *Journal-Herald*:

That is sad news for the flying saucer addicts—what you put in the *Journal-Herald* this morning where the Air Force says there is nothing to this flying saucer business.

But if what the Air Force says is correct, what becomes of all the hundreds and hundreds of sighting of strange moving objects in the skies that so many people have been seeing for several years?

Also, I saw where General MacArthur was quoted recently as saying that he thinks there will be no more world wars, but that the nations will have to unite one of these days to repel an invasion from some race from another planet or from outer space. That sounds to me as though the general thinks there may be something in this flying saucer business after all.

Nothing is more fitting to close out the month of October and top off the Air Force's announcement than the anti-climactic announcement of flying saucers over Florida. The quiet, staid little university city of Gainesville, Florida (Alachua County), reported UFO on the night of the 30th. It was reported in the Gainesville *Sun*, October 31, 1955:

FLYING SAUCERS REPORTED IN ALACHUA COUNTY

That Air Force bugaboo—the flying saucers—appeared in Alachua County again last night.

City police and the sheriff's office reported several telephone calls seeking an explanation on some low-flying aircraft "that were different and made no noise."

Odd "lighted objects in the sky" were reported over the southern section of Gainesville—and were seen by deputies in Williston, Ocala, High Springs, and Gainesville.

A Florida Highway Patrolman also reported spotting the object around Baldwin. All the calls were around 10:00 o'clock.

Air bases in Orlando and Jacksonville reported none of their aircraft were in this area.

NOVEMBER

On November 18, we heard again from Leo Bash, via the San Francisco *Chronicle*. Bash is not easily kidded. Here is his letter:

UFO's

Editor:

In referring to my previous letter on investigations by the Air Force of Unidentified Flying Objects, Leon E. Salanave (letters, November 10) displays exactly the conclusion uninformed people will display, and which the double-talk released by the Air Force is intended to help them reach.

Major Donald E. Keyhoe, several years ago, declared, "UFO's are real". . . . Fantastic, preposterous, impossible as it may seem, overwhelming evidence accumulated since Major Keyhoe's declaration indicates conclusively the Major knew what he was saying.

UFO's are not jet-exhausts, or high-altitude balloons (flying in formation against the wind); or meteors (obviously under intelligent control); or experimental aircraft (tracked at 2,000 mph); or missiles (high-altitude rockets spiraled and out-distanced in flight by UFO's); or illusions and fantasy.

The hundreds of thousands of people all over the world who have witnessed and reported these phenomena are not "victims of fantasy or illusion; in other words, they are not just plain nuts.

Leo K. Bash, Mill Valley

Amen, Mr. Bash!

It does not seem to have occurred to anyone that if, by some remarkable chance, the Air Force is telling the truth, and these hundreds of thousands of people are "nuts," how appalling the obvious implications are.

On November 18, 1955, the *Star-Ledger* of Newark, New Jersey, published the announcement of a new UFO Club. Obviously, plenty of people fully intended to maintain a healthy skepticism of the Air Force announcement:

ORGANIZE TO DISH DIRT ON SAUCERS

The North Jersey UFO Club, an organization assembling material on flying saucers, named a three-man central governing committee today.

Members elected to the committee were William J. Wilson, Lee R. Munsick, and Edward G. Collen.

The parade of mysterious accidents to jet planes is continuing. Here is one of the latest reports, via the New York *World-Telegram and Sun,* November 18, 1955:

JETS COLLIDE, 1 KILLED

Lancaster, California: Two Marine Corps F9F Panther jet fighters collided during maneuvers yesterday killing one flier in the subsequent crash of his plane. The other pilot was able to make an emergency landing.

And, speaking of jets, here is another one of those odd disappearances. It came in a letter. We print the whole letter just as received, and say thanks to Mr. Bell:

Route #1, Box 52
Linden, California
November 18, 1955

Dear Mr. Jessup:

On November 13, an Air Force jet fighter, radioed McClellan Air Base in Sacramento, that it was preparing to land. It has not been heard from since. The whole area of our Central Valley is fairly thickly populated, and it seems highly unlikely that a crashed plane would go unnoticed.

A burned out area, about thirty miles from here was investigated, but yielded nothing. The plane has simply vanished. This seems to follow along with other cases cited both by you and Harold T. Wilkins. Like the ones you have given, it disappeared after asking for landing instructions, and usually very close to its landing point.

Sincerely yours,
David Bell

Here is another letter to the editor of the New York *Herald-Tribune*, November 20, 1955:

The recent USAF announcement that Avro Ltd., of Canada, has a contract to build what looks like a "flying saucer" overlooked one very interesting characteristic of this aircraft, related to the "Coanda Effect," on which its operation is based. This was described on pp. 456-465 of the *"Proceedings of the Fifth International Congress for Applied Mechanics"* (J. P. den Hartog and H. Peters, editors: John Wiley & Sons, N.Y. 1939). One significant application of the Coanda nozzle was its use as a motorcycle engine muffler or silencer.

Not only did it silence the exhaust, but the back pressure was less than when no muffler was used.

This indicates that the Avro saucer will probably be remarkably silent in operation. This feature is a further example of the astounding prescience of the great number of saucer observers who, since 1947, have been predicting the shape and performance of the Avro craft, and have also almost invariably remarked on the amazing silence of "saucers" in flight.

Leon Davidson
White Plains, N.Y.

There is real food for thought in the remarks of the following editorial in the Ironton (Ohio) *Tribune,* November 22, 1955. These polar bases could be for almost anything and certainly a base in Antarctica should be scrutinized rather carefully:

NOTE TO MOON SEEKERS

There may be a significant parallel in the announcements of the plan to establish a permanent occupation of bases in Antarctica and the plans for the first United States world satellites and "flying saucer" type of aircraft.

It is true that in these times scientific progress seems to accelerate at something like geometric proportions, but it might be well to remember that Admiral Richard E. Byrd established Little America on the Bay of Whales in 1929, and only now a permanent base is being attempted.

Incidentally, the first land in the antarctic was discovered for Russia by F. G. Bellinghausen in 1819, although the ice pack had been encountered in 1772 by Captain James Cook of Britain.

While we are preparing for world satellites and flying saucers, and dreaming of space travel, we should recall the long years it has taken to overcome the handicaps of life in Antarctica which is so much closer to home than the nearest heavenly body.

Scholars already have been arguing about the possible religion of the Martians and promoters have been staking out real estate claims on the moon, but the exacting scientific journeys to these distant places may not be realized for a good many years.

Here is another bit about the satellites, from the Washington (D.C.) *Post and Times-Herald,* November 26, 1955:

EXPERT PREDICTS TEST MAY NEED SIX "SATELLITES"

Paris (Reuters). Dr. A. F. Spilhaus, one of the fathers of the United States plan to launch an artificial satellite into outer space, said today it might be necessary to send up as many as six missiles to get satisfactory results.

Dr. Spilhaus, in Paris to attend the meeting of the United Nations Scientific and Cultural Organization, described the artificial satellite project as "not spectacular at all, but merely an extension of the known techniques of rocketry."

Dr. Spilhaus is dean of the Institute of Technology at the University of Minnesota. He said miniature instruments in the satellite would radio results back to earth and all nations taking part in the 1957-58 geophysical year would be asked to pick up its transmissions.

The Cornwall (England) *Local*, November 24, 1955, printed the following discussion. You will be seeing more on this subject in spite of the Air Forces of the United States and Britain:

WHAT ARE THE FLYING SAUCERS?

By Michael Raab

What are the flying saucers? Are they really what they are made out to be? What do they look like? Listen to some of these reports: On July 24, 1948, at 2:45 a.m., two Eastern Airlines pilots, Captain C. S. Chiles, and First Officer John B. Whitted, were flying over Montgomery, Alabama, when a brilliantly lighted cigar-shaped object came speeding toward their aircraft. Captain Chiles said, "it was headed southwest, and it headed toward the left. It veered also, and passed us about 700 feet to the right."

Another report is that of Congaree Air Base, Columbia, South Carolina. On the morning of August 20, the men at a nearby Air Defense Command Post were watching the radar screen when a blip of an unknown object appeared on the screen. When the first sighting of the blip was made it was about sixty miles from the ADC post. Almost instantly the men realized that the blip was traveling at a tremendous speed. In a few seconds the radar sweep went around again and a row of widely spaced spots appeared. While the operators were still watching, the blips slowly disappeared from sight. Hastily, before the blips completely disappeared, they figured out the object's speed. It was making over 4,000 mph! These are reports of cigar and oval shaped objects. Are they dangerous?

Here are some more reports: One of the most famous cases of a person being injured by a flying saucer was probably the Desvergers case. The saucer encounter took place in a woods near West Palm Beach, Florida, on the night of August 19, 1952. Scoutmaster D. S. Desvergers and three scouts were riding home from a meeting when eerie lights were seen in the forest. Leaving the boys in the car, he went into the woods to investigate with a flashlight and machete. Two minutes later one of the scouts saw a reddish-white fireball in the woods. It came from about the height of the trees and seemed to slant down toward the spot where the scoutmaster was last seen. When the scoutmaster failed to return one of the scouts ran to the nearest house and phoned the sheriff. Just as the sheriff arrived Desvergers staggered out of the woods, badly frightened and on the verge of exhaustion. He had reached a clearing he said when he realized there was a disc-shaped machine about twenty-five feet in diameter. An instant later the saucer's turret opened and shot out a ray that scorched his arms and hat. When he regained his balance he realized that the saucer was gone.

Another case was that of two boys of Amarillo, Texas. They had reported seeing a small disc land near them, its top section still spinning. When one boy touched it the rotating part sped up and sprayed out a gaseous spray. Then it took off with a whistling sound and soon disappeared. The gaseous spray left some odd red spots on the boy's face and arms.

Have the saucers any real weapons? Has any human ever seen the inside of a saucer?

Science has become rather complacent as to the extent of its qualitative knowledge, but the depths of the sea and the air will yet bring change to our thinking and concepts of the world around us. Here is an article about what has come from the profundities of the oceans. For a most startling concept of what may be coming from the celestial depths of our mysterious atmosphere, take a look at an article by John P. Bessor in the December issue of *Fate Magazine,* and printed in the Washington (D.C.) *Herald,* November 30, 1955:

VISTAS IN SCIENCE

By Thomas R. Henry

Soviet Oceanographers Make a Find

Russion oceanographers may have found the third greatest depth in the sea, a 300-mile long, 3-mile wide trench between the Kurile Islands west of Japan and the Kamchatka coast.

They report soundings down to approximately six miles. This is approximately the same as that of the three previously known great depths—the Philippine and Puerto Rico depths and the Tonga-Keremec Trench, north of New Zealand.

This depth has been explored partially in several voyages of the oceanographic research ship Vitaz, according to a report of V. C. Borogov, assistant director of the Soviet Institute of Oceanography, in the Russian Voks Bulletin just received here.

The chief interest, Dr. Borogov says, has not been in the area per se, but in the strata of life in the great depths. The greatest abyss from which living animals were obtained was approximately five miles. From the bottom dredges brought up a few bristled worms, fantastic crawling sea cucumbers, and long-legged sea spiders. The latter have been found the dominant animals in the greatest depths in the Atlantic. But, they found, the abundance of life drops sharply with depth in the realm of everlasting darkness and pressures of fifteen to twenty pounds per square inch greater than any known on the surface.

There is a ladder of food available in the sea, they found, and each ocean stratum has its own fauna.

At depths of about four miles the crab-like decapods disappeared. At about five miles there is an end to sponges and star fish.

From depths of about one kilometer they dredged 120 animal species, at five kilometers 50, at seven 40, at eight 20, and at the greatest depth, close to ten kilometers, only six. At the same time the mass of living organisms decreased about 20-fold.

The average depth of the trench they estimate at about nine kilometers.

In these days of flying saucers and the like, lots of queer things are being reported seen.

Some of the queerest, according to an account in the British Scientific Journal *Nature*, have just been reported by Brett Hilder, New South Wales sea captain, to the British Admiralty weather service.

Once last year off eastern New Guinea, Hilder reports, he saw "a loom of light on the horizon extending over an arc of fifteen degrees. It was bright over some submerged reefs. Then it shifted, but still in the direction of the reefs. The light was a brilliant line along the horizon. It showed on the radar screen like a rain squall and covered an area about two miles square.

"It lay in lines and patches like sand banks. Two miles from the reefs we passed through one patch. The light appeared as if coming from a depth of about thirty feet."

Six months later, Hilder says, he witnessed much the same phenomenon off Guadalcanal. There were a lot of oval patches of light, about fifty feet long, and the illumination was quite bright. It appeared as if the source was a few fathoms beneath the surface. This phenomenon showed some traces on the radar screen, but it disappeared as soon as the radar apparatus was switched off.

It is possible, he points out, that the curious luminescence may be that of sea animals which are stimulated by radar in some way. There have been previous accounts of such animals stimulated by reverberations of ships' engines.

Hilder reports seeing at sea "phosphorescent wheels—rays of light radiating from a point and rotating clockwise or anticlockwise over an area of five miles or more. The rays are curved and a few feet wide. They suggest the rays that radiate from northern lights. The wheels travel over the water at a speed of about one hundred miles per hour."

There is a possibility, Hilder suggests, that these luminous appearances may be associated in some way with a disturbance in the earth's magnetism.

Jersey Journal, November 26, 1955:

SOMETHING NEW! A RECTANGULAR FLYING SAUCER!

A new angle to flying saucers is given by Ralph Del Piano, 16, of 66 Waverly Street, Jersey City, a member of the Civil Air Patrol at Carlstadt.

The flying saucer which Del Piano, five other members of the CAP and a Route 46 service station attendant saw, while a tire on their car was being repaired Monday night, was not round, as the classical flying saucers, but rectangular.

The flying angle, which glowed orange, was in the southeast sky, about five miles from Journal Square, Del Piano said.

The C.R.I.F.O. *Orbit,* November 1, 1955, carried the following recounting of the mysterious jet explosion or disappearance of August, over or near Long Island, N.Y. No comment is needed other than that of editor Stringfield:

(Case 109, Shinnecock Inlet, Long Island, N.Y., August 26, 1955.) A veteran pilot for Republic Aviation Corporation, Earl Kane, was killed violently when his Thunderflash mysteriously exploded in a routine flight. The blast tore his plane apart and bits of wreckage were sprayed over the surf and beach—his body was blown to bits. *A Republic spokesman said Kane had radioed to the tower five minutes before the blast,* reporting minor difficulties, but that was the last they heard. Just what happened was not clear. Investigating reporters found a cloak of security dropped over the tragedy. Significant, however, was the report of an eyewitness, John Borucke, of Southampton. He said, "I *saw two planes* flying over the beach, then I heard a terrific explosion." But Republic officials *denied* the report of a second plane. Also, curiously coincidental was the fact that another plane, a private, single-engined Cessna, had crash-landed in the surf at Montauk Point about three hours later. The occupants, unhurt, said their craft developed engine trouble.

Editor: Here's real confusion to say the least! Of most concern, however, is the second plane described by eyewitness, Borucke. Was Republic's denial of the second plane a statement of fact, and the object Borucke saw actually a UFO? My informant comments further, "I talked with employees of Republic. According to what I heard, everybody was trying to find out just what happened. The accepted theory is that engine seizure took place, piling up fuel-air mixture which blew the ship apart. Pilot is said to have reported a flame-out, though. Tower at Republic tried contact *five full minutes* after pilot's last message without success. *How did they know when ship blew up?* Assumption is, pilot tried to bring ship in for landing on beach. If so, why did he not answer—*or why does the radio always go dead when most needed?* I observed *above normal jet activity on day of crash.*" My informant asked Republic if the jets were theirs and the answer was negative.

This is also from C.R.I.F.O. *Orbit,* November 4, 1955:

WERE THESE BALLOONS, MR. QUARLES?

The Secretary of the Air Force had no trouble in sweeping all the bonafide saucer reports into the circular file, but we doubt that he could use the old balloon trick in talking us out of this unique sighting. Our source is Emil Slaboda, columnist for *The Trentonian,* Trenton, N.J. He says in his September 3, 1955 column, "Hurricane Diane is almost forgotten, but there was one incident reported to me by a reliable source that proved interesting. During the furious rain and winds, at approximately 3:00 a.m., two UFO's were sighted over Hamilton skies. They were described as oblong and brilliant. The witness told me the objects seemed to be signalling each other. I realize most flying saucer sightings normally can be explained away as weather balloons and high-flying planes. But through no stretch of the imagination can I believe that two airplanes, or for that matter, weather balloons, braved the furious storm to put on a pyrotechnic display."

Here, in the Philadelphia *Inquirer*, November 9, 1955, is a follow-up of Bob Camburn's letter:

SAUCERS IN THE NIGHT

Robert S. Camburn is right about flying saucers. I, too, have seen one, and it was no illusion, but a real ship—shooting through the night like a meteor.

Take a look at the following report of the herd of whales that beached in formation on the coast at Melbourne, Florida. It come from the Philadelphia *Inquirer*. (Is it any wonder "everybody" reads it?)

What is it that makes this Florida-Caribbean area so mysteriously active? Can it be a ghostly remnant of the lost Atlantis?

MAD WHALES OF MELBOURNE

The sad end of fifty-three pilot whales, which swam ashore en masse on a Florida beach at Melbourne, is a reminder that the world's oceans still represent an abyss of mystery, unfathomed by the modern technology of which we are so proud.

The whales piled up on the sun-baked beach—according to one theory—in order to escape the warm waters of the Gulf stream as they migrated from Greenland to the Cape of Good Hope.

The truth is that we can only guess at what madness or fear it was that drove the whales to their doom, and our guesses are not very convincing or well-supported by scientifically gathered facts. The oceans covering seventy per cent of the earth's surface veil from us myriad forms of life of which we have only the scantiest knowledge.

Many of the whales were devoured where they lay by swarms of voracious sharks. Was it because of the sharks that they would not

turn back into deep water? Or was it some other enemy of the deep
as yet unrecognized by man that forced them ashore?

So far no motive other than curiosity has impelled us to seek
answers to such questions. Eventually, however, when human popu-
lations have caught up with present food surpluses it may be different. Then we may find it necessary to turn to the tremendous
food-producing capacities of the sea and solve its mysteries in order
to survive.

The above article was brought to my attention by Goldie
Sargent, 3704 Hamilton Street, Philadelphia 4, Pennsylvania.

Here are two announcements of the ill-fated ship "Joyita." We
must admit that thousands of people evidently agree that these
disappearances of ships' crews smack of UFO activity. We received clippings of this event from all over the United States
and Canada, and we thank the readers who sent them in to us.

The Washington *Daily News*, Friday, November 11, 1955:

SHIPS

Five weeks ago the 70-ton cabin cruiser *Joyita* left Apia, Samoa,
for a two-day trip to the Tokelau Islands. Yesterday the steamer
Tuvalu came upon the waterlogged *Joyita,* drifting aimlessly and
far off its course near the Fiji Islands, with no trace of the twenty-
five persons aboard. Everything was in perfect order—but the
twenty-five persons had vanished.

This second featured article was sent to us by John O. Wicks
23, Woodrow Avenue, Toronto 6, Canada. (Thanks, John):

ANOTHER MARY CELESTE
MISSING FIVE WEEKS, DERELICT FOUND OFF FIJIS
By Jack Thornton
(Special to the *Globe and Mail*)

Suva, Fiji Islands, November 10, 1955—The disappearance without trace of the 25 passengers and crew of the twin-engined fishing

vessel *Joyita* is shrouded in mystery that recalls the famous and unsolved case of the *Mary Celeste.*

The *Joyita,* five weeks overdue on its 320-mile voyage from Samoa to the Tokelau Islands, was found Wednesday by another steamer off the Fiji Island of Vanua Levu.

Scraps of food were found on the ship and there was an awning which had been erected on deck not long ago. But there was no hint of what had become of the 25 persons aboard. The ship was 800-miles from its Samoan starting point.

The new mystery paralleled the case of the *Mary Celeste* which was found in full sail in the Atlantic in 1872. The ten people who had been aboard were missing, but the ship was perfectly in order. No clue to the fate of the passengers and crew was ever uncovered.

When the *Joyita,* under Captain T. H. Miller left Apia Harbor she was expected to reach the Tokelau Islands in 44-hours. There was only a two-day supply of food and water aboard.

When she failed to put in at the Tokelaus, Royal New Zealand Air Force planes searched 100,000 square miles of the South Pacific. The search eventually slackened and nothing was heard of the *Joyita* until yesterday.

I sailed as a crew member on the *Joyita* on the voyage just before its mystery trip. Twice before I have been lucky enough to sign off ships that have sunk on the next voyage. In this case I feel lucky to have escaped the fate of the 25 passengers and crew who have disappeared.

Yet, after sailing on the ship I can say it was a splendid vessel, well equipped for its route. Its captain and mate were splendid seamen.

The captain, in his forty years, served in the Merchant Navy and then in the Royal Navy during the war. He talked little about his wartime career, but it is known that he was commissioned and probably rose to the rank of lieutenant-commander. In 1947, he went to the Gilbert Islands as a government ship's master. He later resigned his command of a government-owned ship and, after assuming command of the *Joyita,* based his fishing operations at Canton Island.

Last year he fished in Samoan and outlying waters, and for a few months used Pago Pago as a base. He then moved his headquarters to Apia, from which he sailed on the voyage that has ended in mystery.

Miller was regarded by his men as an individualist and a strict disciplinarian but, above all, a superb seaman. Masters of other small ships in the Pacific considered him an expert navigator.

His mate, Charles Simpson, a massive man in his twenties, arrived in Pago Pago last year as deck officer aboard a U.S. ship being delivered to Japan. A North American Indian whose home was near Seattle, Simpson survived three previous shipwrecks.

Recently he married a Samoan. They expected to have their first child around Christmas.

Two natives of the Gilbert Islands were the only permanent members of the crew. For the last trip eight other islanders were added to the crew.

The ship was built in Los Angeles in 1934 as a deep-sea yacht. During the war she served as a U.S. Coastguard patrol ship and was *equipped with a radio-telephone and two radio receivers*—all of which were aboard and serviceable, when she set sail on her last voyage.

After the war the ship was purchased by a woman lecturer at the University of Hawaii. Captain Miller obtained one-fifth share in the vessel, which was registered at Honolulu, when he outfitted it for fishing. When the last voyage was begun, the *Joyita* was up for sale.

When the *Joyita* was found yesterday, *her funnel had been either blown or washed away*. Some of her compartments were so flooded they could not be searched. And the *ship's log was missing*.

The Miami *Daily News*, November 12, 1955, published the following sighting as written by Bella Kelly:

MADE NOISE LIKE SIREN

SAW "FLYING SAUCER," SHORE FOLK REPORT

Twelve persons in Miami Shores reported seeing a flying saucer hover near Biscayne Bay on NE 94th Street last night.

First to sight the saucer was Lucien Brown, 1065 NE 94th Street, "It was a little after midnight and my wife and I heard this siren-like sound," Brown said. "It kept getting louder and finally I went outside to see what it was.

"There, about 300 yards up, was this saucer, sort of oblong shaped and with a weird green light coming out of it. It seemed to bob up and down a while and then went out over the bay."

Brown called his neighbor, Dr. Lynn Whelchel, 1008 NE 94th Street, to tell him about it and Whelchel thought it was a joke and went back to bed.

About half an hour later, however, the doctor said, his wife and two children were awakened by the same noise. They rushed out of the house and there was the saucer. The children started screaming Whelchel said, and his wife started crying.

Asked if the ship might have been an experimental one similar to those revealed by the Air Force recently, Whelchel and Brown said definitely not.

"It wasn't that shape and you could tell from the funny light it must have been something from outer space," the doctor declared.

Whelchel said the saucer was also seen by two other neighbors who live on NE 93rd Street. Another Miami Shores resident, Richard Darnell, 1125 NE 93rd Street, said he didn't know the Whelchels or the Browns, but he saw the thing too around the same time. He said he was reading when he heard a whistling sound, went outside and saw a "green-like saucer." He said about six of his neighbors also witnessed the sight.

Edward Mitchell, a calculator machine salesman, 1123 NE 93rd Street, said he and his two children saw the saucer around 12:45 a.m. They gave a description similar to Whelchel's and Brown's.

The Marine Corps Station said it knew of no saucers or any other type of unusual planes that might have been in that area.

Here is a letter, dated November 16, 1955, just as it was received by me:

Mr. M. K. Jessup:

I just finished reading your book and enjoyed it very much. I wonder if you have time to listen to a small story of a sighting of a UFO. I doubt whether I can relate it with any amount of interest

or whether it's important enough to take your time. I do hope you
will read it.

Kwajalein, Marshall Islands—April 1954—My buddy and I were
lying on the baseball bleachers sunning—a quiet day—the wind was
blowing approximately 15-20 mph, not unusual for the Island. We
spotted an extremely bright object almost directly overhead. I then
started looking intently to find other bright spots which could be
stars as they are sometimes visible during the day. The time of day
was between noon and 2 :00 p.m. There were no other spots we could
see, the object we did see was motionless. After a while I discarded
the possibility of an airplane, there are many in the area but they
just don't stay still. The next thought was a helicopter with a bird's
eye view of the Pacific and the Islands below. There were none
stationed on the Island but we considered it. A balloon would have
been a fine suggestion except that we had then been watching and
talking for ten minutes, possibly longer, but I'm trying to be
logical. There was a tree nearby and some of the foliage was in the
area of vision. Also there were two light wires running angled across
the line of sight. With this time lapse and the wind blowing, the
object still could be located in its initial position. By this time we
were taking into account the object's background. Sometimes the
clouds would hide it and at other times you could see it and clouds
beyond. It was windy up there, the clouds moved rapidly. I had two
pair of binoculars in my locker in the barracks so I told my buddy
to watch it and I would get them for us. After returning I put the
7 x 50 pair on the object, it was still in the same place, still as
bright. The object was round, uniform brightness all over, vivid
white but not a glare. I could see the outer edge clearly, sharply
defined, not hazy or fuzzy. There were no other lines or marks
visible. We would change glasses (the other pair is 8 x 30) but the
appearance of the object remained the same. Shortly, with both of
us looking through glasses, a cone shaped mist, exhaust or whatever,
appeared on the leeward side of the object. The object seemed to
move, I could have shifted my glasses, but at any rate, I lost sight of
it. I said, "What happened to it, I can't see it." Jones, my buddy,
said, "It looked to me like it went straight up." With our naked
eyes again, you could still see the mist drifting off, it soon disap-

peared. The time we spent using the glasses must have taken another ten minutes.

J. C. Howard
7852 Wherry Drive
Norfolk, Virginia

Here is another letter that appeared in the San Francisco
Chronicle, November 1, 1955. Mr. Bash obviously does not intend
to let anyone intimidate him. He is a very alert observer:

Editor: So the Air Force is "satisfied none of the saucer sightings
are in fact aircraft of foreign origin." I think everyone who has
pursued the subject is in complete agreement provided the term
"foreign" is limited to mean other nations of this planet.

As to the statement, "All past sightings of the eccentric craft
being illusions or explainable as conventional phenomena,": that is
to say, if it is unexplainable as conventional phenomena, then it is
illusion.

My answer to that is *"Stendec."* Let's face it. There have been
UFO's in our skies longer than man has kept history. They are not
something new, but they are unbelievably fantastic, and intelligently
controlled.

Man did not put them there. They defy man's explanation. What
power moves, and what intelligence directs these amazing objects
is purely conjectural—but *"Stendec,"* clearly and distinctly, is the
word that came over the radio when a British air liner with its crew
and passengers vanished from this earth without a trace.

Frank Reid of Chicago is an ardent UFO student. In the
Chicago *News* of November 3, 1955, he protests the government's
negative press releases:

HE EXPECTS MORE FLYING SAUCERS
AND PREDICTS SOME WON'T EXPLODE

In the *Daily News,* October 27, you printed an editorial on the
Air Force's latest report on UFO's. The editorial was headed
"Exploded Saucers."

The UFO mystery is far from "exploded." It is true that there are people involved in UFO research and investigation who are in it because of their very strong "craving for the mysterious and supernatural," i.e. crackpots. But you will find such people in any subject or activity that is a bit out of the ordinary.

However, most people interested in UFO's are not wild-eyed mystics and crackpots. The majority, who do not make as much noise as the lunatic fringe, are people who have come to the conclusion that UFO's are real through intelligent logic.

They know that the "small percentage of the sightings not readily explainable on other grounds" are proof that some type of cigar and disc-shaped machines have been seen, and sometimes from close up, in our atmosphere.

One has only to read Major Donald E. Keyhoe's "Flying Saucers From Outer Space" with an unprejudiced mind to realize this. Although Keyhoe has a tendency to over-dramatization of cases, the vast bulk of sightings mentioned are from official Air Force analysis reports.

These are not hoaxes. They are all by reliable observers. In some cases, the UFO's were simultaneously sighted visually and by radar.

Why the Air Force attempt at debunking? In UFO research it has been noticed that reports come in cycles. The years 1951, 1953, and probably 1955, are noted for their lack of reports. But 1950, 1952 and 1954 were full of reports, the number going up each cycle.

At one time in 1954 UFO reports were coming in at a rate of over 700 a week, higher than it had ever been before!

It is obvious that the Air Force is trying to foster a belief that UFO's are hoaxes or secret planes in preparation for the expected increase in sightings next year, an increase that may be tremendous.

Frank Reid
Chicago

Robert S. Camburn has been a good correspondent and supplier of UFO material. The Philadelphia *Inquirer*, November 4, 1955, published a letter from Mr. Camburn, dated October 27. With his usual alertness he has put his finger on the Achilles' heel of the Air Force report:

SAUCER CLUES

Now that the Air Force has issued another of its periodic denials of the existence of flying saucers (while stating it is about to reveal some imitations of its very own), it is timely to raise a few questions.

First, what was it that Kenneth Arnold first saw back in 1947? What did Clyde Tombaugh, the astronomer, discoverer of Pluto, see? He described it as a solid, oval ship of unique character and behavior. Earlier another prominent astronomer had a similar experience. What did Commander McLaughlin, USN, see, and his men track by theodolite (at 18,000 mph) at the White Sands rocket testing grounds, in 1949? What of the strange sightings of many competent air lines pilots?

Or have all these now recanted? Then what of the earlier observatory sightings which author-astronomer M. K. Jessup has shown can only be explained by space craft near the earth? These are but a few of the holes in the Air Force's denial.

It is strange, too, that since the non-existent saucers were first reported, the U.S. has been trying to produce similarly shaped and performing craft although aeronautical engineers then derided the disc form as inadequate because of excessive instability.

Robert S. Camburn

Here, from C.R.I.F.O. *Orbit,* is more evidence of the mysterious Swedish jet disaster:

NEW EVIDENCE ON SWEDISH 4-WAY DISASTER

Looking back over the list of macabre cases mentioned by C.R.I.F.O. we should like to review some new evidence concerning Case 90. It comes by way of an AP dispatch appearing in the New York *Post.* We quote in part, ". . . the aircraft disappeared soon after take-off from a base at Norrkoping, fourteen miles south of the lake . . . the air force could not explain the incident. The formation had just received and acknowledged permission to pass through clouds that should have sent them *upward.*" Our correspondent, Max Schaeffer of New York, speculates, "But if they were fourteen miles from take-off and *going up*, the distance of the melting surface of the lake below them could not have caused the accident.

Thus, despite all denial and pretence, and attempts to confuse the general public, the "saucer" controversy continued unabated. Look forward to the year 1956. It is going to be a busy one.

November passes into December.

DECEMBER

December came in like a lion—and went out like a *lion!* This month made me feel that 1956 may well be a stellar year for UFO, and, who knows, may bring truly startling events to each and every one of us!

The very earliest report in the month is from the Riverside (California) *Enterprise,* and actually took place at the end of November:

AIRPORT HEAD TELLS STORY RELUCTANTLY

A flying saucer in the form of a globe of white light returned recognition signals with a Piper airplane over Desert Hot Springs one recent night, it was reluctantly reported today by Gene Miller, pilot of the plane and manager of Banning Municipal Airport.

Miller and a passenger, Dr. Leslie Ward of Redlands, reportedly sighted the unidentified flying object while returning from a chartered flight to Phoenix, Arizona.

The story of the strange aerial meeting with the phosphorescent globe was related somewhat hesitantly today by Miller, after the Enterprise first heard reports of the saucer encounter through friends of the airport manager.

Miller said he at first thought the object was an airliner and blinked his lights twice as a recognition signal. The fiery globe flipped its lights out twice in answer.

The airport manager was somewhat wary of telling his story to a reporter, "because I remember the way the newspapers hammed up their interview with Kenneth Arnold, when he first spotted the saucers back in the '40s."

"I know Arnold very well and he's a sound and reliable business man," declared Miller. "But the newspaper stories made him look like a crackpot."

Miller said that he was returning with Dr. Ward to Banning at about 6 p.m. on November 14th in a Piper tri-pacer and had reached what is known as the intersection of the Palm Springs airway.

"Off to our right—between us and the Little San Bernardino Mountains—we saw a globe of white light traveling toward us," he continued.

"I thought at first it might be an airliner," said Miller. "It was about six or seven miles away in the night sky."

Miller, following normal procedure, flipped his landing lights off twice as a recognition signal. The globe of light went dark twice in return.

"When the globe blinked out there was total darkness," said Miller. "There were no position lights or red and green lights to indicate an aircraft."

Miller said the strange object continued traveling toward his plane at which he estimated to be a slow speed of not more than 50 miles an hour. About a mile away from the object, Miller switched his landing lights three times and received a similar return signal.

"Both Dr. Ward and I commented that it was definitely not an aircraft," recalled Miller. "At that moment the saucer really surprised us."

Miller said the mystery object suddenly backed up in mid-air, "clear over the hills and went up toward the top of Mount San Gorgonio, disappearing from sight."

Near Whitewater, Miller was forced to turn back his plane because of heavy turbulence and head for Palm Springs airport.

Once more the flying object appeared over the Little San Bernardino mountain range.

Miller said the object appeared to be climbing down the ridges, a white glow suspended about 500 feet above the hills. It then picked up speed, traveling at a low altitude, and cruised off across the desert floor in the direction of Desert Center.

"I would have liked to have followed it," said Miller, "but it was a rough, windy night."

The airport manager said that his sightings took place four days before Desert Hot Springs residents reported on November 18th that a mystery object blazed across the sky and burned on the slopes of Mount San Gorgonio. Sheriff's officers were unable to find a trace of the reported aircraft.

"I don't know whether there is any connection," said Miller, "but it's certainly weird."

Miller said that the encounter was not the first time he has observed flying saucers. He said that he and several other observers sighted a silver object floating in the sky above the Pass airport several months ago.

"I've known quite a few pilots who have seen them," explained the airport manager. "The Army can try and explain away saucers all they want to, but their explanations still don't solve the problem."

Miller, who was a pilot for the Flying Tiger Airlines out of Burbank for several years, recalled that one of the senior captains on the line was paced by a cigar-shaped object one night near Albuquerque.

"It frightened heck out of him and he was almost incoherent over the radio," said Miller. "The object was bigger than his C-46."

"While on the Tokyo airlift, I had a strange bluish light pace our

DC-4 for about 10 minutes one night," remembered the ex-airlines pilot.

Miller said that few of the airlines pilots ever bothered to report their meetings with strange flying objects.

"The pilots I knew used to say that they sure as hell wouldn't report them and get laughed at or bawled out for imagining things," he said.

Miller theorized that the only explanation for flying saucers is that they have an extra-terrestrial origin.

"But whatever their origin," he concluded, "you can't disregard or explain away something you see regardless of who says different."

Miller served as an instructor for the Air Force during World War II and afterwards flew with the Air Transport Command. In 1951, he became a co-pilot for the Flying Tiger Airlines, and served for several years with the company, making a number of flights to Germany and Tokyo.

Published late in the year, but evidently an event which took place much earlier, though certainly in 1955, the following eerie incident was reported in David Grinnell's column. It is reported as sober fact, and we pass it along to you as possible evidence that people are not talking through their hats, necessarily, if they say that visitors from outer space are with us—*now!*

All we ask is that you pause a moment and *think*. And ask yourself again, why doesn't the Air Force wish us to know the truth?

TOP SECRET

I cannot say whether I am the victim of a very ingenious jest on the part of some of my wackier friends or whether I am just someone accidentally "in" on some top-secret business. But it happened, and it happened to me personally, while visiting Washington recently, just rubber-necking, you know, looking at the Capitol and the rest of the big white buildings.

It was summer, fairly hot. Congress was not in session, nothing much was doing, most people vacationing. I was that day aiming to pay a visit to the State Department, not knowing that I couldn't, for there was nothing public to see there unless it's the imposing and rather martial lobby (it used to be the War Department building, I'm told). This I did not find out until I had blithely walked up the marble steps to the entrance, passed the big bronze doors, and wandered about in the huge lobby, wherein a small number of people, doubtless on important business, were passing in and out.

A guard, sitting near the elevators, made as if to start in my direction to find out whom and what the deuce I wanted, when one of the elevators came down and a group of men hustled out. There were two men, evidently State Department escorts, neatly clad in gray double-breasted suits, with three other men walking with them. The three men struck me as a little odd; they wore long black cloaks, big slouch hats with wide brims pulled down over their faces, and carried portfolios. They looked for all the world like cartoon representations of cloak-and-dagger spies. I supposed that they were some sort of foreign diplomats and, as they were coming directly toward me, stood my ground, determined to see who they were.

The floor was marble and highly polished. One of the men nearing me suddenly seemed to lose his balance. He slipped; his feet shot out from under him, and he fell. His portfolio slid directly at my feet.

Being closest to him, I scooped up the folio and was the first to help raise him to his feet. Grasping his arm, I hoisted him from the floor—he seemed to be astonishingly weak in the legs; I felt almost that he was about to topple again. His companions stood about rather flustered, helplessly, their faces curiously impassive. And though the man I helped must have received a severe jolt, his face never altered expression.

Just then the two State Department men recovered their own poise, rushed about, and, getting between me and the man I had rescued, rudely brushed me aside, and rushed their party to the door.

Now what bothers me is not the impression I got that the arm beneath that man's sleeve was curiously woolly, as if he had a fur coat underneath the cloak (and this in a Washington summer!),

M

and it's not the impression that he was wearing a mask (the elastic band of which I distinctly remember seeing amidst the kinky, red, close-cropped hair of his head). No, it's not that at all, which might be merely momentary misconstructions on my part. It's the coin that I picked up off the floor where he'd dropped his portfolio.

I've searched through every stamp and coin catalogue I can find or borrow, and I've made inquiries of a dozen language teachers and professors, and nobody can identify that coin or the lettering around its circumference.

It's about the size of a quarter, silvery, very light in weight, but also very hard. Besides the lettering on it, which even the Bible Society, which knows a thousand languages and dialects, cannot decipher, there is a picture on one side and a symbol on the other.

The picture is the face of a man, but a man with very curiously wolfish features: sharp canine teeth parted in what could be called a smile; a flattened, broad, and somewhat protruding nose, more like a pug dog's muzzle; sharp, widely spaced vulpine eyes; and definitely hairy and pointed ears.

The symbol on the other side is a circle with latitude and longitude lines on it. Flanking the circle, one on each side, are two crescent-shaped moons.

I wish I knew just how far those New Mexico rocket experiments have actually gone.

Your editor received a letter, dated December 4th, from Mr. Herman H. Mitchell of 22 North Street, Huntington Station, New York, in which he reported some very peculiar sun spots. His description is not sufficiently definitive for us to say, with certainty, that a part of the spots were UFO operating in space. However, his description of their movements over a three-day period would seem to indicate movement in the reverse direction to that of conventional sun spots. These spots, or discs, traversing the face of the sun, have been reported ever since the invention of the telescope, and have caused a great deal of comment and contention in the astronomical profession. We cannot say unequivocally that Mr. Mitchell saw UFO's, but we can say that many UFO's have been seen under similar circumstances.

The APRO *Bulletin* of December reported a brilliant spherical globe looking like cast silver. It flew over the town of Guarenas, about 40 kilometers east of Caracas, Venezuela, on August 26th. The flattened silvery ball was seen by hundreds, and made a loud humming noise. It was in view about 40 seconds. It was very, very high and moved erratically at high speed.

(Ed.: These objects which make a humming noise are becoming more common. A few have been reported over the past several years, but more and more sightings are recorded in which this humming sound is prominent. Some correspondents say the objects "sound like a dynamo" others have said like "high frequency vibrations." In some cases observers have been apprised of the nearness of UFO, while indoors, by merely hearing this humming sound. In Miami, Florida, your editor has been told—as recently as December 29th—that a man of peculiar scientific and archaeological attainments told two friends that UFO would pass over their home on a certain night. He visited them on that night, and during the evening this characteristic humming sound was heard. The group went outside immediately and saw a light approaching. A large UFO of round shape drew over the house at about 1000 feet altitude, circled the house once, and disappeared in the distance at terrific speed. Names are not mentioned for the usual reasons, but this was told to your editor by two people of far above average intelligence, and of unimpeachable integrity. This tale lends credence to the theory that some humans may well have a kind of telepathic contact with space people.)

Life featured, in the earliest issue in December, a series of drawings of UFO's and commented that the Air Force had ex-

plained, to its satisfaction, at any rate, about 60% of the sightings, but admitted that the remainder were mysteries.

Under the date of December 7th, a memorable date in American minds, your editor received a letter from Mrs. Gwynne D.
Mack, of Pound Ridge, New York, covering a bonafide sighting
made by three adults and an eleven-year-old boy on May 9th,
1955. Another sighting of the usual orange-yellow light UFO is
reported in the same letter, but without accurate date. In passing,
may we comment that Mrs. Mack is of a distinguished, scholarly
family, one of whom is a prominent physicist and spectroscopist.

Here is Mrs. Mack's letter:

URGENT!
REPORT ON SIGHTING OF UFO

(May 9, 1955—Southern California. Four Observers: three adults,
one eleven-year-old boy.) Group was driving up to Mt. Wilson Observatory from Los Angeles, California. Weather: sunny and clear.
Time: shortly after noon. Place: on road, at altitude between 3000
and 4000 feet, above Arroya Secco Canyon.

High above this very deep canyon, but low enough to be cut off
from our view as we rounded the road-side hills, we saw a *huge mass*
of dozens and dozens of white, elliptical, flat objects. It was hard
to estimate their size, but they were smaller—possibly about two
feet in length. They were circling around one another, in an un-
hurried, steady motion, and at frequent intervals some of them
turned entirely over. When they did this, they flashed dazzling
silver. As we wound up the mountain road, we kept seeing these
objects at each clear curve, and had time to study them.

The effect was like an enormous gathering of sea-gulls, soaring
together in a close mass. However, they were definitely not birds.
Their shape allowed no possibility of head or tail, and there was no
movement comparable to wing-motion. When they flashed silver, it
was almost blinding. Some of them seemed to be dark at each end
of the ellipse.

As soon as we could, we stopped and climbed a small hill to observe better. But when we reached a clear view of the canyon, the objects had vanished!

Earlier in the spring, my young son and I saw—just past twilight —a bright orange light rapidly approaching from the east, low above the treetops. It came almost overhead, then changed course southward, at which time the orange light disappeared and a mass without clear outline was vaguely discernible against the dark sky. This mass was studded with several little bluish and white lights which blinked. There was also a humming sound.

I reported to our nearest ground-observer post which had no knowledge of such a craft flying in the vicinity—nor did the Filter Center.

(Signed)

(Mrs.) Gwynne D. Mack

December 7th, 1955, was also distinguished as the day of publication of Major Donald E. Keyhoe's new book *The Flying Saucer Conspiracy,* published by Henry Holt & Company. It is an emphatic continuation of Major Keyhoe's crusade to force the paternalistic and bigoted government to disgorge its knowledge of the reality and nature of the UFO. The Major has been almost alone in this combat, insofar as organized and systematic opposition to the Air Force is concerned. Again we are mindful of the urgent need for *unity*—for a *Central UFO Agency!*

Major Keyhoe has devoted himself to the urgent task of trying to bring officially concealed information before the public in order that the people of the United States may truly know about the most revolutionary discovery and awakening in all human history.

The UFO Annual is proud to join him in that fight!!

To a large degree, Major Keyhoe's fight has been a losing one. He has been overwhelmed by bureaucratic ponderosity and smothered in obfuscating gobbledegook. Nevertheless, the things which the Major says in his latest book are documented and buttressed by fact. If they were not thus supported, Major

Keyhoe would be open to serious charges—*which have never been forthcoming!*

It can hardly be accidental that the Air Force's massive and stolid report on its "Project Bluebook" was released very shortly prior to the publication date of *The Flying Saucer Conspiracy*. The planned distortion of data and misuse of statistical methods in the government's report are prima facie evidence of deliberate concealment of facts.

There was an effective press conference on the eve of publication of the Major's book, but in line with the general kowtowing of the press to government pressure for suppression, very few newspapers carried the report. We can, to a large degree, pardon the press for its attitude, for—unfortunately and disgracefully— some of our fine publishing houses have been guilty of sponsoring sensational and unreliable reports of contacts with space people, space trips and obviously faked photographs, etc.

A few courageous papers published Major Keyhoe's press conference, however, and we are pleased to give you one of those rare items, this from the Washington (D.C.) *Evening Star*, December 7th:

AF KNOWS FLYING SAUCERS ARE REAL, KEYHOE SAYS

Outer space's most vociferous press agent said last night that the Air Force knows flying saucers are real, but he added they could not possibly be secret weapons devised by the United States.

Major Donald E. Keyhoe, retired Marine flyer, said that, if the saucers were part of our own military, then present jets would be obsolete and we would have no need to fear Russian bombers, since the saucers' terrific speeds and maneuvers prove them to be superior by far to any machine developed by any nation of this earth.

Furthermore, said Maj. Keyhoe, it would mean the United States, with its saucers, had been secretly violating the sovereignty of most other countries, for the saucers have been seen over most areas of the earth every year since 1944.

Maj. Keyhoe made his remarks at a press conference in the National Press Club. His third book on flying saucers, "The Flying Saucer Conspiracy," was published today by Henry Holt & Company.

As for speculation over whether flying saucers are real or imaginary, he quoted Gen. Benjamin Chidlaw, former head of the Air Defense Command, as telling one writer that "we have stacks of flying saucer reports," and "we take them seriously, considering we have lost many men and planes trying to intercept them."

(After first refusing to comment, Maj. Keyhoe said, Gen. Chidlaw admitted he may have talked with the writer but that he was misquoted.)

The Major said one such case of a plane lost while chasing a saucer recently was admitted by the Air Force. This, he said, was on November 23, 1953, when an F-89 jet and two airmen were lost while chasing a saucer over Lake Superior.

Major Keyhoe said that last June 16, every Air Defense Command post in the Nation was alerted, and jet pilots were sent scrambling after unidentified flying objects seen between here and Baltimore, as well as in the Midwest and on the West Coast. The Baltimore Air Force Filter Center that night, he said, "was flooded with 'phone enquiries."

He said flying saucer reports are more numerous during the time of the year when Mars is nearest to the earth.

The Major explained that the Pentagon, fearing hysteria on the part of citizens, has clamped a tight lid on all news regarding saucer investigation. He displayed what he said were official censorship orders which, he said, prohibit pilots, radar men, airport tower operators and other trained observers from disclosing saucer operations.

"Under Janap-146, a chief of staff order," he said, "even airline pilots who report encounters with saucers through official channels are forbidden to reveal them. A second order, AFR-200-2, provides that no unsolved saucer report can be released to the press."

Quoting from Air Force Special Report 14, recently released, Maj. Keyhoe said 21.5 per cent of reported sightings of saucers remain unsolved by Air Force Intelligence.

"These 689 cases," he said, "consist mainly of verified reports from highly qualified officers—armed forces pilots, radar men, guided missile trackers, airline captains, CAA tower and radar operators, and similarly well-trained men."

Maj. Keyhoe urged the press to demand an end to official secrecy on the saucers.

"There is no proof to my knowledge," he said, "that the saucer operations are hostile, but regardless of what the Air Force has secretly learned, I believe the facts should be given to the public."

(Ed.: A number of people have queried me as to how the government could possibly keep such an exciting secret. My answer is always the same: Remember the first atomic bomb? Since you obviously will, just ask yourself how the thousands and thousands and thousands of people involved in its manufacture kept it secret!)

December 12th brought your editor some clippings from the astronomical magazine *Sky and Telescope,* amongst which were the following reports of lights seen on the dark portion of the moon. Readers with access to astronomical publications could render a service by compiling all reports or lights seen on the moon over a period of years. There really should be a "moon patrol" similar to the systematic sun-spot study carried out by professional astronomers. The professionals scoff at such organized observation of the moon, because they are dogmatically certain that no activity of any nature can take place on the moon. If the truth about lunar activity is to be ascertained, it will have to be done by amateur observers, but be on guard that the professionals do not try to take credit for the discoveries you make.

FLARES ON THE MOON?

On August 26, 1955, I was observing the moon with my home-built 6-inch reflector, using an Erfle eyepiece and a Goodwin Barlow lens which gave a magnification of 200X and a 20-minute field. At 7:51 p.m. CST, while examining the neighborhood of the Apennines, I saw on the dark portion of the moon a bright flare that remained visible for about 35 seconds. It appeared roughly as bright as a 2nd-magnitude star does to the naked eye. The terminator region of the moon had been under survey for about an hour, and I am certain that the flare was not present for many seconds before I first saw it.

The position of the flare, as estimated in terms of the diameter of the field of view, was in the neighborhood of the Carpathian Mountains. This seemed to be too far inside the dark portion of the moon for the object to have been an isolated mountain peak catching the sunlight. The flare remained fairly steady in brightness, fading only slightly before it abruptly disappeared.

Reports from other observers who were observing the moon at this time would be of interest.

X. B. McCorkle
1564 Alta Vista
Memphis, Tennessee

Shortly after sunrise on September 8, 1955, I was looking at the moon, high in the sky, through a small 20X telescope. My attention was directed to the Taurus Mountains at the western edge of Mare Serenitatis when, at 7:35 a.m. EDT, I saw two distinct flashes of light, about a quarter second apart, that seemed to come from the edge of these mountains.

There appeared to be nothing that could have caused reflections in my telescope. The sun was hidden behind trees at the time, and there were no aircraft in the sky.

W. C. Lambert
2506 South 10th Street
Ironton, Ohio

The following is an excerpt from a letter sent to your editor by Mr. William S. Hunter, Los Angeles, California. Although reporting an earlier phenomenon, the persistence of "organic" clouds of this nature is of great importance and interest:

Dear Mr. Jessup:

. . . All the debunking the Air Force is capable of cannot shake my firm belief that UFO are created by intelligence.

I am a control tower operator, a commercial pilot with five thousand hours of flying time, and meteorology as a hobby, so opportunities to study and observe unusual phenomenon of the atmosphere come almost daily.

Your chapter on clouds and storms was very interesting, and I would like to tell you about an unusual cloud I observed several years ago.

One warm summer night in 1947, I was working the midnight to eight shift in the CAA control tower at Winston-Salem, North Carolina. The weather observer on duty was Bill Adams who is now a controller in the CAA Tower at Greensboro, N.C. The night was clear and the moon was full and high in the sky. About two-thirty in the morning Bill called for me to come out and see an unusual cloud approaching from the west. I went out on the catwalk around the tower to observe with him and was quite surprised at the sight I saw. The cloud was shaped like a football and the moon reflected off it making it look quite white. The amazing part about the cloud was the intense lightning projecting from the cloud in all directions. The lightning wasn't reaching the ground or any other cloud as it was the only cloud in the sky. Violent thunder was rocking the ground. The cloud went across the airport in an easterly direction and as long as we could observe it the lightning didn't stop. The surface wind was calm so apparently the wind at the cloud level was strong westerly as it moved rapidly along. We estimated the cloud to be about four thousand feet above the ground and two thousand feet long and one thousand feet thick.

I have often thought about the above incident and thought perhaps you would be interested in hearing it. It wasn't just another cloud because one cloud alone can't generate streak lightning without another cloud or the ground to receive the discharge, yet this one did! . . .

Very truly yours,
(signed)
William S. Hunter

A tiny snippet of interest came to light in the San Francisco (California) *Chronicle*, December 13th, obviously in reply to a previously published letter:

Editor: In regard to the letter from Mr. Satanave (December 5) stating that newspapers no longer publish sightings of Unidentified Flying Objects because the public has lost interest in the subject:

As librarian of a public library, I am in a position to know, more or less, what the public wish to read and what they are reading. The books on the subject of UFOs in our library are in constant circulation, the newer ones having waiting lists! Would this seem like lack of interest on the part of the reading public?

Virginia Stewart
San Anselmo

The following phenomenon was recalled to us by an extended discussion in Major Keyhoe's *The Flying Saucer Conspiracy.* These phenomena have been known to close students of UFOlogy for some time, but were soft-pedaled by the press, and are not generally known to the casual reading public. This item is part of a recent account in the C.R.I.F.O. *Orbit:*

THE ENIGMA OF THE ALPHABETIC FORMATION

In the January 1955 issue of CRIFO the writer reported on page four the English incident of radar tracking objects flying in U and Z formations. According to the British Air Ministry, the objects appeared from nowhere, usually about midday, flying at a height of 12,000 feet in an east to west direction. The War Office said, "We cannot say what they are. They first appear in a U or badly shaped hairpin formation. After a time they converge into two parallel lines and then take up a Z formation before disappearing." Migratory birds were ruled out!

While this paragraph in the C.R.I.F.O. *Orbit* refers to sightings made in 1954, we consider the sightings of the greatest importance and believe them worth an echo. Students of UFO phenomena may have heard of this strange affair, but the casual reader probably missed it because of the official blackout.

Chiefly, these formations of about fifty UFO's appeared regularly at noontime for some days, and were discovered by radar on a cloudy day. When they reappeared on a clear day and were being tracked by radar, ground spotters and pursuit planes tried to locate them, but without success—*these intelligently controlled multiple formations were invisible.*

A similar thing occurred during World War II, according to Major Keyhoe, and it has not yet been explained. Your editor agrees with Major Keyhoe on this point: If these reports are true—and we have no real cause to doubt them—then this UFO situation may be very serious indeed!

If, as we said, this and other events documented in the latest books on UFO are true, and our government is keeping it from our people, then in the opinion of your editor, the government is guilty of a monstrous betrayal of trust, something infinitely worse than the commercialized hoaxing with which we have been plagued for some years. If our government is guilty of such malicious mendacity, it might go a long way to explain why commercialized hoaxing has been permitted to thrive. Mind you, *these are opinions only,* and are based on the assumption that statements made by Major Keyhoe and others are correct. If this condition, as assumed, is true, then your editor desires to ask only one question—and that with only one word . . . *why?*

It has been reported that our paternal bureaucrats are afraid we will panic. Where would you panic to if you suddenly found that all of these fantastic reports were true and that the air and space around us are *filled* with UFO? What are you or I going to do about it? The answer is, for now at least—nothing. Our only course is to study, research and try to contact and understand these beings which have suddenly become so plentiful after centuries of association.

And at this point in December, a startling offer came to our attention, made by our friend and co-researcher, Mr. James W. Moseley, Post Office Box 163, Fort Lee, New Jersey.

Mr. Moseley sent out a notice to the effect that he ". . .

personally offers a reward of one thousand dollars to anyone who can produce tangible, conclusive proof that there are flying saucers visiting us from other planets."

Little more need be said. Your editor assures you that this is a bonafide offer, and if anyone will contact your editor, through the publisher, arrangements will be made for the safe and insured transport of the proof and, in all probability, the person possessing the proof to our headquarters in New York, where we shall arrange for experts to make the necessary judgements and studies and will arrange a press conference to make the announcement and furnish the indisputable proof.

The Washington (D.C.) *Evening Star,* December 22nd, carried an amusingly written piece which has overtones for UFOlogists:

FROZEN FLYING FISH SAILS OUT OF SKY TO SMACK CAR

**No Autos in Front, Nothing Overhead,
Occupants Tell Puzzled Officials**

Ichthyologists the world over are going to remember this day, but not so vividly as William Shannon and George Brinsmaid.

This was the day the frozen fish fell out of nowhere and crashed through the windshield of Mr. Brinsmaid's brand-new automobile.

"All of a sudden there was a tremendous crash and this fish, dead and frozen stiff, came through the windshield," Mr. Shannon said with considerable awe still in his voice.

Mr. Shannon, 25, of 1947 North Cleveland Street, Arlington, and Mr. Brinsmaid, 37, of 1832 Biltmore Street, N.W., were en route to work at the RCA Service Co., in Alexandria. The time was shortly before 8 a.m. Traffic was fairly light.

There were no cars immediately in front of them as they drove down Mount Vernon Memorial Highway, 600 yards beyond Memorial bridge. There were no aircraft overhead. They were not passing under an overpass.

The conversation topic was yesterday's air crash at Jacksonville, Florida.

"All at once—*boom,*" said Mr. Brinsmaid.

"There was a big hole in the windshield. There on the floor was this frozen dead fish. I pulled over and stopped.

"I don't know where it came from. Out of the air, I guess.

"The fish? It's in the trunk of the car. I guess I'd better get it out of there."

Mr. Shannon was considerably more shaken. He declared: "That fish looked like it was right out of the river. It was about 10 inches long and a little shredded from going through the windshield.

"We got out of the car and looked around. The place was almost deserted. Nobody was around.

"Nothing like this ever happened to me before."

By mid-morning, the dismay had spread into official circles.

"For heaven's sake!" said Dr. Lionel Walford, head of fish biology of the Fish and Wildlife Service. "Someone must have thrown that fish. That it leaped from the water and froze in the air is incredible!"

When Dr. William Mann, director of the Zoo, was informed of the event and, after he ceased chuckling, he was inclined to agree with Mr. Shannon. "I never heard of anything like that. It's new to me."

"Flying fish inhabit more southerly waters, but it is possible one could be up here. Anything is possible!"

Regardless of its last mode of transportation, this was no flying fish, the two victims contended.

After Mr. Brinsmaid removes the fish from the trunk of his car, Dr. Isaac Ginsberg, ichthyologist of the Smithsonian Institution, would like to have it. Curiosity, you know.

The following fascinating letter is from a school teacher of prominence, and the letter, of December 28th, speaks for itself:

Seeley Lake, Montana

Dear Mr. Jessup:

Your historical approach to the answer behind UFO's appears to me to have exceptional merit. Perhaps you can piece in the following information which I have gathered over the last six years:

After having seen what I thought was a flying saucer in the winter of 1952 and making a report of it to the C.A.A. in Dillon, Montana, and since my report was so seriously received, I have been less afraid to broach the subject to other people.

One group in Missoula, Montana reported this to me after they finished telling me about two "moving lights" which they had seen over Missoula about December of 1953. June and "Bobby" Schlappert told me that their father mentioned having seen a long cigar or zeppelin shaped object across the face of the moon when he was just a little boy. I believe they said that he saw it in San Francisco, California, and the date would be around 1900 or just a bit later.

(Ed.: this will, by now, strike a responsive note! Remember?)

They said that their dad remarked that it took this object about two hours to pass the face of the moon. It was seen with the naked eye. A second report that I have from personal observation follows:

Early in 1954, about the last of March, my wife and I were parked on a hill between Ely, Nevada and McGill about ten in the evening when suddenly I noticed a bright object to the rear and left of us toward Ely. At first I thought it to be a bright headlight or a large spot-light, but immediately changed my mind and shouted "LOOK!" The object we both saw was round and about the size of a basketball held at ten feet distance, its center a copper flame green, toward the outside third, a red-orange hue, and the periphery showered brilliant red and yellow sparks. This was in view for at least three or four seconds, but during the course of time, the object arced toward the earth to approximately 2000 feet above Ely. It then curved upward and disappeared from view over the mountains toward Tonapah. The altitude of these mountains was about 3,500 feet above Ely, and the first altitude I could judge since I was taking flying lessons at the time and was very conscious of elevations in the vicinity. As the "green fire-ball" disappeared, its tail looked deep red like a jet exhaust. We noticed no sound.

Shortly after that, within a space of weeks, Dr. Lincoln La Paz was called to, I believe, Ogden, Utah, to investigate a mysterious explosion that had shattered windows two miles from the scene. After three days, he and his colleagues made only the announcement that the crater created by the blast "was definitely not caused by a meteor."

Sincerely yours,
(signed)
Keith B. Hamilton

And almost in the same mail, the following interesting piece arrived. Mr. John Philip Bessor is a shrewd analyst and a close observer and researcher of UFO phenomena. There have been many interesting theories presented, publicly and privately, as to the true nature of UFO, and your editor feels that each and every theory, if presented with sincerity and intelligence and sufficient insight to be worthy of the term "theory," deserves an airing. What better place, therefore, than in the UFO Annual?

We are pleased to offer, therefore, the following piece from Mr. Bessor:

SPACE ANIMALS

John Philip Bessor
6349 Walnut Street
Pittsburgh 6, Pennsylvania

There is a saying that Nature abhors a vacuum. The microscope reveals all manner of living things in a single drop of pond water; our seas swarm with marine life varying from the barnacle to the whale; our jungles are inhabited by thousands of species of animals, insects and fowl, great and small, some carnivorous and dangerous, others herbivorous and peaceful. Is it not reasonable to assume that the very realms above us—the stratosphere and ionosphere—are likewise teeming with life forms of a highly attenuated substance natural to a highly rarefied atmosphere. Authenticated observations assure us that flying saucers are composed of varying sizes and shapes. Some have been seen as round, and about the size of a base-ball; others the size of a Constellation plane. Flying saucers have been described as spherical, square, disc-shaped, torpedo-shaped, oblong, V-shaped and cloud-shaped. Some change their shape in flight, evincing a non-solid structure. Some of the disk-shaped objects may be likened to the clam or oyster, with an ectoplasmic shell to render its passage through the atmosphere more speedy. "Bands" or other markings on some of the objects may be similar to the bands or markings on the striped, eel-like fishes found in the ocean. The pulsating lights so often observed emanating from the saucers may be analogous to the pulsating light of the fire-fly, or the luminous glow of deep-sea creatures noted by Beebe in his underwater explorations. On May 16, 1808, at approximately 4 p.m. a great procession of dark brown, "hat-crown-shaped" bodies, with tails "three or four fathoms in length," sailed over Skeninge, Sweden, causing the sun to turn a deep brick red. Occasionally, one of the strange objects would flutter to the ground, leaving a jelly-like substance which soon vanished. (Transactions of the Swedish Academy of Sciences, 1808-215.) During the unexplained phenomenon of the purple sun (September 1950) a six foot purple-glowing sphere softly alighted onto a Philadelphia field, not even bending the grass beneath it. Touched by one of the policemen who saw it fall, the object immediately began to dematerialise, and within half an hour was a sticky mass upon the ground. In a short while, the substance had completely vanished, but not before the F.B.I. had collected a sample for examination. Since no report of the analysis was forthcoming, it is presumed that the substance defied analysis, or vanished before subjected to it.

Now, these two cases evince that some (if not all) of the objects popularly termed "flying saucers" (1) do exist, and (2) are of an animal nature. In July of 1947 I submitted my theory that the flying saucers are ectoplasmic "ghost animals" to the Air Matériel Command at Wright Air Force Base, Dayton, Ohio. In August, 1947, Harry H. Haberer, of their Radio and Press Section, wrote me, "— Your theory concerning the flying discs is one of the most intelligent we have received." In studying that monumental "The Books of Charles Fort," I noted that the 1870s, '80s and '90s saw record- and near record-breaking weather, and also a rash of aerial phenomena. Now, since 1944, we have been experiencing record- and near record-breaking weather, and also a tremendous number of flying saucer reports. This leads me to suppose that there is a cyclic recurrence of periods (roughly thirty years each) of freak weather, and aerial phenomena. I think we can be justified in assuming that the solar or cosmic disturbance in space which effects freak weather, also causes the "flying saucers" to "migrate" to more dense atmospheres, coming within our range of observation. Since 1946 there have appeared in our papers numerous accounts of migrations of fishes into waters previously foreign to them, and of the intrusion of wolves, bears and other wild animals into areas in which they had never before been observed.

Oddly, the flying saucers adhere to certain "zones" or "belts." I have found that they predominate along both coasts, and along a "belt" reaching from British Columbia, Oregon and Washington, through Idaho, Indiana, southern Ohio and into West Virginia. Western Pennsylvania appears to be shunned by the mystery objects. I have no reports of flying saucers being observed over the great industrial city of Pittsburgh. An occasional, lone flying disc has been observed over eastern Pennsylvania. A recent survey of ghosts showed that Sussex, England, is the most haunted spot in all that country. Is there some electrical emanation from the earth or sky which effects manifestations of the paranormal? Does the area of Cincinnati, Ohio, for example, emanate some electrical discharge which Pittsburgh does not?

Despite the syrupy platitudes of so-called "mediums" and mystic-minded fiction writers there is no evidence that the flying saucers are controlled by benevolent "masters" from Venus, Mars, Jupiter or Saturn, come to earth to warn us miserable earthlings against the woeful effects of atomic explosions. Indeed, all things would point to the flying saucers being rather severe with those who fly too close to them, and rather fond of abducting whole crews of transport planes, small sea-going vessels, and inhabitants of tiny Eskimo villages. Perhaps the numerous falls of flesh and blood so often reported in the past are the remains of humans, wild beasts or birds caught up by some low-flying "saucer." Indeed, we wonder if these mysterious objects invade the very "realm of heaven"!

It is incredible that the "silence group" of the Air Force persists in deluding the public! Its recent statement, arrived at by armchair speculation, that "97%" of all reports were explainable as conventional aircraft, birds, Menzel's mirages or cobwebs, was designed to

(1) kill off all interest in the flying saucers, and (2) allow a convenient "escape-hatch," by the "3% unexplainable," for the Air Force to save face should some unforeseen spectacular saucer performance occur over a large city. I am certain that the Air Force refuses to admit the reality of flying saucers not from fear of public panic, but for the sole reason that to admit the existence of the paranormal, would be far too embarrassing. It is more simple to deny that which it can not understand.

The letter following is one of the most challenging that we have received. Mrs. Andrew has fired a virtual broadside at us, and if we could effectively answer *all* of her questions, we would certainly know all about UFO—a condition which obviously does not exist. In view of the comprehensive implications of this letter, however, we are going to try to comment at greater length than usual, and for that purpose we have taken the liberty of numbering the points in Mrs. Andrew's fascinating correspondence:

Vienna, Virginia

Dear Mr. Jessup:

I have read your *Case for the UFO* and find some of the theories advanced therein of extreme interest. I wonder if, by chance, you have read the revealing article by Zoe Wassilko-Serecki which appeared in September's *American Astrology Magazine*, entitled "Startling Theory on Flying Saucers." What *is* your reaction to such statements as these?

1. ". . . the theory of the saucers' interplanetary origin collapses before the weight of its own evidence . . . yet, if the UFOs are not visitors from outer space, what actually could they be? Judging from the few authentic photographs, they have a shape which resembles that of the plankton, the smallest creatures living in the ocean. Starting from this observation . . . could they be, perhaps, some kind of gigantic jellyfish of the air, carrying a minimum of dense matter, and, at the same time, a maximum of energy? Their home would have to be in the Ionosphere, the electrical layer of our own atmosphere, which starts approximately 50 miles about the earth's

surface and has temperatures up to 400 degrees Fahrenheit. They would be creatures capable of living within this fiery element and their bodies, glowing with heat, must be almost hollow, and charged with electricity. We know that they are covered with a shining, silvery coloring or skin, and move, for the most part, by rotation . . ."

2. ". . . creatures living in the electrical element of the Ionosphere would, quite naturally, possess a kind of electric sense . . . the tendency of the UFO's to concentrate above big cities and certain types of military installations is no longer enigmatic when looked upon from this new point of view . . . Hence the reason they are attracted to the above mentioned areas is a simple one— these are the places where radio stations and various other installations are concentrated, the places from which electromagnetic waves, which are those creatures' native element, and which they are capable of sensing, are emitted."

3. ". . . The behavior of the UFO's, generally speaking, gives the impression that they are guided by some unusual sense. . . ."

4. "Just as fish will circle around ships, the UFO's approach planes and, perhaps out of curiosity, come quite close."

5. ". . . Like most fish, the UFO's have a silvery skin that reflects the sunlight. Like many deep-sea fish, they glow and glitter in a variety of colors of light, which apparently they can dim and brighten at will. Being creatures of the bright air, their light is stronger, frequently dazzling."

6. ". . . A remarkable feature . . . is the fact that they come in a variety of sizes and shapes which apparently represent different states of development. The smallest disc types observed are only the size of an average dinner plate (8″ in diameter)."

7. ". . . Why is it that no dead UFO ever falls . . . to the ground. The answer possibly lies in the fact that the inconsiderable solid mass of these creatures' bodies may, after death, be consumed by the very heat of the Ionosphere. Yet quite apart from these possibilities there actually have been cases of . . . strange material falling down from the sky. Various reports, dating as far back as the 17th century, speak of gelatin-like, sinking masses, yellowish, oily liquid clots of something like coagulated blood, as well as of ashes—which could not be of meteoric origin."

8. ". . . It would be interesting to have biologists and students of marine life check into the details of the new theory . . ."

9. ". . . Could not these creatures be something like a "missing link" between organic and inorganic life? . . . In judging this possibility we must remember that their home is in the atmospheric "border line," the most outward region of our planet and hence the first to receive the life-giving radiations of the Sun, as well as the first to receive whatever radiations may reach our planet from outer space . . . and there is every reason to believe that these mysterious UFO's are just another of the creatures of our own planet earth."

Any comments you might make in regard to this theory would be of interest.

Very truly yours,
(signed)
Mrs. Rubye Andrew

And now, let us make a few editorial comments anent this most unusual theory.

1. Almost universally, the term "interplanetary origin" denotes origin on other planets, and implies travel between planets. The usage is slightly misleading. We really should speak of "planetary origin" and "interplanetary travel." What the writer of the article evidently meant by "collapsing under its own weight" has already been explained in *The Case for the UFO*, where we have pointed out that the very promiscuity of the UFO precludes mass migration from other planets. We have, therefore, been forced to assume indigenous habitat in the earth-moon binary planet system as the only reasonable explanation for the large numbers of UFO observed. As to their being "jellyfish of the air," we are very open-minded. Mr. John Bessor, as you now know, has maintained ever since an announcement in the *Saturday Evening Post* in 1949 that at least a part of the observed UFO are what he calls *Space Animals*. Your editor does not necessarily agree that *all* UFO are such, but the evidence of both remote control and innate intelligence is overwhelming. Your editor is inclined to think that these entities, or the parent-craft from which they come, may

have their habitat actually in *open space*, or what has been popularly termed *Outer Space*, and that their use of the earth and moon is occasional and incidental. The matter of 400° temperature in the Ionosphere, is academic only, for even at a high *temperature* the atmosphere at that level is too rarefied to contain much *heat*, and is therefore no serious problem. The far reaches of space itself may have temperatures of a million degrees or so, and yet the atoms or molecules may be so far apart that not enough *heat* could be accumulated to melt a drop of butter.

2. There may be much of truth in this suggestion of special sensitivity to some of the more tenuous electrical phenomena about which we are only now beginning to learn. This is a field for serious research by competent—but open minded—scientists. We do not wish to make firm comment; rather merely to acknowledge that here is certainly something to think about.

3 and 4. This suggestion of an instinctive attraction to airplanes, etc., and guidance by an unusual sense is very pertinent. We feel, however, that there may be two kinds of sensitivity involved; one of a very high degree of intelligence and the other of lower, or animal-like level—a kind of instinctive sensitivity. We think there is evidence that the *latter* may be "space animals" while the former are more likely erudite beings who have constructed vast artificial moonlets or, as the Air Force calls them, "space platforms!"

5. The writer makes a very common mistake in assuming that one single explanation will cover all observed UFO. Some do appear to have reflecting or iridescent skins, but some appear more nebulous or jelly-like. We feel, again, that at least two basic types must be contemplated: one of them "constructed," and one of them "natural." In other words, some UFO's are born, some are made.

6. Yes, the variety of sizes and shapes *is* remarkable, but no more remarkable than the variety of moving organisms seen in our oceans, among which is an occasional structure of gigantic size and anomalous texture, obviously made and controlled by

higher intelligence (submarines, ships, etc.). There seems to be a parallelism of conditions and existence between our oceans and the space adjacent to the earth-moon system.

7. This question practically contains its own answer. These devitalized UFO *have* fallen to the ground. There is an increasing accumulation of data on jelly-like, smelly, organic masses which reach the earth's surface and quickly disintegrate. This disintegration must not be confused with dematerialization. The disappearance of dry-ice (frozen carbon-dioxide) is a similar phenomenon, and you would hardly say that the dry ice has dematerialized.

8. Yes, by all means have these new concepts checked by every type of specialists in the fields of natural science—but let's have open-minded investigators, and not sealed minds determined to find only negative results.

9. We do not understand your references to "inorganic life." Such a thing seems meaningless, unless you are merely implying disembodied intelligence, about which we know so little at present. But, what you rather obviously intend is an inference that there are other types of "life" and intelligence in space and the upper atmosphere than those now familiar to us in what we call the vivisphere, and in this case we do lend a most sympathetic ear.

We do believe that UFO are creatures—both born and constructed—of our earth-moon system . . . but there is much to learn.

And December ended with great success when we were successful in obtaining an actual Air Force Regulation 200-2 . . . proof that the Air Force of the United States is working very hard on a problem of which they deny the existence.

What better way to end 1955—and look forward to an exciting 1956—than to reproduce the now famous AFR 200-2!

It can no longer be disputed: ladies and gentlemen, *here it is!*

¦ FORCE REGULATION }
. 200-2   }

DEPARTMENT OF THE AIR FORCE
WASHINGTON, *12 AUGUST 1954*

INTELLIGENCE

Unidentified Flying Objects Reporting (Short Title: UFOB)

1. Purpose and Scope. This Regulation establishes procedures for reporting information 1 evidence pertaining to unidentified flying jects and sets forth the responsibility of Air rce activities in this regard. It applies to all r Force activities.

2. Definitions:

a. *Unidentified Flying Objects (UFOB)*— 1ates to any airborne object which by performce, aerodynamic characteristics, or unusual tures does not conform to any presently known craft or missile type, or which cannot be sitively identified as a familiar object.

b. *Familiar Objects*—Include balloons, asnomical bodies, birds, and so forth.

3. Objectives. Air Force interest in unidentid flying objects is twofold: First as a possible reat to the security of the United States and forces, and secondly, to determine technical pects involved.

a. *Air Defense.* To date, the flying objects ported have imposed no threat to the security the United States and its Possessions. However, the possibility that new air vehicles, hostile rcraft or missiles may first be regarded as flying jects by the initial observer is real. This re- 1ires that sightings be reported rapidly and as mpletely as information permits.

b. *Technical.* Analysis thus far has failed provide a satisfactory explanation for a numer of sightings reported. The Air Force will ntinue to collect and analyze reports until all ghtings can be satisfactorily explained, bearing mind that:

(1) To measure scientific advances, the Air Force must be informed on experimentation and development of new air vehicles.

(2) The possibility exists that an air vehicle of revolutionary configuration may be developed.

(3) The reporting of all pertinent factors will have a direct bearing on the success of the technical analysis.

4. Responsibility:

a. *Reporting.* Commanders of Air Force activities will report all information and evidence that may come to their attention, including that received from adjacent commands of the other services and from civilians.

b. *Investigation.* Air Defense Command will conduct all field investigations within the ZI, to determine the identity of any UFOB.

c. *Analysis.* The Air Technical Intelligence Center (ATIC), Wright-Patterson Air Force Base, Ohio, will analyze and evaluate: All information and evidence reported within the ZI after the Air Defense Command has exhausted all efforts to identify the UFOB; and all information and evidence collected in oversea areas.

d. *Cooperation.* All activities will cooperate with Air Defense Command representatives to insure the economical and prompt success of an investigation, including the furnishing of air and ground transportation, when feasible.

5. Guidance. The thoroughness and quality of a report or investigation into incidents of unidentified flying objects are limited only by the resourcefulness and imagination of the person responsible for preparing the report. Guidance set forth below is based on experience and has been found helpful in evaluating incidents:

a. Theodolite measurements of changes of azimuth and elevation and angular size.

b. Interception, identification, or air search

This Regulation supersedes AFR 200-2, 26 August 1953, including Change 200-2A, 2 November 1953.

action. These actions may be taken if appropriate and within the scope of existing air defense regulations.

c. Contact with local aircraft control and warning (AC&W) units, ground observation corps (GOC) posts and filter centers, pilots and crews of aircraft aloft at the time and place of sighting whenever feasible, and any other persons or organizations which may have factual data bearing on the UFOB or may be able to offer corroborating evidence, electronic or otherwise.

d. Consultation with military or civilian weather forecasters to obtain data on: Tracks of weather balloons released in the area, since these often are responsible for sightings; and any unusual meteorological activity which may have a bearing on the UFOB.

e. Consultation with astronomers in the area to determine whether any astronomical body or phenomenon would account for or have a bearing on the observation.

f. Contact with military and civilian tower operators, air operations offices, and so forth, to determine whether the sighting could be the result of misidentification of known aircraft.

g. Contact with persons who might have knowledge of experimental aircraft of unusual configuration, rocket and guided missile firings, and so forth, in the area.

6. ZI Collection. The Air Defense Command has a direct interest in the facts pertaining to UFOB's reported within the ZI and has, in the 4602d Air Intelligence Service Squadron (AISS), the capability to investigate these reports. The 4602d AISS is composed of specialists trained for field collection and investigation of matters of air intelligence interest which occur within the ZI. This squadron is highly mobile and deployed throughout the ZI as follows: Flights are attached to air defense divisions, detachments are attached to each of the defense forces, and the squadron headquarters is located at Peterson Field, Colorado, adjacent to Headquarters, Air Defense Command. Air Force activities, therefore, should establish and maintain liaison with the nearest element of this squadron. This can be accomplished by contacting the appropriate echelon of the Air Defense Command as outlined above.

a. All Air Force activities are authorized to conduct such preliminary investigation as may be required for reporting purposes; however, investigations should not be carried beyond this point, unless such action is requested by the 4602d AISS.

b. On occasions—after initial reports are submitted—additional data is required wh[ich] can be developed more economically by [the] nearest Air Force activity, such as: narrat[ive] statements, sketches, marked maps, charts, a[nd] so forth. Under such circumstances, appropria[te] commanders will be contacted by the 4602d AIS[S].

c. Direct communication between echelo[ns] of the 4602d AISS and Air Force activities [is] authorized.

7. Reporting. All information relating [to] UFOB's will be reported promptly. The meth[od] (electrical or written) and priority of dispat[ch] will be selected in accordance with the appare[nt] intelligence value of the information. In mo[st] instances, reports will be made by electric[al] means: Information over 24 hours old will [be] given a "deferred" precedence. Reports over [5] days old will be made by written report prepar[ed] on AF Form 112, Air Intelligence Informati[on] Report, and AF Form 112a, Supplement to A[F] Form 112.

a. *Addressees:*

   (1) *Electrical Reports.* All electrical r[e]ports will be multiple addressed to:

     (a) Commander, Air Defense Com[mand, Ent Air Force Base, Colo[rado Springs, Colorado.

     (b) Nearest Air Division (Defense[) (For ZI only.)

     (c) Commander, Air Technical Intell[i]gence Center, Wright-Patterson A[ir] Force Base, Ohio.

     (d) Director of Intelligence, Headqua[r]ters USAF, Washington 25, D. C.

   (2) *Written Reports:*

     (a) Within the ZI, reports will be submitted direct to the Air Defense Command. Air Defense Comman[d] will reproduce the report and dis[-]tribute it to interested ZI intelligence agencies. The original repor[t] together with notation of the dis[-]tribution effected then will be forwarded to the Director of Intelligence, Headquarters USAF, Washington 25, D. C.

     (b) Outside the ZI, reports will be submitted direct to Director of Intelligence, Headquarters USAF, Washington 25, D. C. as prescribed in "Intelligence Collection Instructions" (ICI), June 1954.

b. *Short Title.* "UFOB" will appear at the beginning of the text of electrical messages and in the subject of written reports.

c. *Negative Data.* The word "negative"

eply to any numbered item of the report
nat will indicate that all logical leads were
eloped without success. The phrase "not
licable" (N/A) will indicate that the question
ı not apply to the sighting being investigated.

d. *Report Format.* Reports will include the
owing numbered items:

(1) Description of the object(s):
  (a) Shape.
  (b) Size compared to a known object
    (use one of the following terms:
    Head of a pin, pea, dime, nickel,
    quarter, half dollar, silver dollar,
    baseball, grapefruit, or basketball)
    held in the hand at about arms
    length.
  (c) Color.
  (d) Number.
  (e) Formation, if more than one.
  (f) Any discernible features or details.
  (g) Tail, trail, or exhaust, including
    size of same compared to size of
    object(s).
  (h) Sound. If heard, describe sound.
  (i) Other pertinent or unusual features.

(2) Description of course of object(s):
  (a) What first called the attention of
    observer(s) to the object(s)?
  (b) Angle of elevation and azimuth of
    the object(s) when first observed.
  (c) Angle of elevation and azimuth of
    object(s) upon disappearance.
  (d) Description of flight path and
    maneuvers of object(s).
  (e) Manner of disappearance of ob-
    ject(s).
  (f) Length of time in sight.

(3) Manner of observation:
  (a) Use one or any combination of the
    following items: Ground-visual,
    ground-electronic, air-electronic.
    (If electronic, specify type of
    radar.)
  (b) Statement as to optical aids (tele-
    scopes, binoculars, and so forth)
    used and description thereof.
  (c) If the sighting is made while air-
    borne, give type aircraft, identifi-
    cation number, altitude, heading,
    speed, and home station.

(4) Time and date of sighting:
  (a) Zulu time-date group of sighting.
  (b) Light conditions (use one of the
    following terms): Night, day,
    dawn, dusk.

(5) Locations of observer(s). Exact latitude and longitude of each observer,
  or Georef position, or position with
  reference to a known landmark.
(6) Identifying information of all ob-
  server(s):
  (a) Civilian—Name, age, mailing ad-
    dress, occupation.
  (b) Military—Name, grade, organiza-
    tion, duty, and estimate of reli-
    ability.
(7) Weather and winds-aloft conditions
  at time and place of sightings:
  (a) Observer(s) account of weather
    conditions.
  (b) Report from nearest AWS or U. S.
    Weather Bureau Office of wind
    direction and velocity in degrees
    and knots at surface, 6,000', 10,000',
    16,000', 20,000', 30,000', 50,000',
    and 80,000', if available.
  (c) Ceiling.
  (d) Visibility.
  (e) Amount of cloud cover.
  (f) Thunderstorms in area and quad-
    rant in which located.
(8) Any other unusual activity or condition, meteorological, astronomical, or
  otherwise, which might account for
  the sighting.
(9) Interception or identification action
  taken (such action may be taken
  whenever feasible, complying with
  existing air defense directives).
(10) Location of any air traffic in the area
  at time of sighting.
(11) Position title and comments of the
  preparing officer, including his preliminary analysis of the possible cause
  of the sighting(s).
(12) Existence of physical evidence, such
  as materials and photographs.

e. *Security.* Reports should be unclassified
unless inclusion of data required by d above
necessitates a higher classification.

8. Evidence. The existence of physical evidence (photographs or materiel) will be promptly
reported.

a. *Photographic:*
  (1) *Visual.* The negative and two prints
    will be forwarded, all original film,
    including wherever possible both
    prints and negatives, will be titled or
    otherwise properly identified as to
    place, time, and date of the incident

(see "Intelligence Collection Instructions" (ICI), June 1954).

(2) *Radar.* Two copies of each print will be forwarded. Prints of radarscope photography will be titled in accordance with AFR 95-7 and forwarded in compliance with AFR 95-6.

b. *Materiel.* Suspected or actual items of materiel which come into possession of any Air Force echelon will be safeguarded in such manner as to prevent any defacing or alteration which might reduce its value for intelligence examination and analysis.

9. Release of Facts. Headquarters USAF ' release summaries of evaluated data which ' inform the public on this subject. In respo to local inquiries, it is permissible to inform n media representatives on UFOB's when object is positively identified as a familiar obj (see paragraph 2b), except that the follow type of data warrants protection and should : be revealed: Names of principles, intercept s investigation procedures, and classified ra data. For those objects which are not plainable, only the fact that ATIC will anal; the data is worthly of release, due to the ma unknowns involved.

By Order of the Secretary of the Air Force:

Official:

K. E. THIEBAUD
Colonel, USAF
Air Adjutant General

N. F. TWINING
Chief of Staff, United States Air Force

DISTRIBUTON:
S; X:
ONI, Department of the Navy 200
G-2, Department of the Army 10